The World of Evendaar

Book Two

The Queen Revealed

A. R. Winterstaar

Cover Illustration by Anastasia Ward (akward13@live.com)

First Published 2014

Third Edition, May 2018

ISBN: 0-9914794-3-2

ISBN-13: 978-0-9914794-3-6

Evendaar Publishing

www.evendaar.com

DEDICATION

Simon

Endless, Ageless, Forever Love

CONTENTS

THE PROPHECY OF THE END OF THE WORLD

"A child born into the Golden Age shall be stolen from the Light and hidden from the eyes of the world.

Seek this Hidden Child when the three Signs of the End of the World appear...

...Only the Hidden Child shall defend the Throne from the Favored and cast the Shadows into the Light to restore the Glory of my Chosen Ones on the Throne of my Kingdom.

Beware and rejoice for only in the greatest darkness does the brightest light shine.

The Empress of a Dark God will want to burn the blood of the Lost Child Hidden.

The Child must sacrifice a fear of the Dark and go without a Magek to save the World from an evil pestilence that will destroy all life in its path.

All who defy the Child shall burn to ashes, and those ashes shall feed the North Wind.

Excerpts taken from *The Prophecy of the End of the World*, printed by Pere Manus and dictated by the Child Prophet Celestina and Voice of the Goddess Serena. Translated from the old tongue by Pere Raindor Marchant.

PROLOGUE

The image in the mirror crackled and skipped, making the young man curse. *The magic of that damn queen is getting more powerful by the day!* He could even see the green haze that drifted about her in a cloud, creating static and interfering with his ability to spy on her through the Magic Glass.

The young man sat back and chewed his bottom lip. His long fingers drummed the table in front of him in an impatient tattoo as he thought hard.

This new queen was a puzzle and a problem for him.

He had been watching her closely ever since High Wizard Ohren had dragged the woman across the universe with her three children in tow, to land in the world of Evendaar just weeks ago. Though initially she had appeared as frightened and innocent as a kitten, the Blood Ceremony had revealed her true identity as a half-St Lucidis, half-Marchant bastard, and no misbegotten creature of the Blood, with its evil, reeking, green magic, could be allowed to keep the throne. *She had to be gotten rid of, that was certain, but carefully.*

The first attempt on her life had been during her mission to Sandar to retrieve the Fire Orchid stamens from the Empress Sanda'hani. The Sandarian Mage had promised that he would kill her in the underground Holy Caves, where the queen's magic should have been at its weakest, but the young man had only watched in horror as the queen had called on the filthiest of all dark magic and drained the Mage dry, killing him outright in his own temple.

The young man narrowed his eyes at the Magic Glass and glared at the queen riding her chestnut horse along a dusty patch of the King's Highway. Soon she would return to the Golden Palace holding aloft the life-saving Fire Orchid stamens and casting herself in the role of savior of the Unisian people when the Summer Influenza was beaten back for another year.

But no, he could not allow it!

Already the queen had a dangerous amount of power at her disposal, and whether by accident or design, she had formed strong personal bonds with both High Wizard Ohren and the immortal, Prince Rainere Marchant. To allow her a political stage to garner more support would be fatal to the status quo in the kingdom of Unisia. The status quo *he* had worked so hard to maintain all these years. The queen needed to be removed, yes, but he would not underestimate her as the foolish Mage of Sandar had. First, he would destroy those powerful relationships of hers, and then he would destroy the woman herself.

With a flick of his wrist, the Magic Glass went dark. The young man stared at his reflection in the polished surface. His electric blue eyes shone above his smooth cheeks and his lips were rosy after he had been chewing at them. He smiled and the beautiful reflection smiled back. He loved this face.

Pulling up the black silk scarf at his throat, the young man covered the lower half of his face and said a name aloud. The Magic Glass lit up again. This time, a dark-haired boy stared back at him. The background noise behind the boy went quiet as he moved into a dark corner of some tavern room and gazed back at the young man.

"Yes, Boss," said the boy, flicking his long fringe out of his eyes with a sharp toss in a pathetic attempt at nonchalance. The young man could see the boy's terror as clear as day.

"I have a job for you," said the young man. "You must meet me in the usual place."

The boy swallowed and his cheeks paled. "Now, Boss?"

The young man smiled behind his scarf. "Yes, Charlie. Now."

CHAPTER ONE

"A Storm Rises"

Prince Rainere paced the floor of his laboratory, glass shards crunching under his feet where the wall of windows lay smashed and scattered on the floor. Their destruction was the most violent symptom of his concern for the queen's wellbeing in Sandar. The wind blew in through the broken windows, tangling his long hair and blowing it in his eyes. He wore two spots of color high on his cheeks and his eyes blazed with ill-contained fury.

"Where is she, Grotto?" snarled the prince, as he swung about to continue his pacing in the other direction and impatiently pulled the hair out of his eyes. "I haven't heard from that nasty spider, Schiss, for almost four days. He should have reported back to me on the queen's whereabouts by now. Anything could have happened to her!"

"Perhaps your Queen Adelena killed him, like she did his older brother?" replied Grotto acidly, as he pushed himself off his knees, carrying a pan of broken glass in one hand and a brush in the other. "That would explain his tardiness." He dumped the glass into a waste basket and returned to the floor.

Rainere stopped to consider the option for a moment before striding on again. "No, I told him to be careful with her. He would not have shown himself after what she did to Oki. No, something is wrong, I am sure of it. It's this cursed prophecy, Grotto! I was certain that the wizards had sent her after the wrong empress, but now…"

The prince drifted off, distracted, as he watched the heavy rainclouds billow and chase each other across the skies above the Dark Forest. "If only I knew that Adelena was safe. If only I could see her." Rainere's voice was rough, but Grotto could hear the tortured yearning in it. "If only there was a way I could bring her to me, to have her close again."

With an impatient growl, Rainere turned from the windows and stalked out of the room, slamming the door behind himself so hard that more glass tinkled to the floor from the broken frames.

Grotto sat back on his heels and dropped the pan of shattered glass onto the floor. Now alone, he could let out the deep, soul-weary sigh that had been building in his chest.

His master, the last Marchant prince, had good reason to be fearful, for the full moon was only a scant eight days away. *How was the prince to marry the queen and ascend the throne of Unisia in such a short amount of time, thereby fulfilling the Prophecy of the End of the World and upholding his oath to the Spider Empress Ka-kik?* To make matters worse, the Spider Empress was furious with the queen for killing her beloved son, Oki, just weeks ago. The Goddess only knew what she would do now that her time of mourning was almost over. No doubt, the Spider Empress would scream for the death of the queen after all that she had done, complicating everything all over again.

Although his master was a terribly powerful and intelligent warlock, his poor mind was altogether too fragile. Yes, he had won the heart of the Unisian Queen Adelena, but then he had also foolishly gone and given her his own.

Grotto shivered in the chill wind that blew through the laboratory. Deep down in his gut, Grotto feared that this imposter of a queen could well be the death of his immortal master, and the fact that he was powerless to prevent it made Grotto hate her even more.

*   *   *

Prince Rainere stalked up the dimly-lit staircase of the stone tower, his long legs taking the crooked steps two at a time. At the top of the staircase, a little wooden door leading to the outside rattled on its hinges as strong gusts of wind buffeted against it. Rainere shoved the door with his shoulder, heedless of its rusted joints, and smashed it back against the wall of the tower. He strode to the edge of the palace roof and looked out over the landscape in front of him, resting his hands on the low wall. The stone was cold to the touch, and rough with the embedded grey crystals that gave the palace its name.

The grounds of the Grey Palace weren't large. One could easily see the front boundary fence from the roof. Huge wrought-iron gates marked the entrance and opened onto a white-pebbled road lined with skeletal linden trees. The road led up to a gravel semicircle in front of the palace steps. There was room for twenty carriages to sit there, but as no one was ever invited to the Grey Palace, Rainere had never seen such a sight.

Several stone dragons guarded either side of the dozen front steps, their stone jaws carved into fiercesome snarls. The great, black-lacquered front doors of the palace were pristine, despite the many years that they had stood, and almost hummed with the countless spells and curses that had been set upon them to prevent intruders from entering when they were not welcome.

The prince pulled his hair back as the wind whipped it across his face, and then cast his gaze out beyond the boundary to the thick forest surrounding the palace on three sides. Far away, deep in that dark and forbidding place, the Spider Empress sat in her nest weeping for the death of her son and probably plotting some kind of evil revenge against the queen. What that would be, Rainere couldn't hope to guess. Certainly, the empress would not risk taking Adelena's life before she could fulfill the prophecy by marrying him and making him keep his oath of freeing the Spider People from the Under Lands as the king of Unisia. Rainere knew that was too important to the Spider Empress, even more so than retribution.

Rainere raised his eyes to the Black Mountains behind the palace and stared sightlessly at the sharp and jagged peaks. They were as familiar to him as the features of his own face, but he had never ventured into them, save once. The Marchant Eldars had taken him to the summit of he knew not which mountain, to carve the immortality spell into his unwilling flesh.

Rainere closed his eyes as the memory of the pain they had inflicted washed over him. His mouth formed a hard line. For one hundred and fifty years he had lived in this cruel world, and never had he known the joy that Adelena's love had given him. At first, she had only haunted him in his dreams, making him mad with desire and unsure of his wits, but then she had arrived in Evendaar, brought over from her world by the Wizards Council of the Golden Palace, and they had finally found each other. Now nothing could keep them apart: not the Wizards Council or the prophecy, not even the Spider Empress herself. He and Adelena were fated to be together. The Goddess Serena had told him so herself.

"But, *where is she?*" muttered Rainere as he scanned the horizon and scratched his fingertips against the stone beneath his hands. He had felt secure, though not happy, about letting Adelena journey to the coastal nation of Sandar with her children. He had figured that there, she would at least be safe from the Spider Empress and free of the influence of the High Wizard Ohren and his dangerous meddling with the Prophecy of the End of the World. Unfortunately for Rainere, the wizard's interpretation of Adelena's role in the prophecy was the exact opposite of the Spider Empress's, and therein laid the greatest danger for Adelena. Both sides sought to force her to follow their paths.

Rainere was so deep in thought, that he almost missed the sound of the squelchy *pop* from behind him. The prince spun around to come face to face with one of the children of the Spider Empress. His short, skinny frame was more emaciated than was usual for his breed, and his large eyes bugged out with exhaustion.

"Schiss! Where the devil have you been? I have waited four days for you to show up!" Rainere yelled, advancing on the tiny man and grabbing his arms to stop him from leaving again.

Schiss rapidly blinked his big eyes and cowered in Rainere's grasp. "Don't be angry, m'liege," he stammered. "I couldn't…and it took days…then she…"

Prince Rainere forced himself to let go of the terrified creature and asked him the only question that mattered. "Is Queen Adelena alright, Schiss?"

Schiss looked like he was going to pass out and swayed on his feet as the wind blew him about. He looked up at Rainere with a slightly crazed expression.

"Queen Adelena lives, m'liege. She and her children are riding back to the Golden Palace now. They've been on the road for two and a half days and are passing the turn for the Dark Forest today. I had wanted to return to you sooner, m'liege, but I was captured in Sandar by a Mage. Such a nasty, nasty human. He kept me in a box until…until…" Schiss swayed again and Rainere put out a hand to catch the little man before he fell.

"I almost died in that box, m'liege. The magic was so thick, I couldn't breathe at all, but then she came, and she saved me." Schiss smiled up at the prince. "She told me she would never kill me, ever. Then she let me go with her blessings. I tried to travel the portals back here, but I was too weak, so I jumped aboard her carriage for a couple of days until I got to the Dark Forest and could come back to you."

He grinned again. "She is so beautiful, your queen, m'liege, and so gentle and kind."

"She is over there," Schiss pointed to the distant edge of the forest. "Right there on the King's Highway, just past your lands, barely half a day's ride away."

Prince Rainere dropped the man-spider and turned to gaze in the direction of the highway. *So close!* Rainere thought, as a desperate joy bubbled up from deep inside him. *So close, I can almost feel her.* He closed his eyes and raised his face into the wind, as if to catch the very scent of Adelena, his love.

When the prince's eyes snapped open again, the silver ring that circled his black pupils spun and undulated with the power of his magic. Rainere raised his arms above his head and shouted the incantation that would release his magic into the sky. Hot green explosions of energy shot out from his hands and up into the domain of the North Wind, who shrieked for joy at being given such a dangerous gift and blew with raucous fury and reveled in the uncontained power zig-zagging across the sky.

Terrified, Schiss dropped to the stone floor of the roof and crawled to safety in the doorway of the nearby tower. The tiny man-spider whimpered as the wind howled past his ears with a voice like a devil from the beyond and the air crackled with green sparks of energy. The feeble afternoon sunlight deepened to twilight as heavy black clouds dropped low over the land. Schiss looked up in fear and saw more gigantic clouds scudding across the sky to cover the Grey Palace. He shivered as the first flakes of snow began to fall and pulled his thin shirtsleeves down over his hands.

Schiss had heard that in the days of old, Marchant royals had discovered the magic to control the weather, but he had never seen proof of it until now. Cautiously, he stuck his head out of the doorway to watch Prince Rainere, but a sharp crack lit up the sky followed by an earth-trembling rumble, and Schiss cowered back into his shelter with his hands over his delicate ears.

Prince Rainere stood as if transfixed. His arms raised to the sky and a look of intense concentration on his white face. Only his lips moved as he strengthened and re-strengthened the incantation to bring on the wild and terrible storm. The ground shook as another deep rumble thundered through the sky.

Slowly, Rainere came back to his senses and lowered his arms. Looking about, he watched with satisfaction as snowflakes danced in the eddies and gusts about him. A tiny twitch at the side of his mouth almost suggested a smile.

There is no way Adelena can stay out in this storm, he thought. *She will have to seek shelter now and my home is the only refuge for miles in all directions. Her Queen's Guard will have no choice but to lead her here.*

She will be with me again soon.

CHAPTER TWO

"Blood and Bad News"

"Can you see who it is, General?" asked Adele, as she held her hand up to shade her eyes and squinted at the puff of dust in the distance.

"It's two riders, but I can't make out their livery just yet," replied General Ohrig, his pale blue eyes sharp, despite his years.

Adele and the general were both sitting astride their horses in the middle of the road as the five men of the Queen's Guard and the two nannies, Caitlin and Seraphina, packed up their lunchtime camp in a green field not too far away. The carriage drivers pulled their horses back into their traces in readiness to continue the long march back home to the Golden Palace

Captain Lucky was walking over from the camp with Adele's little son, Aaron, and her son's puppy, Hero Boy. The tall captain was holding Aaron's hand and leaning his blond head down to better hear what her son was saying. Of all the Queen's Guards, Captain Lucky was the most intimidating to Adele's children, and she could see Aaron's shyness in his slight hunch as they came closer. Though he was very kind to the children, Lucky took his authority as captain seriously, and was not as playful as the other, younger Queen's Guards, the red-headed Pepper and handsome Leith. Of course, the two older Queen's Guards, Bear and Owens, were not playful at all, and the children instinctively recognized these two as soldiers and not babysitters. But despite this, there was a comfortable intimacy that had grown between them all from being on the road together, including their stay in Sandar for the past ten days, and everyone was close to her three children now.

"Queen Adelena, if I may interrupt, your son would like a word with you." The young captain smiled and ruffled the little prince's hair encouragingly.

"What is it, sweetheart?" asked Adele, as her son gazed up at her, his hazel eyes serious.

"Hero Boy told me that there is snow coming, isn't there, Mummy?" Aaron finished every one of his statements with a question. His little-boy earnestness always undermined by his four-year-old's insecurity.

"Snow?" Adele raised her eyebrows in surprise.

"Bit hot for snow, I would think," said General Ohrig, frowning up at the cloudless blue sky.

"That's what I said, too, didn't I? But Hero Boy told me that snow is coming," insisted Aaron. "Look, it's making him sad!"

The three adults and Aaron looked down at the large black and tan puppy as the dog cuddled in close to his master's legs. The puppy did look pretty miserable.

"Don't worry, sweetheart," smiled Adele, glancing back up the road as the riders in the distance drew nearer. "We will all be home in two days and we can be safe and warm in the Golden Palace even if snow does come."

"Okay, Mummy," Aaron agreed reluctantly. He pulled the puppy up off its haunches. "Come on, Hero Boy. Mummy said it's alright, okay?"

The puppy and his little master walked back to the carriages and Adele's eyes followed them. It wasn't like Aaron to be so serious. He was normally such a happy little boy.

Absently, she reached into her pocket and touched the letter Ripenzo Shale had left her just that morning. He had spoken of a storm, too. She chewed her bottom lip, anxiety fluttering in her chest.

"Your Majesty?" General Ohrig interrupted her train of thought. "Those riders are St. Lucidis messengers from what I can see, and they are coming in hard. We should ride up to meet them now, and not wait for the carriages to join us until we know what they want."

He turned to the captain. "Captain Lucky, mount up and come with us."

"Yes, General." Captain Lucky sprinted off to get his horse, Redfire.

Minutes later, the party of three trotted down the road to meet the messengers coming their way. Adele could hear the thundering of the hooves and saw the horses were in distress, flicking their heads, as foam flew from their mouths.

"Do men often ride that hard when they are carrying good news, general?" asked Adele, giving Ohrig a sidelong look.

Ohrig's mouth tweaked into a grim smile. "Not in my thirty years of experience, Your Majesty. But there is always a first time for everything."

Adele and her two Queen's Guards stopped at a distance from the messengers, to give them time to safely slow their mounts and approach. The two messengers were riding the dappled grey horses from the St. Lucidis stables, and both were wearing the Gold Lion crest on their tunics. They were definitely from the Golden Palace.

"Your Majesty, Queen Adelena!" called out one of the messengers, addressing Adele directly. "I have a message for you from High Wizard Ohren, Your Majesty."

He thrust a long cylindrical tube at Adele and tried to sit up as straight as his labored breathing would allow him to. Adele noticed his blond curls were plastered to his forehead and that his collar was dark with sweat.

"Please, Captain Lucky. Help these gentlemen take care of their horses and get them some refreshments. They are obviously exhausted." Adele couldn't help but pity the animals more than the men who had been ridden so hard and come such a long way to deliver this message to her.

Captain Lucky led the riders back to the carriages further down the road, delivering them into the care of the other four Queen's Guardsmen, and rejoined his queen and general.

Adele studied the cylinder in her hands. It was the size of a normal scroll and had a golden lion head at each end, and no apparent opening.

"Generally, these cylinders are locked with a Blood Print spell, Your Majesty," said General Ohrig, leaning over from his saddle to examine the cylinder for himself.

Adele looked up. "Then how am I meant to open it? Ohren knows I don't have any magic." Of course, that wasn't exactly true, but Adele wasn't in a place to explain that to her general just yet.

"Well, we use these out in the field for transporting sensitive information and normally the tube has had a drop of your blood embedded in the spell. Another drop of your blood on one of the lion heads should break the spell and open the tube for you."

"Really?" Adele didn't bother to hide her incredulous expression. "Has no one ever heard of a combination lock in this world? Why must we use blood for *everything*?"

She looked down at the tiny dagger that General Ohrig handed her and scrunched up her nose in distaste. "Can you do it for me, please?" She offered him her finger.

General Ohrig tried to hide his amusement behind a stern frown. "Just take the knife, Your Majesty. You only need a scratch to get a drop of blood."

Adele took the blade and reluctantly pushed the tip into her left thumb. The keen edge soon glistened with red. Adele wiped her thumb over the lion heads and watched fascinated as they both began to rotate in opposite directions with a little clicking noise before popping out and hanging off the end of the cylinder, suspended on loose springs.

"It's only a glass cylinder," mused Adele, as she shook the scroll out. "What's to stop someone from just smashing it open?"

"Because it's made of Sticking Glass, Your Majesty. If you just broke it, then the glass would magically stick to you, working its way through your clothes to your skin and then inside you, piercing all your organs and causing internal bleeding. Hence, the magic demands the blood of the receiver to open it properly."

Adele gave Ohrig a long look. She didn't like it when he used that particular lecturing tone with her. It wasn't her fault everything on this world was still such a mystery. She had only lived in Evendaar for a month. She kept her gaze on the general until his blue eyes crinkled at the sides and she could tell he was trying not to smile again. "Thank you, general," she said dryly. "Informative and needlessly graphic, as always."

General Ohrig nodded, accepting the remark as a compliment, then looked pointedly at the curled-up scroll in Adele's hand. Adele looked down at it, too. A jolt of dread mixed unpleasantly with the cold chicken pie she'd had for lunch. Slowly, she uncurled the letter, not at all eager to find out why the high wizard had almost killed two horses to get this message to her.

To Our Queen Adelena,

Please do not be overly alarmed by this missive I send you now, but it is imperative that you do not return to the Golden Palace at this time. Instead, you should head directly to the Belvoir Estate.

General Ohrig can be trusted to guide you along the safe roads.

Prince Bertrand II of Belvoir has been informed of your arrival and will expect you to stay at the estate for the duration of the Horse Carnival. I will have your luggage, staff, and amenities sent directly to the estate for your convenience.

Please know this letter contains my sincere wishes for your health and my hopes that you had success in Sandar.

Please give my fond regards to the children.

Yours in service to the kingdom,

H.W. Ohren St. Lucidis

Thoroughly confused, Adele handed the letter to General Ohrig and looked back at the carriages. Her three children played happily, yelling and laughing as they were chased by the youngest QG, Pepper. The nannies, Seraphina and Caitlin, had finished packing the carriages and watched the children, giggling behind their hands. QG Leith held the three over-excited puppies at bay on leads as the children ran about. Meanwhile, QGs Owens and Bear were off to the side, smoking cigarettes and ignoring the game. And here Adele had hoped it would be uneventful day.

"What in the name of the Goddess?" muttered Ohrig, as he read and re-read the letter, checking the back for more instructions. There were none.

"Well, at least there is no need for alarm, general. Ohren says that right at the start, before he warns me not to return to our home." Adele was trying to be sarcastic, but her nerves betrayed her. When she took the letter back from Ohrig, her hands were shaking.

"Why would he say *imperative* if he didn't want me to be alarmed?" she asked, scanning the letter again.

"I assume we need to change direction immediately," frowned Ohrig. "But, if my memory serves me correctly, the safest road we can take to the Belvoir Estate is at least another day's ride from this point here. Then we would need to travel across country for half a day or so, maybe more. Belvoir is closer to us than the Golden Palace, at any rate, so that is good news, but if time is more critical then we can turn off the highway and travel the back roads through the Dark Forest. It'll be slow, but the distance is almost half, and we will get there quicker in the long run."

"Yes, alright," nodded Adele, as her mind spun off in a hundred different directions. *What could have happened to spur Ohren to write her this letter? Had he heard what had happened in Sandar? Had they already discovered that the Sandarian Mage was missing?*

Her left thumb smarted and, not thinking, she sucked the blood off. It tasted like copper and dust.

"Which choice, Your Majesty?" asked Ohrig, looking over at his pale queen, his expression just as worried as hers. "Should we take the back roads or stay on the public highway?'

"Just give me a minute, Ohrig," muttered Adele as she examined the letter once more. She chewed her bottom lip and thought hard but it was so difficult to know what to do when she had no clue why their plans had changed. *Damn Ohren and his mysterious wizard ways!*

"What's this carnival Ohren mentions here?" she asked.

"It's a horse racing carnival," Ohrig replied. "It's the most famous in Unisia, if not Evendaar. All the royal families of the kingdom gather at Belvoir Estate to race their fastest horses, sell the studs and mares, and drink far too much. It's more of a weeklong party than a proper horse market. I'm guessing the carnival was originally meant to coincide with the end of your royal procession around the kingdom."

"But, instead, I had to spend almost two weeks traveling back and forth to Sandar for emergency trade negotiations." Adele patted the top pocket of her travelling cloak, where she kept the little box of Fire Orchid stamens. "Thank goodness, it was worth it!"

Adele looked at the general of her Queen's Guard. Over the intensity of the past two weeks, she had come to value General Ohrig's sensible advice. He was a man whom she felt had earned her trust, or at least *enough* of her trust. Though his deep-set, pale blue eyes were often shadowed by the worries she brought him Adele knew that General Ohrig never backed down from a challenge, and he did not encourage her to, either.

"What worries me is that the high wizard has said that he'll send my things to Belvoir Estate, but not that he would meet us there. Didn't he say that it was crucial to get these flower stamens back to Concordis to make the influenza tonics immediately?"

Ohrig straightened up in his saddle as Captain Lucky joined them. The carriages were now on the move and were slowly making their way down the road. All the nannies, children, and puppies were aboard, and the other four members of the Queen's Guard were riding beside them.

"My first priority is the safety of the queen and her children," Ohrig said firmly. "So I would not advise us to ride into possible danger at the Golden Palace. Instead, we should travel to the Belvoir Estate. Even if the high wizard can't be trusted, I believe we will still be safe there."

"Why shouldn't we trust the high wizard?" asked Adele quickly, giving Ohrig a curious look. She had a strong feeling that Ohrig knew something about High Wizard Ohren that he wasn't telling her. But Ohrig just shrugged, his closed expression suggesting that conversation should wait for a more private time and fell in beside the first carriage as it came up beside them.

"Everything alright, Your Majesty?" Tilburn's worried face leaned out the window of the first carriage. He had a quill stuck behind his ear and his hands were full of papers.

"Of course, it is," Adele forced a smile to placate her Majordomo. "We have just received an invitation to join the carnival at Belvoir Estate. Sounds like it should be a great party, so we are going to head there instead of back to the palace."

"Really?" Tilburn looked doubtful. "I know it was on the list of duties for you, but I hardly think High Wizard Ohren will believe that a horse festival would be more important than taking receipt of the stamens."

"Well he does think it's more important," interrupted Adele, her own disquiet making her short with Tilburn's sensible question. "And he told us to go to Belvoir, so we will go to Belvoir."

Irritated with her response, the ever-sensitive Tilburn shut his mouth with a snap and retreated back into the carriage and Adele immediately wished she hadn't been so brusque with him. Now he would sulk for hours. Besides, after everything she had been through to get the Fire Orchid stamens for the high wizard it was just too hard to believe he wouldn't want to take them from her straight away.

I killed one man and ruined the life of another to secure these Fire Orchids for Unisia, thought Adele, the memory making her heart drop into a dark pit of shame. *And now Ohren doesn't even want them?*

She shook her head to try and lose these disturbing thoughts. Ohren was one of the good guys. A wizard, true, but a good wizard. *What's done is done,* she told herself firmly. *Besides, all the royal families will be at this carnival. Hopefully, Rainere will be there, too.*

The idea of seeing Prince Rainere again picked up Adele's flagging spirits. She really needed to talk to him about what had happened in Sandar and what it could mean for the two of them. If she had started a war between Sandar and Unisia, he may very well change his mind about wanting to marry her. On this journey she had already had too many experiences with magic to ignore the power that now lived within her. A power she was determined to keep secret until she knew more about it all and she had a feeling that Rainere was the only person who may be able to help her.

Adele decided to take Ohrig's advice and follow the highway to the Belvoir Estate. Out on the open road, Adele felt comfortable enough to ride ahead of the caravan to be alone with her thoughts. It was pleasant enough until a gusty breeze blew up and rattled the branches of the trees that lined the road and sudden chill bit at her cheeks.

In their carriage, the children shivered and cuddled close to their nannies. Down on the floor, Hero Boy whined and looked up at his tiny master.

"I know, too, don't I, Hero Boy?" said Aaron quietly. "The snow is coming."

CHAPTER THREE
"Webs of Deceit"

A strong wind blew in through the broken windows, overturning some tiny glass bottles and rattling the papers that lay strewn across the workbenches in the laboratory. Grotto jumped at the commotion, roused from his maudlin contemplations where he still swept glass on the floor. He shivered as another buffeting gust almost knocked him over. This was an unnatural wind.

He moved to the empty windows and looked out to the front gates and the Dark Forest beyond. Heavy black clouds raced across the sky and piled in great heaps over the Grey Palace. Grotto's nose twitched at the smell of ice in the air, its cold clear scent stabbing at his sinuses.

What was his master up to now?

Grotto cleared his thoughts and quietened his mind to listen to the wind. His long, bony fingers gripped the jagged edge of the windowsill as he leaned out over the edge.

She comes! She comes! whispered the North Wind. *She comes with the breath of a beast behind her. All men be afraid. The queen is coming!"*

Grotto frowned and pressed his thin lips together. *The North Wind was fickle and often spoke in foolish riddles, but the 'breath of a beast'? What new darkness was this? Most likely, it was the Spider Empress of which the wind spoke.*

The queen was close, and his master was finally doing something to bring her to his side where she could fulfill her part of the prophecy. Grotto looked forward to events unfolding as they should, but he couldn't calm the disquiet in his soul. The empress would have her vengeance on the queen, and Grotto feared that his master was underestimating the strength of the empress's hatred. This prophecy was not going to end well for the queen, and Grotto did not want the prince to be in the way when it did.

The Spider People were an ancient and primitive race, but they had long memories. Their ancestors had walked the Above Lands a thousand years ago, nesting in the trees of the Dark Forest and eating all the fresh meat they could catch, animal and human alike. They had been a powerful race, feared by all and nearly unstoppable because of their ability to walk in the light of day, as well as at night. Not many of the Dark Entities shared this ability, but it was the very thing that made them so dangerous that had been so fascinating to the Marchant kings of the day.

The Spider People were a long-lived race. Though not technically immortal, they still maintained their bodies for hundreds of years in perfect health. The Spider People had exchanged their knowledge of the Gift of Life with the Marchant kings for protection from the Goddess Serena when she returned to the world of Evendaar. They had made the Under Lands their permanent home, hiding in nests on the promise of the Marchant kings that one day they would be able to return to the surface of the world. When the Spider Empress and her kind covered the land, other Dark Entities would also rise from the shadows where they had hidden for so long. A new era of darkness would cover the world, and the Goddess Lune would have dominion over the Goddess Serena as she had in the days of old, before the humans had even come to this world.

Grotto gritted his teeth and gazed sightlessly out at the billowing clouds. He didn't even notice as the first flakes of snow drifted in and fell softly about him.

All that imposter queen has to do is marry my master and put him on the throne as the rightful king of Unisia. Then when the Dark Entities take back the lands of the other nations, Prince Rainere will finally rule all of Evendaar. The Marchant blood will once more hold the throne, and my oath to Rainere's late father will finally be fulfilled. Grotto almost smiled at the thought of it, but the moment passed quickly. The task was not yet done.

What we need is more time to get the queen to marry the prince, but the prophecy is being moved to the will of the Spider Empress and she is far too impatient for a resolution. If only the Hidden Child was not this abomination that has trapped my master in her terrible magic, binding him to her with filthy wiles. The quicker he puts her and her mixed blood children aside after the marriage, the better. Grotto thought to himself.

A loud sniff alerted him to the presence of one of the servants who made up the meagre staff at the Grey Palace. The man had slunk into the room and hovered by the door, wearing a dirty apron and a surly expression.

"Barren, call for the glazier," Grotto ordered, pointing to the empty windows behind him. "We will need these windows repaired immediately."

Barren sniffed again and wiped his nose with the back of his hand. The smell of cheap whiskey hung about him like a fog. "The glazier say'd 'e wasna' gonna come agin if 'e's bill wasna' paid from the las' time."

Grotto stared hard at the unkempt servant as he struggled to come up with a cure for the last repair bill, and this expensive new one. "Take the pewter candlesticks from the High State dining hall. There are six of them there. Give them to the blacksmith and then take what he pays you to the glazier. They should both know that the order came from me so there will be no haggling. Am I understood?" Grotto snapped.

"Unner-stood, sir." Barren attempted a bow, but just sort of fell to the side and stumbled out of the door, instead.

Grotto clenched his hands into fists of impotent rage and bit off a curse. *How low the Marchant family has sunk!* They were reduced to selling off priceless heirlooms, just to keep their crumbling home whole. Grotto was not a greedy man and gold held no personal attraction for him, but he did like things to remain as they were. Despite Prince Rainere's willful destruction of the palace's windows, mirrors, and the occasional chandelier, Grotto was determined to keep the palace in good working order until the prince became king and the doors of the Unisian royal treasury flew open to him.

He remembered so clearly when the Grey Palace had been the most elegant and opulent of all the Marchant houses. It did not share the ostentation of the Golden Palace but had been decorated over the years by the Marchant monarchs in an elegant and formal way. From the smallest details in the gold leaf frescoes adorning the walls to the exceptionally rare ice marble that lined the floor of the entrance hall in great square slabs, the Grey Palace had been a vision of wealth and good taste. Of course, there had always been hundreds of servants to clean and polish the rooms in the past. Now there was just Grotto left to care for it all, and his small staff of drunken buffoons from the local village.

"One day soon, I will return things to the way they were," Grotto promised himself aloud. "This palace will again become the beauty that it was and those pewter candlesticks and everything else shall be brought home. May the Goddess Lune bless my efforts."

Newly energized, Grotto knelt down to sweep up the rest of the broken glass with fresh vigor, muttering to himself. "Though that abomination has stolen my master's senses, her marriage to him will give him back all that is rightfully his—his throne and his home."

Grotto caught a glimpse of his reflection in a shard of glass and paused. His vivid green eye glinted back at him. All he had to do was keep Prince Rainere from doing anything foolish until that could happen. Neither Rainere nor the Spider Empress could be allowed to discover the queen's true nature until after the marriage. If Empress Ka-kik found out who Adelena really was, then the prophecy would be nothing more than a happy fantasy and all their lives would be forfeit.

CHAPTER FOUR

"Shelter From the Storm"

They had not been riding the King's Highway for long when Adele took a moment to pull up the collar of her riding jacket. It had been hot on the beaches of Sandar and the sunny days of late spring in Unisia were hardly cold. The turn in the weather seemed ominous after all that had happened today.

Adele glanced over at General Ohrig as he cast a worried look up at the sky where heavy grey clouds were gathering above their heads.

'There is a storm coming. It's going to be bad.'

Damn Ripenzo and his cryptic message, Adele thought, *now that it doesn't seem so cryptic anymore.* This had to be the storm he warned them about in his letter.

"What is it, Ohrig?" asked Adele as she pulled her horse up beside the general.

"Hear that?" he asked Adele.

Adele cocked her head to the side and listened hard.

"I hear nothing but the wind," she replied.

"Exactly," frowned the general. "The birds have stopped singing."

Adele's stomach dropped. That couldn't be good.

"We should take shelter," said Ohrig. "We will be too vulnerable on the road when the weather breaks. I suggest you ride in the carriage with the children, Your Majesty. It's going to get uncomfortable out here."

Adele jumped when a peal of thunder rumbled through the sky and made her horse start. She had only started riding a couple of weeks ago and being on a nervous horse was not yet something she knew how to deal with. A gust of wind blew at them head-on, raising puffs of dust on the road and sending grit into their eyes. Captain Lucky rode up just as Adele's horse shied, making her yelp in fear.

"Easy girl, easy my girl. It's alright. Just a bit of wind," the captain crooned, as he reached over to take the reins from Adele so she couldn't jerk them anymore and soothing the nervous animal as it shook its mane and pawed at the ground.

Adele felt the hairs on her body rise and a shiver wiggle its way down her spine when a flash of lightning cracked the sky, illuminating the densely-packed trees of the forest lining the road to their left. The Dark Forest was unlike the green and sunny forests that were common in Unisia. The trees here were gnarled and ugly, their dark green leaves crowning the forest in a dense canopy that didn't let in any light to the forest floor. There were no paths through the trees that Adele could see.

"Ohrig, where can we shelter? The forest looks impenetrable from here."

But the general didn't answer her. He was looking over into the forest, then back up the road ahead of them. Adele knew Ohrig well enough now to know he was making a serious decision. She waited until he was done, as her own anxiety mounted.

"There is always bad weather over the Dark Forest, but with the densely-packed trees, we will have more protection than if we continue on the highway. It will be much easier without this wind, too." He frowned, as he looked at Adele, but she knew his concern was only for their safety. "As I mentioned before, there is an old road not far from here, which will take us along the back roads to the Belvoir Estate, but without good visibility it's easy to get lost in the Dark Forest. If we took the wrong turn we would end up at the Grey Palace instead of Belvoir, and that wouldn't be wise."

Adele dropped her eyes to her saddle to hide the thrill of excitement that shot through her at the idea of seeing Rainere again. She'd had no idea that they were so close to his home at the Grey Palace. "Wouldn't Prince Rainere give us shelter?" she asked, trying hard to sound innocent, instead of eager.

"He would," agreed Ohrig slowly. "But if we can avoid asking for it, so much the better. Let's just pray to the Goddess Serena that this is just a passing summer storm and move as fast as we can to Belvoir."

"Through the Dark Forest, general?" asked Captain Lucky, confirming his orders, but Adele didn't miss the anxious look he gave his superior.

The general gave a curt nod and pulled his horse around to face the three slowly-moving carriages behind them. "Take the queen's horse for her, then tell the men to prepare for a hard ride. Put your cloaks on and keep your swords at the hip. I want you to take QG Pepper and ride on ahead to scout the trail for us, but not too far ahead. Shouting distance only."

"General," nodded Lucky, who dismounted to help Adele slide off her horse.

"Scouts? Are these woods dangerous, Ohrig?" asked Adele. They all looked up, as the sun was suddenly covered by a thick bank of clouds, plunging the countryside into an early twilight.

"The Dark Forest borders Marchant lands, Your Majesty, and has been left wild for thousands of years. I'm not sure what, or who, lives in these woods, but without a bright sun or a wizard in our party I think it's better to be safe than sorry." Ohrig's voice was grim and Adele could take no comfort from it.

Adele headed back to the carriages. She heard her little daughter, Stella, call out for her and felt anxiety tighten its grip on her lungs, pulling her breath in short bursts. She and her children were in constant danger in this new world and she just couldn't seem to make it stop. The Chime Voices sang magic commands softly in her ears, but she ignored them. She had no need of her odd power right now.

It certainly couldn't control the storm or tell her what she needed to do to keep her children safe. She thought briefly of insisting that they head to the Grey Palace, but a powerful need for secrecy prevented her. No one could know that she and Rainere were involved with each other. Not yet.

So instead, Adele plastered a bright smile on her face and pulled herself into the crowded carriage filled with her three children, their nannies, and puppies. Squashing herself into a seat, she took the baby, Stella, into her arms and cuddled her eldest daughter, Natalie, close to her. Aaron was curled up in a corner of the carriage, his little face white with worry. The sight of his expression made Adele want to weep, but she stayed resolutely cheerful.

"Come on, everyone! It's just a little storm. Nothing to worry about at all. Now, how about a song? *Five fat frogs sitting on a log...*" Adele began singing.

The carriage picked up the pace considerably and they were all getting jumbled around as Adele kept the singing going, her own voice the loudest, drowning out the noise of the storm.

Suddenly, the carriage almost lifted off two wheels when they sharply took the corner onto the forest road. Caitlin, the youngest nanny, cried out in fright and all the children started whimpering. Trying to slow her own racing heart, Adele had just started on another nursery rhyme when Natalie called out. "Mummy, look! What's that?"

Everyone looked out of the windows of the carriage as soft, white flakes spun and whirled in the wind outside.

"My God, it's snow," whispered Adele. She looked over at her little son where he lay curled up on the carriage cushions.

"Hey, Aaron! You were right, sweetheart." She reached over and squeezed Aaron's leg. "We do have snow today."

Aaron returned her smile with a worried frown. "Hero Boy told me, didn't he?"

"Well, then, clever Hero Boy," replied Adele, as she reached down to give the puppy a scratch behind his ears. Adele felt it was important that Aaron didn't see how freaked out she was that his earlier prediction had come true or that he kept saying his dog had told him.

The wind howled ferociously and the carriage shuddered as the wheels bumped and rolled over the pitted road. Soon the delicate flakes of snow had turned into a heavy white cloud and Adele could only presume they were looking at a blizzard. She'd never seen one before on Earth, as they had always lived near the beach. Occasionally, she heard the shouting of her men and the carriage drivers over the howl of the wind, but mostly, she tried to drown it out, singing silly songs and telling stories to keep her children calm. One of the nannies, Seraphina, managed to find a firelighter to light the two tiny lanterns in the carriage. It would have been very cozy, if it wasn't for the demonic screeching of the wind outside.

"Wow! Thunder, lightning, and snow! Aren't we the lucky ones?" Adele told her children as yet another peal of thunder rattled their teeth.

Stella whimpered and cuddled into her mother.

"It isn't right, Your Majesty," whispered Seraphina. "We must be awfully close to the Marchant palace to be getting weather this bad. It is a magical storm. I'm sure of it."

Adele silently raised her eyebrows in a warning gesture to the young woman. She didn't want the children getting more upset than they already were.

Time passed slowly in the carriages and it felt like an age before the carriage slowed and lurched to a rude stop. Stella had fallen asleep in Adele's arms and Natalie was cuddled into her side. There was a knock at the door and Adele heard General Ohrig shout her name. She passed the baby over to Caitlin and stepped out of the carriage carefully, not wanting to let in the frigid air of the storm.

Jumping down, Adele could only just make out General Ohrig and her Queen's Guardsmen through the billowing snow, standing in front of an enormous set of gates. Holding her arms up to protect her face, Adele approached the general just as a huge gust of wind almost blew her over. Panicking, Adele reached out and threw herself at the nearest Guardsman before she was blown away.

Captain Lucky wrapped his arms around Adele, holding her tight. Adele squirmed as the snow blew into her eyes and Lucky's tough leather armor pressed into her back.

"Your Majesty!" General Ohrig had stepped up behind her and shouted in her ear. "We have…a wrong turn, the storm…Grey Palace…too dangerous…road…"

Adele nodded, though she couldn't catch half of what he was saying. Looking over Captain Lucky's protective embrace and through the large wrought-iron gates, a break in the swirling snow lasted just long enough for Adele to see a huge building with warm yellow lights shining in the upper windows.

The Grey Palace.

Despite the cold wind and the icy flakes dripping down her neck, Adele felt a flush of heat.

Rainere lives here.

Adele pushed out of Lucky's arms and reached out to touch the black metal of the gates. The flash of green sparks was almost lost in the flurries of snow as General Ohrig gave a warning shout and threw himself in front of Adele. The three of them gazed in wonder as the gates slowly swung open by themselves. Adele smiled as a deep sense of familiarity settled over her as comfortably as a blanket.

She had been there before.

Chapter Five

"There's No Place Like Home"

Adele stepped through the gates of the Grey Palace with General Ohrig on one side of her and Captain Lucky on the other.

"Your Majesty! Look!" said Ohrig, pointing ahead of them. "The storm stops at the gates."

"That's impossible," whispered Adele as she gazed around at the thick snow covering the grounds. Not a breath of wind disturbed the tiny glittering icicles that hung like jewelry from the trees lining the wide driveway. Even the sky above them was clear and black, littered with sparkling stars and a half-full moon, heavy and white above the turrets of the palace.

"General, this is just too strange," muttered Captain Lucky. "It must be the dark magic protecting this place. I don't like it."

"Neither do I, but we have no choice, captain. The storm is just too strong out there in the forest. We have to think of the children."

Adele heard the men beside her shift and organize the carriages to join them, but she paid them no attention as she walked away up the road alone. Her eyes drank in the sight of the Grey Palace that was familiar and strange all at the same time. The stonework reminded her so much of the baroque architecture of Earth, but with a distinctly alien aspect that was beautiful. She knew this place so well because she had travelled here a hundred times in her dreams when she had still lived on Earth. It had been her happy place during all the lonely nights and bad days of her life as a woman stuck in a loveless marriage with three small children to care for. This palace had been her paradise in all its strange and melancholy glory and this time Rainere would be inside waiting for her.

Adele fought the urge to clap her hands and giggle like a girl. She quickened the pace and almost raced along the wide path. The carriages rattled up to join her at the foot of the front steps of the palace, their wheels sending out sprays of snow that lined the drive. Tilburn cautiously stepped out of his carriage and down onto the gravel. His wig and clothing immaculate despite the bumpy ride.

"I understand that we are here on your orders, Your Majesty," Tilburn said, nervously looking up at the great black doors of the Grey Palace. "But I must beg you to reconsider your decision. No St. Lucidis monarch has stepped foot into the Grey Palace since, well… ever."

Tilburn moved to stand in front of Adele and bring the full force of his disapproval to bear on her, his expression knotting his thin eyebrows and pursing his lips. "Forgive my candor, Your Majesty, but you have no idea what it means politically should you ask for shelter from the Marchant prince. And quite frankly I think we will be safer out in that unnatural storm than we will be by his fireside. And by *we*, I mean *you* of course, Your Majesty. You, and the children."

"We had to stop somewhere, Tilburn," said Adele reasonably and stepped aside to guide the children up the steps. "I had the good luck to meet the prince at my coronation a few weeks ago and he seemed very polite. I'm sure he will give us somewhere to wait out the storm if we ask him nicely enough. Now, if we could all just keep our opinions of Marchants to ourselves while we are here?"

Adele turned back to point at her majordomo. "That means you, Tilburn." Tilburn looked momentarily affronted before dropping the act and nodding in grudging agreement.

Adele looked over at General Ohrig to check his mood, but his expression was stony and he only gave her a brusque nod. She almost sighed in exasperation. *Honestly, they didn't even know Rainere, how could they all fear him so much?*

"Look Mummy, stone dragons!" said Natalie slipping her cold hand into Adele's and grinning with pleasure. "They're so beautiful!"

Adele gave her daughter's hand a squeeze. At least Natalie wasn't frightened of the Grey Palace. Nor was Aaron, who was trying to stare up at the roof, cricking his neck backwards and squinting.

"There is a snow man up there, isn't there?" he giggled. "A man with lots of snow!" He pointed. Following his gaze, Adele accidentally stepped back onto the step below her and into Captain Lucky's arms. There was an awkward moment as the captain tried to hold her steady and Adele tried to pull away from him, resulting in the two of them falling into a rough hug and a bark of embarrassed laughter from Adele. She didn't try to look up again.

When the royal party had all assembled behind her, Adele put her hand on the huge dragon-headed doorknocker and tapped three times. The sound could be heard booming through the house. Adele fidgeted in anticipation of seeing Rainere again.

They waited for one long minute, and then another. The guards started shuffling and muttering in their line behind the women and children. Aaron and Natalie blew puffs of steam at each other as their breath came out in white clouds. Adele stamped her cold feet and stifled a grin. He should be here any minute now.

They waited some more.

"Maybe no one's home?" suggested QG Pepper in a hopeful voice. "Maybe His Highness is out and just left the lights on for...security purposes?"

"Shut it QG," growled General Ohrig cuffing Pepper lightly on the head. "The Grey Palace doesn't need security lights. It's protected by the darkest spells magic ever created."

The general caught Adele's eye when she turned. "We should be alert," he said.

"But not alarmed," countered Adele, and raised her hand to knock a second time just as the doors began to swing ever so slowly inwards. Adele's breath caught in her throat, fighting for space with her heart.

The doors had completely opened before Adele could finally make out a single tall figure walking towards them from the dim interior of the entrance hall. He stopped just inside the doorway.

It was Grotto.

Adele's heart sank back down into her chest and she felt the smile on her face turn wooden. Rainere's manservant, Grottonski, was the only other person who knew about her relationship with the prince, and he hated her.

"Good evening," Adele began, before Tilburn almost pushed her out of the way, stepping to the front and pulling himself up as tall as his diminutive height would allow.

"Sir, Her Majesty the Queen of Unisia requests the hospitality of the royal Prince Rainere of Marchant. We have been caught up in a dangerous storm and need to shelter for the time it takes to blow over. We have with us the queen and her royal children in our party and insist that succor be given in their time of need. Of course it is a great honor to the prince, and Her Majesty expects the best of care, despite the late hour."

During the entire speech, Grotto remained stock still, his face frozen as if carved from the same grey stone that framed the doors. Adele smiled warmly to try and take the chill out of Tilburn's pompous attitude, but Rainere's manservant never spared her a glance. Finally, Tilburn fell silent and looked expectantly at the servant before him.

"This way if it please you," was all Grotto said in his deep, hoarse voice as he abruptly turned on his heel and stalked off into the cavernous entry hall. Tilburn huffed and pulled his vest down with a sharp tug. Giving Adele a quick *I told you so* glance, the majordomo led them all inside, following Grotto.

"Wow!" said Aaron, her son echoing Adele's thoughts exactly as they made their way through the entry hall. "This house was made for giants, wasn't it, Mummy?"

"I really think it might have been, sweetheart," Adele answered as her eyes travelled up to the incredibly high ceilings. Leering gargoyles and fierce griffin-like creatures perched on top of every column and corner, looking as if they might pounce down on them at any minute.

The entry hall led to an even bigger foyer. The floor of the foyer was made up entirely of black and grey marble tiles in a checkerboard pattern. Suits of armor complete with helmets and swords lined the walls. Some polished to a high sheen while others were rusty and beaten up.

Grotto was standing at the foot of one of the two enormous staircases before them. The royal party assembled before him silently, in awe of the somber grandeur of the Grey Palace. The children, sensing the mood of the occasion, clung to Adele's legs.

"This staircase leads to the upper levels of the west wing, and the chambers where you may stay for the time being. The other staircase leads to the upper levels of the east wing. No one is permitted to go there." Grotto glared heavily at their little gathering, daring them to say anything in response to this edict. Then he turned and climbed the stairs too rapidly for such an old man as he appeared to be.

Adele tripped several times on the steps as she couldn't help staring about herself at the intricately carved stone of the balustrade, and the tapestries that lined the staircase. She had never come inside the palace in her dreams before, so everything was as fascinating as it was unfamiliar.

As Grotto led them down a great hallway, Adele couldn't help but notice the air of neglect that hung over the place. The carpet beneath her feet was faded and worn through in patches. The gloomy lighting of the lamps lining the walls only served to highlight the dusty paintings and peeling wallpaper.

"Mummy, this place is so spooky!" whispered Natalie to Adele as they passed yet another full-size portrait of a glaring Marchant monarch. "Do ghosts live here?"

Adele hushed her daughter and squeezed her hand. An instinct told her Grotto probably had ears like a bat. Besides, Adele needed all her concentration to remain calm as they moved further into the Grey Palace. Her nerves were growing more fragile as she expected to see Prince Rainere at every turn.

Grotto eventually stopped in front of a set of wide doors. To Adele's surprise they were covered in delicate engravings and glowed a very soft green. Marchant magic protected these doors.

"The royal suite, for Her Majesty and the infant royals," announced Grotto as he pushed the doors open. "Maids sleep in the chamber adjoining the suite. There are closets down the hall for your men-at-arms."

Grotto barely glanced at Adele as he snapped a bow in her general direction and then turned and marched off into the gloom of the long hallway.

Adele tried not to feel completely crushed that Rainere hadn't shown himself. *Maybe he is asleep in bed? It is very late in the evening, after all.* Adele turned to Tilburn to ask him the time, but wisely decided against it when she saw his face.

Tilburn's cheeks had puffed out dramatically and a vein throbbed at his temple. Her majordomo was apoplectic with rage at the casual treatment of the royal family at the hands of a Marchant servant and he was about to express his feelings loudly. Adele quickly pushed Tilburn into the apartment and closed the doors before his anger could explode down the hall.

General Ohrig and the Queen's Guard soon returned from giving the apartments a quick once over. "All clear, general?" asked Adele.

"All clear from a safety perspective, Your Majesty, but I can't say your majordomo is going to be any happier when he sees the state of these rooms."

Adele gave the general a quick grimace as Tilburn surveyed the sitting room, spitting with fury and only managing to speak in garbled half sentences.

"Why, of all the…! How dare they? Abominable treatment of the royal…never have I ever!"

Seraphina had found a tray of refreshments on the dining table and quickly poured Tilburn a goblet of wine. He downed the cup in one draught and carefully put it down on a side table before pulling his waistcoat straight with a sharp tug. His expression showed he had regained some of his self-control.

"Your Majesty, I can only offer apologies for your awful, *awful* treatment at the hands of the Marchant family. It is unforgivable that our royal family should be treated like common houseguests, and not with the honor that your visit should entail. Of course, you will now see why I was so reluctant to put ourselves in this position of asking for hospitality," said Tilburn.

"Tilburn, honestly, it's all right," said Adele, not without a little exasperation. "We have caught Prince Rainere by surprise that's all."

They all looked at the trays of food and wine laid out on the dining table. Their preparation didn't entirely support her argument, but Adele decided to look past the point.

"We didn't really have any choice Tilburn, with that storm out there. And look, the children are happy, at least." Adele said, as she gestured to her three little ones as they careened from one room to the next, screeching happily. The dusty floorboards were perfect for sliding about on their knees. "Let's just get settled and everyone can get to bed. It's been such a long day."

Given instructions, Tilburn finally had an outlet for his anger. He set himself to unpacking the few trunks that the drivers had brought up behind them, ruthlessly employing everyone not of royal blood to dusting mantles and tables, and lighting fires in the enormous grates.

Adele followed behind her children and explored the ancient suite they'd been given. The sitting room was the first room they had entered, but on either side of it were two large reception rooms, one of which was filled with furniture as if it had been set up for a concert. Rows of spindly wooden chairs sat facing a narrow podium where tapestries hung from the ceiling, suspended from horizontal rods, creating a stage area. The pictures on the tapestries depicted scenes of worship and what looked like ritual baptism, but instead of water the white robed figures were walking through a great fire, embroidered in red and gold thread. The acolytes on the other side of the fire held their hands aloft, their clothes burnt away and a green halo about their bodies. Their little thread faces showed expressions of terrible rapture.

From the little naked people dancing about in such wicked glee to the strange writing that ringed the image with letters sharp and unreadable, something about the images felt unwholesome. Adele didn't feel comfortable studying the tapestry with her children by her side so she quickly shooed them away to the next room, which was a large bedroom. A huge canopied bed rested in the center of the room, and several couches of various sizes had been pushed haphazardly against the walls. A large wardrobe sat in the corner. An image of an ugly goblin face had been engraved in the doors and it scared the little girls, so Adele decided that her Queen's Guard could have this room.

The second reception room was all the way on the other side of the sitting room and was almost completely bare of furniture. Tattered grey silk curtains hung at the floor-to-ceiling windows, and a huge stone dragon glared menacingly from above the fireplace, perched as if it had just climbed down from the ceiling. A single leather armchair sat in the center of the room, facing the windows. A stain lay spread at the foot of the chair, marring the floorboards darkly, and Adele didn't want to look too closely to see what had caused it.

Through this empty room, Adele found the bedroom where she was to sleep with the children and their nannies. As she ran her fingers over the heavy black furniture, it felt cold to the touch. Everything was made of iron, and the sharp metallic smell of it filled the room. Adele looked up as Seraphina's lantern threw shadows into the dark corners and studied the walls searching for any hint of secret doors or passageways. Rainere had shown her that the Golden Palace had been full of such secret tunnels when he had stayed there and she guessed that his own home would be the same.

Caitlin bustled into the room with the children running ahead of her and their night things in her arms. Adele helped to bathe the children in the cavernous bathroom attached to the bedroom. The soporific effect of a hot bath was working well to calm their frazzled nerves after a stressful day of travelling, and as they had already filled up on the snacks that had been laid out, the children were ready to sleep quickly.

Adele kissed each of her little ones good night as they snuggled down under the surprisingly fresh sheets of the great bed. The three puppies had piled into their basket under the bed, already snoring. Adele leant down and gave Hero Boy a little pat. The dog stirred and whined in his sleep.

It had been so odd today when Aaron had claimed that Hero Boy had told him about the snow. It wasn't like Aaron to make up stories like that. *Is it possible that I'm not the only one to have magic wake up inside me, now that we live in this new world?* Anxious, Adele chewed her bottom lip as she headed for the door.

"Are you going to see the prince, Mummy?" asked a little voice behind her.

"I don't know, Aaron. Maybe," whispered Adele, turning back to the bed to see her son sitting up between his sleeping sisters. "You should rest now, sweetheart. I'll be back later though, and I'm going to sleep right next to you, I promise."

"Tell him I like his snow, don't I, Mummy?" said Aaron and thankfully fell back on his pillows ready to sleep.

"I think it's beautiful, too, Aaron," whispered Adele, as she breathed a sigh of relief at the innocence of the comment. She couldn't take any more puzzles tonight. *Perhaps he had heard the QGs talking about*

Ripenzo's storm earlier, she thought. *Maybe one of them suggested that it meant snow was coming.*

Adele made her way back into the central sitting room.

"Everything alright, Your Majesty?" asked Seraphina, as the young nanny put down her fork to stand for Adele.

"When you've finished your dinner, could you please stay close to the children?" asked Adele. "The girls are already asleep, but Aaron is still a bit unsettled."

Seraphina bobbed and sat again, ready to bolt down her food and do as she was asked.

"Can't say I blame the little tyke," said General Ohrig as he made his way across the sitting room from the opposite doorway. No doubt he had been looking at the strange set up next door. "I will station guards at your bedroom door and at the front here throughout the night, Your Majesty."

"Do you really think that's necessary, General?" protested Adele. "I'm sure the men are all exhausted from the hard ride today, and everyone could do with a good night's sleep."

She also couldn't think of how she was to sneak away to find Rainere if there were guards all over the apartment. "I'm sure there is no reason to be overly alarmed," she said, making a play for humor.

General Ohrig gave her a skeptical look. "Your Majesty, there is something you should know while we are here in the Grey Palace," he began, but was interrupted by a loud knock at the door.

Tilburn scurried to answer it and stepped back in surprise as Grotto strode past him into the room, searching the group until his eyes alighted on Adele. She almost flinched from the venom in his glance.

"His Highness, Prince Rainere, extends a cordial invitation to Her Majesty the queen to dine with him in the High State dining room this evening," he said stiffly, almost choking on the word *cordial.*

Tilburn was incensed and jumped in front of the prince's manservant. "Surely the prince would not expect Her Majesty to join him for dinner at this late hour, with such little notice?" he asked in a scandalized tone. "It would be most forward and outside all manner of protocols to even suggest such a thing!"

Grotto's expression told the majordomo what he could do with his protocols. "The Marchant *prince* has invited the *queen* to dine with him *this* evening," insisted Grotto enunciating each word and leaning over Tilburn menacingly.

"I accept the invitation!" interjected Adele before Tilburn could explode into righteous fury once again. "Thank you, Mr. Grotto, please tell Prince Rainere I can be ready to join him within the hour."

Grotto snapped a shallow bow and turned smartly, exiting the room and banging the doors loudly behind himself.

Adele looked about and saw everyone in the room was staring at her with varying degrees of horror on their faces. She laughed nervously. "What? He's our host! I have to be polite." She smiled as the butterflies began batting against the sides of her stomach. "Besides, I've already told you. I've met the prince before, and he isn't as scary as everyone seems to think."

Adele turned away to avoid General Ohrig's gaze, pretending not to see the hand he raised to stop her as she moved off towards the bedroom.

"Girls, I'll need some help getting ready," she called back to Seraphina and Caitlin. "Please find my nice dress for me, the red I think? And get the make-up and things out. I need to wash the smell of horse and dust off me before dinner."

The moment she had been waiting nearly two weeks for was about to happen. No grumpy general was going to stop her from seeing Prince Rainere tonight. Nothing was going to keep them apart now.

Chapter Six

"No Good Sense"

At the appointed hour, Adele was washed and groomed for her dinner with the prince. She was pleased that she had brought the red silk dress with her. She hadn't worn it once in Sandar, so it was still clean and relatively unwrinkled. Adele loved this dress. Its tight bodice gave her waist a wonderful waspish shape and pushed her small breasts up prettily. It made her blush to wonder what Rainere would think of it. Following Grotto down the dark corridor, Adele let a grin dance across her face. Her heart thudded in her chest and she clenched her hands together to hide her damp palms. She was so excited that she almost passed by Grotto when he stopped in front of a large open doorway and gestured for her to enter ahead of him.

The High State dining room was large, but by no means as cavernous as the one at the Golden Palace. It had been decorated for the dinner with hundreds of fresh candles sitting on white china plates stacked three rows deep on each of the dozen buffets lining the walls. A fire roaring in the grate took the chill off the air and provided most of the light in the room. A long dining table stood in the center with twelve chairs lining each side and heavy chargers sitting at either end.

Adele stepped into the room and made her way over to the table, her slippers clicking noisily on the bare marble floors. Though her eyes roamed the room, she was not sure she would have seen him if he hadn't moved.

Prince Rainere was leaning against the mantle of the fireplace, his velvet coat camouflaging him against the dark wood. As he turned to face her his long black hair fell to either side of his face, framing his chiseled cheeks and sharp chin. His gaze found hers, and his frozen expression became colder still.

Blithely, Adele headed straight for Rainere and almost fell over Grotto again as he pulled out a charger from the table directly into her path. "Wine, Your Majesty?" he asked. The question was also a curt demand to sit down.

Remembering herself and where she was, Adele sat down on the offered chair and blushed furiously. Of course, she couldn't just throw herself at Rainere here in the dining room. *Anyone could be looking!* She quietly thanked Grotto as he poured her a glass of ruby red wine. She fingered the base of the crystal goblet and bit her bottom lip, feeling suddenly and completely out of her depth. Rainere had neither moved from the fireplace nor said a word to her.

Perhaps he is only waiting for the servants to leave? Adele thought, but then watched in dismay as Grotto took his place by a buffet against the wall opposite her. *All the better to glare balefully at me*, she supposed. How could she be feeling this unwelcome in Rainere's home?

"Your Highness, thank you for taking us in tonight, the storm in the forest was quite fierce," Adele began and risked a glance up at Rainere, and then another over to Grotto. "I'm sure that we would have frozen solid if we'd been out there any longer." She tried for a smile but it caught uncomfortably in a lopsided grin. She quickly straightened her lips.

"Queen Adelena." Rainere's voice was one of her favorite things in this new world and its deep rasp sent a warm thrill through her. "I am so glad that I could be of assistance to you and your party tonight. It is indeed such good fortune that you were so near the Grey Palace when the storm hit."

He moved towards her as he spoke. His arms were held behind his back, and he reached the table in a few slow strides. Rainere was dressed simply but elegantly, as always. The velvet jacket was long and fluted at the back, his leather trousers were tight and the silk shirt was only half-way tucked in, as if he had just gotten dressed this minute. Adele looked up into the prince's dark green eyes as he came to stand next to her.

"It's good to see you, Rainere," Adele said softly. "It's been such a long time and so much has happened. I have much to tell you."

Adele couldn't disguise the wobble in her voice. She had been tired and scared for too long during the two weeks they had been apart, and she didn't want to play games with Rainere right now. She held her chin high and let him see the tears that shone in her eyes.

Rainere pulled out a chair and sat close, the silver ring around his black pupils pulsed and flashed. *Was he angry?* "By all means, Your Majesty." Rainere inclined his head and continued to stare at her coldly. "You have my fullest attention."

Adele couldn't speak. A gut-wrenching disappointment held her mute. She shook her head and stifled a sob. Rainere leaned forward and Adele felt the menace even before she heard it in his voice.

"Careful, my queen," he growled. "An unguarded moment like this could be your undoing. You should be aware that I have seen *everything* you have done since entering my grounds."

Adele dashed away the tears and frowned up at Rainere, confusion swirling with the hurt inside her. *What did he mean when he said, 'unguarded moment'?* A warm rush of anger dried her tears as suddenly as they had sprung up. She needed to know what was making Rainere act like this. Now.

"I can't talk to you properly here," she whispered. "You need to tell me what is going on with you, and I need to tell you what happened to me in Sandar." She could see his restrained emotion in the slight shake of his hands on the table, and the defensive tilt of his chin.

Prince Rainere's eyes flashed at her. *"Going on* with me?"

So, he was going to keep up this charade, was he?

"Now, Rainere!" hissed Adele impatiently, throwing a dark look at Grotto who had approached the table to refill their still-full glasses of wine and listen in. She stood up, pushing the heavy chair back with difficulty. Adele fussed unnecessarily with her skirts as she avoided looking at Rainere and waited for him to rise. She knew she was being rude, and she had no idea how far she would have to take this *I'm the queen, do as I say* act, but she was desperate to get Rainere alone.

Something was very wrong with him, and her instincts told her she was the only one who could fix it.

Rainere stood slowly and led Adele out of the dining room, along so many dim and deserted corridors that she soon lost all sense of direction. The only comfort Adele could take in their heavy silence was that they had left his manservant Grotto far behind them in the dining room.

Finally, they stopped in front of a single door that was glowing greenly and that sparked a little when Rainere pushed it open. Adele entered the room with a confident step. She was determined not to get teary again, now that she had Rainere alone. She let her guard down so often with this man, and they had too much to discuss to waste time with tears, but her decision didn't stop her from jumping a mile when the door slammed shut behind her. She glanced at Rainere, but the prince had stalked off to a cabinet in the corner of the room and was fiddling about with glasses and a bottle.

Adele looked around the chamber and saw that a huge bed dressed in white silk sheets and heavy fur blankets dominated the room. She had to hide her smile when she realized that Rainere had brought her to his bedroom. Obviously, there was hope for them left.

She watched as Rainere moved to the fireplace and set down two tiny glasses of golden Firewhiskey on a table by an armchair. He leaned against the mantelpiece and gazed moodily into the flames, the firelight warming his features and illuminating his dark green eyes.

"I don't know why you are so angry with me, darling," began Adelena, as she made her way to settle in the armchair. She had to stay confident, after all she hadn't done anything wrong that Rainere could be aware of. "I was so looking forward to seeing you again."

"Were you, my queen?" snapped the prince, turning on her in a fury. "Perhaps, if you expected me to believe that, you should have hidden your lover from me better!"

Adele was genuinely stunned. "Lover? Rainere, you are being ridiculous."

"I'm being *ridiculous?*" Rainere snarled and stepped forward to tower over Adele where she sat on the armchair.

Adele caught the intoxicating scent of cold smoke and rich spices that only Rainere could smell of and didn't even have the good sense to be afraid. She felt a tug deep between her legs and the gentle ringing of the Chime Voices in her head reassured her that in spite of his size and anger, Adele was still very much in control of the prince. She could drop him where he stood with just a single word of command.

Adele squared her shoulders and looked up at Rainere. Her face was distractingly close to his hips. She enjoyed the warmth that swirled up from her pelvis and pressed her knees together. "Yes, you are," she smiled.

"Then tell me. Who is that blond gentleman who held you so tenderly in his arms at my very gate this night?" asked Rainere, his voice tight and cold.

Adele blanked. *Blond gentleman?*

"Who? Captain Lucky? Rainere, he's the Captain of my Guard." She laughed in relief at the misunderstanding. "He was only holding me because the wind was blowing me over outside the gate. You might not have seen how strong the blizzard was on your grounds, but out there the wind was terrible."

Rainere narrowed his eyes at her amusement. "Is that his name? Lucky?" he asked darkly.

Adele smiled. Rainere had seen Lucky catch her in the wind and thought they were lovers. *Was he really that jealous?* Though Adele could see from the flashing rings in his eyes and the stony set of his mouth that Rainere took anyone touching her very seriously indeed. She needed to reassure him that she was his again. Obviously, this separation of theirs had been just as hard on him as it had been on her. The thought of that made her very happy.

"Rainere, give me some credit, please! He is just a boy," she said as she smiled at his serious expression. "You know I need more than that."

Adele placed her hand on the back of his knee and gave a playful tug. Rainere flinched at the touch but didn't move, his expression still hard. "Then he held you again on my steps and made you laugh. I saw you both there. Was that nothing, too?"

"Rainere, I would never do that to you, to us," Adele said keeping her eyes on his. She could see the war between relief and hurt still swirling in their troubled green depths. She had never played the seductress or even tried to exert any kind of feminine charm on a man before, and she was entirely unsure it would work with Rainere now. But she *was* sure that he loved her and she could tell that he desperately wanted to be convinced of her faithfulness. In any case, of all the terrible things that Adele had done in the last two weeks in the nation of Sandar, being disloyal to Rainere was not one of them.

She leaned forward to close the gap between them, her face a mere inch from his belt, and looked up at him.

"Rainere, I missed you so much," she begged him. "Please don't do this to me." She ran her hand up the back of his thigh and let it slide up under his shirt, touching the cool skin at his waist, her fingers tracing the tattoo that was engraved there.

Rainere caught his breath sharply and pressed into her hand. His eyes closed in a moment of pleasure before he jerked away.

"So, he is nothing to you, this Captain Lucky?" he asked softly.

"He is just one of my Queen's Guard," she reassured him, placing her other hand in his, and squeezed his fingers.

"Adelena, *cara mia*," he whispered, and just like that he was hers again. Rainere ran a tender hand along her cheek and caught her chin in a gentle pinch. "Forgive me, my love."

The relief that flowed through Adele was so strong it made her head spin. She felt giddy with happiness and decided to enjoy herself now that the drama portion of the evening seemed to have passed.

"You are so cruel, Rainere," she tried to pout over her grin. "I've had to suffer two weeks without you, and *two weeks* without so much as a word from you since our last night together at the Golden Palace. I've been here for hours in your palace, and you haven't even kissed me once. Then I have to listen to your accusations? It's just too much!" Adele paused for dramatic effect and threw herself back in her armchair determined not to look at her prince, but her smile betrayed her.

Rainere threw his head back and laughed. The deep wicked sound of it made Adele blush all over again. She pulled herself up to stand in front of him, pressing close. He was tall, much taller than her, and the top of her head barely brushed his chin. He smiled down at her and it was like sunshine on her shadowed heart.

"As your queen, I order you to kiss me, Prince Rainere of Marchant," she requested, and slid her arms around his waist. "Also, I want you to take your shirt off." She bit back her giggle when Rainere raised one perfect eyebrow at her.

"You order me, Your Majesty?"

"And the pants," she insisted and tried to match his look with her own.

Suddenly, Adele found herself caught up in a puff of green sparkles and flew through the air only to land softly in the middle of the enormous bed, yards from where she had been standing. Belatedly, she shrieked in protest and hit Rainere on the shoulder when he landed next to her.

"You *order* me, Your Majesty?" Rainere's tone was imperious, but his gaze was soft with longing. He caught up her hands as they batted at him with just one of his own and pinned them over her head. "You have no authority here my little St. Lucidis queen, my darling *cara mia*. We are in the Grey Palace now, which is Marchant territory, and I am the only sovereign ruler here." He bent down and lay a lingering kiss on her neck.

"Oh my, whatever shall I do?" Adele laughed, enjoying this playful side of Rainere that she had seen so rarely. "The wicked Marchant prince has me trapped. Poor little me! Who can save me?"

Rainere's smile faltered and died in an instant. "If Captain Lucky came in here now, I would kill him, *cara mia*. I want you to know that."

Adele rolled her eyes and huffed. "Rainere, you are so jealous! Seriously, it's insulting."

She struggled and pulled against his hands that held her firmly, very much aware that the movement made her breasts rise in her low-cut bodice, and of the effect this had on Rainere. He bowed his head over hers, his lips poised over her mouth but she turned her cheek just a moment before they touched.

"I believe I *ordered* you to take your clothes off," she said, and smiled at Rainere's frustrated growl.

He raised his hand and with a warm flash of green they were laying in a cloud of black silk and velvet feathers. Rainere was now completely naked and gorgeous beside her, his clothes disintegrated. She wriggled as his hand rose up over her own dress.

"No, stop!" she protested with a yelp. "I like this one, and it's the only decent dress I have here."

Rainere let her hands go and slid back a little to kiss the top of her chest as he ran his hand down the front of the bodice. Adele felt a tickle as all the laces and buttons undid themselves and her dress became very loose. Her giggle died when she saw the intensity of the passion in Rainere's expression. She could tell he was only just barely in control of himself.

She did that to him. She was the one who could make him lose his tightly held control and submit to her completely. Adele reveled in the power she had over Rainere, the power that he gave her with both hands. It made her feel beautiful, strong and adored. She had never felt so much like a woman before than she did with him. It was like she was a new person and she had been born again in Rainere's gaze.

Adele ran her eyes over his perfect musculature, taking in the way he was braced up on his arms over her like a lion ready to pounce. His passion was fierce, intense and now she knew, jealous. A sensible part of Adele's brain knew she should feel frightened of the prince. He was a hundred and fifty-year-old immortal wizard living in exile from the kingdom of which she was the queen. His magic was supposed to be dark and wicked as much as hers was supposed to be light and good. Nothing about the two of them being together was right or safe, but as she looked up into the gaze of her hungry prince she heard the Chime Voices in her head singing their sweet and eager commands. The magic deep inside had grown in strength after Rainere had shown her how to find it, and to use it, and this magic craved Rainere's touch. She needed him now like she needed air to breathe. She couldn't resist a moment longer. Adele slipped her hands behind Rainere's neck and pulled him close. His long dark hair fell about them in a curtain of black silk as his face came down to hers.

"Kiss me," she whispered.

CHAPTER SEVEN

"Wicked Steps Come Softly"

Grotto slumped in the charger at the head of the dining table that had recently been exited by Queen Adelena and sipped at the wine that she had not tasted, hoping it would calm his shaken nerves. It had taken all of his self-control not to run after his master as the prince was led away by that dread woman like a lamb to the slaughter just moments ago.

Guilt fueled by anger burned hotly inside of Grotto's old chest. He was swamped by memories of the past and the terrible mistakes of Rainere's father when he ruled this Grey Palace. For it was Prince Rainold who had in his lust and pride, brought the Marchant family to their lowest ebb in all the centuries. It was he who had brought the monster within their midst so long ago.

Grotto remembered the fear of that time, living with the monster who had changed the fate of the Marchant family and the damage she had done to his precious charge, the baby Prince Rainere. He could remember it all as if it were just yesterday.

Grotto had never before met a creature so ambitious and evil as that demon who had called herself Rainestra Marchant as if she had a right to that name, as if she was a human!

It had not even been a year after the death of Rainere's mother, Princess Rainella, and Rainere's birth, when the demon had moved into the Grey Palace under the cover of darkness and married the wayward Prince Rainold in a midnight service, assuming the position of princess of Marchant and adopting Rainere as her son, as if Rainella had never existed. The prince himself had been so completely bewitched by the demon that he had been blind to what his foolishness had wrought. But then, Prince Rainold had never much cared for his duty to the name of Marchant.

Grotto had woken one night not long after the wedding with a fierce pain in his chest and a heavy cloud of premonition hanging over him. It must have been the Goddess Lune herself who had guided him to the baby prince's bedchamber while he stumbled, still half asleep.

The door of the nursery had been pushed open, and the first thing Grotto saw was the insensible body of the nanny on the floor, her cheek red and swollen where she had been struck. His gasp disturbed the figure bent over the baby prince in his bed.

She had smiled as she looked up at him, but her eyes had been as dark and cold as her soul. Her expression became more sneer than smile when she recognized the fear on his face before he could hide it.

"What is it, elf?" Her voice was melodic, beautiful. Grotto could feel it swimming about his ears seeking entry into his head, seeking to control him with its charm. "I was kissing my sweet new son goodnight, so have you come for your own kiss?" She had laughed then, a high, tinkly laugh. "I bet you taste delicious."

Grotto had forced his feet forward, determined to meet the monster with his head high. He had never known terror like that which was pounding through his bloodstream at that moment. His instincts were screaming that he should run from this creature, run as far and as fast as he could, but his love for the boy held him firm and he pushed himself forward to the bedside of his prince, close enough to the creature to touch her should he choose, or kill her if he had been able. But he only knew of one weapon that could control her.

"I'm sure his father, the prince, will be pleased by the way you dote upon his only son. Even in the small hours of the night you grace him as a mother might. He will be told of your visits, Your Highness, please be assured." His voice was only a croak but his meaning was clear.

The thinly-veiled threat hung in the air between them. For one terrified moment Grotto was sure the demon would reach across the bed and suck every last ounce of life out of his long-lived bones and his bowels turned to liquid, but she merely blinked at him and turned back to gaze down at the tiny boy asleep beside her.

Grotto was close enough to see the sparkling puff of green that was the essence of Prince Rainere's spirit hover in a little cloud at his rosebud lips.

"His dreams are so small," she'd murmured, her tone curious. "He dreams of Rainold, and drinking milk in his arms, and he dreams of you, elf."

The demon raised her hazel eyes to Grotto's.

"If I wanted him, you could not stop me," she said, and this time her expression was almost apologetic.

"I know." Grotto's answer was so soft he wasn't sure he had even really spoken the words.

The demon rose from the bed then and moved to the door of the nursery, stopping just before the threshold. "I will leave him to your care for now, elf, but my people will have him one day. A prize like him cannot not be hidden from the Temple for long." She touched her belly. "And if it cannot be me then I swear it will be my daughter who will take him for her own."

Grotto watched her leave, and his trembling only started when he heard the door click shut behind her. Dashing to the other side of the bed, he pulled the baby prince to his chest and hugged him hard. He waited until he felt the little boy squirm and grizzle in his sleep before he lay the boy gently back down on his pillows. Tears of relief flooded his eyes as he saw the last traces of essence flow back into Rainere's tiny mouth. Only a few green sparkles still glittered on his lips.

Grotto stroked the black curls off the boy's forehead and ran his palm along the dimpled cheek, feeling the chill of dark magic on the baby's skin and seeking to warm it away. Having his essence sucked out by that she-demon would deplete the boy of his strength and vital warmth, and he would need to sleep for hours to recover it. As he was not yet a year old, it was hard to know if his wits or power would be affected by the draining.

Biting the inside of his cheek caused the tears in Grotto's eyes to spill over, and with a long finger, he wiped them off his cheeks and painted them onto Rainere's lips. It wasn't much, but the magic in his tears should be enough to help the boy heal more quickly and deter the demon, should she come calling later. More tears fell as Grotto thought about what it would mean to him if anything fatal should happen to this beautiful boy. He continued collecting his tears, wiping them onto the baby's cheeks as he tried to focus on finding a solution to the problem of a rogue demon in the Grey Palace. How was he to protect the young prince from his evil step-mother?

Prince Rainold loved little in this world more than indulging his own pleasures, but unlike many Marchant fathers he took a great interest in the child from his first marriage. Though he had not cared for the mother, Princess Rainella, at all, even annulling their marriage contract just weeks after it was made, Rainold was enamored with the son she had given him before she had died. Surely, even a demon would not risk the wrath of a Marchant prince just to sate her appetite for young blood? *Grotto would need to tread carefully, but he had to find a way of warning the prince about his new wife's night-time visit to the baby and her promise that she would have a child by Rainold himself. As reckless as the prince was, even he wouldn't allow the birth of a half-Marchant, half-demon abomination.*

The little prince sighed deeply and turned over in his sleep, taking Grotto's hand and pulling it under himself as he would a comforter. Moving slowly so as not to disturb him further, Grotto laid down next to the boy and wrapped his long limbs around the prince's, counting his little breathes and feeling the warmth slowly return to his body.

He remained like that for the rest of the night and every other night until the cursed demon princess was murdered by the Marchant Eldars and the Grey Palace was delivered from her control.

Pulling his mind back to the present, Grotto snarled and dashed the crystal glass down on the table. The red wine sloshed over the side of the glass and splattered on the white cloth.

Grotto had been so sure that Prince Rainold would put Rainestra aside when she started her affair with the St. Lucidis king. Just as he had been so sure that the Eldars had killed Rainestra's baby, when they had killed her after the birth, thinking she had made a St. Lucidis and Marchant half-breed. Yet the demon had succeeded where the wizards of the Golden Palace and the Eldars had not: she had forced her St. Lucidis abomination into the Prophecy of the End of the World and fooled them all.

Grotto alone knew the truth. Queen Adelena was the very image of her demon mother, Rainestra. He recognized her the moment he first saw her at her coronation at the Golden Palace. But it was such a bitter reward that all he could do now was follow the prophecy and push his dear master into a marriage with this abomination that was his new love.

Grotto ground his teeth. The demon Rainestra might have won the battle by manipulating the fates so that her daughter married the last Marchant prince, but Grotto was determined that she would not win the war. Instead of fighting circumstance, Grotto now felt it was only right that the Spider Empress Ka-kik be persuaded to eat the queen in revenge for killing her son, Oki. Then all would be set to rights when Prince Rainere was king of Unisia and the queen was dead.

The old manservant set his mouth in a grim line and pushed himself to his feet. As he began to collect the unused plates and cutlery from the dinner service, he shook with a sudden chill that rattled the china in his hands.

If only he didn't have to wait helplessly on the sidelines while this abomination had her evil way with the prince on this very night. Grotto shuddered at what she might be doing to his poor master.

Soon, master, he promised himself silently. *Soon, I shall free you of this dreadful lust and insanity that she has fired in you. Soon, she shall die.*

CHAPTER EIGHT

"Sweet Love Speaks Softly"

Adele and Rainere fell back against the damp silk of the sheets, panting loudly, chests heaving.

"That was…" Adele gasped, waving her hand in the air as if to make the right word appear.

"I know," Rainere agreed and caught her hand, pulling it back down to entwine in his.

They lay there for a long moment just catching their breath and holding hands as the aftershocks of pleasure slowly ebbed away. Adele recovered first. She rolled over onto her side, facing Rainere, and smiled. "You have no idea how much I've missed you, my love," she said, and lay a kiss on his chest.

Rainere looked down at her and brushed a wisp of hair out of her eyes. "I think you gave me some idea, *cara mia.*" He smiled his gorgeous half-smile, but then winced as he moved his shoulders. "Your magic is getting stronger, though. I'm sure of it."

Adele ran her hand down Rainere's chest to his rippling abdominals. *Was it possible that he was the most perfect specimen of manhood ever made?*

"I'm sorry, my love. Did I hurt you?" she asked and moved to drape herself across him, luxuriating in the feeling of his skin on hers. "I'll be gentler next time."

Rainere laughed and the sound was throaty and wicked. "Don't even think it," he warned her and moved Adele to sit astride him as he shifted himself to lean against the bedhead. Face to face now, Rainere tangled his hands in her hair and pulled her in for a kiss. As the kiss became deeper and her hands travelled his body, he pushed her away again.

"Just let me look at you," he said gently when she frowned at the interruption. "It was too long ago that I had your beautiful face before me."

Adele smiled as Rainere stroked a hand down her cheek and pushed her long dark hair back over her shoulder, smoothing it down her back. Her eyes travelled to the small bedside table and saw a sheaf of papers piled haphazardly on it. She leaned over to examine one more closely. "Rainere, these are pictures of me!" she said in surprise. "Where did you get them?"

Rainere shrugged, almost embarrassed. "I drew these when I saw you at the Golden Palace, during all those abysmal meetings. I knew I did not want to forget any detail of your face."

Adele looked at the elegantly-wrought sketches and smiled at the flattering likeness. "I'm sure I don't look quite like this," she grinned and raised an eyebrow at her artistic prince. "My breasts are not really *that* big."

"I draw what is in front of me." Rainere smiled as he took the picture from her hand and put it back on its table. "But I see you have changed so much in your weeks away from me that I will have to start all over again." He touched her cheek. "You got some sun, and your skin is more golden than it was before."

"The beach was so beautiful, Rainere. The children and I loved it! Have you ever been to Sandar?" Adele winced at the look he gave her. No Marchant monarch would ever be welcome in Sandar. "Sorry. Of course you haven't. But it was amazing."

His hands travelled to the top of her thighs. "There are muscles here that weren't before," he commented.

"Really?" Adele was pleased he had noticed. "I have been learning to ride a horse for the first time in my life," she said proudly. "And I did a lot of walking and swimming in Sandar."

Rainere's hands slipped around to cup her buttocks and gave them a squeeze. "There is more of this than there was before," he remarked appreciatively.

"Well, I did eat a lot more than usual, I guess," Adele admitted ruefully. "On the road it gets so dull and we had brought so many sweet biscuits and cakes with us for the journey. I probably overdid it." Her pleasure with Rainere's examination was fading a little if he was going to point out flaws, too.

"No," said Rainere, giving her behind a gentle pinch. "I mean I *like* it. You are far too fragile as it is, with your tiny bones and diminutive size. I like to feel that there is more of you in the world. I like that you are stronger now and less likely to blow away in the wind than you used to."

The memories of the dreams that they had shared for so many years together before she had come to Unisia swam between them. Only Adele had been able to travel to Rainere's world on the dream winds that blew her there, but she had been a ghost in his dreams and the winds had always blown her home again, back to the reality of her life on Earth. It was the same reality that Adele wanted to return to one day, though she knew that Rainere could never join her there. Melancholy edged in around their warmth.

Rainere picked up Adele's hand and placed it on his chest. She felt his heart beating fast and strong, and looked up into his dark, green gaze.

"You must never leave me for that long again, Adelena." Rainere's voice shook with emotion. "I could not do anything when you were gone. I couldn't eat or sleep. Even work held no pleasure for me. I can't...I just can't live without you now."

Adele leaned forward and kissed Rainere softly on the lips. Once. Twice. He pulled back to look at her again. His eyes bore into hers, searching them for anything he might have missed before.

Adele blinked and bit her bottom lip. *Could he see the wicked things she had done in Sandar carved into her soul?* Now was the moment she should tell him about what had happened in the Holy Caves with the Mage. She should ask his advice on how to fix the problems she had wrought. *He understood this world so much better than she did. Surely he could help her now?*

But would that change how he felt about her? Would he think what she had done to Ripenzo Shale was justified or just plain cruel? Adele could not bear it if Rainere turned away from her. She needed him so desperately to be on her side now that she had doubts about High Wizard Ohren and his plans for her back at the Golden Palace. She still didn't know why the wizard had warned her not to return when she knew that the fate of Unisia depended on her delivering the Fire Orchid stamens to him.

It was all just too confusing. Adele wanted something in her life to just be simple and beautiful for once. She loved Rainere with all her heart. *Maybe it was better that she protected him from what she had done? Anyway, it would do no harm to tell him tomorrow instead of tonight.*

Adele took his face in her hands and kissed her prince. She felt him grow ready for her again.

"Promise me that you will never leave me again, *cara mia?*" Rainere whispered, his lips against hers. "Promise me you will marry me now so that we can always be together."

Rainere tightened his hands around her buttocks and lifted her to hover over his erection still pressed between their bodies. Adele gasped as he slowly lowered her onto himself. She rose and dipped, pleasure coursing through her at the movement.

"Promise me," insisted Rainere, a fierce note underlying the sweet words as he pulled her down harder.

Adele groaned as too much of him was inside her at once. He was so big, and it took time to be ready for him. "Rainere, please."

Relenting, Rainere let her rise up again, the new muscles in her thighs giving her the control she wanted as she dipped back down again and again. His hand slipped between her legs and found the swollen sweet spot where she needed his sensitive fingers. As the pleasure intensified, Adele dropped her head back and moaned. Rainere's hot mouth found her neck and he pressed his teeth against her skin as his body took her to the edge of her control.

It was too fast. Adele released a thread of her magic into Rainere's chest and she instantly felt his responding gasp against her throat.

"Oh, *cara mia,*" he groaned as the magic wormed its way deep inside of him, tightening around his own power and binding it. "It hurts so much."

He collapsed onto his back. "Please, don't stop."

His beauty, his power, his vulnerability, and his love for her completely overwhelmed Adele. She felt hot tears leak down her cheeks as she let the rhythm of their bodies take over. Arching back, with Rainere completely filling her, Adele sobbed the word of command that the magical Chime Voices were singing in her ears and cried out as it took them both over the edge in a hard, rolling orgasm that lasted forever and no time at all.

Finally released, Adele fell onto the bed beside Rainere, both of them panting and glistening with sweat. As Adele lay with her eyes closed, she felt Rainere's hand move gently along her cheek. She smiled as bliss made her feel silly.

"Find me a priest," she said, with a satisfied groan, and trembled from the orgasm that shook her still. "I'll marry you as soon as we have one."

Adele didn't open her eyes, so she didn't see Rainere's expression and the pain in his eyes. She didn't see that he still didn't believe her.

Chapter Nine

"To Look Upon Hope and Smile"

Rainere led Adele back to the apartment, holding her hand the whole way. The empty hallways and corridors were all so dimly lit that the brightness of the lanterns outside the suite doors almost dazzled Adele.

She pulled Rainere back around the corner so they were in the dark again. Rainere looked at her quizzically and pressed in close so she would only have to whisper. Adele slipped her hands under his untucked shirt, enjoying the smoothness of his tightly-packed muscle under her hot hands, but she forced herself to focus on something else for a minute.

"Rainere, tomorrow you are going to meet my children," she murmured. "They might be a bit… if they don't like you, you must be gentle with them, okay?"

Adele bit her bottom lip and hoped that Rainere would take her advice in the way that she intended it. If he really wanted them to be together, then he would have to work hard to earn her children's trust.

"I will be a perfect gentleman, I assure you, Adelena." He lifted her chin with his finger. "*Cara mia*, I know how important this is to you, and to us."

He kissed her in farewell and his tongue flicked lightly in her mouth. Stifling a moan, Adele reached up to pull Rainere closer and felt him stiffening against her in response. She pressed into the kiss and reached between his legs.

"*Cara mia*, no." He broke away as he pulled her hands off his body and gave them back to her. "We cannot."

"It's not my fault. You started it!" whispered Adele, unable to keep the embarrassed pique out of her voice. "If you didn't smell so good…"

Adele could almost feel the smugness radiating off Rainere at her compliment and lack of self-control. She resolved not to kiss him again before she walked away as a petty punishment for his ability to resist her right now.

"Good night, Your Highness," Adele said loudly and stepped out from the dark corner, away from Rainere, and into the light of the hallway. "Thank you for a lovely evening."

"Good night, Your Majesty," replied Rainere formally. "I shall look forward to seeing you and the royal family tomorrow for lunch."

"Very well," answered Adele haughtily, and didn't glance back over her shoulder, even though she was dying to. "I shall see if I have the time for it."

She almost giggled at his answering growl and blew him a quick kiss before she opened the apartment door and fell onto Captain Lucky.

"Oh, Your Majesty!" said her handsome captain with his customary smile. "We thought maybe the prince had eaten you, you've been gone for so long!"

"No, no, I'm quite alright," replied Adele quickly, stepping into the room and shoving Lucky out of the way. She cursed her bad luck, *Dammit! Why couldn't it have been Bear who opened the door? He wouldn't have said two words to me.*

"Our sympathies have been with you all evening, Your Majesty," said QG Pepper, standing up as Adele entered the room, and stifling a yawn. "When Mr. Grotto came to tell us that His Highness had taken you up to view the observatory, we knew you would be doing your duty for the Crown all night."

Adele forced a laugh at her young guard's comment. "The prince certainly can talk! As soon as we got onto the topic of what the

Marchant family is owed by the Crown, he wouldn't shut up," she blathered before shutting *herself* up.

"Shall I wake Caitlin for you, Your Majesty?" asked QG Pepper, a little too eagerly. Adele caught Captain Lucky rolling his eyes and hid a grin. Perhaps there was more romance than just hers going on in the royal party.

"No, I can do it. I'm sure she's in with the children by now," she explained, but felt mean when she saw Pepper's face fall. With a quick 'goodnight', she hurried away to her room before her friendly façade could crack.

Fortunately, Caitlin was too sleepy to notice anything wrong with Adele's dress or hair. She only yelped when she broke a nail on the too-tight lacings that Rainere had done up for her with magic.

"I'm sure I didn't tie them this tightly, Your Majesty," Caitlin grumbled, but said nothing else. Adele kissed her three children in their sleep and lay down in the enormous bed amongst them all, finally resting after an exhausting day.

As she lay there, Adele stared through the holes in the ragged curtains at the dark night. The stars seemed so much lower in the sky here in Evendaar than at home on Earth. The wind howled and rattled at the balcony doors, making Adele shiver at the memory of its biting chill in the blizzard today.

How fortunate the storm had hit right at the moment they had turned into the forest and that their wrong turn had led them right to Rainere's home. Adele thought of Ripenzo Shale's warning about a storm in his letter this morning.

Well, if that was the worst of it, we should be alright now, thought Adele. *It was a terrible storm, but Rainere saved us from freezing to death.*

Aaron made a little squeak in his sleep and nestled closer to his mother. Adele gently stroked the hair off his forehead and pulled the covers up to his chin before turning back to the window.

Adele wondered how she could be so lucky to have the love of such an incredible man like Rainere. She smiled when she recalled his earlier jealousy of Captain Lucky. But he didn't scare her at all with his glares and dark frowns. His anger had just made her feel more cherished. No one had ever wanted her with the intensity that Rainere wanted her. No man had ever made her feel this special. Adele closed her eyes and re-lived the memories of the night while she waited for sleep to come.

CHAPTER TEN

"To Curse the Lover of the Beloved"

Down deep in the bowels of the Grey Palace, Schiss stared up at the ceiling of the dusty little office room where Grottonski had taken him. He knew the queen was somewhere in the Grey Palace tonight, but to his sadness he had yet to see her. He directed his attention back to Grottonski, hoping to dissuade him from his current action.

"But Mr. Grottonski, sir, should you sign it in the prince's own hand? Won't he know what you have done?" Schiss asked. He watched over the old man's shoulder as Grotto scratched out a letter, replicating the handwriting of Prince Rainere perfectly. Though Schiss wished he could read the human language better, he could tell the letter was about the queen and her children.

Schiss quailed under the sharp glare that Grotto sent him, but he was feeling uncomfortable for more than one reason. Grottonski was writing to the Spider Empress and Schiss had no desire to act as a delivery boy tonight.

His mother the empress was probably furious with him for leaving the nest to follow the queen on her trip to Sandar. It is true that the prince had not given Schiss much choice in acting as his personal spy, but the empress would not care about that. She was as unreasonable as she was insane. He could only hope she would still be too preoccupied with grieving the death of Oki, her favored son, to be too concerned with Schiss right now.

Still, any journey into the nest would be dangerous. His brothers and sisters continued to battle over the position of power on the Nest Council that Oki's death had opened up. Any conversation with the empress could be seen as an attempt to ingratiate himself with her and would earn the wrath of his larger and stronger siblings.

However, Schiss knew that any effort to appeal to Grottonski's kindness would fall on deaf ears, so he instead tried to reason with him.

"I cannot guarantee that I can even get this letter to the empress tonight, you know," said Schiss, his reedy voice plaintive. "There is a war in the nest and it is still bloody. Someone might steal that letter from me and let it drop in the mud. Perhaps…"

"You will take a talisman," snapped Grotto and his tone brooked no debate. Schiss paled as he caught the small object that Grotto tossed at him.

It was a long stick, a finger bone by the looks of it, with a black crow feather tied to the end, bound by a string of gut. Schiss sniffed at it and recoiled quickly. It smelled of death and dark magic. Schiss gave it a cautionary wave and a shot of green sparks flew out the end of the finger bone:

"Beware the carrier of this talisman," boomed a disembodied voice. "Death visits here!"

Schiss shrieked and dropped the bone. It fell to the floor, clattering on the tiles. It didn't break, though the voice and the green sparks disappeared.

"It's a little dramatic," remarked Grotto drily. "But it should get you to the center of the nest for an audience with your mother unmolested. Just don't wave it about too much or it could explode. It's very old."

Nodding, Schiss cautiously bent to pick up the bone and placed it in his pocket, his expression showing his distaste. "What should I expect from the empress when I give her the letter?" he asked. "Should I wait for one in return or do I have your permission to return to the Grey Palace?" Schiss sent Grottonski what he hoped was a winning smile, but the manservant was shuffling through piles of papers at the desk and his effort was wasted.

"It should be here," muttered Grotto, searching a pile of small cards in a little wooden box. "I had the name of the priest right here… ah-ha, here he is!"

Grotto looked up at Schiss and the little man-Spider almost flinched from the malevolence in Grotto's smile. "You should hurry back to me, Schiss, because I will have another letter for you to deliver as soon as you can."

Schiss didn't like the creaking sounds coming out of Grotto as the old manservant attempted a chuckle. "Priests are dangerous humans, Mr. Grottonski. He's not going to hurt the queen, is he?" he asked as a feeling of foreboding swamped him.

"Hurt her? Why, no, little spider, but even that abomination will need a priest at her wedding, won't she?" Grotto cackled, but quickly choked it off to turn back to his work.

A wedding! The beautiful Queen Adelena will marry the Marchant prince? Well, he is a lucky man, though he couldn't deserve a lady such as her. Perhaps, Schiss thought hopefully, *I might even be invited.*

He would so love to see the queen again, and he would love for her to see him in his human form so he could thank her properly for saving his life in Sandar. If she hadn't released him from that little box he would have died horribly from the magic that was singeing his fur and eating away at his innards. *On that day, the queen had arrived like a vision of the Goddess herself. She had shaken him gently to the ground right next to a portal and blessed him with a promise never to kill him. Obviously, she had thought him special above all others. Obviously, she had seen something in him that she hadn't in Oki, because he had died by her hand whereas Schiss had been preserved.* They had a bond, he and Queen Adelena, Schiss could feel it right down to his bones. *Maybe it had something to do with this prophecy that was so important to Empress Ka-kik and Grottonski?*

Schiss had always liked humans, and he liked living above ground. He liked the sun and although he knew it wasn't healthy he felt most alive when he was sitting in a tree, casting his web between its swaying branches. It was how Prince Rainere had first found him. Schiss had been napping in his web when he felt the cold sides of the glass box enclose him. It had been the old man, Grottonski, who had convinced the prince to let Schiss out of the box and transform into his human form to plead his case for life. Ever quick, the prince had recognized a fellow outcast in Schiss and had taken pity on the little man-spider, but it was Grotto who had negotiated Schiss's freedom in exchange for a steady stream of information from the nest.

Schiss wanted to be out of the nest so badly. He wanted to live free from the politics of the Nest Council, controlled by his most bloodthirsty siblings, and he wanted to be free of his mother, the empress. Her insanity had grown with the years, and it had been passed on to the new hatchlings. Now, there was a bloodbath every other week. Schiss hated the sound of the screams of the dying babies as they were pulled apart and eaten by their stronger siblings. The empress should have stopped the violence but she only responded with rewards for the victors.

When the Days of Darkness finally came, only the strong would rise from the nest to reclaim the Above Lands. The strong and the crazy.

Seeing that Grottonski was occupied with his next letter, Schiss took the chance to slip away. He tucked the folded letter next to the nasty talisman in his threadbare jacket and made his way back up the dark corridors and stairways to the ground floor of the palace where he could find an open window. Schiss morphed back into his spider form with a squelchy *pop* and crept up the wall to the window ledge. He had to be cautious here, though there were many portal entrances floating around the palace there were also sharp-eyed ravens watching for small creatures to eat.

A wispy portal, transparent and fragile, drifted over to the window as if blown by a breeze, and Schiss braced himself to leap into its tiny opening. The portal was a gateway to the ancient paths that the Spider People had been travelling for millennia in Evendaar, well before the humans came and found the magic to create their own human-sized ones. He would be at the nest in a matter of minutes.

Schiss sent a prayer to the Goddess Lune that he could deliver this letter and be back at the palace by dawn.

Despite his grim mission, Schiss's heart lifted. He would be with the queen soon.

CHAPTER ELEVEN

"The Next Adventure in Love"

Another night had passed so quickly.

Adele opened her eyes and watched as the grey wash of dawn lightened the room. She was positive she hadn't slept at all. Adele felt Aaron settle himself at her shoulder and start playing with her hair. "Are you awake, monkey?" she whispered and pulled him into her arms for a cuddle. He allowed her to squeeze him for a moment before he shifted away and sat up, staring down at her.

"Your eyes are different, Mummy, aren't they?" he whispered. "You have shiny rings in them, and diamonds, too, I think."

Adele smiled. "I have *diamonds* in my eyes? Are they pretty?"

Aaron frowned. "You're beautiful, but I don't like you being different. You should make your eyes the same as before."

Adele reached up to stroke the hair off her son's face and tried to smooth the little worry lines that creased his brow with her thumb.

"We are all a bit different on this world, my darling," she said. "I've got glitter in my eyes because of the magic that is inside of me now, but I am still your Mummy and nothing will ever change that. I love you, my sweet boy."

"I had a dream last night, didn't I, Mummy?" said Aaron. "The man came and held my hand. He said that I was his family, that I had a light in me. Is that like magic, too?"

"What man?" asked Adele more sharply than she meant to and pushed herself up on an elbow. "Did he wake you up?"

"He wasn't really a man," replied Aaron and pursed his little lips, thinking hard. "He was floating on the air, and I could see the window through his body. But I wasn't scared, was I Mummy? I knew he was a nice ghost," Aaron finished proudly.

"Mum-mee?" Stella was awake now. "Hung-gee."

"Yeah, me, too!" said Aaron and his shout woke a grumpy Natalie.

Adele refrained from asking Aaron any more about his dream, as the nannies woke up with the chatter of the children and the puppies roused themselves from under the bed. Adele threw a robe over her nightdress and followed the children out to the dining room. A plain, but generous, buffet had been laid out for them: boiled eggs, platters of sliced ham, fresh rolls, and bowls of soft, creamy cheese, jugs of syrup, and piles of sweet, tart apples.

Once again, QG Bear was stuck with puppy duty, as he took the dogs out on the terrace for some exercise and morning poops. Despite his sour expression, Adele got the feeling that her guard actually enjoyed the chore and watched as he played with the pups, throwing sticks and chasing them about. Adele told herself to remember that Bear must have a softer side if he could be so gentle with the puppies, she just rarely got to see it behind his narrow-eyed glares and muttered cursing.

As soon as the children were finished with their breakfast, they wanted to be out playing in the snow too. Seraphina and Caitlin took the children out and left Adele to drink her cup of tea in peace.

As she poured another cup, General Ohrig made his way over to join her at the table, standing stiffly to await permission to sit down. Adele smiled and waved for him to relax. "General, please. We don't need to be so formal when it's just us."

General Ohrig nodded as he sat down but said nothing. The general was freshly showered and dressed in a clean white shirt under his pressed jacket. Adele noticed a touch of shaving cream by his ear and resisted the urge to wipe it off. General Ohrig would not appreciate the contact. He, like all the men of her Queen's Guard, treated Adele with a formal chivalry that she had never experienced before. It was polite, but it made her feel lonely too, and never failed to remind her that she was the queen and therefore different.

"Sleep well, general?" asked Adele as she buttered another warm roll and attempted to lighten the dark mood the general had brought to the table with him.

General Ohrig gave Adele a sharp look, his pale blue eyes watching her intently. "Well enough, Your Majesty." His answer was clipped, almost brusque, a sure sign he was unhappy about something. "As I understand it, you had a rather long night with His Highness, the prince?"

Adele shoved the roll in her mouth and nodded, hoping Ohrig didn't notice her blushing cheeks. As he continued to stare at her, his eyebrows beetled low over his eyes.

"Your Majesty, though it is not my place to ask what was discussed with the prince, you did mention to Captain Lucky that the prince raised the issue of reparations for the Marchant family and that the Crown owed the Marchant family in some financial way. Is that right?"

Adele nodded again. Yes, she had told Lucky that lie.

The general stiffened in his chair, his hands unconsciously clenching and unclenching into fists on the table. Adele could tell that Ohrig was trying to be diplomatic in this conversation and for such a straight-talking man, this was almost painful for him. She took a sip of her tea and braced herself.

"Spit it out, general. What do you want to say?"

"Frankly, Your Majesty?"

"Please."

"Your Majesty, I don't think it has been made clear to you yet the danger we have put you in by agreeing to stay in the Grey Palace as guests." Ohrig's voice was low and his tone was serious. "The

Marchant prince is not only in political exile from the court of the Golden Palace and St. Lucidis society, but he is also a bachelor. Just as you are unmarried." Ohrig cleared his throat, obviously uncomfortable with what he was about to say next. "If anything should…If he were to force himself upon you…Well, the consequences could be disastrous."

"What?" Adele choked on her tea. "Are you saying you think the prince would, or could, do that? That he would force himself on me, sexually?"

General Ohrig leaned forward and looked Adele directly in the eye. "We are in the Grey Palace, Your Majesty, on Marchant land. This property does not fall under the authority of the Crown. If anything should happen to you here, then the court would have little or no recourse to detain the prince. On his land, Prince Rainere is the king."

Adele chewed her bottom lip. Rainere had said much the same thing to her last night, but she had been too distracted to really pay attention to him.

"If the prince should decide to, he could take you to his bed and claim the act as a betrothal agreement. He could then marry you without even needing your consent, and lay claim to your throne as your legal husband. Such is the way of Marchant law."

"You make it sound so simple for him," whispered Adele, feeling guilty and horrified all at once.

General Ohrig nodded grimly, and stood up, satisfied that Adele had understood his warning. "Your Majesty, we are dealing with a man who is not only a prince of the realm, but also an immortal wizard, not to mention the rumors about his lack of sanity and morals. We must be vigilant at all times in his company."

"Right," agreed Adele wanly, dismissing Ohrig with a small wave, and he took his leave. "Vigilant."

Adele felt ill. The cup of tea went cold in her hands and she stared hard at the breakfast things as if they might be to blame for the turn the morning had taken. Yet again, Rainere was painted as a horrible villain and her as the innocent queen to be caught up in his schemes.

But she knew such a different side of him.

Rainere had insisted on her marrying him as soon as possible. Was it because he wanted more than her love? Would he really be happy sharing the throne with her, or did he want it all for himself? Adele looked over at the moth-eaten curtains that framed the balcony doors and saw in the light of day just how old and ragged the suite was. The servants who cleared the table were surly and unkempt, their aprons stained and tattered.

It was clear Rainere could certainly use the money their marriage would bring him.

But he won't just get money if he marries me, she thought. *He'll get my children, the kingdom, and probably a civil war when the other royal families learn what I have done.*

It was a lot to risk if she was making the decision for the wrong reasons. The marriage itself was still a thorny issue for Adele. After having her heart shattered by divorce back on Earth, it was tough to think about giving her trust and commitment to another man again. And he wasn't just a man; he was an immortal wizard. And she wasn't just a woman anymore; she was now a queen. She had a bigger responsibility than just to her heart.

The surety she had felt in Rainere's arms last night had dissipated in the cold light of Ohrig's warning. Adele rose from the table and went to dress. She had so much to think about and no time to do it in. She had to prepare the children to meet Rainere today. Though he made her body tremble with a look, Adele was very aware of how cold and intimidating Rainere appeared to most people, and she had no idea how the children would respond to him, or how Prince Rainere would behave with her children. She could only hope that he would love them as much as he loved her, because if he couldn't then there was no future for them regardless of all the royal laws and crowns in Evendaar.

Chapter Twelve

"Lunch in the Glassroom"

"Natalie, do *not* pull your hair out!" Adele ordered, as the royal family followed Grotto down the dark hallway to the Glassroom, where Prince Rainere had invited them to take lunch with him. The Queen's Guard followed close behind them while Tilburn skipped ahead, struggling to keep up with Grotto and his much longer legs.

"But the pins are poking me," whined Natalie, scratching at the braids pinned to her head. They were all back in their travelling clothes of pants and shirts, as they had nothing left that was clean, but Adele had made an effort with the children's hair for this special occasion.

Adele tried to calm her racing pulse with a deep breath and resisted the urge to snap at Natalie again. It would do no good to yell when her daughter was determined to be contrary.

"Remember we all need to be on our best behavior today," Adele warned the children as she watched Natalie unwind her braids and pull out all of Caitlin's hard work in seconds. "Anyone who is naughty will be in very big trouble with me later."

When the party finally reached the Glassroom, Grotto flung open the double doors with such force that they banged against the walls making everyone jump. "The Glassroom," he announced. "Also known as the Queen's Orchid Room." He sent Adele a poisonous glare to let her know that she definitely wasn't the queen he was referring to.

Ignoring Grotto's patent displeasure, Adele stepped into the room and looked about for Rainere, but it seemed he hadn't arrived yet.

By the looks of it, the room had once been a rather glamorous greenhouse. The shelves and pedestals decorating the walls were littered with the dead descendants of what would have been a magnificent display of orchids. Thin irrigation tubes were pinned to the walls and shelves and fed into hundreds of empty vases. Despite the grey and dismal appearance of the withered vegetation, the air was perfumed with a floral earthiness that was quite pleasant. The crystal candelabras dotted about the room had been lit to help brighten the weak sunlight that filtered in through dirty windows.

Adele dropped Stella lightly to her feet and gestured for Tilburn to come closer so she could whisper questions to him, but he refused.

"Your Majesty," Tilburn said, "I was not invited to enter the Glassroom nor to take lunch with the prince, despite being the highest-ranked servant in your entourage. I shall take my leave if it pleases you and see you back at the suite afterwards." He turned with a sniff and left, stumbling a bit in the gloomy hallway.

Adele sighed and rolled her eyes. As if there wasn't enough drama in the day without Tilburn getting all upset about protocol again. General Ohrig assembled the Queen's Guard by the doors, half of them facing into the room and half facing the hallway. He gave Adele a loaded look and when she turned back to watch over the children, she was surprised to see them talking to Rainere who had entered through a door in the corner of the room that she hadn't notice before.

Rainere looked up when he felt her eyes on him. Their gazes locked across the room and Adele felt desire sweep through her with a deep, ripping need. Blushing, she let her eyes drop and tried to focus on her little ones. She smiled as Stella put her arms out and scooped up her baby girl.

"You look like somebody I know, don't you?" Aaron was staring at the prince, fascinated.

Prince Rainere turned his dark eyes on the little boy. When he spoke Adele barely registered his words as his sonorous rasp spread shivers all over her body.

"As we have never met previously, I cannot answer that for sure, Prince Aaron," replied Rainere, regarding Aaron seriously but the little boy just broke into giggles.

"He'd said you'd say that you can't answer my questions, didn't he?" Aaron chortled at his private joke.

Grotto announced that lunch was served and servants pulled back chairs as the royal family and Prince Rainere sat. Soup was served immediately.

"As much as I would wish to answer you, Prince Aaron, it is very difficult for me to understand if your remark is a statement or a question." Rainere's tone wasn't severe, but his manner was firm. "Perhaps you could just say what it is you mean."

"Yes," replied Aaron, sitting up straight and immediately knocking over his water glass with the effort. A servant loped over to tidy the mess. "Yes, you are right, aren't you? I like to say what I mean, don't I?"

"I think that indeed you do," agreed Rainere.

"I say what I mean all the time," interjected Natalie, casting a superior look at her brother. "I never ask silly questions when I speak, and I always mean what I say."

"Interesting," mused the prince, turning to the little princess. "I wonder how it is that you ever learn anything of importance without asking questions of others?"

"Why?" added Stella, enthusiastically slopping her mushroom soup about.

"Quite," agreed Rainere, raising an eyebrow in the baby's direction. Stella smiled broadly at him.

"Well, it's because I already know most things about the things I want to know," replied Natalie with the supreme confidence of a six-year-old diva. "And things I don't know don't matter to me."

"Then that makes you a very dangerous person," said Rainere crisply. "It is only by asking questions that one learns how very much one doesn't know. It is those who live in ignorance who bring darkness to our world."

"What's ignorance?" asked Natalie.

"Ignorance is when one doesn't know enough about a subject to understand it at all," replied the prince.

"I don't want to bring darkness to our world." Natalie's eyes went wide and her expression serious.

"Well then, you must ask each and every question you can think of to better understand the world about yourself."

Aaron started giggling again at his private joke and wriggled about on his seat.

"I will, I promise," vowed Natalie, dropping her soup spoon on the table as she gestured it in the prince's direction.

Adele sat silently in shock as her children happily interacted with Rainere, his presence and gravelly voice commanding their full attention. Even Stella was beaming at the prince and throwing him coy glances from her chair. Adele had no explanation for their comfort with him, except perhaps that he didn't talk down to them or try to amuse them. He spoke to them as if they were adults or equals.

Which I suppose they are, thought Adele in surprise. *My children and Rainere are all princes of the realm and equals like no one else is here.*

The thought disconcerted her more than she would like. *They were political equals, sure, but could he be a father to them?*

The meal continued with the children and Rainere chatting like old friends while Adele sat quietly. The only other person who watched the children with the prince as intently as Adele was Grotto. At times, the manservant waited on the table and skulked around the edges of the room, supervising the other servants as they brought in dish after dish on silver trolleys. At other times he stood frozen in the doorway as still as a statue, with only his darting eyes betraying any movement. Occasionally he'd catch Adele's gaze and instinctively she would glance away. Grotto's hatred of her was almost palpable, and Adele waited in protective readiness for him to dare send her children one of the deathly glares that he gave her.

"Your Majesty, Queen Adelena," called Rainere from the other end of the table. The children giggled when she started in surprise. "I was just asking if you would perhaps like to accompany me on a tour of the Grey Palace. The prince and princesses have suggested that they would enjoy the experience."

"Of course. That would be wonderful, thank you." Adele forced her dark thoughts away with a smile. She shouldn't be looking for trouble when everything was going so well at the moment.

CHAPTER THIRTEEN

"Sometimes Magic Is Simply Sweet"

General Ohrig had insisted that the entire Queen's Guard join the royal family on the tour of the palace. Adele knew he was trying to gather as much information about their host as possible in case an emergency should arise, but she thought Ohrig could be slightly subtler in his methods. The general watched the prince like a hawk, following his every movement, though Rainere seemed completely unaware of her officer's scrutiny.

Grotto actually led the tour, escorting their party from one great hall to the next, passing through so many echoing chambers that after the first hour Adele was sure that they were walking in circles. She soon gave up asking polite questions of Grotto during his monotonous and very detailed monologue on the history of each room and the artifacts contained within them. It just seemed to infuriate him to be interrupted, and even the children were uncharacteristically silent, sensing the old man's hostility. The tour ended in Rainere's laboratory.

Adele marveled at the light that streamed in through the clean, shiny windows of the long galley room. Workbenches stood in parallel rows, and at either end of the room there were large blackboards covered in scribbled diagrams and numbers. More benches and shelves lined the walls piled with books and odd paraphernalia and the air smelled like chalk and chemicals giving the room the feeling of a school science classroom.

Adele wandered to the windows and looked out over the white carpet of snow to the Dark Forest beyond the boundary of the palace. It was the oddest thing to see the dark storm clouds piled high over the forest and the fierce blizzard shaking the trees while the grounds of the Grey Palace lay calm, the sun shining down on the glittery snow.

"It's so strange," murmured Adele as General Ohrig stepped up behind her shoulder. "It looks so miserable over there but here it's like a little winter wonderland."

"Yes, strange," agreed the general in a tone that suggested he thought otherwise.

"You think he created this storm, Ohrig?" Adele whispered, she had no need to specify who *he* was. "But how did Ripenzo know it was coming when he warned us in his letter?" She tilted her head in Ohrig's direction without quite looking at him. "I think *that* is stranger than what…"

"Yes, the grounds are beautiful, Your Majesty," agreed Ohrig in a much louder voice as they were approached by Aaron. He was followed by Grotto with a tray of refreshments. Adele took a glass of warm spiced wine and a shortbread biscuit from the tray and smiled at her son. Aaron was beside himself with excitement at all the fascinating things in the prince's laboratory, and he dragged General Ohrig away to show him something that shot out sparks when you touched it.

Adele was left on her own to sip her wine and nibble her biscuit, but her gaze was irrevocably drawn back to Rainere. The prince stood by a workbench, chatting with the children as they ran from one table to the next, their exclamations of delight and awe filling the room. There was a softness about his mouth that might have been a smile. Adele breathed an internal sigh of relief.

Adele only realized she was staring at Rainere when he caught her eye and gave her a polite nod. She felt her smile tighten and falter. Rainere was so much better at the poker face thing. He looked cool and calm, his manner appropriately reserved. She, on the other hand, felt flustered by the constant hot flashes of desire that swept through her every time she looked at him or walked by him. It was awkward, to say the least, surrounded as they were by her entire Queen's Guard and her three children.

"But how does it *work?*" Natalie was being persistent in getting a clear answer from the prince, but Adele could see no wear on his patience yet.

Rainere crouched down to better explain himself to the little girl. His long, dark hair fell over his shoulder as he pointed to the tiny machine on the table in front of them.

"Here," he said, his raspy voice gentle. "Here, there is a thought locked inside this little box. Inside the box is a little wheel and the thought has nothing to do but spin it round and round. The wheel then moves this little mechanism, causing a spark to fire, which ignites the flame and projects the image onto the glass plate."

"It looks like a movie," said Natalie. "Like at home. Except we have cartoons and not just pictures of fire." Aaron joined his sister to get a closer look at the tiny image projector.

"Can I see the thought please, Prince Rainere?" asked Aaron as he prodded at the box.

"No." Rainere's voice was firm. "It is a bad thought, and if it were to escape it could easily get lodged in one of our heads, which would be uncomfortable."

"Because it's the bad thoughts that spin round and round," said Adele from her place at the window, surprised by the poetic simplicity of the magic.

"And what's this?" Natalie asked, opening a little metal box on the bench before her. Adele wandered over to see what her daughter had found but the box was only filled with pale green sand.

"Ah! One must be careful with this, Princess Natalie," said Rainere and took the box out of Natalie's unsteady hands. "This sand comes from a very special place in Evendaar, and it is very rare. In fact, I believe it is the last of its kind. It is a conduit for powerful magic useful for transporting dangerous spells. I have yet to find a need for it, but I can activate it to show you."

Rainere muttered a quiet word or two and the sand rose up, sparkling in the sunlight, and hovered above its box, before forming a ribbon and doing a quick loop-the-loop before dropping back into its box. The children all cheered and instantly demanded another performance. Rainere patiently obliged, until they were distracted by something else.

The day continued happily until the light in the room faded and the lamps and candelabras were lit. Suddenly, a huge cacophony swept through the palace. The chimes of a hundred different clocks echoed through the halls, from the deep sonorous *bong* of the grandfather clocks to the delicate chiming of the timepiece the prince carried in his pocket.

"What's that noise for?" asked Aaron, fascinated by the sound as it continued for several minutes.

"Twilight," said Rainere. "The clocks ring at the exact moment the sun has set, and the night is upon us. It is a very special time for magic, as the flow and flux are disrupted when the sun sinks and the moon rises. Every wizard needs to know when twilight has come."

"And it's also time for children to have their dinner and get ready for bed," smiled Adele as she scooped up a sleepy Stella and collected Aaron's hand. "I think we should all thank Prince Rainere for a lovely day and promise to see him again tomorrow."

The little chorus of thank-yous was interspersed with the children's' routine complaining about not being hungry, tired or ready for bed. Promises of piggyback rides from QGs Pepper and Leith got the children to head out without too much trouble.

Adele couldn't look Rainere in the eye as she thanked him for his hospitality. As the formal words left her lips, she felt a sudden urge to leap into his arms and kiss him. She clutched her hands together tightly until the moment passed and she was almost relieved when Rainere bowed politely and left the room before she could make a fool of herself. Her lack of control was almost frightening.

Walking back to their suite with the others, Adele remembered she had left her jacket in the laboratory.

"I just have to get my coat," she told Ohrig as she turned to go back the way they had come. "I can get it myself, general, no need to be overly alarmed," she joked but Ohrig gave her a worried frown. She could tell he didn't want her out of his sight for a second.

Adele walked quickly back to the laboratory hoping Ohrig wasn't going to follow her. As she approached the door, it glowed greenly in the dim light of the corridor. It was a wonder no one had noticed it before. As Adele placed her hand on the doorknob, she felt a slight sizzling sensation under her hand. The knob turned slightly of its own accord.

Adele let out a surprised "Oh" and snatched her hand back.

"It won't open for you," came a low voice to her right and Rainere stepped out of the shadows. "It's protected by magic."

"But it was tur…" Adele's voice drifted off as Rainere came closer. She hid her trembling hands behind her back. "I forgot my jacket in there," she said.

"Of course. Allow me," said the prince politely. He opened the door for Adele and she stepped into the room. When she heard the door click shut behind her, she spun around to face Rainere, taking a step back in surprise as he swept her up in his arms and sat her on a workbench.

His mouth was hot and hard on hers and it took all her strength to pull away and gasp a breath. Rainere trailed hungry kisses down her neck.

"Rainere!" She pulled his hair to get his attention. "Rainere, I have to get back. They're waiting for me."

Rainere reluctantly stopped kissing and rested his forehead against hers. "I miss you every moment that I'm not with you," he groaned.

"But then when I see you and you are wearing these clothes, and I can't touch you. To resist such temptation is agony."

Adele grinned wickedly. *So, he had felt as frustrated as she did today? Well, good.*

"You like these pants?" she asked, looking up at Rainere through her eyelashes. "But these are just my old travelling clothes."

"Like them? They are obscene!" he glared at her. "When you bend over I can see every curve of you."

Rainere cupped his hands around Adele's behind and yanked her even closer, pressing hard against her.

"Rainere, you are making me crazy," whispered Adele, even as she tightened her thighs around his waist. "We have no time for this."

Rainere ignored her as he pulled the laces on the front of her leather trousers. He slipped his hand inside and quietened her gasp with his kiss. With his tongue against hers and his fingers stroking deep inside Adele was at the brink of her control in a matter of moments.

"Sweet Christ, Rainere! Please, stop," she moaned as her body's will fought her commonsense.

"You are so delicious," murmured Rainere as he kissed her neck and bit gently on her earlobe. Adele could only hold her breath as the rush of bliss from deep inside built up, taking her higher and higher.

In that moment of silence, she heard Grotto's voice call out "master."

Adele swore and wrenched herself away from Rainere, looking around wildly to see where the manservant was and if he had anyone else with him. Grotto was standing by a second doorway, with his eyes trained on Adele.

"Get out!" snapped Rainere as he cast a vicious glare in Grotto's direction.

"Very well, master," replied Grotto, turning to leave. "I just had to tell you that General Ohrig is waiting at the other door for his queen. I believe he is getting impatient."

"I have to go," whispered Adele. Her cheeks glowed red as frustration and shame sought dominance over her distracted state.

Rainere tied her pants for her and kissed her roughly. He felt it, too. "If not now, when?" he whispered.

Adele squeezed him between her thighs before pushing the prince away to jump down off the bench. She shook her head.

"They are watching me too closely. I don't know how we can," she answered and grabbed her lost jacket from a nearby stool. "You'll have to think of something." She gave him a rueful smile.

Adele opened the door just as General Ohrig was about to knock.

"Sorry, general," said Adele, smiling brightly. "I only found it in the last place I looked." She waved her jacket at him, as if he needed proof. But the general was craning to look over her shoulder to see if anyone else was in the room with her, thankfully Rainere had already disappeared. Until that moment Adele hadn't realized just how little the general trusted her. She felt the blush fade from her cheeks as a cold sensation flooded her gut. Ohrig knew something was up between her and the prince, and he wanted to know what it was.

Damn it! This was going to make everything so much harder, thought Adele.

CHAPTER FOURTEEN

"And Sometimes It Is Wicked"

It felt like forever before the children were all settled into bed that night.

Natalie had been rifling through Adele's things looking for a present for Prince Rainere, ready to declare her undying love for him after their wonderful day, and Adele had only rescued the little coconut-wood box that held the Fire Orchid stamens at the last minute, giving herself a heart attack and giving Natalie a severe telling-off. Adele couldn't remember where Natalie had found the precious box, but she hid it in her travelling cloak up on a high shelf for safe-keeping. Aaron had been skittish, too, talking about the strange man of his dream again and hoping he would visit again tonight. It was well after the sun had gone down before all the children finally stopped chatting and had given in to sleep.

Adele closed their bedroom door behind her and walked through the empty reception room to the middle sitting room. Most of her Queen's Guard were all sitting about playing a card game. Coins were clinking on the table, but only QG Bear was smiling. This wasn't unusual, as QG Bear apparently had a gift for cards, though it didn't stop the rest of the men trying to beat him at it to their own repeated misery. General Ohrig sat at the dining table and had laid out his weapons to polish. The gold handles of his knives and sword winked and glittered in the candlelight, looking festive despite their wickedly sharp edges. QG Pepper was sitting opposite the general with his own weapons to polish and was chatting away, oblivious to his general's stony silence.

Seraphina and Caitlin both stood to attention as Adele approached the couch they were sitting on, so she changed direction to a nearby armchair and waved for them to sit again.

"The children are asleep, girls. Just take a break," said Adele as she pulled off her boots and curled her feet up under herself.

Tilburn came over with a tiny glass of golden liquor on a tarnished silver tray. She thanked him and took a small sip and enjoyed the radiant warmth that spread through her, releasing the tight knot of tension in her shoulders. She rolled them out and took another sip.

God bless Firewhiskey, Adele thought, leaning back in her chair and staring at the heavy logs blazing in the fireplace.

"Your Majesty…?"

Adele looked up from her daydreaming and realized that the room had gone quiet. Her guards were only whispering to each other as they played now, and Seraphina and Caitlin were just exchanging giggles behind their hands while they cast glances at QG Pepper. Though they had all been so much more relaxed with each other camping on the road to Sandar, now that they were in a palace again it looked like protocol had returned to the company. Adele wasn't just herself anymore, she was back to being their queen. No one wanted to let down their guard when she was around, in case they offended her. She was like the parent showing up at the party: no fun at all.

"Your Majesty?" Tilburn tone was more insistent this time. "While you were in with the children, Mr. Grotto came by to extend an invitation to dinner with the prince. I took the liberty of declining on your behalf."

Adele's head snapped up. "You did *what?*"

The entire room fell silent, all the men looking up from the card game. Adele felt a flash of fury at her bossy majordomo, but when she looked across at Ohrig he was watching her reaction so closely she forced herself to take a breath and hide her temper.

"What I mean is, Prince Rainere is our host, Tilburn. What reason did you give him for declining? I hope you weren't rude."

"Of course not, Your Majesty," sniffed Tilburn, affronted by the accusation. "I was as polite as custom dictates I need to be to a Marchant servant."

Adele raised an eyebrow at the equivocation.

"I merely said that you were exhausted by the day and the lateness of last night and needed to rest, Your Majesty. Surely the prince should understand the need to let you rest," Tilburn added hurriedly. "Now if it please you, Your Majesty, I have a much more important issue that requires your attention. I was wondering if perhaps you could request that Prince Rainere send a messenger to Belvoir Estate on our behalf to let them know we are marooned here at the Grey Palace. I would feel much better for knowing that one of the other royal families knew of our whereabouts, if not the entire High Wizards Council and the court of the Golden Palace, too. Our wise General Ohrig has decided that we cannot spare any man of our party for the job!" Tilburn spun around to glare at Ohrig, who returned his cold expression. This was obviously a sore point for both of them.

"I will not diminish our force by a single man," agreed Ohrig and turned to Adele, his pale blue eyes daring her to protest. "Should we have the need to protect our queen and her children, we are already at a severe disadvantage."

Adele rubbed a hand across her forehead and interrupted Tilburn before he could get started on his answering argument.

"I'm sure that the prince will have somebody available to send to Belvoir, Tilburn. Besides I think the storm was calmer today. We should be able to leave as soon as it has stopped, perhaps in a day or two."

"Unless, of course, it is an unnatural storm with an unnatural cause, Your Majesty," remarked Ohrig. This time, Tilburn agreed with him

Adele had suddenly had enough of the general and Tilburn and all of their suspicions. She felt a buzz start in her head as the Chime Voices whispered words of command she had never heard before, but which she was tempted to use just to release the tension she felt building in her body. The frustrated sexual desire of an hour ago scratched at her temper and Ohrig's thinly veiled accusations against Rainere made her want to snap. She knew Ohrig only saw her as a victim before the predatory prince, someone to be protected from her own ignorance and naiveté. Logically, Adele could see that Ohrig only wanted to protect her, but he was trying to control her, too, and she couldn't stand that.

Rainere is just as much a slave to me as I am to him, Adele thought rebelliously. *He loves me and needs me. He wants to make me happy. Ohrig is too prejudiced against Marchants to understand that Rainere is more than his bloodline.*

She ended the conversation before she could say anything unwise by getting up to leave and saying "good night" to the room. More than anything, she wanted to walk out into the dark hall and search the palace for Rainere, but reason prevailed and instead she headed to her bedroom. Tense, she barely paused to register all of the relieved "Good night, Your Majesty's" from her company as she left. But as soon as she stepped out Adele heard the noise level in the room return to normal and QG Bear's rough voice asking: "What's up her knickers, general?"

"Shut your mouth, Bear, before I shut it for you," Ohrig retorted. She heard a thud of an object being thrown and contacting then an "Ow!" from Bear.

"Serves you right, watch your manners with our queen," scolded Captain Lucky. But laughter followed soon after.

They are all nice enough, but no one in there is my friend thought Adele, her irritation melting into loneliness. *I'm just the queen to them, not a person.*

As quietly as she could, Adele crept through the bedroom where the children were asleep and headed for the bathroom. Just this morning, she had discovered an actual shower system with three rain heads shooting out glorious hot water. Maybe a long soak would make her feel better?

Adele carefully shut the door behind her and turned the heavy lock. Seraphina and Caitlin had a bad habit of coming in to help her undress and wash. After having done a competent job of it by herself for twenty-nine odd years, Adele found the whole process intrusive and uncomfortable.

Undressing quickly, Adele shivered in the cold air and crossed the stone tiles to the shower wall. The taps were stiff and squeaked loudly as she turned them. She heard an ominous clanking and gurgling from the pipes, but soon hot water gushed out in a huge waterfall and she could step her cold body into the blissful warmth.

A groan of pleasure escaped Adele as the hot water cascaded down her body. With two hands she slicked her hair down her back, pulling it smooth. The fragrance she wore perfumed the air as it escaped into the steam cloud that surrounded her.

Yet, Adele couldn't relax.

If anything, Adele felt even more keyed up now that she was on her own and had time to remember her interrupted dalliance with Rainere this afternoon. She tried to puzzle it out while the Chime Voices hummed and whispered in her ears. Of course she'd had unsatisfying sex before, in fact more often than not during the seven years she had been married. Sex with no orgasm for her had been disappointing, but it had never left her feeling so frustrated and so incredibly *pent up* before. She ran her hands over her breasts and down to her stomach but paused before she went lower. *No, that just wasn't going to be enough.* She needed something powerful, something hard and strong, to take away this craving. She needed what *he* could give her.

Adele caught her breath when she *felt* Rainere enter the room, even before she could see him through the clouds of steam. Like a dark angel, the prince made his way across the bathroom from the shadows in the corner, leaving ajar the door he had entered through. Of course! There was the secret door she had searched for here in her bathroom.

"Come here," said Adele and her voice was an unfamiliar growl loaded with intent.

Rainere didn't stop until he was standing right under the spray with her. His silk shirt soon plastered to his body reminding her of how good he looked naked. Adele ran her hands over his chest and pulled at the buttons, breaking them off in one heavy rip. She hadn't known she had the strength to do that, but right now she didn't care.

With one fluid motion, Rainere bent low and slipped his hands around her behind he lifted her up and held her solid as a rock as she wrapped her legs around his waist.

"*Cara mia,* my queen…" he whispered.

"I don't want to be your queen," snapped Adele with a fury that surprised Rainere. She nodded at the door to the outside. "I'm *their* queen, but tonight I just want to be *your* lover."

The rings of silver lit up in Rainere's eyes as his arousal spiked and sent a thrill shooting through her. She wanted to use her magic on him, make love to him and control him. She wanted to make him love it.

"Not in the water," she said before he could put his lips to hers. "I want you on the chair."

Hot pink spots colored Rainere's cheeks and she knew that it was from her order as much as his excitement. Rainere had always been the king of his own castle and no one had ever told *him* what to do before.

Rainere walked them over to a chaise longue by the washbasins and carefully sat back on it, stretching out his legs and pulling her to sit astride him. Laid back against the damp silk, Rainere's eyes flashed and burned, he waited for her next command, but the anticipation was uncomfortable for him. She needed to guide him before he took over out of sheer impatience.

But first, Adele had to get herself under control.

As she sat naked and wet on top of her prince, Adele tried to resist the instinct to plunge her magic into him immediately. She trembled with raw need as the Chime Voices directed her not just to invade Rainere and hold his magic firm in her own, but they told her how to take it from him and absorb its delicious flow. The strength of the silver in his eyes was like a window into his power, and she was the thief who could take it from him. Sexual desire was confused with a dark hunger to have Rainere, to take him completely inside of her, until there was nothing of him left. The Chime Voices wheedled and cajoled, asking her to do this for them, but before tonight they had never done any more than give her the commands she needed to act. Right now, it was as if they were a separate entity and her magic was a creature to be appeased instead of a part of her.

"Rainere, I don't want to hurt you," whispered Adele, and heard the darkness in her own voice. She squeezed her eyes shut tight. "But you have to stop looking at me like that. You are making me... hungry."

Rainere just moaned and pulled her mouth against his, stopping her protests with a kiss that shook her control and fed her need. Adele flinched at a warm flash and felt Rainere naked beneath her as particles of his black pants floated about them. He pulled her up until she crested his erection and then tugged her gently down until he was completely inside her. Rainere groaned with pleasure, his head thrown back and caught up her breasts in his hands.

Adele leaned forward to lick at the pulse on Rainere's neck that fluttered frantically under his white skin.

"Here," the Chime Voices tinkled. "Take him here. Pull it! Rip it! Suck it out of him!"

"Adelena, *cara mia*, I want you, too," Rainere's rasp seemed to answer her hesitation. "I want to be inside you. I want you inside of me."

Adele trembled with desire but knew that he didn't understand what he was asking of her. This time was different. This time it wasn't just about sex, it was about magic. She tried to resist, but the sound of his groans of pleasure crumbled her resolve and the temptation was too strong. Planting her hands on his chest and riding him hard, Adele sent the fine tendrils of her power into Rainere's chest: twirling about and gripping his heart, curling up his neck and down to his groin, finding all the points that conducted the flow of magic around his body. The sensation was overwhelming and exquisite all at once. Adele was drinking in his wickedly green magic until she was swimming in it. The sensation that gripped her was less an orgasm than it was a relief, like water on a parched tongue. She fought for control of her thirst, making deal after deal with the Chime Voices to just take a bit from Rainere's magic, and then just a bit more.

She promised herself she would stop when Rainere asked her to, but his gasp of complaint came too soon.

She pushed deeper inside him and promised herself she would stop when he said "enough," but he had to *really* mean it. But his pleading moans were too soft to hear.

Adele promised herself she would absolutely stop when Rainere cried, and then groaned in frustration when his sobs rattled through her.

Steeling herself to pull away was harder than she thought. She had to disentangle the strands of magic that she had bound so tightly through him, retracting them back to her core and trying to calm the excited chanting of the Chime Voices.

Adele felt drunk and unfocused as the world rushed back in and she pushed herself off Rainere's body. The dim light of the steamy room outlined only the shapes of things around them. She was too hot and fought for a breath, trying to gasp air back into her lungs. It was a long moment before she thought to turn and look at Rainere.

The prince lay on the chaise longue, his arms hanging limply by his sides, and his eyes staring up at the ceiling. He only moaned softly when Adele shook his shoulder and kissed his cheek.

"Rainere!" Adele choked on her rough throat. "Rainere, are you alright? Darling, say something."

Guilt swept through Adele in a horrible black wave. She had hurt him, really hurt him! Rainere could barely move. She had taken more from him than he could give and now he was broken.

"I'm a monster," she whispered to Rainere. "Darling, please forgive me. I'm so, so sorry I hurt you!"

Rainere moaned again but his eyes became more focused and he managed to push himself up to sit. He rubbed his hands over his face and pulled his knees up to his chest, hesitantly, as if it pained him, and rested for a moment.

Adele swept his long hair off his face and gathered it at his shoulder. She stroked her hand over the expanse of his well-muscled back and watched the ripple of the jet-black tattoo engraved on the skin there. Even weak he was so beautiful. Adele mentally slapped herself at the warmth that sprung between her legs again at the sight of his skin. She put her arm around Rainere's shoulders and hugged him, whispering her apology a hundred times. It took another minute before Rainere roused himself enough to pull his legs off the chaise and plant them on the floor. He didn't speak, but he grabbed Adele's hand as it stroked his arm. She looked into his eyes and saw the silver rings around his pupils were tarnished now, slowly spinning in lazy circles. She gave a little sob and touched his cheek, only realizing after a moment that Rainere was leaning into her hand.

"Darling…" she wept, with no words to express her guilt.

"Don't…don't cry, *cara mia*." His voice creaked like an old man's. "I saw *her*…I saw the Goddess in you, my *cara mia*. She is in you. She craves…"

Rainere drifted off, eyes closed, as a dreamy smile floated across his lips. When he opened them again, they were clearer.

"I love you, Adelena, so much," - he wouldn't let her interrupt - "What you showed me tonight proved we are fated. We will be forever together, entwined and bound in the arms of the Goddess Serena. Tell me you saw that, too, my beloved?"

Adele looked into Rainere's dark green eyes and saw the bloodshot veins staining the whites. The shadows beneath his eyes seemed deeper and spread further, but his hand gripped hers with strength and the look he gave her was fired with the light of the fevered. She swallowed, and remembered the hunger that had consumed her, the taste of the cold *green* of Rainere's essence as it slid into her own soul. She didn't know how or why she had done it, but she hadn't felt any ethereal presence, and the guilt that weighed on her now was a clear sign her feeding had not been sanctioned by any deity she knew of. Rainere's smile broke her heart, as he wiped away the tears that leaked from her eyes and put them to his lips.

"Don't think of the pain, Adelena, think of the power you showed us both. It was a gift," he pulled himself to his feet and staggered a little. "Nothing we have done before has ever been like that."

Adele sat silently as she watched her six-foot-four, muscle-bound prince limp to the secret doorway. He held his ribs with a hand and reached out to hold the wall with the other when he turned back to blow her a kiss.

Adele stifled a sob then leaped out of her skin when the doorknob rattled at the bathroom door, followed by a quiet knock.

"Err, beg pardon, Your Majesty, but the door seems to be locked. Can I get help you get ready for bed?" asked Seraphina, barely audible over the noise of the shower.

Adele swore quietly, but when she looked back Rainere had gone, the secret door clicking shut behind him.

She remained sitting on the couch. The sweat had dried on her skin, but her hair still dripped in a steady patter of drops on the silk couch behind her. Adele looked down at her hands, hands that had vibrated with so much power tonight, the same hands that had betrayed Rainere. Despite what he thought Adele could not think of what she had done to Rainere as a good thing. *Good things don't cause so much pain, do they?* She wrapped herself in a cotton towel.

"Your Majesty? Are you alright?" Seraphina sounded worried. No doubt Ohrig had given them instructions to not let her out of their sight for too long.

Adele took a deep breath and shoved away the knowledge of what she had just done to Rainere so she could pretend to be normal. She thought grimly that Ohrig might have the wrong royal to watch. Rainere wasn't the monster. She was.

"I'm fine," she said out loud and walked over to unlock the door, surprised at her steady voice. "Everything is fine."

CHAPTER FIFTEEN

"When Love Does Not Stay Behind"

Adele had spent a long night waiting for dawn to come quickly, but it stayed resolutely dark until the proper time. Eventually, though, the grey light turned brighter and the birds started their morning songs.

All night she had tried to examine what it was that had happened to her and what it was exactly that she had done to Rainere. The experience of, for lack of a better word, 'feeding' on Rainere had been nothing like the sensation she had felt when she killed the Mage in the Holy Place of Sandar. That had been a horrible, violent stabbing of power. The word of command that killed the Mage had shredded her throat to ribbons, but last night with Rainere the commands had been whisperings of soft, sweet poetry and the sensation had been overpowering, but exquisite. Other than the guilt that sat like rocks in the bottom of her gut, Adele felt strong, rested and full of energy. But that only confirmed it for her: she had *taken* something from Rainere, and by how he had looked after they had finished she had given him nothing back. *Then why had he been so happy?*

Adele shook her head. It was no use. She cleared last night from her mind and smiled at the little ones around her as they roused themselves to whisper and cuddle into her. *She wasn't a complete monster if she could make children this angelic, surely?*

It suddenly struck Adele that she had never heard birds singing in the morning yesterday. She climbed out of bed and went to the window. The trees of the Dark Forest sparkled like Christmas decorations in the morning light.

The storm had broken.

Adele threw a robe over her nightdress and left the bedroom with all three of her children in tow. Caitlin and Seraphina were already dressed and waiting outside the bedroom door.

As Adele entered the sitting room, she saw the general with Captain Lucky and QG Owens talking to a man she had not seen before. He was wearing riding livery, and his coat carried an insignia of what looked like a wolf in the colors of bright green and brown. *A messenger from Belvoir was already here?*

"So if we leave within the hour we can be there by nightfall?" Ohrig was asking.

"Yes, general." The young man nodded, but his eyes skipped over to Adele, still standing at the door, holding her robe closed with both hands.

The messenger stepped towards her and bowed immediately. "Your Majesty Queen Adelena, I bring greetings from Prince Bertrand II of Belvoir. We have been searching for you and your party ever since the St. Lucidis messenger arrived at Belvoir Estate yesterday morning. Thank the Goddess you found shelter from the storm."

The messenger's voice had a deep and pleasant timbre. He had pushed his hat to the side as he spoke, and Adele saw dark curls hidden beneath it. She approached to take the scroll he offered her.

"It's an invitation from Prince Bertrand II of Belvoir, Your Majesty," said the messenger needlessly as Adele broke the seal and unrolled it anyway. "You are welcome to come to the estate at your earliest convenience, but as the carnival starts tomorrow I would advise that we leave today to make it back in time."

"Is that right?" asked Adele, her tone sharp as her stomach dropped away and she pretended to read the scroll in her hands. She didn't want to leave Rainere today after what had happened last night. She had to know that he was alright first and make it better.

Adele looked up as she realized a silence had fallen over the group. The Belvoir messenger looked stricken, terrified he might have offended her. Adele noticed his eyes were a light sea-green and his lashes were long and dark.

"I'm sure no disrespect was intended, Your Majesty, it is wise advice," Ohrig said with a frown at the same time that the messenger blurted out an apology.

Adele folded the letter and pulled the sash on her robe tighter as she gave Ohrig a cold glance. There he was, telling her what to do again and scolding her in front of a room full of people. His attitude was really getting irritating.

"I know what you meant, no apology necessary…um, what's your name?" said Adele and noted the messenger's blushing cheeks.

"My name is Benjamin, Your Majesty."

He couldn't have been more than his early twenties, maybe not even that old. Her body responded to his shy smile and she almost blushed herself as a surge of warmth swept through her.

Stop it right now! Adele admonished herself. *He's just a boy, not Rainere, for God's sake.*

She looked away from Benjamin's pretty sea-green eyes and over to Tilburn who entered the room dragging a heavy trunk behind him. "How long will it take us to get ready to leave, Tilburn?"

Tilburn dropped his trunk with a loud thud and approached Adele wearing a beaming grin. "Well, I'm already packed so I should say an hour at the most, Your Majesty." He rubbed his hands together in satisfaction. "I've already been down to the stables to ask the drivers to prepare the carriages. We will just load them and be out of here by the time the royal family has finished breakfast."

"Oh, that quickly? Wonderful," said Adele and bit her bottom lip to hide its quiver. That left her no time at all to see Rainere. She turned her back so no one could see her disappointment and sat down at the table with the children.

She didn't even hear the knock at the door, but Tilburn skipped off to answer it with a bright "Coming!" Two miserable-looking Marchant servants entered the apartment pushing squeaking trolleys covered in hot breakfast dishes, which they arranged on the dining table to the delight of the hungry children.

Adele didn't realize that Grotto had followed the servants into the apartment until she heard Tilburn imperiously informing the Marchant manservant that he was to tell Prince Rainere that the royal family was leaving within the hour.

Grotto turned his piercing eyes on Adele and gave her such a loaded look he might as well have said what he was really thinking as it was so plain in his expression. "I shall inform His Highness that the queen wishes to leave the Grey Palace immediately and refuses any further hospitality he could extend to her."

Adele paled. Grotto was being so awful when he knew she couldn't say a thing to defend herself. Leaving hurt her as much as it did Rainere.

"Err, quite right!" replied Tilburn wishing to cause as much as offence as he politely could. "The prince can meet us at the gates for a farewell. Or not, if he has business elsewhere, of course. I'm sure we have taken up enough of his time."

Grotto turned his poisonous gaze on the little majordomo and remained silent for a moment longer than was necessary, allowing the intensity of his loathing to be felt by everyone in the room.

"*His. Highness*," enunciated Grotto through clenched teeth. "Will do as he sees fit and accord the occasion exactly the time it deserves. I shall let you know his will before you leave."

With that, after giving Adele the shallowest of all bows, he spun on his heel and left, slamming the door loudly behind himself, as was his way.

"Ugh!" Tilburn shook himself. "I'm sure that man has magic in his eyes. Such a troubled soul I have never met before."

"Was that Grottonski, the prince's man?" asked the Belvoir messenger with wide eyes. "He looks just as ferocious as he is described in the stories we have at home."

"You don't know the half of it, Benjamin," replied Tilburn snippily. "Now I've no more time for you to stand about gossiping, you'll need to help us get ready to leave this morning."

Adele turned back to her children and picked a boiled egg from the plate before her, though she didn't want to eat it as her stomach felt full of sawdust.

"What was that Tilburn said, Mummy?" asked Natalie, giving her mother a hard look. "We aren't leaving, are we?"

Caught up in her own sadness, Adele hadn't thought how the children might react to leaving the Grey Palace with such short notice, so she was shocked by the height of hysteria that followed her announcement. Natalie burst into howling tears and screeched to be allowed to stay, while Aaron cried and threatened to hide himself where no one could find him. The prince had promised to show Aaron the dungeons today, and her son was desperate to see them. Poor little Stella didn't understand the reason behind the fuss but cried in sympathy with her big brother and sister.

"You can't make me go!" shrieked Natalie and dashed from the table. Adele heard Caitlin squawk in surprise from the next room. "Princess you can't pull all that out, I've just packed it!"

Adele sighed, but was at a loss at what to do. Her children's grief mirrored her own. She couldn't believe that she and Rainere could be separated so easily from each other by circumstance. A hundred times she wanted to call out. "Stop packing, we will stay here instead!" but a hundred times common sense stopped her. It was just too dangerous for anyone to know about their relationship.

Natalie stalked back into the room, ignoring the nanny who hovered nervously behind her and with all the dignity she could muster announced:

"If you are going to make me leave, then I am going to make Prince Rainere a present." She wiped her tears away with the back of her hand. "And it's going to be something really, really special, so he knows that I will miss him. I will need a pencil and paper and other stuff." Natalie swept out again but Adele waved Caitlin to leave her daughter alone. Natalie needed time to cool down. Seraphina managed to convince Aaron and Stella to come outside on the terrace to play with their puppies, which always cheered them up.

Adele got herself a cup of tea and dropped her chin to her hand as she poured it. She tried not to look as dejected as she felt, but it was too hard.

"The little ones seem sad to leave the Grey Palace, Your Majesty," said Benjamin cheerfully as he edged his way over to her, earning himself a sharp glance from Adele. She took a sip of tea instead of biting off the sarcastic remark that was on the tip of her tongue.

Calm down, she told herself again. She needed to be kinder. The boy was obviously excited to be in the legendary Grey Palace, where no Belvoir had stood for generations, and by the look of his shy smile and shining eyes he was pretty excited to meet her, too.

Adele stifled a sigh. Everyone was excited to meet her at first, just before they started telling her what to do. "Benjamin, will you be riding with us back to the Belvoir Estate?" she asked, forcing her tone to be pleasant.

"Absolutely. Yes. I, yes, will be coming with you, Your Majesty!" stammered Benjamin, his cheeks going even pinker. "I promised to show the boys… um… your Queen's Guard the best road through the forest. It's very easy to get lost if you don't know the way."

"Well, it will certainly be good to have someone who has experience to show us the way to Belvoir this time," replied Adele in a voice she was sure would carry over to Ohrig, where he was organizing trunks with the other QG. "God knows we could have done with some proper directions two days ago."

She glanced over at Ohrig and smiled with satisfaction when she saw that he had stopped talking and was shaking his head. He sent her a small grin and tipped his head at her, acknowledging her needling, and just like that the invisible tension between the two of them dissipated. Smothering his smile, Ohrig turned back to Captain Lucky. Adele returned her gaze to Benjamin and saw that he was beaming with pleasure at her compliments.

"Your Majesty's faith in me is an honor," he said proudly and swept into a deep bow. His hat fell off and black curls spilled over his forehead. Grinning in embarrassment, Benjamin picked it up and jammed it back on his head, pushing the curls into his eyes.

Adele gave him a smile. He really was very charming.

"You, boy! Belvoir Benjamin!" shouted Tilburn from the door. "If Her Majesty is finished with you, you must help take these trunks down to the carriages. I'm not waiting for those good-for-nothing Marchant footmen to help us. Such a sorry lot they are."

Benjamin looked expectantly at Adele, perhaps a little too eagerly as his eyes flashed to the front of her exposed nightgown before returning to her face.

"You had better do as he says," said Adele. "He'll only get louder and more insulting if you don't."

"Your Majesty, I'm at your service." Benjamin bowed a little less extravagantly this time, giving her a wide smile and the tiniest of winks.

Adele upgraded Benjamin from 'very charming' to 'incorrigible flirt' and instantly felt less special. If she had been in a better mood, she might have been amused by the sharp word that Captain Lucky gave the messenger as Benjamin joined the other QGs. The captain's look said, "What the hell do you think you're doing? Don't flirt with our queen!" And Benjamin's nonchalant shrug and grin said, "Hey, just because you boys aren't up for it, don't blame me for trying," earning himself a clip over the ear from QG Owens. It was sweet how her

Queen's Guard protected her virtue. Sweet, but unnecessary, as her virtue had long since been given to Rainere.

Adele pushed back her chair and headed out of the room to get changed and prepare herself to do the one thing she wanted to least of all.

She was leaving Rainere yet again.

Chapter Sixteen

"The Unrequited Distance of Circumstance"

As she walked out onto the front steps, Adele squinted in the sunlight bathing the Grey Palace. Their arrival two days ago had been in the dead of night during a dangerous snowstorm. But now, as they were leaving, the sun shone and the blue sky was studded with soft clouds, innocently scudding about in the breeze. Adele gave them a baleful glare. Though it was ridiculous, she felt completely betrayed by the weather. She would have been so much happier if the storm hadn't broken.

Adele knew Rainere's eyes were upon her and she bit her lip to stop the tremble that would lead to the tears she couldn't show. It killed her to see how tired and hollow he looked in the harsh light of day. Though he was standing upright and tall, Adele could see what his dignity was costing him in the tightness about his eyes. She had hurt him so much last night and she couldn't forgive herself for it, though he had already said there was nothing to forgive.

"Prince Rainere, it has been an honor and a pleasure to stay at the Grey Palace with you. We can only thank you from the bottom of our hearts for your generous hospitality in our time of need, and I hope you will accept my open invitation to the Golden Palace whenever you have a chance to visit the capital." Adele forced herself to be formal, but couldn't resist stepping closer to Rainere, if only to search his face for the damage she did last night. She was relieved to see that his eyes had returned to normal at least. The whites were clear and the silver rings of magic were spinning about his black pupils again. If only his cheeks weren't so haggard and his face so pale.

"Your Majesty, the honor has been all mine," replied Rainere and bowed as low as he could without actually putting his forehead against hers.

"I cannot tell you how much we've enjoyed ourselves." Adele drifted off as she could hear her guards muttering behind her. What she wanted to do was throw her arms around Rainere's neck and kiss him, kiss him hard enough to make last night disappear, and give him all the pleasure he deserved without any of the pain she had inflicted on him. It was so wrong that they had to be apart after such an upsetting night.

But it was impossible.

Their gaze grew longer. Tilburn coughed politely.

"Prince Rainere?" Natalie had pushed between them and was pulling on the prince's sleeve. Rainere knelt down on one knee so he could be closer to Natalie's eye level.

"Yes, Your Highness," he said, a wisp of a smile pulling at his mouth.

"I have a present for you to say thank you, and to say I want to come back here one day," said Natalie as tears trembled in her voice. "I love your Grey Palace." She thrust a clumsy little package at Rainere.

"That is very kind of you, Princess," said the prince formally but his eyes were clouded with an emotion that Adele didn't recognize. "I – ah - I shall treasure it."

Suddenly, Natalie threw her arms around the prince and hugged him with all of her might. "I love you!" she howled and started to cry in earnest.

"Okay, Natalie, let's just calm down, darling girl." Adele was close to tears herself but was aware of how strained the atmosphere had just become as her Queen's Guard advanced back up the stairs to her and the children. Rainere kept his own arms open and free of the little girl so as not to confuse anyone as to whom was hugging whom.

"Come on, darling." Adele managed to pry her weeping daughter off Rainere's shoulder and hugged her tight. "Come on, sweetheart, we don't want Prince Rainere to see us sad. He must know that we are happy because we got to stay at his palace and how much we enjoyed the lovely things he showed us."

"Okay," sniffed Natalie, trying to be brave and looked up at Rainere with wet eyes. "Do you want to open your present now? I got it for your labor-atormy. Mummy said it is really, really special."

Prince Rainere looked down at the lumpy gift in his hand.

"That's okay, sweetheart, Prince Rainere can open it later," said Adele, flushed with her own barely contained emotions. She hustled Natalie down the stairs to the waiting carriages and almost threw her daughter in with the other children. They had to leave now before she copied Natalie and lost all self-control.

As the carriages pulled away Natalie started weeping loudly again and Stella and Aaron almost fell out the window as they waved and shouted goodbye to the prince. Adele peeked out and saw Rainere raise a single hand in farewell. She ducked back inside the carriage and hoped no one could hear the sound of her heart breaking.

CHAPTER SEVENTEEN

"It Always Rains Here"

Rainere stood on the top of the palace steps long after the royal carriages had left the Grey Palace grounds. He stood perfectly still, as if he had been carved from stone, and he watched and he waited for the impossible.

But Adelena did not come back.

Thin grey clouds crept across the sky over the palace, dropping lower and lower until they covered the parapets and towers in a misty haze.

All his joy had left with Adelena, and there was no more sunshine.

Fat drops of rain had begun to fall, splashing onto the ground before him, when Rainere felt Grotto's light touch on his shoulder. "Master, come inside. Please."

Distant thunder trembled across the sky as Rainere slowly turned away from the road and walked back inside his palace, Grotto following a step behind wearing a worried frown.

The prince stood in the entrance hall and looked about as if he didn't recognize the grey and black checkerboard tiles beneath his feet, or the suits of armor that lined the walls. He gazed up at the tattered pennants of his ancestors fluttering in the breeze from the open door. Just minutes ago, the sun had warmed this floor, and the voices of children had rung in the hallway echoing with shouts of joy and sadness combined. Now, silence had reclaimed this world.

Rainere felt the loneliness so acutely that it almost made him gasp.

Adele had taken all the noise, all the feelings, and all the laughter away with her. That was her world, and it didn't stay behind when she moved on.

Rainere thought of Natalie's arms clutching tight around his neck as she whispered "I love you" in his ear. Her little arms had felt like twigs, so fragile that he had been afraid to hurt her if he had tried to pull them off. Her breath had been hot and swirled about his head, smelling of fresh bread and soap. Rainere looked down at the package still in his hands. He pulled at the rain-spotted paper and the stiff parchment sprang apart revealing a penciled image: a little girl wearing a crown was holding hands with a much taller man also wearing a crown on his head. Both figures had long dark hair and big smiles on their faces. Above the sketch written in a labored cursive were the three little words Natalie had professed with such passion: *I love you.*

A distant memory awoke somewhere deep in Rainere's mind and struggled to the surface of his consciousness.

He must have been tiny, as his father's desk had seemed as big as a mountain. The few steps to stand next to the old man's knee took forever. He had worked hard to reach out and touch his father's leg. A large white hand had come down to cover his baby one. Dark purple splotches of ink had stained his father's fingers as he wrote letters at his desk. He felt joy at the thrill of his father's green-eyed gaze and being lifted high and held to the warmth of his chest. "My son," and his voice filled Rainere with a fierce pride. He belonged to this man, he was a sun...

The prince's mind travelled back to the present and focused on the simply wrought sketch of himself and Princess Natalie. He cast a glance at the little wooden box that had been wrapped in the paper, coconut wood by the look of it. He pushed it down inside a pocket and wandered up the stairs. Last night had been hard, but this morning, watching Adelena walk away had been worse. He needed to give his heart a moment to recover from everything that she'd done to him. Today he needed the Blue Tonic to take away the pain.

*   *   *

Grotto remained standing in the entrance hall for a minute after Rainere had left. Shaking himself out of his deepening panic, Grotto forced himself into motion, slamming the great front doors shut. The *boom* reverberated around the entrance hall and shook the tapestries on their ancient strings. He lay his forehead against the back of the lacquered wood and pressed his lips tightly together to prevent a scream of sheer frustration from escaping.

The prince had let her go! He had let the queen slip right through his fingers and only watched her as she drove right out the front gates of the Grey Palace, and out of his control. After all Grotto's shouting and all his warnings, the prince had let the abomination go free!

Grotto banged his head against the great door causing green sparks of energy to flash and burn him. He moaned in despair.

Now the queen was heading even further out of their grasp to the cursed Belvoir Estate. No magic could be worked within the boundaries of Belvoir, none at all. Not even a creature of powerful magic like the Spider Empress could survive for long on those cursed lands. The queen would be untouchable there, but she would also be in a different kind of danger. Her kind could not last long within the boundaries of Belvoir as the curse forced her magic to turn on itself, corroding her from the inside out. This was the very reason the Marchant kings of the past had created Belvoir estate. It had been a neutral site where the various factions of the family could meet without fear of magical attacks from each other or the entities that used to roam Evendaar freely. Even immortals were rendered human again as the curse prevented even the most powerful of spells from working.

If only the old masters knew how their cursed estate would be used to protect those unworthy and weak in magic from the Marchant prince who should be their king by right of the Blood. Grotto's lip curled in disgust as he thought of the sacred halls of Belvoir being used to house the impure Belvoir family. Those who were once serfs and vassals were now play-acting as princes and lords. The wrongs of the distant past needled Grotto as if they had just happened yesterday.

We have only six days to put my prince on the throne, thought Grotto, as anxiety melted his insides like acid. *Why would my master have lessened the storm to allow a messenger through? Why would he have let the queen escape to Belvoir when he had her in his bed, all tangled up in her appetites.*

Grotto's stomach turned at the memory of finding the prince in the laboratory with the queen. The prince, with his arm wrapped around her, his other hand doing something unmentionable in her trousers. The expression on his face had been ecstatic, and he had smiled as he kissed the abomination. He had smiled.

Grotto's hand flew to his mouth in shock. *No, it couldn't be! His master couldn't have let the queen go to Belvoir on purpose. Was he really preparing to sacrifice himself to the Spider Empress?* Because when the empress found out the prince had betrayed her no one would be safe from her fury and Rainere would have given his precious life for nothing.

Grotto shook himself into action a second time and raced up the left staircase following the prince. He headed straight for the Great Library, cursing all the while. Instinct told him that the Prince would have sequestered himself in the only room in the entire Grey Palace that Grotto couldn't enter.

The door of the Great Library was open just a crack, and through it Grotto could see Prince Rainere slumped in an armchair, a small bottle filled with blue liquid hanging from his hand, gazing into space. How did Grotto not notice how hollow his master's face had become? How did he not see the prince was on the verge of collapse? She had done this to him! The abomination had sucked the life right out of him. Grotto had seen it too many times before with Rainere's father to not recognize the symptoms of a wasting of the spirit now that it was staring him in the face.

What hell was this life that he now had to do the thing that would hurt his precious master the most?

"Master," pleaded Grotto, panic coloring his voice as he pressed his face to the gap in the door. "Master, you have to get the queen back! We only have six days left to fulfil the prophecy. The Hidden Child must have you at her side at the time of the full moon. The throne of all Unisia will be yours if you just force her to marry you."

"And what will happen if I don't, Grotto?" Rainere's gravelly voice was low and barely carried to Grotto.

Grotto ripped his hands off the door and blew on them. The runes that protected the sanctity of the Great Library were burning him. He took a moment to order his scattered thoughts. Now that he had Rainere's attention, he had to make his words count. He thanked the Goddess that Rainere had yet to drink the blue opiate in the bottle.

"Master, there is no telling what will happen if we do not follow the words that the Goddess Serena herself passed down to us. '*Only the Hidden Child shall restore the Glory of my Chosen Ones to the throne of my kingdom*'," Grotto quoted. "You yourself have spoken with the Goddess, master. She brought you back from death and she saved you for a reason, did she not master? Master?"

The prince did not answer, but his head rose off his chest.

Grotto pressed his lips to the door and ignored the burning runes. "The Goddess Serena favored you above all others, master, for you are the very last of her Chosen Ones!"

Grotto became excited as he saw Rainere rise and walk unsteadily towards him. Finally, he was listening! "It is your sacred duty to follow the words of her prophecy. You must stand by the queen, master, and take her throne for your own. It is the only way that the glory of the Marchant family will rise again."

Grotto's eyes were wide and lit by a fierce hope.

Rainere opened the library door wider and stared into the face of the servant who had raised him since he was a baby, the servant who had trained his infant prince to become an adult king. He saw the twisted belief that had shaped Grotto's whole life up until now. This prophecy had tainted his mind as it had tainted the Spider Empress and the wizards of the Golden Court.

In that moment Rainere realized that Adelena would never find any peace in the world of Evendaar. He could let her escape to the Belvoir Estate for a time, but without his protection Adelena would simply fall prey to the wizards of St. Lucidis and be pulled back into the fray of this imaginary war. Rainere pulled the door open and such was Grotto's distraction that he almost stepped over the threshold to grab the lapels of his master's jacket in relief.

"Please master. Get her back! I know a priest. He does not live far from here and is recognized by the Crown. He will marry you, and in six days you can show the Spider Empress her will has been done. Your oath to her will be fulfilled, and the prophecy will be complete."

"I will bring Adelena back to the Grey Palace, Grotto, but I will only ask that she marries me if she would wish it. I will not force her to do anything," growled Rainere in a warning tone. "I will not make my love unhappy for all the thrones in the world. If the Spider Empress tries to…"

"All will be as you say, master," interrupted Grotto hurriedly. "Now, please go and chase the queen down."

Rainere frowned. "On what pretext? Don't be a fool, Grotto. Her men would not let her acquiesce to me, even if I found her outside the Belvoir boundary." Rainere stepped past Grotto into the hall. "No, I have a better idea. Send a letter to Prince Bertrand II of Belvoir, telling him I will be attending the racing carnival. I will prepare the horses tonight for the journey and we can travel by portal as soon as I recover my strength to make one big enough."

"But master, the Belvoir curse! What about your immortality spell?"

Rainere shrugged and leaned against the wall as though the effort of the small movement was too much for him. He looked exhausted. "I can sacrifice a few days of my endless life if it means that Adelena will be safe from the empress while I convince her to see this marriage through. She promised me…" Rainere drifted off uncertain then shot Grotto a defiant look. "I truly believe she loves me, Grotto."

Grotto bit his lip until he tasted blood. The coppery tang filled his mouth and made his stomach turn over. He tried to think of practicalities and not the prince's words. Rainere would need something to recover his strength, and there was nothing else that would aid his health more quickly than the thing Rainere hated most. "Master, I shall fetch the Gift of Life for you."

Grotto dropped his eyes but not before he saw the look of disgust roll across Rainere's face, making his pale face whiter.

"I have no need," the prince protested, but knew as well as Grotto that it was futile. The Gift of Life was the only answer to his weakness: the weakness that Adelena had brought on him. With the barest of nods, Rainere pulled himself off the wall and handed the bottle of Blue Tonic to his servant.

As he watched the prince stagger down the hallway, Grotto sent a quick prayer to the Goddess Lune and another to her sister, the Goddess Serena, praying that she would be merciful to her Chosen One as he was the last hope of the Marchant family. After hundreds of years of waiting, there was suddenly no time at all to do what needed to be done to get Rainere on the throne. Grotto bit his sore lip again. *Now all I need to know is where that little man-spider is.*

Schiss hadn't yet returned from delivering the letter to his mother the empress. Perhaps he was killed like he feared he might be. Grotto sniffed. If was of no account. If Rainere was headed to the Belvoir Estate then the prince could find the priest himself and none would be the wiser.

CHAPTER EIGHTEEN

"The Belvoir Estate"

Adele swigged back her tiny glass of Firewhiskey and then quickly poured herself another. She took a deep breath and enjoyed the fact that she was finally alone. It was after midnight, but she was still too wired to sleep. It didn't help that every time she closed her eyes she saw an image of Rainere's stricken expression, his hand raised in farewell, fused to the back of her eyelids.

The journey to Belvoir had been long and uncomfortable, bouncing around in the carriages as they raced to the estate before the weather could turn again. But Prince Bertrand II, or Bertie, as Adele had come to know him at the Golden Palace, more than made up for the trip with his warm and generous welcome. He was extremely relieved to see Adele and the children arrive on his doorstep alive and in good health.

Adele hadn't quite realized the extent of the hysteria their disappearance had caused. When the messenger from the Golden Palace had arrived with a letter announcing both the royal party's imminent arrival and the news of the terrible storm that would prevent their passing, it had thrown Belvoir Estate into a panic. The snowstorm had made it difficult for search parties to travel very far into the Dark Forest, and it hadn't been safe to search in the night. Only Benjamin had been successful in entering through the gates of the Grey Palace for reasons that weren't properly explained to Adele.

Adele looked around her new chamber and couldn't help but compare it to the bedroom at the Grey Palace. The Belvoir Estate was less a palace than it was an enormous manor house, but it was far richer and more comfortable than the threadbare grandeur of the Marchant palace. Here, the carpets were deep and thick, the silk on the walls was hand-painted and the drapes at the windows were rich velvet brocade. Large white candles burned, scenting the air with fresh pine, and vases of flowers crowded every surface on the desk and side tables. Paintings and tapestries decorated the walls, depicting pastoral hunting scenes and white-dressed figures having picnics on green hills. Dogs featured prominently in all the images and, in fact, most of the cushions and pillows on the overstuffed chairs and couches were covered with the faces of dogs at play, dogs chasing ducks or dogs curled up with other dogs.

Adele sat on the end of her bed, sipping at her second glass of Firewhiskey more carefully and trying very hard not to cry. She would give her right arm to be back with Rainere in his spooky old home right now, even with Grotto lurking about. She missed him so much, the pain almost felt like it was burning her from the inside out.

Bertie had thrown them a wonderful welcome dinner tonight, but she hadn't been able to eat a thing. Every time she thought about how she had left things with Rainere, her stomach roiled and she felt dreadful. The children had been put to bed next door with Caitlin and Seraphina, and also Siobahn, the third nanny, who had arrived from the Golden Palace with the St. Lucidis party just yesterday. Adele felt they were safe enough without her sleeping by their side, and, in some ways, she welcomed the peace and quiet, but she missed them, too. *Perhaps she could sneak next door and kiss them one more time as they slept?*

A quiet knock at the door interrupted her thoughts. "Come in," she called.

Lady Olivia poked her pretty head into the room. "I'm sorry to bother you, Your Majesty. I just saw the light on and wondered if you needed anything."

Adele smiled at the young woman curtseying in the doorway and welcomed her inside. "I'm fine. But thank you, Lady Olivia."

Adele walked to the bay window and marveled at the warm breeze drifting in. It had been snowing at the Grey Palace and now she was sweating in the heat of a hot summer's night at the Belvoir Estate. "I'm just having a little trouble going to sleep after all the excitement of the day."

"So am I!" giggled Lady Olivia, busying herself with turning down the bed, removing all the decorative pillows by the armful, and dumping them in baskets under the bed. "I have never been to the Belvoir Estate as a guest before. It's so much bigger than I thought and nothing runs on magic, so they have so many funny contraptions everywhere. Have you *seen* the bathrooms?"

Adele shrugged. They hadn't really caught her eye.

"Oh my! Well, let's just say they are *not* what I had expected," Lady Olivia giggled again and the sweetness of it made Adele relax a little. Olivia was such a cheerful presence amongst Adele's rather dour ladies in waiting, Lisbeth and Cara, and the subservient nannies. Adele had liked the young woman instantly when she had met her just weeks ago at the coronation ball and was so pleased to have someone a bit more interesting and fun in her entourage. Lady Olivia also had a real talent with couture and had helped design a beautiful new collection of dresses for this week-long carnival, adapting the more dated and frankly awful designs Adele had been shown at the Golden Palace before her trip to Sandar. For that alone, Adele was grateful to Lady Olivia.

But Adele only listened with half an ear as Lady Olivia gossiped good-naturedly about who had turned up today from the other royal families. Apparently the Carparells had come in very late and had made a huge fuss about their accommodations, as they had brought too many squires with them to house in the manor. But there were no more arrivals from the Golden Palace and no High Wizard Ohren or Mrs. Dolores Ollenby, the only two people who Adele really wanted to see.

As she drained the tiny glass, Adele felt a sigh build.

"Listen to me prattling on," said Lady Olivia, sensing Adele's shift in mood with a quick glance. "I shall see you in the morning, Your Majesty. I believe there will be a late breakfast served at the tenth hour, and the horse show won't begin until the afternoon."

Adele nodded. "Tilburn filled me in, but I'm sure the children will wake me regardless."

Olivia curtseyed again and left through the door to the hall, but before the door could even close, Adele heard another knock. She glanced at the clock on the mantle. *It was almost one in the morning and her room was as busy as central station!*

"Yes," she called out warily, hoping it wasn't Tilburn with more work for her.

The messenger, Benjamin, stepped into the room and bowed, giving her a charming smile. "Good evening, Your Majesty. I have just come on duty and wanted to let you know I will be on guard until well after dawn. If you should need anything, anything at all, please do not hesitate to ask."

Adele didn't like the warmth that spread inside of her at Benjamin's words, or the nausea that soon mixed with it. His shiny eyes and keen glance left her in no doubt as to what he was suggesting she could ask for. If she didn't already have an incredible lover for whom she pined even now, then the attentions of a young man like Benjamin might have made her blush and stammer. As it was, Rainere had given her so much more than amazing sex. He had given her his heart and she would never betray that.

Still, it was hard to avoid feeling flattered by young Benjamin's obvious attraction to her. At twenty-nine and as a mother of three, Adele sometimes felt decades older than she was. But when Benjamin stepped toward her until he stood just a foot away she started to feel very unsure about how far he was going to take his flirting. Being much shorter, she had to tilt her head to look up into his pale green eyes.

"I don't need a thing, Benjamin," Adele said firmly. "Thank you anyway."

Benjamin's breathing hitched a little and his smile slowly morphed into a sexy pout. He leaned in, forcing Adele to lean back or risk becoming uncomfortably close. *Was he really going to try to kiss her, here in her bedroom?*

"Really?" He nodded expectantly, a black curl of hair flopping into his eyes.

Adele swallowed hard, stepping back and away from the gorgeous young man. She forced herself to frown. "Actually, could you please make sure I am left *alone* from now on, and that you remain on the outside of the door for the rest of your shift."

To his credit, Benjamin immediately snapped back to professional form. "Yes, Your Majesty, of course." He gave her a cocky grin before he bowed and retreated to the door, opening it only to see QG Owens on the other side.

"Your Majesty, excuse me, I…Benjamin! What do you think you are doing in Her Majesty's room?" asked QG Owens, suddenly irritated, as he caught sight of Benjamin with the queen.

"Benjamin is standing guard with you tonight," replied Adele, telling Owens how she felt about that with her crossed arms and cold expression. "But I really would like to go to bed now, so I would appreciate it if you could keep him on the other side of this door."

QG Owens gave Benjamin a hard look but answered Adele politely. "I will personally deal with anyone who steps beyond the boundary of this doorway, Your Majesty." As he pulled the door shut Adele saw him give Benjamin a quick clip over the head.

Adele almost smiled as she pulled off her robe and climbed into the bed. Her Queen's Guard took their duties very seriously, but she could only imagine how furious Rainere would be if he saw someone actually flirting her. Adele's smile died. Actually, that wouldn't be funny at all.

As she lay down, Adele tried to get comfortable on the bank of fluffy white pillows and closed her eyes, but her mind would not stop racing.

Why isn't Ohren here? She wondered. She had expected him to be in the St. Lucidis group to see how she had fared in Sandar or, at the very least, to take the precious Fire Orchid stamens out of her hands.

Adele tried to remember the last time she had seen the coconut-wood box containing the stamens, but her brain was a little fuzzy. Surely they would still be where she left them, in her travelling cloak, as she hadn't touched them since hiding them there?

Adele's stomach dropped away when she thought of everything that had happened not even a week ago. Ohren had to know what she had done to the Mage of Sandar and the promises she had made to the Empress Sanda'hani. She had no idea where Ripenzo Shale was, or whether she should have looked for him when he disappeared.

Here I am drinking champagne with the Lords and Ladies of Unisia, and my actions could well have started a war we are not prepared for. Adele quailed at the thought and sat up in bed, hugging her knees. To make matters worse, she hadn't even told Rainere what she had done in Sandar or spoken to him about this crazy prophecy that High Wizard Ohren had told her about.

Now the magic that was boiling up inside of her was getting out of control Adele had to face the truth: with her magic she had killed a man and had hurt Rainere badly. She was becoming dangerous, and she didn't know how to stop it.

But it wasn't only the power of the magic that scared her, it was her desire to use it again. Her stomach flipped at the idea of having Benjamin under her right now, his throat exposed and her hands pressed against his chest to find that gorgeous, cold power swimming in the darkness. *Would he taste different than Rainere?*

Adele swallowed as sour water filled her mouth. *Why am I even thinking about wanting to hurt a young man like that? I would never betray Rainere.* Adele scolded herself. She was an awful person to let anything like that cross her mind when Rainere was so wonderful and when he forgave her for everything she had done to him.

Adele groaned and threw off her covers.

She had so many other things to think about right now. She was constantly surrounded by people but she felt so alone. Her problems were unique even in this alien world and she had no one to talk to about any of them. Adele had been queen of Unisia for just over a month, and she still had no idea who to really trust in this world.

Adele remembered the life she had left behind and once let out of their box the memories of Earth washed over her. Memories of croissants, Sunday papers, shopping at supermarkets and nothing more complicated than the children's routine had filled her days. Even her recent divorce had been like everything else in her life, and had been shoved in around the corners of her time. Raising three kids on her own hadn't left room for anything more. She hadn't even had time to properly grieve for all that she had lost.

And now she had an immortal wizard begging for her to be his bride, and the fate of a nation weighing on her shoulders. Adele started to tremble as adrenaline-fueled anxiety shook her overtired body. She hadn't slept in days and she didn't know why, but it had to be something to do with the magic that was growing inside of her.

The clock on the mantel chimed gently. *Damn.* It was already three am. Adele hated this time of night. All her anxieties and worries screamed their loudest at three am. She huffed and threw herself back on the bed and pulled the covers up again, determined to calm down. Adele resolutely closed her eyes and ignored the hot tears which wet her lashes and escaped down her cheeks.

She lay like that until the sun rose three hours later.

CHAPTER NINETEEN

"What Lurks Behind Doors?"

It was early in the morning, not long after dawn, when the royal children came squawking into the kitchens with their three nannies in tow—two red-heads and a dark-haired beauty. Charlie, who was chatting to his cousin, Mary, and eating hot rolls, looked up at the commotion.

"Gawds, 'elp us! What is the royal children doin' in 'ere?" screeched the Head Cook, as she lurched her bulk across the busy kitchen to the little party. "What's the meanin' of this? If you needed summink fah the children you should've rung down, not come you'selves!"

The Head Cook looked aghast, as Aaron accidentally stepped in front of a maid carrying a tray of hot bread. "'Ere, 'e almost died then, and we would've wasted all that bread!" she shrieked, blue eyes bulging over her quivering cheeks.

Always confident, Charlie's cousin, Mary, stepped forward to intercede before things got out of hand. "Calm yourself, Colleen. I'll see to the bairns, never mind." She soothed the hysterical Head Cook, patting her arm until the lady walked off still grumbling and casting the children dark looks.

Mary turned back to the nannies and children, checking her cap and smoothing her apron, a warm smile dimpled her cheeks. "Good morning, Highnesses and nannies. What is it you'll be wanting?"

The black-haired Beauty looked down her nose, eyeing Mary's cook's apron in a haughty way.

Which is a bit rich for a nanny, thought Charlie, though he also thought she was gorgeous enough to get away with it.

"The bairns are hungry and we didn't know your ways at Belvoir so we thought we'd come down ourselves. I know the breakfast party is at the tenth hour, but the children need to eat now."

"What would they like?" asked Mary.

"Sugar buns!" the children squealed in unison, the baby just a beat behind.

"Yes, *please*," agreed one of the little red-heads, the one with the nice curves, softening the dark-haired nanny's more imperious attitude. "But some fruit and milk too if these children want to grow up big and strong." She grinned at the children's answering groans.

Mary waved the little party to sit at the table next to Charlie and she hurried off to collect a tray of food. Charlie stared with unabashed curiosity at the children. They were very clean and well-fed looking, he decided, the baby was positively fat. They all had something of the queen about their faces, especially the eldest girl, Natalie, with her long, dark hair and serious expression. The baby was as blonde as any St. Lucidis princess, but Aaron, the boy, had lighter brown hair and a pointy little face. Charlie blinked in surprise when Aaron turned his hazel eyes on him and gave a wink, then another and another.

"Oi!" said Charlie, slightly perturbed. "What are you doing with that winking business? Don't you know not to wink at a man?"

Aaron frowned. "You're not a man, you are a teenager, aren't you?"

Charlie bristled at the comment and his cheeks flushed when he realized that Beauty was watching them both with a grin. Charlie had to recover some dignity and not let this royal kiddling throw him off his game with the ladies.

"What are you all doing down here anyway? Shouldn't you be up with your mum, the queen?" he asked gruffly.

"I like kitchens," replied Aaron with a shrug.

"Our mum is still in bed right now," clarified Natalie.

"I'll bet!" muttered Charlie and earned himself a sharp look from one of the redheads, the other one with freckles on her nose.

"Her Majesty was up late with her duties at the dinner, she's entitled to some rest," said Freckles crisply, her pale blue eyes staring Charlie down. "Not that it's any of your business, *boy*."

"Alright, alright, don't get your knickers in a bunch," Charlie replied with a grin. "Wasn't saying anything about Her Majesty. Just heard it was a proper party that's all. Lots of Firewhiskey I suppose?"

He gave Freckles a wink, which got the desired reaction, and he chuckled when she turned away in a huff.

Mary returned with another serving girl carrying trays of sugar buns, cut fruit and a large jug of icy cold milk. Charlie nabbed himself a sugar bun before Mary could stop him and earned a giggle from the children. He grinned back at them.

"What's your name, teenager?" asked Natalie.

"Charlie. What's yours, kid?"

"Natalie Serena Marlock St. Lucidis," she replied grandly.

"Nice name. Bit long isn't it?" sniffed Charlie, as he pinched a piece of fruit off the tray.

"And she forgot the princess bit," agreed Aaron.

Natalie frowned at her brother. "Princess is not my name. It's my station in life. That's what Mrs. Ollenby says."

"That's where trains go," added Aaron, conversationally. "To stations."

Natalie opened her mouth to retort when Beauty shoved a bun in it. Aaron fell about laughing at his sister's wide eyes.

"It's a bit early for that kind of talk, Princess Natalie," said the nanny, though not unkindly. "Now, eat your breakfast so we can get you to your horse riding lesson."

"Who'll be up and about to give them a lesson?" asked Freckles. "The whole estate is asleep."

"Benjamin will be ready," said Nice Curves confidently.

"How do you know?" asked Beauty as she fed small bits of fruit to the baby.

"He said he always gets up early, no matter how late it was the night before," replied Nice Curves.

Beauty and Freckles exchanged a glance before breaking into laughter. Aaron joined in though he didn't know why.

"Oooh, well, it's nice to know someone understands the handsome messenger so well," teased Beauty.

"He's not just a messenger, you know," blushed Nice Curves, but looked pleased despite the comment. "He is a groomsman and a house guard too. He was on duty for the queen last night," she added.

"Aye, aye, got a fella then, nanny?" smirked Charlie though his heart sunk just a little. Nice Curves had a friendly look about her that a man like him could appreciate.

"Her name isn't Nanny, its Caitlin," corrected Natalie, pointing to each girl in turn. "And that's Seraphina and that's Siobahn, as in *sha-vorn*."

"Oh, don't tell him our names," huffed the dark-haired Siobahn. "He's just a cheeky kitchen boy."

"I'm not!" said Charlie in an injured tone. "I'm a cheeky squire to a nobleman of Carparell."

He winked at the children and was rewarded with more giggles.

"Well, we need to be on our way," said Caitlin, scooping up the baby and swinging her onto her hip. "Everyone say good-bye to Cheeky Charlie." But she smiled and her blue eyes twinkled.

Aye aye, thought Charlie, *maybe Nice Curves will be for me after all?* He grinned back and jumped off the bench to bow low to Caitlin and the children.

The little party left the kitchen with as much noise as they had entered with after Aaron knocked over a tower of empty oven trays.

"So that's the royal children," said Mary next to Charlie's shoulder. "I never saw them up close yesterday. Pretty lot, aren't they?"

"Hmmm, yeah, pretty," answered Charlie, distracted. Aaron had worn an expression on his face so familiar to Charlie, but he couldn't for the life of him place where it came from. He concentrated hard for a moment, but the memory slipped away just as he thought he had it. With a sigh, Charlie focused back on Mary's prattle.

"…though I don't know why they are so high and mighty, they're only nannies. I could've been a nanny you know, but the sound of babies crying sets my teeth on edge…"

"Right then, Mary. I'll see you later, alright?" Charlie lay a quick kiss on his cousin's cheek. She smelled of flour and something sweet, like candied fruit. "I'll go see if my lord's awake."

"Right you are, Charlie," replied Mary, mildly. She'd believe anything he said. "See you later." She bustled off about her business.

Charlie left the kitchens. Blending in with the other servants, he quietly made his way to the royal wing.

Here, things got a little trickier.

Charlie ducked behind a suit of armor as two guards passed him, one in the green of Belvoir house livery and a big fellow in the Queen's Guard gold and white.

"I'm telling you, Owens. The queen has a real thing for me," the one in green was prattling. "If I'd just had a few more minutes with her, I'm sure I could have…"

"Shut up, you *idiot!*" replied the Queen's Guard testily. "I'm sick of hearing about it."

Charlie peeked round the suit of armor, as the two guards made their way down the hall and around the corner. He checked the other direction, but there was no one else around. Obviously, these two had decided to go off duty early.

That meant the door to the queen's bedroom was unguarded. Charlie counted the doors along the side of the hallway to make sure he had the right one to her bedroom, following Mary's information.

Slowly, Charlie crept toward the door, ready to scarper, should anybody come by unexpectedly. He ran a hand down his stolen clothing. He was dressed head to toe in the dark blue and grey of Carparell and looked every inch the squire he was masquerading as. Listening hard at the queen's door, he heard the distant sound of running water, and decided she must be in the bathroom.

With one hand on the door handle, Charlie automatically palmed the blade he held up his sleeve with the other. He took a quick breath and ducked into the room, silently opening and then closing the door behind him. His eyes quickly adjusted to the dim light in the room, which was good, as he only had a minute or two at the most. Her Majesty was surrounded by people day and night, so this quiet in her room wouldn't last long. He cast a quick glance at the bed, which was rumpled and empty. The clock on the mantle ticked loudly, counting his seconds.

Charlie stepped into the center of the room, pulled the little box from his pocket and pressed the catch that released the lid. The sand within sparkled greenly, glittering in the dim light. Charlie muttered the brief incantation and then held his breath as the powder in the box rose in a cloud and hovered for a moment before drifting slowly away from him to the open door of the wardrobe.

"That's strange," said a voice from behind him. "What's it for?"

Charlie's heart clutched hard in his chest and he whipped round to face the figure who had uncurled from the window seat. Not bothering to consider how he had made the mistake of missing an actual person in the room, Charlie put all his energy into fixing his problem. His eyes raked the woman in front of him. She looked young, maybe mid-twenties, with long, dark hair pulled back in a ponytail, dressed in a loose shirt and riding breeches. Her face was pretty, but her eyes were a magnetic rich hazel framed by dark lashes, and they scanned him with an intensity that sent chills down his spine. He remembered the warning he had been given and looked away from her face. Queen Adelena was dangerous.

"Who are you?" she asked, her voice soft, with an unfamiliar lilt.

Charlie made a snap decision. He flicked his hair off his forehead and stepped backwards to bow, having deftly put the box back in his pocket.

"I'm Charlie, Your Majesty," he gave a cocksure grin that he knew didn't reach his eyes. He glanced at the green cloud of sand, but it still hovered benignly at the wardrobe. "It's a real pleasure to meet you."

"Likewise," replied the queen, nodding in response to his bow. "What's that green sand doing in here?" she asked, but Charlie thought she looked more curious than angry. Charlie hoped she wouldn't try to touch the powder. He had no idea what would happen if she did, but it wouldn't be good.

The blade slid back down his wrist to lay against his palm. Holding his blade helped Charlie to think. He ran through all the scenarios he had come up with if he had been caught by anyone but the queen. The green powder should have been invisible to all but those with the strongest magic. He decided to risk it all and stall for time, hoping the powder would find the object he had been sent to steal so he could escape with the queen being none the wiser. It was an ambitious and stupid plan, but that was Charlie's usual style.

"That's a very good question, Your Majesty, and I'm glad you asked," Charlie dressed his face with an easy smile. "You see, we are currently conducting safety checks in the manor house at this time. Your room should have been cleared yesterday, but I only just found out that the lout who was supposed to check it didn't. I'm so sorry to disturb you this early in the morning, but I was keen to get it clear straight away. I'll only be a moment and then I will leave."

The queen raised her eyebrows. "Are you using magic to check the room? I thought that was impossible on the grounds of Belvoir Estate."

"Ah, yes, it is," agreed Charlie, as he edged over to the wardrobe where the powder was hovering. If the object had been found, it should have turned silver. Charlie felt the sweat drip down his neck and his eyes flicked back to the queen, who was staring at him with something close to suspicion on her face. His ruse was not working. Desperate now, Charlie began to rummage through the pockets of the cloak that the green powder hovered nearest.

"It must be here," muttered Charlie and swore under his breath as all the pockets turned up empty.

"What are you looking for? Maybe I can help?" asked the queen, but a tremor in her voice caused Charlie's head to snap up. He watched her inch toward the door. His time had just run out.

"There are no guards outside, Your Majesty," he said quietly, not bothering to smile anymore. "I came here to find something and it's not here. I didn't come here to hurt you, I promise. So, if you let me go, I will let my boss know that you are safe and there will be no trouble."

Charlie moved slowly, so as not to startle her, and walked backward toward the door.

Curse it all. It should have been such a simple matter! But the powerful magic in the sand had failed him, and now the Boss was going to kill him if this nervy-looking queen didn't order her guards to do so first. Despite his bravado, Charlie had no illusions about how difficult it was going to be to sneak out of the Belvoir manor in broad daylight with soldiers on his tail. He'd grown up on the city streets of Concordis, not the low country of Belvoir, after all.

"Who sent you?" whispered the queen and for some odd reason, a smile bloomed on her face. "I know him, don't I?"

Not likely! thought Charlie but answered politely. "Yes, you know him." It was always better to agree with powerful people.

She took a step toward him and reached out a hand to stop his backward movement. Charlie froze in his tracks. He didn't know quite what she was capable of, but he knew it was bad. The queen wasn't any taller than him, and with experience and fear on his side he was sure he could take her if it came to a fight. He just had to trust that none of her power would work in Belvoir. If it did, he was dead.

But as she got closer, Charlie saw that it was concern and not anger that filled her eyes. He felt a strange and powerful compulsion to throw himself into her arms and sob on her shoulder. He even had a vision of himself doing it. As the last time he had cried he had been wearing swaddling clothes, Charlie felt dazed by the intensity of the emotions that swept through him.

Don't let her touch you. Don't ever let her catch your gaze. It'll be the last thing you ever do, m'boy, the Boss had said. The warning rang in his mind now. Charlie felt his defenses falling before the queen as she edged ever closer to him. The blade dropped lower in his hand until he grasped the hilt of the knife.

The door of the bathroom flew open and both Charlie and the queen spun in surprise.

"I cannot thank you enough for allowing me to use your bathroom, Your Majesty," gushed a gorgeous blonde as she skipped into the room bringing the scent of roses with her. "It's so hard having to share a bathroom with the other ladies-in-waiting. I cannot tell you how long Lady Cara takes… oh, hello!" The blonde had finally caught sight of Charlie and Adelena frozen in their poses.

Charlie quickly shot the blade up his wrist again. One woman he could take; two and he was stuck. Better to run and risk capture, than to kill the queen and have a witness scream bloody murder. He saw the queen shoot him a glance before straightening herself into a more relaxed stance.

"This is Charlie. He was just delivering a message from the Prince of Carparell," said the queen, gesturing at Charlie's uniform.

"In your bedroom, Your Majesty?" Blondie said in a scandalized tone and gave Charlie a look she might share with a cat turd she had just stepped in. "Get out of here, you cheeky boy. Queen Adelena only receives messengers in her study."

Charlie dropped his head to hide his pretend shame and turned to the door.

"Oh, it's not his fault," said the queen kindly and Charlie almost jumped out of his skin when he felt her hand slip around his elbow and hold it firmly. "I'm sure he was just lost. He's from Carparell, not Belvoir."

Charlie's instincts screamed at him to push the queen away with both hands and scarper as fast as he could, but instead, his feet betrayed him and allowed the queen to pull him into the next room. His head buzzed with the confusing emotions that had swamped him before, making it hard for him to focus his thoughts and come up with a new plan. But things went from bad to worse when they walked into the adjoining sitting room and Charlie saw the General of the Queen's Guard standing by a window, while three burly QGs relaxed on armchairs close by, their weapons glinting all shiny and dangerous in the morning light. They all fell silent at the arrival of the queen.

"Oh, general. Thank the Goddess you are here! We found this boy lurking in the queen's bedroom," trilled Blondie, as she made her way to a tall guard who had stood to attention, a captain by the look of his lapels, and attached herself to his arm. She wore her fear like an ill-fitting costume and Charlie wondered absently why beautiful women were almost always evil before he felt the temperature in the room plummet as four sets of icy blue eyes took his measure.

"Oh, Lady Olivia, that's rubbish," said the queen, her voice quiet and soothing as she patted Charlie on the arm before abandoning him to walk to her desk. "The boy was just lost and had been knocking on my bedroom door for some time. Apparently there were no guards in the hall to tell him which way to go."

The queen looked up at the general, who in turn gave his captain a hard look.

"That is true, general," said the blond captain a picture of dignified shame. "QG Owens and that Belvoir guard, Benjamin, were not here when QG Pepper and I came on duty."

"It's fine, captain. I'm sure there is no danger in the manor. After all, he was just a messenger with a letter, not an immortal wizard!" The queen laughed lightly and the tension in the room eased, but Charlie thought it was an odd comment to make.

"Well, no need to worry about that, Your Majesty," said a little man who had just bustled into the room with a scribe scurrying after him. "Belvoir Estate is blessedly free of any and all magic. Not even the Marchant prince himself could break the ancient curse within these borders."

"Really?" said the queen, disbelief coloring her tone as she threw Charlie a glance. "Not even Marchant magic can be used in this house?"

The little man looked irritated and hid it badly behind a stiff smile. His curly blond hair was unnaturally perfect, no doubt a wig. "No, of course not, Your Majesty. I just *said* that. But I, for one, am extremely relieved to stay here after our time in the Grey Palace. That place made my skin crawl. I barely slept a wink the two nights we were there."

An icicle of fear inched its way down Charlie's spine. Though he kept his eyes on the ground, he used his peripheral vision to scout an escape. In a room full of people, it should have been easy to drop his shoulders and slink away, but his failed mission had left him in a quandary. Perhaps if he kept up the messenger routine, he might get another chance to find what he had been sent here to steal, especially as the queen seemed strangely eager to cover for him?

"No magic at all," mused the queen and her hazel eyes caught Charlie's gaze.

Charlie felt his face tighten. This was it. He was done for now. No way the queen was going to keep a secret of the spell he'd done in her bedroom. He braced himself for discovery.

"What was the message for Her Majesty?"

It took Charlie a minute to realize that the bossy little man was addressing him. His mouth gaped open, but no sound came out before the queen interrupted him.

"Oh, Prince Claudio wanted me to sit in the Carparell pavilion at the start of the races, Tilburn. Impossible, I imagine?"

"*Absolutely* impossible, Your Majesty. Why, just the nerve of asking on this very morning is…"

"Ah, Mr. Tilburn!" Blondie piped up from her position, draped on the arm of Captain Handsome. She made her way over to the queen, her big skirts sweeping over Charlie's feet as she passed him. "Queen Adelena needs to prepare for the breakfast party this morning and then the opening ceremony this afternoon, and we are already behind schedule. Perhaps your paperwork with her can wait?" She gestured to the scrolls and folios Tilburn had just dropped on the queen's desk.

"The business of Unisia will not wait for a horse fete, my lady," said Tight Curls snootily, but Blondie didn't give up. She clasped her hands together in front of her half-exposed bosom, boosting it impressively, and looked up at the little man through her eyelashes.

"But Mr. Tilburn, it's the opening day! The whole court will be out, and the queen's hair alone will take us at least an hour."

Lady Olivia and Tilburn both examined the queen with a critical eye. She looked uncomfortable at the scrutiny and Charlie saw a hand self-consciously pat her hair in its messy ponytail.

"Well, I suppose you are right," said Tilburn with a dramatic sigh. "Her Majesty will go and prepare. I will finish what I can myself and we can work tonight before the evening party starts."

Lady Olivia clapped her hands and cheered the announcement. It made the queen frown and Charlie thought Blondie had over-played it a bit. *Beautiful women were used to getting what they wanted, when they wanted it. No surprise there.*

The queen stood and walked to the front of her desk.

"General, I assume you are going to look for QG Owens and Benjamin now," she said. "Don't be too hard on them. Does Benjamin have a rank I should know about or is he just a… Benjamin? I know he is giving the children riding lessons now."

"He has no rank that I'm aware of, Your Majesty," replied the general. "But that is usual here at Belvoir Estate, they function with a different hierarchy than at the Golden Palace. But I shall let him know how we do things where we are from, especially on guard duty. And Owens should definitely have known better."

Charlie had avoided looking at the general too closely in case he caught his eye. The man was old to Charlie's young eye, but heavily muscled and strong. His bearing was impressive and he radiated the kind of authority Charlie had spent his sixteen years avoiding. He almost felt sorry for the Benjamin down in the stables. The lad might have the eye of Nice Curves the nanny, but Charlie didn't envy him the glacial blue glare of General Beefy.

With a nod the queen dismissed the general who left with two of his QGs in tow and Mr. Tight Curls and his scribe hustling behind. That just left Blondie and Captain Handsome in the room.

"Lady Olivia, could you go and tell Piers and the other dressers to set up everything that they need in my bedroom? It's more comfortable in there," the queen asked Blondie, who curtseyed and skipped out, but not before sending Captain Handsome a pretty smile.

"Captain Lucky…"

Charlie almost snorted, *Of course he is! Captain bloody Lucky! Too perfect.*

"… if you could find my children down at the stables and let their nannies know that they must be ready and dressed for the breakfast party soon. Also, I want them to come up to me and tell me how their riding lessons went, I missed them this morning." She smiled and her face softened when she spoke of the children. Charlie thought it looked like genuine emotion and was confused.

"QG Pepper will guard the door for you, Your Majesty, but would you prefer I set another QG with him while I'm gone?" asked Captain Handsome, his face creased with respectful concern. Charlie hated the just-too-perfect do-gooder type, and in a normal situation might have set himself to baiting the captain, but right now he was just praying he would stay. However, the queen shook her head and Charlie watched in dismay as Captain Lucky snapped a bow and left.

Charlie turned to the queen as she leaned against the front of her desk and folded her arms. She gave him a look which sent a shiver down his spine. "Now, Charlie. Finally, we are alone, so you are going to tell me exactly what it was you were doing in my bedroom this morning."

Chapter Twenty

"And What Hides in the Light"

Adele regarded the young man who called himself Charlie.

He was about her height but hunched like a boy not yet used to his body. His face was so thin that his cheekbones stuck out sharply and had obviously never needed a razor. Though he was clean, his hair was badly cut and it stuck to his forehead at odd angles. The clothes he was wearing hung on his frame, looking as though they belonged to a much taller boy. A passing glance wouldn't have revealed much, but Adele could now see this boy definitely wasn't who he claimed to be. Charlie was too rough and starved-looking to be a palace squire.

"I know who sent you, Charlie," said Adele, breaking the silence and keeping her voice low. "We don't need to say his name, but that little box thing you used looked like one of his things."

Charlie's white face blanched even further. "You know *him*?" he whispered.

Adele smiled. "I do, and I will need you to deliver a message back to him for me."

Charlie became suddenly animated, shaking his head and backing away. "I won't let him know that you said anything, Your Majesty," he promised her fervently. "Please, I know how to keep my mouth shut!"

Adele gave Charlie a curious look and dropped her head to the side, to measure him from another angle. Perhaps Rainere hadn't trusted this boy with the knowledge that they already had a relationship. "But Charlie I'm sure he wouldn't mind if you were just doing as he had asked. The prince won't be angry with you, I promise."

Charlie froze again. "The prince?"

"Yes, Charlie, the *prince*. But we are running out of time. Let me write a quick letter and you can take it back to him. The Grey Palace is just a day's ride away, so you can get it to him by nightfall."

Adele snatched up a quill and paper from the desk and began writing. She was too engrossed to notice the look of shock that was plastered across Charlie's face.

"I wish I knew a spell to seal this thing so only he can open it," muttered Adele. It was frustrating not to have such a simple spell at her command when she could do so many bigger things with her magic. She looked up at Charlie and smiled. "I guess I'm just going to have to trust you, Charlie. If he does, then I can too."

Adele held out the letter to the boy but snatched it back just before his fingers could close over it. She noticed his hand was shaking. "Do you know, Charlie? I've just realized how brave you were breaking into my room this morning to carry out this little task for the prince. How did you know that the magic would even work with the curse on this house?"

Charlie swallowed. "My boss, the...uh, *prince*...has tricks up his sleeve those old wizards never thought of. He has magic no one else even remembers how to use, Your Majesty."

"And did it work? Am I safe from magic here?" she asked.

"Safe as houses, Your Majesty. There was nothing here," said Charlie, but his voice was curiously flat and his eyes avoided hers.

Adele just couldn't shake the feeling that this boy was terrified of her. She handed over the letter and watched as Charlie slipped it beneath his coat. She picked up a wooden messenger token from the desk drawer and flipped it to him.

"You'll need this to get a fresh horse from the stables and food from the kitchen," she said, "and then you can be on your way." Adele's smile faltered. "Only the prince is to read that note Charlie. Only him, you understand? If anyone else finds it...well, it would be big trouble for both of us."

After a quick thought, Adele pulled a thin gold bracelet off her wrist and held it out to the boy. She watched with a growing sense of disquiet as he slowly inched back over to her and took it, careful not to brush her skin. *What was Rainere thinking, sending such a skittish boy to do his errands for him? The kid looks about as tough as Aaron,* she thought.

"There will be more gold when you bring a letter back to me, Charlie. I can be very generous when people do their jobs properly," added Adele.

"Yes, Your Majesty," Charlie nodded, his dark fringe swinging low across his forehead. "I will be back as soon as I can be."

His shrewd eyes rose to meet hers and they were the only adult thing in his young boy's face.

A moment later, Lady Olivia swung back into the room calling out '*Your Majesty!*' and their time had run out. Adele smiled at Charlie before giving him a little push toward the door.

"Off you go, Charlie, and pleasant journey."

CHAPTER TWENTY-ONE

"The Carnival Begins"

The hot sun beat down on their heads as Adele pulled her children close and surveyed the huge crowd spread out across the green fields of the Belvoir Estate. She could just about make out the racetrack between the raised, open-sided pavilions that surrounded it. The colors and flags of each royal family decorated each pavilion in a gaudy show of family loyalty and wealth. The pavilions of the lesser families were behind their richer cousins at ground level, but Adele could see that the parties under these canopies were already in full swing. Music drifted on the breeze as it ruffled the pennants and brought the scents of popcorn and roasting meat, boiled sugar and horse manure.

Hundreds of aristocrats mixed with the landed gentry and the wealthier merchant families from the capital, Concordis, and other nearby towns. Money and connections spoke louder than bloodlines and crowns when it came to the horse market at this all-important carnival.

Bertie held Adele's arm in the crook of his own as he introduced her to the most famous horse traders and husbanders in the kingdom. He bored their audiences again and again, telling the story of his reaction to Queen Adelena choosing the Belvoir Estate stables to provide horses for her royal sojourn later in the year. At the time she had chosen the beautiful chestnut striders, Adele knew she was granting an honor to the family of Belvoir, she just had no idea how seriously Bertie took the appointment. By the time the opening ceremony was due to start she was almost convinced these Belvoir horses would be the backbone of her new court as well as the beasts that would pull the carriages.

The royal family settled with relief under the Belvoir pavilion when the time came for the parade to start. The heat of the day was becoming stifling as the breeze dropped and the dust in the field sat in a hazy cloud over everything.

Up on the high stage of the royal pavilion, Prince Bertrand opened the carnival with a longwinded speech about the competing horses and the more technical aspects of the coming races but the crowd listened politely enough and laughed graciously at Bertie's more pointed comments about the superiority of the Belvoir breeds. He held by his side a boy with rusty red hair and a serious expression. Adele recognized him as Lance, the young man Bertie had chosen to succeed him as the prince of Belvoir.

Personally, Adele knew nothing about horses, but the pageant before her was very beautiful. Both horses and riders were dressed in colored silks, trotting in a well-organized parade before the crowd. Her own children began bouncing in their seats, cheering and choosing their favorites based on the color of the horse's socks, or how tall the riders' hats were. Behind her, Adele could hear her Queen's Guard swapping tips and hints for bets to be laid later, and as always QG Owens held the book. Surprisingly, though, it was the youngest QG, Pepper, who sounded the most knowledgeable about what to look for in a winning horse, and for once the other men listened to him closely.

"The betting should be fierce this year, Your Majesty," said Bertie gleefully as he rubbed his hands together and eyed the horses going past on their second turn. "My rider this year is a young girl from the Blue Hills, and she is a natural on Blue Streak. She handles him beautifully. Truly, they could be one animal when you see them ride together. But she'll be underestimated by the punters, I just know it!"

Adele could only smile wanly as the smell of horse manure under a hot sun had her fanning herself with a scented handkerchief.

"Shall we go down to the yards, Your Majesty?" asked Bertie, extending his arm to Adele as he stood. Adele fought not to grimace at the idea of heading out into the heat again and closer to the fresh manure. "We can look at all of the horses more closely and I'll introduce you to our rider on Blue Streak. I imagine Golden Pride, the St. Lucidis stallion, will be down there too, and I suppose you have an obligation to look him over as well."

Adele did smile this time at Bertie's feigned indifference to the St. Lucidis offering. She had no doubt at all that he was already very familiar with the pride of the St. Lucidis's family stables.

The children begged to come with Adele to the horse yards where the champions were all on display. A thick crowd had gathered at the bottom of their pavilion and Adele had to ask QG Pepper to carry Aaron and QG Leith to hold Natalie so the children wouldn't get stepped on. She took Stella herself as the baby was getting fussy having to miss her nap and only wanted her mother.

The crowd cleared a narrow path for the royal family as they made their way over to the horse yards, cheering good-naturedly and calling out to the children, forcing Adele to nod and smile in return, despite how uncomfortable the celebrity made her.

In the yards the horses had been lined up facing the crowd, while their trainers were perched up high on chairs with long, stilt-like legs. Each trainer had a metal megaphone which they used to great effect haranguing each other and trying to drown out their competition. The language and the humor were slightly coarse as the ritual shouting and bragging of the horse trainers whipped the crowd up into a competitive fervor, but it was very amusing.

Adele was so preoccupied with the entertainment that she didn't really register Stella struggling to get down to her feet, and then pulling her hand out of Adele's. It was only when she heard a loud scream that Adele realized her baby was gone. It had only been a matter of seconds.

Frantically, Adele searched the crowd of people packed in around her until she saw that all eyes were on the enormous stallion Golden Pride, who was stomping and snorting in the ring, her tiny Stella standing directly beneath him. With a shriek, Adele threw herself under the fence but before she could take another step Adele felt herself pushed out of the way as Captain Lucky stepped in front of her, and slowly approached the horse. "Get back, Your Majesty," ordered Lucky in a low voice. "I'll get her."

"Careful boy, he is going to rear if you spook him," said the trainer from up on his perch. Adele noted the man's white face and felt her heart contract with fear.

Captain Lucky ignored the advice and advanced on the horse as its eyes rolled to the whites and its tail flicked aggressively. Lucky crooned quietly, keeping his stance relaxed and calm as he reached out a hand to let the animal catch his scent. Still crooning, he reached under the horse, his shoulder sliding against the horse's neck, and quicker than the eye could follow he had snatched the little girl up into his arms. Lucky leaped back, rightly anticipating that the motion would startle the already-nervous stallion and Golden Pride reared, whinnying in fear at the strangeness he'd just encountered having a little girl crawl under him.

Adele was pale and trembling with fright as Captain Lucky brought her baby back over to her and they all climbed back through the fence. Incredibly, Stella was giggling in Lucky's arms and trying to hold the face of her rescuer in her little chubby hands and when he bent his face to hers she planted a wet kiss on his cheek. It was only when Stella saw Adele's stricken expression that her bottom lip began to tremble, and she put her arms out for her mother.

"And Princess Stella has awarded her brave captain with kisses!" shouted Bertie to the silent crowd. A cheer started to swell, until the sound of a thousand people shouting for joy was all Adele could hear. Unfortunately, her heart was still frozen with shock. She looked at Lucky and saw sympathy in his clear blue eyes.

"She is alright, Your Majesty." He kept his voice low and caught Adele's arm gently, as she started to sway a little. "The children will never be in any danger when we are here to protect them, I swear."

Adele cast her eye back to the rearing horse as three stable hands tried to get him under control. Captain Lucky had risked his own life to save Stella just now.

"I can never thank you enough," she whispered and gripped his hand, but Lucky only bowed in response and stepped away as Adele was suddenly enveloped by a flurry of hysterical royal ladies, all excited beyond words by Stella's near-death experience. Whether it was the multitude of perfumes that surrounded her or the horrible fright, Adele started to sway again and saw dots before her eyes. She pulled Stella tighter to her chest as a hundred hands stroked and petted the both of them.

An arm went around Adele's shoulders just as she was starting to panic, she turned quickly and looked into the lavender blue eyes of Lady Olivia, who gave Adele's shoulders a squeeze before turning back to the jostle surrounding them.

"Let's move this crowd!" cried the young woman in a very un-ladylike voice. "Queen Adelena needs air. Move away, for the love of the Goddess! People, please! Stop gawking and move!"

Still shouting, Lady Olivia managed to pull along Adele and shepherd the other two QGs, Pepper and Leith who were still carrying the older children, out of the fields and back through the gardens of the manor. The further they got from the horse yards the thinner the crowd became and the smell of horse manure finally abated.

Back in the house, their group was joined by the general and the rest of the Queen's Guard who followed them to a quiet courtyard room. The Queen's Guard waited as Lady Olivia settled Adele and the children with hot tea and biscuits. After checking that Stella was indeed healthy after her incident, they left the room to give Adele some peace.

The room was light and airy and Adele finally felt the cold fear melt its grip on her insides as she watched Stella playing happily with her older siblings. Her baby really was okay despite the terror of just a few minutes ago. She took a deep breath and let the giggling of her children soothe her.

Adele looked over at Lady Olivia, who sat holding her cup of tea and smiling at the children playing. She was younger than Adele, maybe no more than nineteen or twenty, but she seemed older than the other young women of the court because of her poise and confidence. Normally, Adele found women as beautiful and glamorous as Lady Olivia intimidating, but there was something so fun about Olivia. Her quick wit and sweet laugh made Adele feel like perhaps they could be real friends one day and not just servant and queen.

"Thank you for your help just now, Lady Olivia. That crowd was getting just too much for me," Adele smiled shakily as Lady Olivia gave her a pat on the shoulder and poured her more tea.

"Oh, it was nothing, Your Majesty, where I'm from we are used to being loud and obnoxious!" Lady Olivia laughed. "Back home on the farm."

Adele realized suddenly how little she knew about the people who worked for her. Lucky's bravery today and Lady Olivia's care made her feel ashamed she had never inquired more closely about who they all were, and where they were from.

"How long have you been at the court of the Golden Palace, Lady Olivia?" Adele asked.

"I had only really just arrived before you yourself did, Your Majesty," she replied. "I had been invited to stay with my Aunt Oliphant in the St. Lucidis quarters. My aunt is the Lady of Templeton, on my Father's side, of the St. Lucidis Templetons."

Lady Olivia saw Adele's eyes glaze over as she recited her pedigree and smiled. "It doesn't really matter! Anyway, I was working as her lady-in-waiting for just two weeks before I met you at the coronation ball and you invited me to apply for the position of dress designer in your entourage."

Adele scrunched her forehead, trying to remember actually doing that. "I did, did I?"

"Oh, yes, Your Majesty. You said you needed help with your Unisian fashion sense, and you liked my dress, the purple one?" Lady Olivia didn't seem to mind Adele's confusion. "I took my portfolio and approached Mrs. Ollenby for the job. She is quite a formidable lady and I was so nervous in the interview. I believe you hadn't mentioned our previous conversation, so I had quite a bit of convincing to do, let me tell you." Lady Olivia giggled. "But I won her over in the end!"

"Well, I'm glad you did," said Adele firmly, putting any doubts to rest. "Now I've got someone to help me with all of those massive gowns that were sent from the palace. Not all of them were your choice, I imagine."

Lady Olivia laughed and the sound reverberated around the room. "Are you thinking of that hideous pink one with the puffy roses across the shoulders?"

"I am," nodded Adele with a grimace.

Both women laughed in easy comradery.

"I'll fix it for you I promise, Your Majesty."

Just then, Aaron started dancing a little jig and chewing his bottom lip in what Adele called his "Wee Dance." "Sweetie, do you need to go?" she asked him and sighed at his vigorous headshake. *Why did her son always have to deny his need to go to the bathroom?*

"I'll take him, Your Majesty," offered Lady Olivia, getting up and taking the little boy's hand in her own. "We'll be back in just a moment, won't we, Aaron?"

Adele settled back in her armchair. It was so rare for her to be left alone with just her daughters for company these days, and she soaked up the moment of peace before someone came in to ask something of her or insist on her leaving the girls with their nannies.

The girls were happily tracing patterns from the carpet onto sheets of paper with pencils, and Adele was relieved to see Natalie sharing so nicely with her baby sister. Looking out the bay window Adele could see the roses in full bloom climbing over the walls and mossy stone of the outside courtyard. It was so pretty here at Belvoir Estate. The shade of the trees outside sheltered the room from the worst of the afternoon sun and the open windows let in a cool breeze. The room was so private and quiet that as the girls fell silent, concentrating on their work, Adele could hear the murmuring of male voices outside her window in the courtyard.

"What do you think would have happened, general?" asked Captain Lucky, his voice was soft, but his tone so serious that Adele couldn't help but focus on it.

"If she had lost the child? I think we might have lost her as our queen," replied Ohrig and Adele froze at his words. "Didn't you find it just a bit odd, captain, that the queen would bring her children to Sandar and then be so happy to keep them at the Grey Palace instead of the Golden Palace? I have been thinking that perhaps there is something she knows about the wizards at the Golden Palace that she is not telling us, something that makes her afraid to leave her children alone without her there."

"But the wizards are the ones that put her on the throne in the first place," argued Lucky. "Surely High Wizard Ohren has only her best interests at heart."

"Best interests? Or perhaps he is holding her there against her will," suggested Ohrig drily. "Have you ever met a more reluctant monarch than our little queen, Lucky?"

"I hadn't met any queens at all until Queen Adelena, general," said Lucky. "But are you suggesting that the Wizard Ohren might have threatened her children as a means of making sure Queen Adelena sits on the throne and does what he tells her too, which is why she takes them everywhere with her?"

"In a word." And Adele could imagine General Ohrig's sardonic smile, even as he spoke. He always looked like that when someone surprised him.

"Yes, it had occurred to me too," replied Lucky, and Adele could hear his frown in the words as he spoke them. "And I think you are right, there is something that we do not know about why she was brought here from her world and made queen. Something that has to do with the wizards maintaining their stranglehold on the power of Unisia."

"Exactly. In fact, I have heard rumors…" answered the general, but Adele heard no more as Lady Olivia came back into the room with Aaron.

"Your Majesty, I hate to disturb you, but it's time we started getting ready for the ball tonight."

Unfortunately, Adele couldn't feel less like dancing, as the words of Ohrig and Lucky flitted about her head. *They thought she had lied to them?*

Adele was shocked it had never occurred to her to ask Ohrig about the Prophecy of the End of the World. He was obviously smart enough to question her exalted appointment to queen by the high wizard, and he had a clear mistrust of those in charge of the court of the Golden Palace. She had picked up on that before.

But, Adele wondered *can I trust him?*

If Adele revealed herself, her real worries and fears, to Ohrig, could she trust that he wouldn't go running back to Ohren to tell tales about her as a terrible queen? *I haven't even told Ohrig what had happened in the Holy Cave of Sandar or the truth about Ripenzo Shale,* thought Adele. *Will he be angry or frightened of me? Would he join the awful Lord Orgustus in wanting me deposed?*

Adele's life, and those of her children, would depend on whether or not Ohrig could be relied upon to protect her if High Wizard Ohren should turn on her, or even if she should marry someone whom Ohrig hated - like the Marchant prince. Was General Ohrig really her man, or was he the kingdom's?

CHAPTER TWENTY-TWO

"Footsteps in the Night"

Grotto paced the floor of his little office deep in the bowels of the Grey Palace. He had no windows in the room and only two green-flamed lanterns turned down low and perched on the shelf above his desk. His eyes preferred the dim lighting as the sunshine of this morning had given him a nasty headache. He was too distracted now to even register the distant sound of the thousand clocks chiming the twilight hour as it swelled through the palace.

"Master, my poor master," muttered Grotto to himself as he paced the few feet of his office one way and then back again. "What madness this abomination has caused in him."

Grotto kicked his foot against the wall and knocked the covered object leaning there. The coarse sheet fell off the golden frame of a large portrait.

"This is all your fault you know!" Grotto hissed at the painting of Rainere's wayward father, Prince Rainold. "If you hadn't been so obsessed with your own lust then that monster, Rainestra, would never have hurt the little prince. She damaged his wits that night! And she gave him a taste for her special brand of agony." Grotto gave the priceless frame another kick but was careful not to touch the painting itself.

Prince Rainold grinned back at him, his expression one of cocky self-assurance. His young face was unlined and his smile was open, as if he had just finished laughing. Nothing he had done in the past could hurt *him* now.

"Bah!" spat Grotto in disgust and covered up the portrait with its sheet again. He couldn't stand even the painted gaze of Prince Rainold on him, mocking his anger and his efforts to save the young Prince Rainere from a fate worse than death.

Grotto returned to his pacing but a quiet knock at the door made him freeze. No one disturbed him in his office. Ever. He pulled the heavy wooden door open and cast his eyes about the quiet hallway but no one was there. Shutting the door again, he turned back to the interior of his room and folded his arms.

"Schiss, that better be you," he snapped.

The little man-spider appeared before him with a squelchy *pop*, and immediately cringed into a bow. "Mr. Grottonski, I've just got back from the nest this very minute." He looked up to gauge Grotto's mood. "I had no trouble getting out, but I had to watch myself in the daylight hours. The sun was out in the Dark Forest, and the ravens were hunting. The human search parties were still in the forest, too, looking for the royal family."

Grotto waved his hand to silence Schiss's prattling. "What of Empress Ka-kik? How did she receive the news that the queen was in the Grey Palace?"

"The empress was very pleased," replied Schiss, but shuddered at the memory of his mother's malevolent joy with the news. "But she told me to caution the prince that she would require proof of a wedding, and not just the queen's word that they were married. When I told her that you would call a priest, she was happy."

Schiss shifted from foot to foot nervously. He had relayed all the information he had been given to Mr. Grottonski but still the man glared at him.

"We have bad news, Schiss," said Grotto, and Schiss flinched at his tone. "Unfortunately, the prince has let the queen leave the grounds of the Gray Palace and go to the cursed lands of Belvoir Estate. They left this morning, and the prince himself is planning to go after them as soon as he can."

Grotto thought of the prince. He had left him only a few hours ago, lying on the couch in the clinic room, taking in the Gift of Life. He hadn't stayed to watch after helping Rainere hook up the needle to his arm, but he hoped that Rainere was taking as much of the Gift in as he could possibly tolerate. Grotto needed his master strong for the conclusion of the prophecy.

"But I've told Empress Ka-kik that there will be a wedding, Mr. Grottonski," stammered Schiss. "She will be very angry if the prince breaks his word to her, maybe worse than angry. The council in the nest will want her to take revenge."

"Yes, revenge," mused Grotto and headed for his desk, reaching it in a few short strides. He pulled out a fresh scroll and a pen filled with ink. "I think I heartily agree with your mother this time, Schiss. She must remember that this queen is the woman who so heartlessly killed her son, Oki. And that this queen is the woman who will be able to bend the prince to her own will after they are married. Perhaps this St. Lucidis queen will decide not to honor the prophecy after all and will keep your people in the dark in the Under Lands. Wouldn't that be just terrible after all the kindnesses that the empress has shown the Marchant prince?"

Schiss felt his mouth fall open in shock. *Surely the good Queen Adelena would let the Spider People walk free again?*

"I find it only prudent to warn the empress that the queen has left the grounds of the Grey Palace," muttered Grotto and Schiss wasn't sure the manservant was talking to him anymore. "After all, the prince is in no fit state to communicate with her. It is my solemn duty as his servant to help my master in keeping his sworn oath to obey the empress in all things. It is the queen who is fighting the conclusion of the prophecy, and it is she who will pay if she doesn't keep her word to my master. The empress deserves to keep that false queen for herself if our abomination can't keep her hands off my prince's power. My master may have to marry her, but he won't have to…"

The old manservant wrote furiously on the scroll, breaking the nib of one pen and grabbing another, all the while growling to himself. He finished the letter with a flourish and grinned ghoulishly at Schiss, who had backed up to cower by the door.

"Here, Schiss, take this to your mother, Empress Ka-kik, tonight. She must be kept informed of every development. But be careful and hurry back. I wish to hear how she takes this news of Queen Adelena's latest foolishness." He thrust the letter at Schiss.

Schiss took the letter and backed out of Grotto's office without a word. He had the clear feeling that Grottonski didn't like the good Queen Adelena and it worried him that the manservant was so insistent Empress Ka-kik know that the queen had gone to Belvoir. This could only go badly for the queen with the empress.

Schiss hoped Grottonski wasn't trying to hurt the queen that he loved. *Grottonski didn't have that power, did he?*

Schiss hardened his frail courage and made a brave decision. He found his way to the upper floors of the Grey Palace with long-practiced ease, though his nerves made him trip and stumble. Schiss stayed in his human form to knock upon the prince's door, but he heard no answer over the sound of his own wheezing. He knocked again and held his breath. Nothing. Squeezing his eyes shut tight, Schiss clenched his fists and disappeared.

Opening his eyes again, Schiss looked around where he had appeared in the corner of the prince's room, but Prince Rainere was nowhere to be seen. Schiss sighed with disappointment. He supposed he would have to search the palace now, but then he would run the risk of bumping into Grottonski again, who would ask him why he hadn't left for the nest yet. Maybe the canny old man would even guess that Schiss was looking for the prince to warn him of what the manservant was up to. Schiss shivered at what would be done to him if that happened. These humans could be as cruel as spiders.

Perhaps he could leave a note? Though it would have to be somewhere only the prince could find it. Schiss wandered over to the prince's bedside table, where he saw a pile of papers. Picking one up he saw the face of the queen staring back at him, a knowing smile playing on her lips, her dress draped low over her chest and her long hair swirling over a shoulder.

Schiss almost gasped in delight at the likeness. Here she was, his very own queen, wrought in carbon and paper but so detailed he felt as if she might speak at any moment. Schiss pressed his thin lips to the portrait in his hands and then quickly folded it into the smallest square that he could and jammed it into his inside pocket next to the letter that Grottonski had given him. What a treasure he had found!

A noise at the door made Schiss jump a mile and fear decided his next choice. Running for the window, Schiss transformed with a squelchy *pop*, squeezed out of a crack in the window frame, and threw himself into the darkness beyond.

Chapter Twenty-Three

"The Swirling Pain of Power"

Adele smiled tightly at the rousing applause in response to her little speech. She hated being back at court for this reason alone. Standing at the center of attention, for all to stare and clap at while she, in turn, watched them nudge each other and talk about her. It was just horrible. What she wouldn't give for a quiet night tucked in bed with a hot cup of tea, or better yet, Rainere. The idea almost made her smile, until she remembered what had happened the last time she had had Rainere in her bed.

She hoped he got her note soon. He had to know how sorry she was and how much she wanted to be with him. She had left him so suddenly and there had been no time to plan their next meeting. It made her ill to think about how long they might be apart this time, really ill. In fact, Adele felt a swell of nausea rock her empty stomach and had to grab Bertie's arm to steady herself.

"Ready to dance, Your Majesty?" asked the rosy prince. The sun and a liberal amount of beer had turned Prince Bertrand into a young man again, and he swung Adele firmly into the circle of dancers without waiting for her answer. A band of twelve musicians with drums and guitars played a rousing rhythm with a strong beat, and the dance floor was soon full of swirling bodies.

Luckily the steps of the dance were simple and repetitive and Adele had to do no more than follow her partners as she was pulled about the floor until she was too tired and thirsty to follow anymore. Grabbing a respite, Adele threw herself into a wicker chair under a tree covered in twinkling lights and caught her breath.

The Belvoirs definitely knew how to throw a party. It was far more rustic than a ball at the Golden Palace, but it was also a lot more fun. A large flat area of the garden had been laid with a wooden dance floor, and above their heads hundreds of strings of fairy lights made a glittering canopy. (Adele knew they had some form of electricity at the manor, but she wasn't sure how it all worked yet). Cheerful servants in bright green vests circled the party with trays of red wine and golden beer. A buffet of food provided dinner and long trestle tables, decorated with fat white candles and fragrant flowers, had been set up under the trees next to the dance floor. There, guests could rest their feet and eat as much as they liked of the roast duck, dozens of different kinds of salad, fresh fruit tarts, and bowls of pink custard flavored with rosewater. Adele was tempted to eat something, but her stomach had been sensitive all day and she didn't want to risk it with all the dancing she was required to do.

Adele wasn't left alone for long as Lady Olivia soon joined her along with several of the younger ladies of Prince Bertie's court. The young women favored a green punch that tasted of limes and hit hard only after Adele had drunk two of them. Her head was swimming unpleasantly and the gossiping and giggling soon began to get on her tired nerves. However, escaping the party proved to be more difficult than Adele first thought as she ducked and pulled away from the dancing groups who wanted her to join them. To avoid saying 'No, sorry!' again, Adele found herself wandering off the path around the dance floor and entering the trees. She thought she knew the way through the dark garden to the kitchen entrance at the rear of the manor, but in the dark, she took a wrong turn somewhere and ended up by the side of the garden sheds. She stepped into an alleyway lit only by a few lanterns and tried to get her bearings despite the buzzing in her head.

A high-pitched giggle and a deeper voice whispering alerted her to the couple she had almost stepped on.

"Oh God, I'm so sorry," stammered Adele embarrassed as she tried to avert her eyes in time not to notice that the girl's skirts were rucked up to her waist or where the man's hands were.

"Your Majesty!" the girl shrieked and wrenched herself away from her boyfriend.

Adele squinted in the dim light. "Siobahn?"

"Oh Goddess, I'm so sorry, Your Majesty! Oh Goddess, oh Goddess!" whimpered Siobahn as she furiously straightened her clothing. "I'm so humiliated. I am so sorry."

"Um… it's alright, Siobahn," said Adele with her own deepening embarrassment. "Caitlin and Seraphina are on duty. It's your night off, so…"

She gestured weakly toward the dark figure next to Siobahn, who was buttoning himself up quickly.

"It's Benjamin, Your M-Majesty," said Benjamin stepping forward into the lantern light.

Oh, he really didn't have to do that. Now Adele felt like the old lady busting teenagers at a party. How could she get out of this fast?

"May I please be excused, Your Majesty?" begged Siobahn, her voice shaking with tears.

"Of course you can," replied Adele. "But I'm leaving, too. I'm sorry to have disturbed you both."

But it was too late. Siobahn gave a wrenching sob and fled the scene as fast as she could. Adele felt awful, but as she turned to leave in the opposite direction Benjamin called out.

"Please, Your Majesty! She's a good girl. It was my fault you found her here." Something in his tone made Adele stop and turn back to him, which unfortunately made her head spin. She staggered, prompting Benjamin to step forward and grab her elbow. Standing only a step apart, Adele looked up at Benjamin and examined him in the dim light. His hair was rumpled and his open shirt revealed a strong chest and the gentle waves of his stomach muscles. He was so young even his skin looked soft. She could see the pulse at the side of his neck and knew it would feel delicious against her lips. Adele inhaled and could smell sex in the air. A lingering heat swept her body.

"Of course it was your fault." And she could hear the hunger in her voice. "Siobahn is only a teenager and you are what twenty-five?"

"Twenty years, Your Majesty," coughed Benjamin. He was totally without his usual confidence and stood hunched in front of her, his eyes on his shoes and his hands moving to pull his shirt together.

Adele looked at him and a weird sensation reared its ugly head up inside of her. A gorgeous man was cowering with fear in front of her. The sort of man who would never have even looked at her on Earth before she became a queen was now bowed and ashamed, waiting for her word of forgiveness. Adele put a finger under his chin and raised Benjamin's face to her own. Even in the dim light she could see his pupils, huge and black, and the tiniest shred of silver ringing them, almost too fine to see, but there nonetheless. She wondered if he would taste younger than Rainere when she delved into him.

Adele felt a sick thrill of desire as she realized that her lips were just a breath from Benjamin's and that she was going to take every ounce of the power from his body.

All at once a wave of nausea swept over her. This was so wrong. She shouldn't be enjoying this man's fear so much. She shouldn't want to make him groan in pain as she plunged her magic into him again and again.

"It's alright, Benjamin," Adele whispered as the nausea made her throat close over. "Just leave Siobahn alone, oh-okay?"

Then Adele turned and ran off into the garden, catching her dress on a thousand branches, trying to get as far away from Benjamin as she could before the heaving took control. Adele dropped to her knees in the dirt and lost everything she had drunk that night.

"Great," she whispered morosely when the heaves finally slowed their irresistible rhythm and she could sit up again. She leaned back against the rough trunk of a tree and let the tears course down her cheeks. "I'm turning into a monster and I'm allergic to my own evil desire. Oh God, Rainere…"

Adele knew instinctively that her reaction to Benjamin had everything to do with what had happened between her and Rainere the other night. But it was just too awful to think that she would want to do that again to anyone else. Shuddering, Adele hated herself for what she had nearly done.

Adele dragged herself off her knees and staggered to her feet. She felt empty and completely sober. All she wanted now was to go to bed and forget what had just happened. Walking slowly, she was very careful to avoid the garden sheds and this time found the kitchen entrance to the house and made her way up to her room managing only a nod to her QGs on duty before she shut the door and fell on her bed.

Whether or not it was the illness, or the strength of her denial, but Adele finally got her wish and slept for the first time in days.

CHAPTER TWENTY-FOUR

"The Price of a Dark Past"

Rainere was not surprised by his intruder. He had been aware that he was being followed as he walked through the east wing from the clinic, but he was impressed that the would-be thief had made it to a dark corner of his private chamber so fast. Rainere had only taken enough of the Gift of Life to make himself feel whole again, as he had been reluctant to do more than heal his injuries. Still, he was confident that he wouldn't get much of a fight from his stealthy visitor.

As he sat at his desk, the prince mixed a softly glowing potion together from the myriad of tiny bottles that sat in wire frames before him, neatly pouring a little from each into a glass tube. He waited until he heard a slight intake of breath from his intruder before speaking.

"I applaud your efforts," he said and almost smiled at the shocked silence. "To break into the Grey Palace is no small achievement. One must have a certain control of one's own dark magic as well as a level of stupidity that is hard to come by. Why, just to brave the Sleeping Guards lining my hallways is quite remarkable."

"I didn't see any guards, Your Highness." The voice was young, but Rainere could feel the smirk from across the room. The prince enjoyed his moment.

"I didn't mean human guards, boy. Don't you know anything about your heritage?" Rainere turned to face the corner where his intruder had hidden in the shadows. "Thieves don't break into the Grey Palace because they *can't*, but because they don't *dare* to."

He let the silence deepen for a moment.

"You bravely walked through at least six different curses just getting to this chamber. No doubt, you are already feeling the effects." Rainere paused, a finger in the air, and listened to the silence. "I think I can almost hear your heartbeat slowing. And now...now I imagine the sweat is leeching out of your body as a worsening lethargy weighs down your limbs. You might know that these are all classic symptoms of the human body gradually petrifying."

The prince sat back in his chair, hands entwined, a finger to his lips to watch as his intruder staggered from the shadows. Only a raised eyebrow indicated his surprise at the boy's youth.

"Please," gasped Charlie, falling to his knees. "Help me!"

"Why?" The prince watched the boy with a gaze that was as intense as it was dark.

"I'm...we have a...friend." Charlie's hand clutched at his throat and he could only manage to choke out the words his panicked brain was feeding him.

"Who?" asked Rainere, surprised again, despite himself. There was no one whom he called 'friend'. Rainere's eyes studied the boy, looking for a sense of familiarity, but he only saw a brown-haired street urchin, half-starved and filthy, now slowly dying on his bedroom floor.

Charlie's arms clutched his chest in a futile attempt to stop the creeping pain crushing his lungs. Then he lay perfectly still. "The queen," he whispered through his stiff jaw. "Message...you."

Prince Rainere pushed himself up and out of his chair. He walked over to the boy and dropped to his knees beside him. He slipped a hand under the boy's head and held the small vial of glowing liquid to his cold lips.

"If you are lying, child." Rainere's voice was a low growl. "The pain you are in now will feel like a mother's embrace in comparison to what I can do to you later."

The boy couldn't talk at all, but Rainere read the desperation and rage in his expression. He saw a ring of silver flash and spin around his pupils as the boy fought the magic with all his strength.

The prince poured the liquid between the boy's parted lips and was careful not to spill a drop. He waited a moment to make sure the potion had slid down his victim's throat before laying the boy's head back on the cold stone floor. He rose and walked to the window to examine the early twilight stars and wait for the antidote to work. It wouldn't take long, and Rainere had important things to think about.

Adelena had written to him and Rainere allowed himself one bright minute of hope trying to guess the contents of the letter.

Maybe she was writing to tell him she was on her way back to him, so he would not have to make the journey himself to Belvoir and risk his immortal life in the process? Or maybe that she had organized a priest and they could be married soon? But of course, that would be too much to hope for. She had no idea how to do such a thing, so he would have to do it for them.

Suddenly, Rainere felt the weight of his responsibility to Adelena press heavily on his shoulders. She was so innocent of the danger that lay in wait for her in the Dark Forest. In five days, the Spider Empress would demand her marriage to Rainere and she would have to relinquish control of her kingdom to him. For the sake of their love, Rainere was determined to ensure that Adelena would trust him enough to give him everything. He needed her to trust that it would be for the best for both of them, as well as her beautiful children. After their last incredible night together, when he had laid himself open to her and she had taken everything from him that he could give, Rainere just couldn't believe that Adelena wouldn't believe in the love between them. He had let her drink the power from his very soul, and he had heard the voice of the Goddess Serena as she urged him to give every ounce of himself to the woman he loved with all his heart.

Adelena must want to see him now. She had to be suffering as much as he was without her by his side and in his bed. To be without her was an agony that only the boy on the floor could sympathize with.

Behind him, Rainere could hear the gasping and coughing which meant the boy could breathe normally again. He turned and looked down at his intruder. His poverty was obvious. Certainly, he wasn't an official St. Lucidis messenger, which could only mean that he wasn't here on official business. Adelena was still keeping their relationship a secret.

Prince Rainere's doubts resurfaced like a punch to the stomach. His voice was hoarse with disappointment when he spoke. "What is her message?"

Charlie could feel all the blood rushing about his recently frozen limbs. The pain and itch of it was excruciating. He struggled to his knees and risked a glance up at the prince.

Charlie realized the hollow-eyed man before him was so much more dangerous than he had been told, and that bloody queen hadn't mentioned a word about the traps laid in the Grey Palace. *Mind you, she was operating under the mistaken belief that he already worked for the prince so that was probably why...but still, damn!* Charlie sensed the prince's growing impatience with how slowly he was moving, but it took a minute before his brain could convince his hand to work again. With numb fingers, he managed to free the little envelope from beneath his shirt.

"Here," he croaked, holding it up and recoiled as the Prince's long white hand reached out to snatch the letter.

The prince broke the purple wax seal and breathed in the fragrance of the scented paper, hesitating a moment before unfolding it. Charlie watched as the prince's eyes read and re-read the letter. When the prince flicked the paper over to check the back of it, Charlie flinched so hard he fell over onto his side, his nerves stretching a little tighter at the prince's obvious displeasure with the note.

Suck a cat's tit! Charlie swore silently as he wiped his sweaty palms on his pants and surreptitiously scanned the room for an escape or a weapon of some kind. He still had his knife up his sleeve, but he didn't quite trust his hands to maneuver the narrow blade just yet.

What the hell is so important that she had to send me all the way here just to piss off the black prince? Doesn't she know he is insane?

Charlie cursed his bad fortune. He thought of the queen's kind eyes and how he had decided to trust her, just a little bit. If he could remain in her good graces, he had a chance to find the object the Boss had sent him to steal from her. But deciding to do that had put him in an even worse situation…just another one of his mistakes in the long line of them that had been his life up until this painful point.

"Is this it?" the prince almost hissed, eyes narrowed. He looked as though he was accusing Charlie of holding back something. "No word? No spoken message?"

Charlie swallowed on his dry throat and managed to shake his head. He fought the urge to pee himself as the prince took a step nearer to him.

Prince Rainere ran his hands through his long hair and closed his eyes. He looked as though he was making a mighty attempt to control his temper. Charlie didn't dare to breathe in case he disturbed him. Suddenly, the prince's eyes snapped open and he cursed so graphically it made Charlie blink. Impressed despite himself, Charlie tucked the phrase away in his memory in case he survived long enough to use it later.

Prince Rainere took another step toward Charlie and grasped his chin in his hand. He moved Charlie's face back and forth, examining the light in his eyes.

"You have a lot of the Blood in you, boy," he growled but his tone was more analytical than angry. "Where did she find you? At the Belvoir Estate I suppose? It's a veritable nest of bastards and ill-breeding there."

He dropped Charlie's chin and wiped his hand on his leg, as if to clean off some impurity he might have picked up from the contact.

"I have a return message for the queen," said the prince as he slowly tore the queen's letter into four pieces and watched as they fluttered to the floor. He seemed calm, but the hairs on the back of Charlie's neck stood up at the restrained violence of the gesture. *Holy hell!* "But it won't be a letter and you must deliver it to her hand only. Am I clear?"

Charlie could only nod.

The prince left the room then, stalking out and slamming the door so hard it made the windows rattle. Finally alone, Charlie dropped to his back on the floor and groaned. He was in so much pain, he couldn't even name all the places that hurt. *That cat-tit-sucking arsehole of a black prince will pay for what he's done to me!* He swore as he let the fury and frustration flow through him, hoping the energy would strengthen his feeble limbs. But despite his best efforts, it took Charlie long minutes before he was able to stand on his own two feet again.

"Sleeping Guards, my sweet arse," Charlie grumbled to himself, stretching out his sore back and neck.

He looked properly around the room for the first time. The air was chill as the large fireplace had been left cold, and only green-flamed lanterns lit the shadows. The room was tidy, but most of the furniture was battered and shabby. There was a great crater in the stone ceiling above the bed, as if made by a small explosion.

Charlie jumped as he caught sight of a figure in a mirror by the dressing table. It took him a moment to recognize himself in the white-faced boy who stared back. His clothes were dark with sweat from his ordeal, and his hair stood to attention in patches all over his head. The day-long ride to the Grey Palace had left him exhausted and filthy, never mind almost being turned to stone. He thought longingly of his knapsack with its clean Carparell uniform hidden behind the Grey Palace stables with his horse. At least with that he could get back into the Belvoir manor without much trouble.

But if this is working for royalty, they can forget it! thought Charlie bitterly, trying without much success to smooth down his hair. *I'm not doing another thing for the witch queen after tonight. I'll just take this thing, or whatever it is, back to her from the prince and then I'm gone.*

But even as he thought it Charlie's practical side came to the fore. It wasn't as if he hadn't done dangerous work before, and at least this time he was sure his employer was good for the money. He felt under his shirt where he had secreted the gold bracelet the queen had given him. *It was a hell of a lot more than the Boss had ever handed over to him.* Charlie's bowels cramped a little when he thought of what the Boss would do to him when he returned without the object.

Charlie tried to work out his sore muscles with some stretches, but only succeeded in hurting himself more. He limped over to sit on the lone armchair by the fireplace, wishing there was a fire there to warm his damp clothes. He sighed loudly and, for company, counted his miseries one by one.

The spell Charlie had been entrusted with by the Boss was very rare and very expensive. He had only had one chance to find the object of his boss's desire and yet the spell had only found a dirty travelling cloak. It would have been easier if Charlie had been told what the object looked like, but the Boss gave out information like a miser did coins, that is to say little or none at all. Charlie had been working for the mysterious Boss on and off for several years, but all he could say about him was that he was a young man, educated by his accent, and crazy as a cut snake. The Boss always wore a long-hooded cloak and a black silk scarf across the lower half of his face to disguise himself, but Charlie wasn't laughing at the get-up. It wasn't just the dangerous work that the Boss demanded that set him apart from the other bosses in the underworld of Concordis. When the Boss called, you came. When the Boss asked, you did.

Charlie had seen what had happened to another kid who hadn't answered the Boss's call. Ellery had been strong too, the Blood showed up clear in his eyes, and he knew how to use his magic. But the Boss was stronger and Charlie had never forgotten the sight of his friend lying naked in the gutter, strangled by his own entrails, his hands tied behind his back with a black silk scarf.

So, when the Boss gave Charlie an expensive spell and told him to find a small box in the room of the Queen Adelena, Charlie went to get that box, no questions asked.

But now the spell was gone, and Charlie was sweating it out in the bedroom of the mad black prince as a favor to the witch, Queen Adelena. Charlie was left wondering if the Boss would torture him first before letting him die or whether he would feed him to the Eldars as he had once promised.

The Boss had assured him that those ghouls from the children's fables were very real, and still searched the world for unfortunates with the Blood coursing through their mixed-blood veins. Charlie fingered the amulet the Boss had given him to hide him from the supernatural sight of the Eldars. With the Blood humming in his veins and the silver ring that sometimes flashed about his pupils, Charlie figured they would come for him right quick if they ever knew where he was. The amulet was his for as long as he worked for the Boss, marking him as taken, and it protected him from all the other thugs and goons who would want to exploit a street kid with dark magic in his hands. But it still didn't make Charlie feel safe.

At least while I run between the Grey Palace and Belvoir Estate, I can tell the Boss I'm searching for his object. Hopefully, he'll let me live long enough to find it, thought Charlie, but he hadn't seen enough of the Boss's mercy to really believe in it.

The problem was, he hadn't gone back to the Boss today, which meant the Boss would come looking for him soon. Charlie wondered if the ancient curse against magic at Belvoir would protect him from the wrath of the Boss, but he doubted it. The Boss knew far too many non-magical ways to kill a man.

A gust of wind rattled the window, seeking entry to the chamber. A tiny finger of air reached in under the frame, swirling around the room and lifted the corner of one of the shreds of paper still on the floor. It caught Charlie's eye, and though it hurt like hell, he bent over and picked up the fragments of the letter, quickly checking the door before assembling the pieces together.

Dearest Rainere,

The hours pass so slowly without you. I am so sorry about what I did to you on that last night. I promise it will never happen again.

I miss you my love.

Adelena

Like the prince before him, Charlie read and re-read the lines. He committed them to memory before scattering them back on the floor just as he had found them.

A love note? Thought Charlie, horrified. *I almost* died *because of a cat-sucking love note?*

Charlie straightened just as the black prince stalked back into the room. The prince's expression was quite blank, but it made Charlie nervous all the same.

The prince ignored his guest and walked to the desk with something dark in his hands. As always, Charlie's insatiable curiosity overcame his more feeble good sense, and he stood up to see what it was the prince was doing. Using one hand to steady himself, Charlie leaned forward to look around the prince's shoulder, but his limbs were still too stiff and Charlie's arm folded making him fall against the mantle, jostling the small objects that cluttered the shelf. Charlie hurriedly tried to straighten the things he'd knocked over, setting back a little wooden box covered in engravings, and the piece of paper that was set behind it, with a child's drawing on it. The picture caused Charlie to raise an eyebrow but the next object he touched made him yelp as if he'd been burned.

The prince looked up at the noise and strode over in a few long steps. "Don't touch anything!" he snapped and took the small glass sphere out of Charlie's shaking hand.

"Is that what I think it is?" asked Charlie, aghast, pointing at the small blue flame that danced within the glass ball.

"It's not for children to play with," replied Rainere coldly and rearranged all the things that Charlie had touched, as if to reassure himself they were all accounted for. He touched the little wooden box, coconut wood by the looks of it, and Charlie thought he saw a flicker of a smile twitch at the prince's mouth, but his fear might have been making him hallucinate.

"Take this." The prince's tone was at once imperious and defensive as he thrust a small black box at Charlie. "Put it in the queen's hand and no other's. It is essential that only her hand opens the box. Tell her…tell her I was serious about us."

Charlie tried not to tremble under the prince's dark glare. "The queen's hand. I understand, Your Highness."

"You will return to Belvoir Estate tonight," ordered the prince, immediately turning on his heel and heading for the door. He stopped when he realized Charlie wasn't following him. Turning only to speak over his shoulder Rainere said:

"I will show you a much quicker way back. At least your blood will *probably* be able to tolerate the portal if you remember not to linger. Now come along, she must receive my gift tonight."

Charlie swallowed a curse. He had been taught about portals by those who knew such things and was told in no uncertain terms not to mess with them, ever. What the hell was he going to do if 'probably' wasn't good enough to get him through it. As Charlie followed the black prince along the dusty corridors and down into the dank and musty bowels of the Grey Palace, he began to consider his immediate future. It was only a little upsetting to him that torture at the hands of the Boss had now slipped to third place on his list of ways to die. Death by Marchant portal or death at the hands of the witch queen he was heading back to seemed to be his two unhappy options.

Charlie sent a silent prayer to the Goddess Serena to look after one of her Chosen and hurried to catch up with the prince.

CHAPTER TWENTY-FIVE

"Fear's Intrigue"

The prince had accompanied Charlie right up to the underground entrance of the Belvoir manor. A professional curiosity made Charlie force himself to remember the route through the Grey Palace and then along the dark tunnel. The portal had scared the pants off him, but the prince had ended up guiding him through anyway. He had obviously changed his mind about leaving Charlie's survival to chance.

Charlie had wanted to watch the prince's reaction to the weight of the curse as their magic fell away and left them walking as two normal men, but in the dim light of the lantern, he couldn't discern any physical changes in the immortal wizard beside him. He almost smiled at his own childish hope to see nothing but a pile of dust and bones on the ground.

But life was never that easy.

Charlie pulled himself through the little door carefully concealed in the wainscoting of the queen's bathroom. He was grudgingly impressed by the directions Prince Rainere had given him through the secret passageways of the Belvoir manor, considering the man had never been in the manor himself. Charlie waited, holding his breath and listening hard before he dared to close the door. He made a note of the indentation that, when pushed, would open it again later.

Looking around the room, Charlie was happy that a covered candle had been left burning for the queen, but by its light he could see how filthy he really was. Covered in dust and dirt, Charlie could not escape the fact that he smelled of horse sweat and stank of fear.

There was no way he could approach the queen in this condition.

Deciding to take the risk of a quick wash, Charlie carefully set down the little black box on a dressing table along with his knife and holster and pulled off his clothes. His whole body shook with tremors and Charlie silently cursed the prince again as he lowered himself into the prepared bath. Blessedly, the water was still warm and smelled fragrantly of sweet oils and flowers. Unfortunately, every pleasant scent reminded Charlie of food and his stomach growled loudly in the silence of the room. He sank down deeper in the water and dunked his head under. Scrubbing with his hands as quietly as he could, Charlie washed off all the dust and grime of the last day. The warmth of the water helped release the shock in his exhausted muscles and when he climbed out of the bath he felt very slightly better.

Reluctant to put his filthy clothes back on Charlie thought wistfully of the doublet and trousers he had left at the Grey Palace. It had been a useful uniform and it was going to be tricky to steal another one. He looked about the bathroom and saw the cast-off blouse and trousers of the queen. The blouse was white with simple embroidery on the front, and the trousers were narrow and dark blue. Charlie shrugged. It would have to do.

After dressing himself Charlie put the little box back in his pocket and the knife up his sleeve and quietly opened the door to the bedroom, peeking inside. He stepped through silently enough but his still-clumsy hands let the door slam shut behind him. He froze in the darkness and stared at the bed until his eyes watered, but the queen didn't even roll over. *Right, she was definitely sound asleep.*

This was going to be the tricky bit, because now he had to wake the solidly-sleeping queen without letting her scream and call the guards' attention. No doubt there were a couple outside the door.

Charlie tip-toed to the side of the bed and looked down on the queen as she slept. He put his hand out to shake her shoulder but hesitated at the last moment.

Even though he had been told she was a witch...

Even though she had sent him into the death trap of the Grey Palace and the hands of an insane immortal prince for a pathetic love note…

Even though he knew all of these things…

The queen looked so sweet as she slept. Her eyelids moved in a dream and a tiny sigh escaped her lips. One naked arm lay outside of the covers and her skin was milky white and unmarked in the soft moonlight from the window.

I'm going soft in the head! Charlie gave himself a shake. *All I have to do is wake her, give her the box and then run like hell before she opens it.*

Charlie slipped his hand inside his pocket and touched the lacquered sides of the black box. Whatever was inside couldn't be good. The prince had not been happy with the letter from the queen. No doubt, inside this box was something to teach the queen never to do it again. It was probably going to hurt her, maybe even kill her.

Charlie felt curiously conflicted as he looked down at the queen and watched as her mouth pursed in a rosebud then ticked up at the side in a smile. Whatever she dreamed about it was pleasant.

Not like Charlie's life had been.

I've got nothing to feel bad about, Charlie silently chided himself. *I don't owe this witch anything. In fact, she owes me an object for the Boss. Why do I care if the black prince hurts her? It's not my business if she is pining after an insane wizard. Maybe with this box she'll learn her lesson?*

The queen murmured quietly and turned her head from side to side. The scent of flowers wafted up to Charlie's nose. They had shared the same bath water.

I'll give it to her, but warn her not to open it, he decided. *Then she can make her own choice, and it won't be on my neck whatever she does.*

Newly determined, Charlie reached out his hand to shake the queen's shoulder.

"You lay one filthy finger on our queen and you will lose it!" hissed a voice from close behind him, and Charlie felt a jab in his side.

Instinctively, he turned to dart away, but hands wearing hard leather gloves clamped down on his upper arms. "Quiet, or you will lose your tongue too, boy."

Cat shit! The Queen's Guard! Charlie cursed his bad luck. He was so used to having his magic-heightened instincts to alert him to trouble, it was odd to feel like a normal man must do. Odd and bloody dangerous! His mind raced. *Even if they let him talk, how in the name of the Goddess was he going to explain being in the queen's private chamber in the wee hours of the night?* And that was presuming they didn't beat the stuffing out of him first.

He was a spy, and carrier of something obviously magic. He couldn't imagine the queen was going to risk her reputation to save his scrawny neck. He could only hope to blackmail her in some way. But that was going to be difficult to do if she was asleep.

Charlie was dragged into the sitting room with the big desk in it. His heart sank down to his feet when he saw who was sitting on the couch: *Captain bloody Handsome again and two other guards with him as well,* thought Charlie and groaned inwardly. Their impeccable uniforms of white and gold were cut close to make the most of their broad chests and tall frames. Charlie fought hard not to be intimidated but was intensely aware that he was standing in bare feet and wearing women's clothing.

The hands holding Charlie pulled him up short and shoved him down onto a puffy footstool. It didn't hurt, but he braced himself for worse.

"Captain Lucky, I found this young man here about to lay hands on the queen as she slept," said the guard standing behind Charlie, keeping firm hands on his shoulders.

All the soldiers stood immediately making Charlie jump. He tried to shake off the tremor of fear at having three large men glare down at him, not to mention the faceless guard at his back, but he felt his bowels clench. Charlie sat up straight and assumed his most nonchalant expression.

The handsome Lucky was bigger up close than Charlie remembered. He trained his sky-blue eyes on Charlie and Charlie was the first to look away despite his bravado.

"So, what's a half-dressed lad like you doing sneaking round our queen's quarters on this fine morning?" Captain Lucky's tone was conversational, but Charlie watched as the captain gripped the hilt of the sword at his hip.

"What does it matter?" growled one of the burly ones. "Let's take him out back and ask questions later."

Charlie gulped and shifted to get a look at the guard who spoke. The man was enormous, with huge arms straining the fabric of his dress coat. He was glaring at Charlie with narrow blue eyes, but his mouth was stretched into an eager grin.

Captain Lucky raised a hand, gesturing for silence. "Would you like to answer my question, boy, or would you prefer QG Bear here beat it out of you?"

"I'm not a boy," said Charlie, attempting to sound indignant. "I'm twenty f – two." He lied, but not quickly enough. His brain was still sluggish after being petrified earlier tonight.

"Twenty for two?" exclaimed Captain Lucky with mock surprise. "Does that mean no more than fourteen where you are from *boy*?"

Charlie lifted his chin stared down the chuckling men but he was relieved to note that the atmosphere had relaxed just a touch.

"So it looks like QG Bear gets to take you downstairs to kick some of those lies out of you after all," smiled the captain. The one called Bear stepped forward and cracked his knuckles.

"Wait," Charlie almost shrieked. His mind raced frantically to come up with a reasonable explanation that would save him from a beating. "I can't tell you why I was in the queen's chambers." He lowered his voice to a stage whisper. "She asked me not to say anything." He added a wink for good measure.

Captain Lucky's composure cracked. "Why you little gutter cat!" he snapped and leaped forward to grab the front of Charlie's borrowed shirt. He pulled Charlie to his feet.

"I'm telling the truth," squawked Charlie, his bravado falling away. "Goddess truth! Ask her yourself. Please?"

Captain Lucky snapped an order for someone to go and wake the queen, but the men only shifted uncomfortably.

"Sir, the only reason I entered Her Majesty's chamber was because I thought she was already out of bed but it was this intruder moving about," said the guard behind Charlie. "I…um…are we allowed to wake her?"

Captain Lucky dropped Charlie back onto the footstool. "Right, I'll do it then. Keep him here."

Charlie waited, holding his breath. He had no idea if his pathetic plan was going to work, but he had seen the desperation in the queen's eyes when she had given him the letter for the black prince. Hopefully, she was just as desperate for his response. Charlie chewed the inside of his cheek and tried to think of a way to let the queen know he had told her guardsmen that he had spent the night with her. It was the only thing he could come up with to explain why he was dressed in her clothing, in her chamber, with her naked and in bed.

He jumped again, skittish as a kitten, when Captain Lucky re-entered the room with the queen in tow. As she pulled up the collar of her robe and pushed the hair off her face she looked dazed and worried. But even with the shadows under her eyes and her pale cheeks, Charlie thought he wouldn't be ashamed to be thought of in 'that way' with the queen.

"So, Your Majesty," Captain Lucky gestured at Charlie. "This is your intruder."

The queen's eyes found Charlie's. She looked visibly relieved.

"Oh, it's just Charlie." She turned to the captain. "It's okay, I know him, of course. But why is he wearing my clothes?"

The queen smiled at Charlie and his heart-rate ratcheted up its pace. She looked around the room at all the guards standing stiffly at attention and Captain Lucky who was now looking everywhere but at her. Charlie watched as it dawned on her that these men required more of an explanation from her for the boy being in her room. He could tell as her smile died that she didn't want to expose him, or his work for her.

Cursing his suicidal tendencies, Charlie decided to help her out. "Majesty, I was just telling the good captain here that you expected me in your chambers tonight when you knew that we would be *alone*."

Adele's confusion was obvious to all except Captain Lucky who stared at his feet. "What?"

"The Goddess knows these men would be well within their rights to kill me if I wasn't in your room for a legitimate reason, my Queen, alone and privately." Charlie couldn't have raised his eyebrows any higher. "With you - in bed." He added for good measure and earned himself a ferocious glare from Captain Lucky.

Charlie looked beseechingly at the queen and thanks be to the Goddess he saw the penny drop as she finally grasped what he was suggesting. Her cheeks flushed pink.

"Well, I, um, don't really think it's necessary to explain the situation any further. It is just that Charlie is... um..." she drifted off, clearly dying of embarrassment. "But I would appreciate it if my personal, um, business was kept quiet. I mean, I would hate for gossip to spread about something private..." The queen gazed about the room but couldn't make eye contact with anyone.

Charlie recognized his chance for escape. "I'll just return to your chambers than shall I, Majesty?" he asked quickly and was up and past her to the doorway before she could say otherwise.

"Right then, well…I, err…will see you all downstairs later," said the queen choking on her discomfort and stepped back following Charlie out of the room.

As the Queen shut the door to her bedroom Charlie spun to face her and prepared to defend himself. The queen pressed her back to the door and stared at Charlie in shock. He stared back at her from where he was standing, half-hiding, behind a bedpost.

The queen burst into hysterical giggles. "I have never been so embarrassed in all my life!"

Charlie thought the queen must have cracked completely as she broke down but her laughter was so deep and infectious that soon a grin stole over his face and he felt the urge to join in.

"Did you see their faces?" he sniggered. "When I said I'm with you in that way. That captain looked like he was going to drop dead."

A genuine laugh bubbled up and out of Charlie. The relief of the situation being over was heady. He was safe, for the time being, and the queen wasn't even angry, she was actually laughing about what a joke it all was. Again, Charlie found it hard to reconcile what the Boss had told him about this woman being an evil witch when she was laughing so hard she could barely stand. The tension melted from his bones as his body shook with laughter.

The queen was holding her ribcage with one hand and had the other propping her up against a desk. "They couldn't look at me," she gasped between outbursts. "They thought you and me had sex, together!"

"I know," Charlie rocked with mirth. "They were like…" He boggled his eyes in comic imitation of shock and they both fell about in peals of laughter.

"Oh, sweet Christ," the queen gasped and wiped the tears away as she threw herself down on a chair. "After all these gorgeous men who throw themselves at me, they think I'm sneaking around with a boy young enough to be my son."

She giggled, calming down.

"Yeah, me! Of all the men in the realm," Charlie agreed guffawing and sat down on the bed. "But I'm not that young, I'll be seventeen in a few months."

The queen froze, her smile cracked.

"They think I'm a pedophile," she whispered. "They think I sleep with…oh, they must be so disappointed in me."

It was as if all the warmth had drained from the room and had been sucked back down inside the queen. Though Charlie's ribs still hurt, the memory of their shared laughter was already fading. As he gazed upon the queen's stricken expression, Charlie felt wounded to the core, though he couldn't have explained why. He mentally hefted his emotional armor back on. How did he let this woman get to him like this?

"Well, Your Majesty, you are still bloody lucky it's only me they think you bed. If they knew about the black prince, you'd have to run and hide faster than I would." Charlie's voice was sulky and he only looked up when she didn't reply.

Her Majesty was gazing out the window as dawn break lightened the sky and didn't react to his thinly veiled threat. "Yes, thank you Charlie. That will be all."

Charlie resented the dismissal though he knew he deserved it. He thought briefly about disappearing into his secret tunnel in the bathroom, but he knew it was wiser to be seen leaving the rooms now that his presence was known. He didn't bother to bow to the queen as he left and slammed the door behind himself for good measure. She might be a witch, but she had hurt his feelings now more than scaring him.

Charlie turned to walk away in a huff but saw all three guards and Captain Lucky standing along the hallway. Lifting his chin, he decided to brazen it out. He straightened his ladies blouse and walked the longest five yards of his life.

"Lovers' tiff, boy?" he heard QG Bear snigger as he passed.

"At least I'm getting some," snapped Charlie over his shoulder. "And I'll bet she's hotter than your tart."

Like a coiled, spring four men stepped forward to surround him, swords drawn. Charlie almost emptied his bladder and cursed his quick temper, which was determined to get him killed today.

"You want to watch that mouth of yours, boy," said Captain Lucky, his tone was sharp and cold. "Our queen is the leader of our kingdom, and a lady at that. Learn to be more discreet."

Captain Lucky waved a hand to his men so they sheathed their weapons, though nothing stopped them glaring at Charlie. "We are to let the royal consort pass until Her Majesty tells us otherwise. You have my word, Charlie."

"Many thanks, captain," mumbled Charlie. He managed to walk the rest of the hall at a dignified pace before turning the corner and sprinting down the stairs and corridors that led him to the little room he had found for himself under the laundry. He lay on his dusty pallet for several hours before his heart stopped hammering in his chest. It was only then that he remembered he hadn't delivered the prince's black box to the queen.

Charlie cursed, and cursed, and cursed.

CHAPTER TWENTY-SIX

"Surprising Sources of Cool Hope"

The crowd cheered as another race came to a close. Though it was only the first of the afternoon races, Adele was already bored of watching horses run around in circles. The once-green grass of the paddock within the track had turned yellow at the edges and looked as dry and crispy as Adele felt.

The air was so hot that Adele found it hard to breathe even in the shade of Prince Bertrand's pavilion. Today the pavilion was filled with his extended royal family and though they all made a lot of noise everyone was too shy to speak to her. To make matters worse, Benjamin was off duty and sitting in the next pavilion just yards away from her. He had the attention of two pretty blondes and a group of young men surrounding him, but he kept looking over at her in a way that was extremely irritating to the female company he was already with. After a polite "hello," Adele had steeled herself to ignore him, but all his staring was wearing on her patience.

Adele gulped at her water and tried, unsuccessfully, to wish away the memory of this morning's fiasco, which was still fresh in her mind.

What in God's name had she been thinking agreeing to go along with Charlie's disgusting suggestion? Surely he could have come up with something better than *sleeping* with her? Adele hadn't been able to look any of her Queen's Guard in the eye all morning. It was all so humiliating! Again, Adele wondered at Rainere's choice of go-between. Charlie was a cute kid and his neglected air pulled hard on her maternal heartstrings, but she hardly thought he had handled anything well since she had met him in her bedroom casting a spell yesterday. But now, she was stuck with his horrible "royal consort" story and had no idea how to back out of it without exposing what Charlie actually did for her.

Adele noticed Bertie shooting her concerned looks and took another gulp of water. She was being too serious; she should be more polite with her host.

To distract herself, Adele searched out her children in the little fenced off area that had been set aside as a playground for all the children of the Estate. It made her smile to see Natalie deep in conversation with three other little girls her own age and Aaron playing a game involving sticks and little balls with a mixed group of boys. The sight struck her as unusual since they had arrived in Unisia. She had rarely seen other children at the Golden Palace. She leaned in to ask her host about it, speaking loudly over the roar of the races and crowd around them.

"Bertie, you have so many more children running around your court than we do in the Golden Palace. Why is that?"

Prince Bertrand smiled with obvious pride and gazed down upon the children playing close to their pavilion. "I would attempt to answer modestly, You Majesty, but we are indeed blessed here at Belvoir with the proficiency of Belvoir women to carry and deliver healthy babes. Our child mortality rate is the lowest of all the royal families, due in no small part to our old-fashioned views on mixing the bloods and cherishing those babes born out of wedlock as much as those born within legal unions."

He shifted to the edge of his chair, obviously warming to a topic close to his heart. Bertie pointed down to the children. "Though probably not one of those kiddies could claim a straight line of succession from either Prince Bertrand I, or even Prince Bartolomus V from the southern Belvoirs, they are all considered to be as much kin as anyone of my own royal progeny, and therefore are all in line for the throne of Belvoir when I pass into the Garden of the Goddess."

Adele nodded, pleased to hear a monarchy who's views she could actually understand, and not the complicated mess of bloodlines and hierarchy of the St. Lucidis family which Tilburn had spent many hours trying to explain to her.

"That all sounds very modern and democratic to me, Bertie," she smiled.

"Quite the contrary, Your Majesty," demurred Bertie. "I believe we are considered to be the most primitive of the families at the genteel court of the Golden Palace."

But he waved his hand as if all of that meant little to him. "In the Belvoir family we have always believed that the best amongst us should be those to rule the family. That a man, or woman, needs only to be strong of heart and mind to be a true Belvorian leader, regardless of the purity of their blood, or the strength of their magic. We stand by our beliefs not because they are old fashioned but because they *work*, even in these modern days. The large number of happy and healthy children in our midst proves this to us daily."

By now, Adele understood that the people of Unisia had a slightly different biology to the people of Earth. Their fertility cycles were shorter and came further apart, giving them fewer chances to conceive children in a year. It was also complicated in the royal families with the problem of inbreeding, as extended family members married often to try to keep the bloodline as pure as possible. High Wizard Ohren had explained that the magic in their blood had something to do with the low birth rate, too, and that with all of the inbreeding the magic was becoming weak or even dormant in many of the younger generations. As a result of this, the court of the Golden Palace had tried to make magic amongst the families seem unfashionable and suspect. Adele's arrival and rumored magical strength with the blood of her powerful parents running in her veins, had thrown all of that up into the air. Adele was very aware of how impressive she was supposed to be and had looked into Ohren's disappointed gaze as she had completely failed to manifest even a hint of the power within herself.

If only they knew that it was Rainere who made her magic come alive.

Bertie leaned in conspiratorially and lowered his voice. "We have some very interesting bloodlines in our family, Your Majesty. Some of our children have quite the *mixed* heritage,"—he mouthed a word that looked like *Marchant* at her, surprising Adele— "But we value brains and brawn over magical abilities. After all, it would do no good to rule from the Belvoir Estate with magic, because of the curse, you see." He tapped the side of his nose to indicate it was a discreet matter and gave her a friendly wink.

Adele nodded again and sipped at her glass of water. Her head had started swimming when she thought of Rainere and magic, and the two things together. A hot flush swept her, but it felt more like a fever than passion. Adele wondered if she was becoming ill. It would certainly explain her roiling stomach and light head.

"You see Lance down there?" asked Bertie, pointing at his young successor. "At just sixteen, not only is he a strapping young man, but he is very quick and bright as well. Look how gentle he is with the little ones. He is a true leader in the making there."

Adele craned her neck to see Lance and watched as the boy knelt in the dirt and dried Aaron's tears when he lost a match, handing over some of his own sticks and balls to make the little boy happy. Aaron was completely enamored at the older boy's generosity and threw his arms around Lance's neck. Adele smiled and waved as Aaron sought her out in the crowd from Lance's arms. Her son looked ecstatic. "He looks like a lovely boy, Bertie. I can see why you are so proud of him." Bertie gave her a pleased grin and turned back to watch the races.

Adele heard a cough behind her and turned to see QGs Bear and Owens exchange a look with each other, suggestive smirks on their faces before they noticed her watching and turned their eyes immediately back to the front.

It took Adele all of five seconds to register the reason behind that look. Her cheeks burned and she felt tears prick sharply at her eyes. *They think I'm a child-raping monster* she thought miserably. *And now that I've said Lance is lovely, they think I'm going to attack him. They'll probably take bets on it.*

Adele bit her lip and berated herself again for trusting such a young, hot-headed boy like Charlie with something as important as her privacy. *He obviously has no idea about boundaries and why the hell had he been in my room while I was asleep anyway? Did he have a message from Rainere and, if he did, why hadn't he given it to me when we were alone?* Because Charlie had been able to perform green magic in front of her in the Belvoir manor, Adele had figured that he had more to hide than she did. *He is obviously some kind of Marchant wizard - just a stupid, half-starved, boy-wizard.*

Adele let out a huge sigh and wiped the perspiration from her brow with a handkerchief. Her nausea was ebbing and surging with the heat, making her almost wish for the chance to finally throw up and be done with it. She had been feeling steadily worse ever since she had arrived two nights ago.

Bertie gave her a sideways glance as a particularly exciting race came to a close. "Feeling the heat, Your Majesty?"

Adele grabbed the excuse with both hands. "You know, I am feeling a bit light-headed, Bertie," she said screwing up her face. "I might get out from under this tent and head inside to check on Stella. She should be waking soon."

Bertie nodded and patted her hand in a fatherly way, already entranced by the next race.

As Adele made her way out of the pavilion, she couldn't help but look over at the two guards behind her. Neither caught her eye but they both turned to follow her. Adele's stomach dropped at the very idea of having to put up with them a minute more.

"Stay here, please," she told them. "I'm going inside but I'll need you to keep an eye on Aaron and Natalie for me." It wasn't necessary, of course, as Seraphina and Caitlin were with the children, but Adele died a second time when the QGs exchanged another smirk as they did as she asked.

See! She thought. *It's not just my imagination. They are judging me for what they heard this morning. Oh God, who else have they told about me and Charlie?* The injustice and shame of it all flared in Adele's chest. Her eyes filled with tears again, and she stumbled on the last step getting down off the pavilion's stairs. A strong hand caught her arm and helped her back onto her feet.

"Thank you, I'm fine," she said without looking up at the kind stranger.

"Your Majesty?" his voice held a familiar timbre, but when she glanced up at the man, she saw a face like no other. He had deep-set eyes above a large, beak-like nose. His cheekbones stood out like craggy cliff edges and his chin seemed unnecessarily sharp. Oddly, his face was entirely hairless, with no eyebrows or beard, and his smooth head glinted in the sunshine. Adele might have been shocked by such a face, but the smile that lit his visage was so bright that she instinctively smiled back, despite her tears.

"Your Majesty, my dear Queen Adelena!" The gentleman stepped back and bowed deeply. "How I have longed to meet you since you came to our shores of Unisia! Please allow me to introduce myself. I am Pere Raven, humble priest and Father to the little flock at our church here in Belvoir. I declare myself your servant."

Adele blinked at this strange looking man's clear excitement at meeting her and suddenly she felt too exhausted for words. She just couldn't bare another person's baseless adoration when it could all be lost with a few words or a nasty suggestion. Adele lost her patience as her stomach lurched uncomfortably.

"It's very nice to meet you, Father, but I'm heading inside now." She hadn't meant to sound rude, but it was all she could do to be civil as she swallowed down on bile.

"Well then, may I accompany you back to the manor, Queen Adelena?" he grinned disarmingly and fell into step beside her anyway.

"Please just call me Adele," Adele insisted. "In my world, I was taught that priests are the equal of kings and queens."

Pere Raven let out a belly laugh so loud and joyful that it almost stopped Adele in her tracks. "Your Majesty's reputation for beauty and kindness have preceded you, my queen, but no one told me you were funny!" Pere Raven grinned down at her. He was taller than she was, but not by much.

Adele grimaced. "Well, there is a lot to learn about me, Father," she said thinking of the horrible rumor circulating her Queen's Guard and wanted to cry again.

"Bad day, my queen?" asked Pere Raven gently as he noted her change in expression.

"Please, just call me Adele. And yes, it's not been a good day," sighed Adele, as they continued on the long walk back to the manor. Adele forced herself to wave and smile at the groups of people they passed. She felt bad not stopping to talk to them as they so desperately wanted to catch her attention, but she didn't have the strength right now. But as they got closer to the manor, the crowd thinned and Adele felt it was only polite to chat with her escort.

"Why is it we haven't met before, Pere Raven," she asked. "I didn't see you at the welcome ball, did I?"

"No, no. I'm sure you would have remembered my charming face if you'd met me before. Most do," joked the Priest. "No, I was out on a mission to aid the passing of one of my parishioners. Lovely man by the name of Brent."

"Oh, I'm sorry for your loss," said Adele automatically.

Pere Raven flapped his hands to wave away her wooden sympathy. "He was a good man who had lived a good long life," he said reassuringly. "He had no reason to fear the beyond, our Goddess Serena has him in her Garden now."

"Ah, that's…good." Adele always felt awkward when faced with other people's religious beliefs and death had always unsettled her.

"Yes, it was good," agreed Pere Raven with another happy grin. "We had a chance to celebrate his life together before he passed. It was a wonderful opportunity for those of us he left behind to remind ourselves of what we want from this short life of ours, and how important it is that we find and give joy as much as we can while we are in this world. Despite my sadness at losing Brent, I'm grateful that he gave me this lesson."

He nudged Adele in the ribs with his elbow. "And his widow threw an excellent wake."

Adele smiled and was relieved that Brent's passing had been peaceful, and that she wasn't going to be expected to continue the philosophical side of this discussion. Who knew how many ways she could insult a priest from a different world?

"You know, Queen Adelena, I have a little keg of cider set up under a tree over there if you would like to rest a while with an old priest?" he gestured at a shady spot in the garden next to an enormous tree.

Adele hesitated. Should she go and check on Stella, who was no doubt still fast asleep, or could she take a drink with this kind old man? Her heart clenched as she wondered if the gossip about Charlie had spread any further in the manor. *Oh God, if Lady Olivia finds out I'll lose my only female friend, all over a lie I helped make.*

"A drink sounds great," she said.

It was lovely under the trees, and although the cider was sour it was very refreshing and helped settle her stomach.

Pere Raven prattled on about the recipe which was a family secret, but not his family's, he had added with a laugh. As they chatted, Adele found herself enjoying a normal conversation with a normal, albeit hair-free, person who made her laugh and shared her disinterest in horse racing. After a while, she began to relax a little as Pere Raven entertained her with gossip and stories from behind the scenes of the carnival. Apparently, the Carparell party were accusing the Belvoir laundry of losing their squires' uniforms and were now keeping their dirty laundry under lock and key. Adele chuckled until she remembered that Charlie had first appeared in the Carparell livery, and almost groaned at another of his indiscretions. That boy was nothing but trouble.

"Is it the heat that is bringing you low, Your Majesty, or is something else making you sad?" Pere Raven asked, his expression gentle. "I'm sorry if it's too intrusive to ask a queen's business, but the affairs of the human soul are a specialty of mine, and I sense a heaviness in yours at present."

Adele was instantly swamped with insecurity. "What can I tell you?" she said drily. "My life is not my own and there is so much I'm not allowed to say."

Pere Raven nodded knowingly. "I can only imagine what a tough road it is being queen, let alone when we must all seem so foreign to you. It is a burden I do not envy you."

Adele looked into the man's guileless expression and her eyes filled with the tears that had threatened to fall all day. "You have no idea," she whispered, but was scared to say more in case she lost her composure completely.

"You are right there," agreed Pere Raven somewhat morosely. "But then I have always suffered from a crippling lack of imagination. It's why I had to turn to religion, so someone else could give me all the answers to my 'whys?' and 'what comes afters?'."

Adele smiled despite herself, but it died quickly on her lips. "It has been difficult to adjust to this new life so fast," she said, looking down at her lap. "I feel like I'm always disappointing someone whatever I do."

Pere Raven sat back in his chair and clasped his wooden cup of cider between his hands. "Of all the things I have heard about you since your arrival, Queen Adelena, most tell of you being a beautiful and kind woman. That your ways are gentle and that you are an uncommonly doting mother," he looked over at her, his naked brows raised. The expression was much less disconcerting now she knew him better. "Are these things true?"

"I suppose you might describe me that way on a good day," she said. Compliments made her feel as awkward as talking about death.

Pere Raven smiled enthusiastically and sat forward again.

"Well!" he said, slapping his knee. "Then some people understand you perfectly. On a good day of course," he added with a wink. "As I understand it, you were not a queen on the world of Earth?"

Adele shook her head.

"It must have been a dreadful shock to land on our world and be immediately crowned and worshipped then." He guffawed loudly. "I can only imagine what a dunce I would be if that happened to me." He let out another hoot. "Or would if I could!"

A giggle escaped Adele before she could squash it back down. The man's good humor was infectious.

"I say, give yourself a break, Your Majesty!" proclaimed Pere Raven throwing his hands in the air, and spilling cider on his brown cotton robe. "You strike me as a person who cares very much about the world around her. I could think of no better person to be my surprise queen, or should I say *surprised* queen." He chuckled at his own joke.

"You are very kind," said Adele. "But I think that many people are relying on the fact that I can be more than I actually am." Her expression turned haunted as she thought of how little progress she had made in finding out about the prophecy that was controlling her life her in Unisia. "Too much depends on me."

"Ah, yes," nodded Pere Raven. "Well, my queen, if I may give you some advice? Take a leaf from the book of the Belvoir family. They believe that leaders are made and not born. They work together as a family to ensure that all of their children are brought up to take their duties and family honor seriously. But not all are made to rule, some are educated to learn to support from behind the throne. My advice to you, my dear queen, would be to find yourself a good support for behind that big throne of yours. No monarch has ever ruled this kingdom alone." He leaned forward and touched her arm. His hand was warm and the skin was rough. "Though perhaps you already have found that support and you just have to let yourself believe in the good of it." He smiled and Adele smiled back. The priest had flecks of green in his murky brown eyes.

"I really should check on my baby," said Adele, rising from her chair. "But thank you, Pere Raven, for the cider and the conversation. I feel so much better than I did before meeting you and I didn't think that feeling better was an option today."

Pere Raven chuckled again. "That is one of the grander compliments I've had in a while, my dear Queen Adelena, and the pleasure was mine alone I assure you."

As Adele parted from the happy priest there was a slight spring in her step. All of his positive words had given her a new energy.

There was very little on this new world that Adele could control. She was a human queen in an alien world, after all, and though her magic was changing in ways that frightened her it was also exhilarating to know that she had a strength that could protect her should she need it. Yet she was underestimated everywhere she went. The only people in all of Evendaar who knew that she was more than a puppet queen were her Queen's Guard. They had seen what she had accomplished in Sandar with the Empress Sanda'hani there, forging a new relationship and ensuring peace between their two realms, however fragile that might be. She had earned the respect of her men then, and, Adele decided, she would be damned if she lost that respect because of a stupid lie.

It was time she embraced the help they could give her instead of shying away from it. She needed to trust the one man her instincts told her was honest and true. So now it was her turn to be honest.

At least, honest enough.

CHAPTER TWENTY-SEVEN

"When Loyalty is a Curse"

"He did *what?*"

Poison from the fangs of the Spider Empress flew out and sprayed the cowering Schiss. He patted at the smoking patches on his old coat and shuffled backwards on his knees. The shaman who had read the letter melted back into the crowd of watching councilors. The entire Nest Council had gathered for this momentous occasion and the mood was very tense.

"Please, Mother of Us All, please understand. The prince, he…" Schiss stammered and trembled under the empress's thousand-eyed glare. He silently cursed Grottonski's honesty, telling the empress everything that the prince had done. Didn't he know this would only make his mother angry?

"He let that little queen escape him and hide in the black lands the humans call Belvoir!" The empress shivered her fangs again and this time Schiss caught a droplet just below his eye. He bit down hard on his lip to keep from crying out.

"He has betrayed me and he has betrayed us all!" shrieked the empress and her cry caused every spider in the cavern to drop and cover their ears. The breathy clicking and popping language that was their native tongue was horribly shrill when screamed aloud in anger.

"No, no, no Spider Empress!" Schiss protested. "The prince has found a priest and he will marry the queen like he promised he would." Schiss crept forward on all fours. His human form felt uncomfortable on the dirt floor as pebbles and sharp bits of bone pressed into his knees, but he couldn't mind the pain now. The empress was crazy with rage at Prince Rainere, and if he wasn't careful with her now she might just command the death of the

Marchant prince and then all their plans would end up on the dung heap.

Schiss shivered. Grotto had promised him a place at the foot of the king when Rainere took the throne. A place at the foot of the king would also be a place at the foot of his beautiful queen, the gentle and kind Adelena, the woman who had promised never to kill him. The very idea that the empress may try to hurt Queen Adelena made Schiss take a firmer hold on his courage and slowly climb back to his feet before his mother.

"Empress, you must understand, these humans above us have many complicated ways of doing very simple things. Prince Rainere merely sent the queen to the Belvoir Estate to get the blessing of her people before she is to return to the Grey Palace and marry him. He has told me he will fetch her back himself. She is a good queen, empress, she will not break her promises to us."

Schiss ran his lying tongue over his dry lips. He had no idea what the Queen Adelena was doing in Belvoir, but he was convinced that the prince wanted to marry the queen and would definitely try to get her back to his side as soon as he could. Grotto had told him so. He held himself taller, buoyed by the hope that what he said was true.

"Empress, by the time the full moon rises, the prince will be a king and all our people shall rise from the Under Lands, just as the prophecy predicts." Schiss watched his mother carefully, as her animal instincts warred with the more cerebral part of her ancient brain.

"But he had lied and betrayed us this…this deceitful prince." The empress snapped and clicked her jaws irritably. "This letter tells me he had fallen in love with the Hidden Child and will keep her as his own after they are married. It irritates me that he has said this. She is the Lost Child, the Hidden Child, but she is also the murderer of my son, beautiful Oki."

The empress shifted on her sodden mess of pillows and glared about the cavern, seeing betrayal everywhere. She clicked again and muttered to herself, "He said he would have this queen by now, but instead she runs all over the Above Lands, hiding in the cursed Belvoir and pulling the prince along by a string. My string! Well, it is time I pulled that string back out of her tiny hands. Prince Rainere must learn that when he promises me a thing, it is a thing he must do immediately. I hold his oath, I hold the true power over him and I can take away what I have given him just as easily."

Empress Ka-kik turned her attention back to Schiss and he cowered beneath the strength of her fury.

"Tell our Marchant prince that on the day of the full moon he will give his bride to me. Then and only then will his oath to me be fulfilled. Only after he has proved his faithfulness as our king will I let him have the *good* queen back," she cackled. "Or what is left of her bones."

"Yes, Spider Empress," whispered Schiss, bowing as his cold blood ran even colder. There was no reasoning with his mother when she was like this. He had to get word to the prince immediately and warn him of the empress's plans.

"Go now, little son," ordered the empress and waved her forelegs at him. "Go do my bidding and tell the prince he has only the wedding night with his bride, then he must bring her to me, or otherwise." Her eyes glittered malevolently. "I will add his bones to the little queen's."

"Wait, empress!"

Schiss froze at the interruption. He saw his older brother, Ki-ok, one of the Favored, step forward wearing the robes of a councilor. This was a new appointment, and it didn't bode well for Schiss at all. His brother was a bloodthirsty cretin.

Ki-ok bowed low to the empress and moved to stand beside Schiss. "My little brother seems to be full of information today," said Ki-ok in his wispy voice, as he placed a cold hand on the back of Schiss's neck, holding him firmly. "Perhaps before we send him back to his master, the Marchant prince, we should try and discover how it is he can be so sure the queen will come back to the Grey Palace."

Ki-ok turned to Schiss and leaned over him. "For such an insignificant spider, you seem to be very well informed about the humans. I think perhaps there is more you could tell us, hmm? Or is it that you wish for only the Marchant prince to hear all of your talking?"

Schiss looked up into the black-eyed glare of his brother and saw the calculation in his eyes. Schiss almost sighed at the inevitability of the pain that was to come even before the fear of it turned his guts to liquid. His first mistake had been to defend the prince. His second had been to call the queen *good*.

Schiss cast a glance at his mother, the empress, and fell to his knees. "Empress, please, let me deliver this message as you have given it to me. I will return afterward." His voice was drowned out by the maniacal laughter of his mother, and he knew words were useless. As he was dragged from the cavern, Schiss sent a prayer to the Goddess Lune that he would only live long enough to see the Queen Adelena again, even if it was in the hour of his death.

CHAPTER TWENTY-EIGHT

"And Loyalty is a Promise Made to Be Broken"

It wasn't until well after dinner that Adele had a chance to put her newly made resolution into action. She had tucked the children into bed hours ago and was finishing up some paperwork with Tilburn when Captain Lucky entered the office.

"You called for me, Your Majesty?" The captain stood to attention in front of her desk, every inch of him polished and neat despite it being close to midnight.

"Yes, I did," said Adele and hoped no one could hear her heart thudding as she screwed up her courage to confront Lucky about the humiliation this morning. "Thank you, Tilburn. That will be all tonight."

She rarely dismissed anyone who hadn't already decided to leave and she could see Tilburn was keen to argue with her, but she silenced him with a stern look she normally reserved for her children. It worked just as well on the majordomo.

Tilburn ducked his head and gathered up all the papers and scrolls into his arms. "Certainly, Your Majesty."

There was a knock at the door and General Ohrig stepped through just as Tilburn passed him. Adele waited until the door was closed before she sat back in her desk chair and gestured for the two men to sit. The general was just as polished as his captain, but there was an air of ruggedness about him that made him seem as if he had just come in from the outside. His chin was rough with a five o'clock shadow and his eyes were tight at the edges, as though he was squinting into the sun. He was the first to speak over the ticking of the clock in the quiet room.

"Apologies for being late, Your Majesty. I was at a security meeting for the big race tomorrow. There has been a change of plans and security will need to be tightened significantly." His look was slightly accusing, and it puzzled Adele.

"Anything I should know about?" she asked.

General Ohrig shifted to the edge of his chair, his hands planted on his knees. "The Marchant prince is arriving tomorrow with his horses to join the race."

Adele had no chance to hide her surprise. "What? Why?"

General Ohrig sat back in his chair and crossed his arms over his broad chest. He regarded her with a look she found hard to return. "You weren't aware, Your Majesty? I thought it might have been one of the many things you discussed with His Highness during our stay at the Grey Palace."

Adele's heart dropped into her stomach. "He never mentioned it," she replied stiffly. "If you are suggesting that I invited him, Ohrig…"

"I'm not suggesting anything, Your Majesty," said Ohrig politely, but his gaze remained intense, reading her every move. "I merely thought His Highness might have given you fair warning that he was about to break a three-hundred-year ban on Marchants crossing the boundary into Belvoir land, and for the life of me I can't think of why he would do that now."

Adele's stomach churned uncomfortably with a mixture of desire and anxiety at seeing Rainere tomorrow. She had a very good idea as to why he was coming to Belvoir, but she couldn't think of anything more dangerous he could do. *Surely, he didn't mean to expose their relationship here, with most of the court attending the big race tomorrow?*

"I found the prince to be very polite and friendly at his home, Ohrig, but I would never presume to know what he was thinking. I don't know him that well," said Adele and firmly brought the conversation away from the topic of Rainere and back to the reason she had called the meeting, before she lost her nerve. "In fact, if the truth be told, I don't know anyone in this world that well, which is why I wanted to talk to you and Lucky tonight."

Adele turned to the captain. "Lucky, do you remember the boy you met in my rooms this morning?"

"Yes, Your Majesty, Charlie." Lucky focused on a point just to the side of her head and his cheeks flushed slightly. Adele almost sighed with impatience. This man was supposed to be a solider for God's sake!

"That's right, his name is Charlie," she nodded and turned to General Ohrig. "Lucky will have told you that there was a boy discovered in my room this morning dressed in my clothing, after he had taken the luxury of a bath in my chambers. What you might not know is that this boy is the exact same boy who was discovered in my bedchamber yesterday wearing a Carparell squire's uniform."

She let the silence hang for a moment as both men stared at her.

"I can tell you that Charlie did not have my permission to be there at either time, and both times, he was armed with a weapon."

Ohrig and Lucky exchanged an alarmed glance.

"Surely not, Your Majesty!"

Adele frowned at her captain. "It does strike me as fairly odd, Lucky, that a young boy could completely avoid detection despite the fact that my bedroom is guarded at night by my own Queen's Guard. The boy wasn't even apprehended until he had almost touched me as I slept."

Captain Lucky's blue eyes were clouded with confusion. "But Your Majesty, you were the one who defended the boy. It is not my business to investigate those who you wish to keep secret from us…"

Adele held up a finger. "But it is your business, Lucky. It is very much your business to know exactly who comes and goes from my private rooms while I am asleep! Or my children's rooms, for that matter. It frightens me to think that a mere boy managed to slip past you twice."

"With all due respect, Your Majesty," interrupted Ohrig. "While I understand what you are saying, you also helped to hide this Charlie character from us by giving him an alibi both times. Though I am disappointed not one of your QGs managed to recognize the boy from yesterday, they can hardly be blamed for not examining the situation too closely. But I presume you have a point to make?"

Adele raised her eyebrows at Ohrig's surly tone. Her instincts told her he was close to boiling over. The bombshell of the prince's imminent arrival and this conversation were making him feel very anxious.

Well, welcome to my world, thought Adele grimly. *My whole life is a dangerous bloody surprise in Evendaar.*

"I do have a point actually." Adele smiled tightly at Ohrig and tried not to let him get under her skin. "Gentlemen, I know that you are both new to your posts in the Queen's Guard and that you have an actual queen to guard now, just as I am new to being a queen. But remember, Evendaar is not my world. It is your world and I do not have the luxury of living as though my life won't get turned upside down again. I need to be able to keep an eye on things around me where people do not suspect I can see them, and I need to have ears where people will not expect I can hear them. The safety of my children depends on the fact that I remain vigilant at all times. Charlie is someone I have very recently found who is in the right position to help me in this regard. I kept him secret from you because trust does not come easily to me and I wanted to be sure he could do the job I have given him. But after Leith caught him in my room this morning and Charlie invented the cover of being the royal consort I realized it will be impossible to hide him from you."

"So, the boy is not, err…?" Captain Lucky asked cautiously, still not able to say the words.

"So the boy is not my consort, no, Lucky." Adele grimaced in disgust. "Rest assured, I much prefer men to children in my bed. But unfortunately, it was the only story that Charlie could think up on the spot to match the circumstances he found himself in, as humiliating as it was for me."

Lucky nodded. Adele was surprised at the expression of relief on the young captain's face, and how much it affected her. She understood now how much he needed her to be a perfect woman as well as a perfect queen. She could only imagine how his idealism would falter if he knew about her and Rainere. Adele looked back to General Ohrig. His expression was shrewd and combined with something that looked like admiration.

"I understand your position completely, Your Majesty," he said. "In fact, I think it's one of the wisest things you could have done, and in your place, I would act in the same way."

Adele almost smiled and enjoyed basking in the glow of Ohrig's tacit approval for a rare moment, though she could hear the "But" too loudly in his voice to ignore it.

"But with all due respect, Your Majesty, you are choosing to trust a young man who was stupid enough to get caught in your bedchamber in the night, with you in it. I hardly think that this Charlie is capable of the discretion that you are entrusting him with. Perhaps you should allow me to choose a better candidate for the position. There are organizations who deal in such things, and you need someone with proper training and connections."

Adele frowned at Ohrig and he frowned right back. It was disconcerting when Adele realized with a start how quickly she had gotten used to people agreeing, no matter how dishonestly, with every word she said. But General Ohrig's face was free of guile. He was just as concerned about her safety as she was, maybe more so as he didn't even trust her to vouchsafe for herself.

"I want to meet this Charlie and have a chance to interview him before you get in much deeper with all this," said the general. "It could be that the boy is working well for you, or it could be that he is selling your secrets on to the highest bidder."

"Ohrig, I don't want you scaring him," said Adele. She panicked slightly at the idea of Ohrig interrogating Charlie, but also at the idea that he might be right. Adele knew nothing about Charlie except that he worked for Rainere. "Charlie and I have a delicate relationship based on a simple understanding. I don't know how he would react to an interview with you."

She cast a glance at Lucky to gauge which side he was on, but the captain had become fascinated with the patterned carpet at his feet. It was clear he had no desire to add to the heated discussion.

"Is that a no, Your Majesty?" Ohrig asked and his eyebrows beetled even more tightly down over his pale blue eyes.

Adele forced herself to take a breath and calm down. She had too much to lose to reveal her whole hand to Ohrig now. Rainere was coming to Belvoir and who knew what that could mean for her in the days ahead.

"It's not a 'no', general, but it's not a free run with Charlie, either. I will speak to him and explain the situation before you meet him," Adele relaxed back into her chair. "Thankfully, only the QGs saw Charlie coming out of my chamber this morning and I would like to keep it that way. I don't want to hear any gossip about me having a taste for teenagers traveling through the manor while we are here. Can we rely on the discretion of your men, general?"

General Ohrig looked very much like he wanted to say something else, but he held his tongue and for that Adele was grateful. "Yes, of course, Your Majesty."

"Your honor is safe with your Queen's Guard, Your Majesty," agreed Captain Lucky a smile coloring his formal tone.

Adele couldn't help but be pleased by his rekindled pride in her. She felt a rush of maternal responsibility to her young captain and smiled back. "Now, are there any changes to the schedule to discuss, with His Highness coming tomorrow?" she asked, changing the subject.

"Nothing that can't wait until morning, Your Majesty," replied Ohrig and his tight tone let her know he was still upset with her. "I'm sure Mr. Tilburn will be able to inform you about any changes to the day and the welcoming ceremony that will be held in the prince's honor. I believe Prince Bertrand is still working out all the protocols now for breaking the ban."

"Wonderful," said Adele, pointedly ignoring Ohrig's attitude and stood up to let both men know the meeting was over. They followed her lead.

"But, please be assured, Your Majesty, that even though His Highness the prince will be rendered powerless by the curse on Belvoir manor, we will not underestimate his strength in other ways." Ohrig gave Adele a knowing look which made her stomach clench. "We will keep eyes on Prince Rainere at all times of the day and night. He has no legal authority here, so we will be able to accompany you with him at any, and all, times."

"Great," Adele forced herself to smile at the general. *Ohrig doesn't know anything*, she consoled herself, *there is no way he would be able to keep quiet about it if he did.* As bad as she felt lying to Ohrig, she knew she needed to protect Rainere more. If anybody knew about them, he would be the one who would bear the brunt of the danger.

The general and Captain Lucky both bowed and took their leave.

Adele sat back down in her chair and stared absently at the desk before her, her fingers tracing the whorls of the wood, dark and light grains blending and separating again in a natural paisley. The meeting had not gone as well as she had hoped. Adele only now realized how much she had wanted Ohrig to support her decision to trust Charlie. It hurt her feelings that he obviously did not. Being more honest with the general had also left the door open for Ohrig to be more honest with her, too, and she wasn't sure she was going to like where that door led. It was going to be very difficult to laugh off this last disagreement they now had with each other.

A warm breeze blew in through the open window and lifted the damp stands of hair at the back of her neck.

Oh God, Rainere is going to be here tomorrow! A heady flash of desire shook her body and she felt a pulse of pleasure deep inside as her magic responded to the thought of seeing Rainere again.

Adele grabbed the waste bin just in time to heave violently.

Chapter Twenty-Nine

"Decepting as Love Tastes"

Charlie had been waiting for hours behind the secret door in the queen's bathroom. Though his little timepiece didn't work in this magic-free house, he guessed it was some time after midnight before he judged it safe to creep out and conceal himself in the window seat of the queen's bedroom. She wasn't yet in bed, but he could hear her talking next door in the study, so he figured it wouldn't be too long.

His wait was only interrupted by Blondie, who came in bringing a tray laden with biscuits and hot tea for the queen's late supper. Charlie watched with interest from his place inside the drapes as the blonde beauty turned back the covers of the queen's bed, studying the sheets for longer than was necessary and sniffing at the pillows, before she moved off to quietly lay her ear against the door to the queen's office, straining to hear what was being said. The sound of a door slamming in the next room sent her running to the bedroom door, where she abruptly stopped, patted her hair, and calmly left the bedroom.

Curious, thought Charlie. *What game is Blondie playing at?* But the chiming of the clock on the mantelpiece reminded him why he was here and what he had to do tonight.

Just give her the box and leave, he told himself firmly. *Don't dawdle, and don't get caught, and* don't *watch her open it.* He thought of the bundle of stolen clothing and food he had left under his little pallet in the basement room downstairs. With that and the gold bracelet, he had a chance to make it to the border of Unisia and maybe to the farms beyond. There he could disappear, far from the clutches of the Boss and far from the bizarre love story of the witch queen and the black prince.

He tensed as the queen entered her bedroom. She was carrying a wicker wastebin and looked exhausted. She took the bin into the bathroom and Charlie heard the sound of rushing water before she returned without it and threw herself down on the couch nearest the window seat. Charlie watched as she poured herself a cup of tea and screwed up his courage to confront her. *Maybe she was furious with him for getting caught, or maybe she was going to laugh about it like she had before?* Whatever her reaction, he needed to do this one last thing before he could be done with her for good.

Charlie stepped out from behind the curtain and silently hopped down from the window seat. "Evening, Y'Majesty!"

The queen almost jumped out of her skin at hearing his voice behind her. Charlie couldn't explain why her fear made him smile, but it did.

"Charlie!" she scolded, making him grin wider. "How the hell...?"

"I was just behind this curtain, Y'Majesty, taking in the view." He risked a wink. The queen looked even prettier when she was all pink and embarrassed. His sharp eyes noticed that she had loosened the ribbons on the front of her gown, and her slip underneath was decorated with gold flowers. Charlie flopped onto the chair opposite the queen and forced himself to look at her eyes. They'd parted badly last time, and he needed to know she wasn't going to kill him after he handed over the prince's gift.

"So, Charlie?" began the queen. She said it in a funny way, with her lilting accent, *char-lee* instead of *char-lay*. "Did the prince ever tell you that he was coming here himself? Because that is something I really could have done with knowing." She clenched her hands together tightly in front of her chest and obviously didn't realize that it pushed her breasts together in a thoroughly distracting way.

Charlie leaned forward and took a handful of biscuits off the tea tray and shoved them in his mouth. He belatedly remembered his manners, asking, "May I?" and sprayed out a few crumbs from his too-full mouth. The queen gave him a look but nodded before she stood up and started pacing the room with small quick steps, speaking in confusing half sentences.

"I know that Rainere wants to..."

"But what can he be…?"

"This is so dangerous for both…"

Charlie slipped his hand into his pocket and found the little black box. His fingers slipped over the slick lacquered sides of it, automatically feeling for a join in the edges. His moral misgivings flooded back from where he had managed to keep them at bay in his mind as he watched the queen work herself up into an anxious frenzy, her expression was heartbreaking.

What in the name of the Goddess did this sweet woman want with a nasty, great wizard like the black prince when she can have any man in the kingdom? Maybe she is as crazy as the Marchant prince? The Devil himself knows that the Boss had warned me so many times that she is an evil witch.

But the Boss was a liar, and Charlie's instincts were usually pretty good when it came to people. The queen didn't set off any of his internal alarm bells. She just didn't look that evil. Mostly she looked scared, and sort of like she was going to be sick.

"Charlie, please tell me?" begged the queen. "Did the prince give you a message for me? Anything at all that might help me to understand why he is risking coming here now?"

"Well, he wasn't happy," began Charlie slowly. He had an odd and unhelpful desire to protect the queen from the truth.

"Why?"

"Well, after he brought me back to life, he read your note and seemed a bit…err…disappointed with it…and by that, I mean, very pissed off." Charlie grabbed another handful of biscuits to avoid looking at her stricken expression.

"I made him angry again," she whispered. "But why? How could he expect more from me when I couldn't even be sure it was safe to write?"

Charlie raised an eyebrow at her and the expression in his eyes was wise though his chin was speckled with crumbs. "I don't think reasonable reactions are the black prince's strong suit, Y'Majesty," he said drily. Charlie tried to ignore the stab of guilt in his gut at what he was about to do. "But he did give me a present to give to you, and he said to tell you that he was serious about you and him. Though his tone was a bit dark at the time."

He produced the prince's gift from his pocket. Their eyes met over the little black box as he stood up and held it out to her. Charlie had the uncomfortable sensation that she could see through his eyes, right down into his soul.

"I know it looks horribly sinister, Majesty, but I'm sure it's fine to open," he said, doing his best not to break his word to the prince, but he couldn't help the urge to warn her. His arm shook a little as he held it out, but the queen only stared at the box.

"Good things do come in small packages," replied Queen Adelena mysteriously.

Charlie frowned. "And so do a lot of dangerous things."

"Are you trying to warn me about what's inside this box, Charlie?" whispered the queen, her hazel eyes opening even wider.

I don't care what happens to her. I only care about what will happen to me if I don't give it to her, Charlie reminded himself firmly. He forced himself to smile. "Just take the damn box, Y'Majesty," he said mildly.

The queen reached out and took the box out of Charlie's hand. Charlie worked hard not to flinch but he took a step away as the queen examined the box, turning it over and over again.

"How do I open it?" she asked. "Is it magic, or a blood seal or something?"

Charlie shrugged. "Maybe. I didn't see what he put in there and when he came back I was still in quite a bit of pain from almost dying so wasn't at my most observant."

"Oh, that's right you said Rainere saved your life!" the queen gasped. "Charlie, I'm so sorry, what happened?"

Though he appreciated her sudden, if somewhat belated concern, Charlie was gobsmacked that the queen had got completely the wrong end of the stick. "He was the one trying to kill me!" he said incredulously, but the queen was distracted by a noise at the front door.

She turned to him, her expression panicked. "Charlie, that might be Ohrig so go hide, I'll find you later." She looked about wildly for a place to hide the box and ended up shoving it under a dressing table covered in make-up pots and various crystal ornaments.

Charlie stood slowly and brushed the crumbs from his shirt. He felt an odd reluctance to leave now he knew this was the last time he would probably see the queen as he was running away tonight.

"You wouldn't happen to have another box about that size in your possession would you, Y'Majesty? Probably made of wood and filled with something incredibly valuable?" Charlie felt no real hope as he asked, but he had to try one last time to find the object the Boss had sent him to steal in the first place.

The queen looked at him in confusion and irritation. "What? Are you crazy Charlie? Go, it's time to go!" She pointed to the door, but Charlie shook his head.

"There is a better way out through your bathroom," he said. "Come and see."

The queen followed him into the bathroom and he smiled at her surprise when she peered into the open door in the wainscoting. She was standing so close to him that he could see the lavender blue of the shadows beneath her eyes, and the palest freckles that dotted across her nose. Her hair brushed against his shoulder.

Charlie didn't even know his hands had slipped around her waist until she pulled them off.

"Charlie!" she whispered crossly. "You have to disappear for a bit. Go and do your Carparell squire act, and when the prince is here you can carry messages for me. We will be watched too closely to be able to do much more, I'm sure."

She handed his hands back to him. Charlie melted at the touch of her skin against his and a delicious lassitude fell over him. He had something to do…it was important…what was it? But all he could focus on were her soft pink lips that beckoned him forward.

"Come and find me tomorrow," whispered the queen, as she disappeared back into her bedroom, leaving the scent of flowers behind. It wasn't until the door clicked shut that the spell was broken and Charlie stood shivering in the bathroom, completely confused and mightily uncomfortable. He adjusted the front of his trousers and shook his head to dispel the last of the fog of desire that had gripped him so hard.

Goddess be damned! he thought as he stumbled out of the bathroom and into the secret tunnel in the wall. *That woman really is a witch.*

Chapter Thirty

"Anticipation is the Fuel for Love's Fire"

Adele shifted slightly, so no one could kick her in the face, but then accidentally put her hand onto a puddle of drool pooling by her knee and almost gave the game away by groaning in disgust.

Aaron giggled and was quickly shushed by Natalie. Even the three very overgrown puppies lay with their heads on their paws, quiet as mice. Stella burrowed her face deeper into Adele's neck as the royal family all grinned gleefully at each other.

"I won't ask you again!" Tilburn was shouting, thoroughly incensed. "Where are Her Majesty and the children?"

"I don't know Mr. Tilburn, really I don't," replied Lady Olivia calmly. "But I'll thank you to stop shouting at me."

"Really, not very gentlemanly, Sir, yelling at a lady like that," interjected Captain Lucky. From under the table the children watched Lucky's boots shift as he re-crossed his ankles. "I've already told you that just as soon as I finish breakfast I'll go and look for them."

At this Natalie clapped both hands over her mouth to keep from laughing.

"Well, I never! In all my life! Breakfast, when there is so much to be done!" Tilburn blustered. Adele could almost hear him turning purple.

"You have my word as a captain, Sir," answered Lucky.

"Breakfast, indeed! Well you have your *breakfast,* Captain Lucky," snapped Tilburn. "I shall find Her Majesty myself, and she will hear about this insubordination, you can be assured of that!"

Everyone under the table listened hard as Tilburn stalked from the room still muttering threats.

"Is it really insubordination, captain?" asked Lady Olivia curiously. "Can Mr. Tilburn get you into trouble?"

"Not at all, Lady Olivia," answered Lucky. "No one commands the Queen's Guard but the queen herself. Speaking of which, where is our royal family? Are we certain they haven't disappeared altogether? Perhaps they are hiding in the tea cups?"

"No, but I do hear giggling, captain," said Lady Olivia. "Perhaps we should try and find the source of it?"

"Hmmm, could they be…" Captain Lucky swung up the tablecloth, surprising the children. "*Under the table!*" he shouted.

The children screamed so loudly it set the dogs off barking and Adele had to cover Stella's ears to stop her from wailing in fright.

The family climbed out from under the table, the children ecstatic with the success of their game. Driving Mr. Tilburn mad was becoming a popular pastime with them. Lady Olivia tried to settle the children back down to their breakfast, but with the dogs stealing bacon off the table and Aaron insisting Captain Lucky repeat the "under the table" gag, it was an exercise in futility.

Adele smiled at all of the noisy chaos in the sunny breakfast room and pulled Stella in for a firmer cuddle. The nannies had already been dismissed to organize the children's clothing for the big day, so Adele didn't have to share her baby's cuddles with anyone else just now. Despite how useful they were, Adele still felt a lingering jealousy that her children had been so happy to replace her affection with the three nannies. She had never had to share her children with anyone before and it always hurt her feelings a little when the baby, in particular, went to another woman.

Adele noticed that Natalie was drawing with a charcoal pencil on her cloth napkin and leaned over to tell her to stop making a mess but stopped when she saw what her daughter had drawn.

"Natalie, darling, that is beautiful! What is it?"

"It's the little movie box from Prince Rainere's labora-tormy," Natalie replied, looking up at Adele with a proud smile.

"Laboratory," Adele corrected her as she examined the intricate sketch of the machine from the Grey Palace.

"Yes, labora-tormy," agreed Natalie. "See, that's where the bad thought goes."

Adele looked at her daughter with new eyes. When had her little six-year-old started growing up so much? "Natalie, it's one of the cleverest things you've ever drawn."

Natalie smiled but her expression turned wistful. "I wish I could go back to the Grey Palace again," she said.

"So you can see the laboratory again?" Adele touched her daughter's hand.

"So I can see *him* again," Natalie sighed and continued with her sketch.

Adele blinked. Obviously, Natalie hadn't forgotten her professed love for the prince, as she often did with the others like, for instance, QG Leith who had passed very quickly out of her affections for one reason or another.

"Natalie…"

Suddenly the breakfast room doors banged open and General Ohrig came striding into the room, his dress boots clumping on the floorboards. "What's all this I hear about the royal family going missing? Tilburn is shrieking fit to bust up and down the corridors searching for you all."

He approached the table and greeted Adele's smile with a bow. "But I can see you are all accounted for, except for Prince Aaron. May I ask if you ate him for breakfast?"

A loud giggling from under the table spoiled the surprise.

"Or is he...?" General Ohrig snapped up the tablecloth and shouted: "*Under the table!*" making Lady Olivia drop her tea-cup and sending Stella whimpering into her mother's neck again. But Natalie and Aaron were both crying with laughter as their puppies went berserk. Adele giggled along with her children. Whatever else that could be said about the people of her court, they all loved children dearly.

The dogs had just about calmed down when Bertie and Pere Raven came bursting in and set them off again. Aaron slipped under the table when he saw the newcomers, but Adele tried to head the game off before it went too far.

"Bertie, Pere Raven, how nice to see you this early in the morning," she said warmly. She was in a good mood today and could barely keep in her seat with excitement.

"And you, Your Majesty," smiled Bertie, looking around at the chaos of his breakfast room. "I have to say you are some of the noisiest and troublesome guests we've had in a while. I've only just heard this morning that you'd all disappeared. Yet here you are, yelling up a storm and eating all my good breakfast bacon."

Bertie and Pere Raven took seats on either side of Adele and General Ohrig sat at the end of the table opposite her. Despite his good humor with the children he looked tense and Adele avoided his eye.

"Uncle Bertie, are we really your worst guests?" asked Natalie curiously. Prince Bertrand II had insisted the children address him as Uncle Bertie when they arrived. He said that being called "prince" in his own home felt like carrying an umbrella inside, silly and unnecessary.

Bertie chuckled. "Not at all, my girl! We had some smelly cowherds from my wife's family come down from the high country to stay with us for two weeks. They all smelled of cow poop and refused to take baths. It was disgusting! You all smell quite lovely."

Natalie giggled and returned to her drawing.

"So, Your Majesty, I am quite ecstatic that you could be with us on this most momentous of racing days." Bertie was pink and shiny with glee, his eyes sparkling with excitement as he piled his plate high with bacon and soft rolls. "It's been almost three hundred years since the Marchant family has participated in our carnival. Three hundred! And today we will make legal and racing history by repealing the ban on Marchant royals crossing our borders. It really is wonderful that your presence in our humble home has been the reason for Prince Rainere to finally come out of hermitage and race his famous chargers alongside our own today."

"Oh, I really don't think it was me…" Adele protested, but felt her words catch in her throat as General Ohrig's gaze fell on her.

"But, it absolutely was, Your Majesty!" Bertie blithely continued. "He stated in his letter that he felt that your presence at Belvoir marked a new beginning for the nation of Unisia as well as a new…what was it?…*integration* of the Marchant family back into society. Pretty thrilling if you ask me!"

Bertie rubbed his hands together and grinned around the table. "This is going to make the horse market so exciting next week. Everyone is going to want to stud my Blue Streak when he beats a Marchant charger."

"Are you so sure that Blue Streak can win against a Marchant horse, Bertie?" asked Pere Rave doubtfully. "I've never seen one run, but I've heard of their legendary speed, as everyone has. Apparently dark magic was bred right into their bones."

"Pah!" Bertie waved away the very idea. "It won't matter a jot when they are on Belvoir land. His horses will only have their breeding and training to rely on, just like everyone else." He held his finger in the air, a proud grin on his face. "And that is how I know Blue Streak will take the prize!"

Adele sat back in her chair. She was still stunned that Rainere was risking so much to come to Belvoir, but a little part of her couldn't help but feel thrilled that he would act so recklessly just to see her again.

"Uncle Bertie what will happen to Prince Rainere when he comes here? He told me he is a creature of magic. Won't the curse in Belvoir hurt him?" Natalie asked and looked so stricken that Bertie immediately calmed himself to soothe her.

"Oh no, my poppet, I'm sure Prince Rainere will be fine. According to the good doctor, Pere Raven, the prince will just age like you and me when he gets here. He was such a young man when he received the immortality spell that I'm sure a few days won't matter much to him."

"But do you know for sure?" insisted Natalie.

"I know for sure, Princess Natalie," interjected Pere Raven. "As a student of magic, a priest of our Goddess Serena's church and a doctor of health I can tell you that Prince Rainere will be fine. And I'm sure he won't mind being two days older if he gets to see you again."

The priest beamed at Natalie until she smiled back.

"He won't mind," she said. "He is so strong and clever."

"Do you like His Highness, Princess Natalie?" asked Bertie curiously. "You didn't think he was scary when you met him?" Bertie glanced over at Adele to gauge her reaction to the conversation, but she was too busy shoving toast in her mouth to say anything.

"I love him," said Natalie with a shrug. "He is so handsome and his Palace is full of so many interesting things. Some things he lets me touch because I am big, but other things he says I can study when I'm older. He is very magic, you know, but he doesn't scare me."

A nervous laugh bubbled up and out of Adele and filled the silence that had fallen over the table at Natalie's answer. Lady Olivia was the first to join in with her and soon everyone was chuckling. Even Aaron, who was still under the table.

"Well, if that's the case, you must be at my side to greet His Highness when he arrives later this morning, because he doesn't scare me either," said Bertie with a wink.

"Yes, but I'm not scared because I love him. You aren't scared because he doesn't have his magic here," said Natalie with her usual sledgehammer wit.

"Natalie!" Adele was mortified by her daughter's reply. "Apologize to Uncle Bertie immediately. That was a rude thing to say."

"But he's laughing," protested Natalie, pointing at the old prince.

"It's fine, Your Majesty. Princess Natalie has my measure," chuckled Bertie. "I think we shall make a fine team when we greet Prince Rainere and present him to your mother."

Adele smiled quickly at Bertie but shot Natalie a look to let her daughter know this wasn't over despite Bertie's forgiving nature. She signaled for Lady Olivia to help her gather the children together. She really needed a minute to get her emotions under control and sitting at the table with General Ohrig watching her so closely wasn't helping. As the royal family hustled from the room, Ohrig managed to catch Adele's eye, though she did her best to avoid it.

"Majesty, if we could take a quick meeting?" He kept his voice low but Lady Olivia heard him as she walked past on the arm of Captain Lucky.

"Oh, general, can it wait please? Her Majesty has got so much to do to prepare for the day," begged Lady Olivia and fluttered her eyelashes prettily.

General Ohrig's icy blue gaze proved he was immune to the lady's charms, but Lucky was already bowing, his cheeks pink.

"It's about a certain issue that we discussed last night," insisted the general.

"I'm sorry but it will have to wait," said Adele. "Maybe you can see me before the prince arrives in a few hours?"

General Ohrig gave a tight-lipped nod and Adele tried not to feel chagrined by his anger. There *was* too much to do this morning. Rainere was coming and Adele had to find another wastebin before her breakfast could show itself again. Sidestepping the general, Adele hurried out after her children and their puppies, praying she made it back to her room in time.

CHAPTER THIRTY-ONE

"And Look How It Burns"

Prince Rainere was vibrating from the radiation thrown off by the power of the portal in front of him. He almost couldn't stand it. He put a hand on the neck of his horse, Titor, who stood beside him and steadied himself. The beast had closed its eyes to the brightly shining portal, but that was the only discomfort it showed at being so close to it.

"Three days, master," Grotto was saying. "That is all we have until the next full moon. Three short days to get the marriage ceremony underway and your ascension completed before Empress Ka-kik requires you to bring the queen before her. You must not dally in Belvoir but bring her back to the Grey Palace immediately. I sent a message to the priest to join us before the sun sets today."

Rainere didn't bother to concentrate too closely on what Grotto was saying. He had heard it a hundred times by now. Instead, he flexed his hands into fists and felt a jolt as the power of the Gift of Life surged through him in an intoxicating stream. Grotto had convinced him to take in as much of the Gift as he could the second time, not only to heal after Adele had depleted him, but also to give him the strength to suffer the absence of the immortality curse when he stepped onto Belvoir lands again. His little experiment crossing the portal with that urchin messenger had let him know how weak he would become. It had taken a huge effort just to keep on his feet as all the magic had dropped away from his body. He would need all the strength he could get to last an entire day, and possibly a night, without his magic.

Rainere examined the portal before him for faults. He'd had to work hard to make it big enough to fit Titor, and he still wasn't sure that it would be able to maintain its integrity as such a large creature passed through it. The spell he had used was from the time of the last great war, when portals had been used to move huge warships across the lands of Unisia, and he wasn't sure he'd read it correctly. He gave one of the seams a cautious poke and it made an angry fizzing noise. Rainere shrugged mentally, it mattered not. He would use the portal regardless of the danger. Adelena was waiting for him on the other side, and the two days they had been apart had been agony. He refused to be away from her any longer, even if he had to walk to Belvoir from here himself.

His heart ached in his chest and adrenalin skittered through his blood at the thought of her. Ever since their last night together when she had ripped into him so deeply and he had heard the voice of the Goddess whispering words of love to him, Rainere had felt like a different man. He had agreed to imbibe the Gift of Life with a recklessness that had never been his way, soaking it up until his blood was saturated with power. He never once thought of the cost involved as he had always done, but instead only thought of the carnal pleasure it would give Adelena to drink this much power from him when they next lay together. The memory of Adelena's gasps whispered in his ears, making him shiver and roll his shoulders.

Grotto touched his arm lightly. "Please, master. Be careful. There will be no wizards at the carnival, but the queen will still have her guards to protect her."

Rainere laughed and the sound was slightly crazed, even to his own ears. "What will they protect her from, Grotto? I'm just a humble man over there." He chuckled again and the sound reverberated around the deep caverns and tunnels of the portal station under the palace. The surrounding archways of other portals, dead from disuse, gaped darkly and returned his laughter back to him in echoes.

"Master," whispered Grotto and his voice was infused with all the worry and hope that was contained in his old frame. "Just please, bring her back."

Rainere gave his manservant a nod and pulled his jacket down firmly. It was old and the fit was slightly too small for him, but it was important that he wear the proper racing attire at the carnival. Rainere gave the portal another once-over. If only he had had Schiss here to test it for him, but the little man-spider had not been seen for days.

The prince firmly grasped the bridle of his horse. The drunken giddiness that threatened to overwhelm him finally passed, and he took a step toward the glittering portal, green sparks showering him already. He stepped through, pulling Titor by his side, and was gone.

Chapter Thirty-Two

"Running Out of Time"

A dry breeze danced through the banners and flags of the pavilions surrounding the racecourse, chasing up puffs of fine dust and drying out throats. The green canvas walls of Prince Bertrand's pavilion snapped and cracked in the breeze, making the children's puppies bark and whine.

"Do you think this wind is going to have much of an effect on the horses, Bertie?" asked Pere Raven anxiously, his naked brow furrowed with concern.

Bertie grinned widely. "Only on that sorry lot of Carparells!" he cackled and stuck his finger in the air. "Ah-ha, it's the North Wind! The North Wind always favors the strong. We are champions for sure, my poppets. Err…may the best house win, Your Majesty," said Bertie in a nod to Adele's St. Lucidis heritage. She waved away his insincere words, and searched the crowd of racers for the huge, black charger and its rider. Adele shifted in her seat and took a sip of water. The temperature had climbed after lunch, bleaching the blue sky and dissolving the clouds. Adele was so hot she could hardly breathe in her pretty, but very tight, bodice.

Natalie and Aaron cheered along with all the other Belvoir children in the royal pavilion as the horses and their riders assembled at the starting gates. Adele heard the murmurs of her Queen's Guard swapping bets from where they stood in a line behind her. The Marchant prince had only brought one horse with him, and his doubtful success on running an untried animal was the cause of much excitement. Only the general was silent, and Adele could swear she felt him watching her every reaction to Rainere being on the course. He had remained no more than a few feet away from her the minute the prince had materialized a yard from the boundary of the Belvoir Estate and been welcomed to cross in an inordinately complicated ceremony involving prayers to the Goddess, the sprinkling of some sort of holy water and of course the spilling of blood, a few drops of Rainere's and Bertie's combined. Rainere had remained cool and aloof, but Adele had been a sweaty mess of desire by the time it was all over. Rainere was wearing a jacket so tight she could see almost every muscle of his arms and back deliciously outlined. The only proof she had of his own internal conflict was the slight tremor that shuddered through him when she took his hand to ceremoniously pull him over the boundary between Marchant lands and the Belvoir Estate.

"Look, there he is, Your Majesty!" squealed Lady Olivia in excitement as Prince Rainere and Titor rode into their starting gate. The tall black horse walking steadily and not showing any of the skittishness of the other mounts as their riders struggled to get them into their own gates. Adele felt a moment of pride that Rainere's horse was as exceptional as the man who rode him.

"My, doesn't he look handsome in his black velvet," sighed Lady Olivia, and giggled at the sharp look that Natalie gave her. "Never mind, Princess Natalie, I'm sure Prince Rainere would choose you over me any day!"

Adele forced a smile, but her stomach was flip-flopping uncomfortably, and she prayed hard that she wouldn't need to be sick during the race. A rush of desire licked through her veins when she caught sight of Rainere through the bars of the starting gate. She was sure that he was looking at her up on the stage of the pavilion, but an answering roll of nausea soon swamped her stomach again and filled her mouth with sour water, forcing her to look away.

Once the riders had assembled, there was a moment of unnatural silence as thousands of people held their breath. A loud crack like a gunshot rocked out over the crowd, and the horses were off. The noise of the crowd was like the sound of an ocean swell, but it faded into quiet as Adele watched Rainere and Titor leap out of the starting gate. They had started a few lengths behind the leader, Blue Streak, with Golden Pride running forward to claim the second place, and remained in the middle of the pack for the first straight and going into the bend. As the pack rounded the bend and headed down the second straight Titor pulled away, seeming to leap over and above the other horses in his way. Rainere lay low against his mount with his chin down and the black ribbons of his saddle streaming out behind him. The crowd went wild as the Marchant team leaped into the lead, taking the second bend and streaking down the last straight, heading to the finish line.

When Titor crossed the finish line he was in front of the pack by at least three lengths and dashed away as if the race would continue on. Adele watched as Rainere fought to pull his mount under control, eventually slowing the creature and heading back to the finish where the last horses were still crossing the line. He was sitting up tall in the saddle and had thrown back his head, laughing. Adele smiled and tears sprang to her eyes when she saw the entire crowd cheering and calling for Rainere, chants of "Mar-chant! Mar-chant!" filling the air down near the fences. Rainere looked over at her from the course and raised a hand in salute. Adele waved back.

"He won! Prince Rainere won, Mummy!" Natalie was as happy as Adele felt, but for a different reason.

If this is how Rainere is received at the carnival, maybe it won't be so bad for him at the court of the Golden Palace next time, she thought hopefully. *If he can find acceptance here, then...* Her positive thoughts trailed away when she turned and caught the eye of General Ohrig. His blue eyes bore into hers and his mouth was set in a grim line. Adele straightened her shoulders. He could stare all he liked, but the general lived with a prejudice against Marchants that Adele would never share. In fact, perhaps it was time he learned to move on, embrace the new world, and get the hell off her back.

Adele turned her attention to her right and the morose Prince Bertie. Adele thought it was the saddest she had ever seen him and she patted him sympathetically on the arm. It seemed ridiculous to her that the outcome of a five-minute race could be so important to him, but she squashed her smile and tried to look downcast when Bertie took her arm and commiserated with her over Golden Pride's third-place position. Blue Streak had come in second, but obviously that meant little more than an outright loss to Bertie.

Tilburn interrupted them as he swept by, arranging the stage for the winner's awards. He handed Bertie the silver tray with the satin rosettes, but Bertie passed it on to Adele, and only pulled himself to his feet as the riders approached the pavilion. Adele fought not to roll her eyes at his petulance, but found it amusing nonetheless.

The royal party descended the few steps down to the winner's stage that had been built this very morning in front of the royal pavilion. The fresh wood had yet to dry out in the heat and the platform trembled as the children jumped about on it making Adele feel slightly seasick.

The winning three riders rode their horses to the front of the stage, pausing to bow to Queen Adelena and Prince Bertrand before dismounting and handing their reins to waiting stewards. Adele found her vision swimming in and out of focus as Rainere climbed the stairs and stopped mere feet in front of her. She forced herself to breathe and wiped away the sweat running down her temple with a silk handkerchief. Her magic sparked and surged within her, making her shake, and she needed to hold Bertie's arm to remain upright.

Rainere looked regal and dignified despite being covered in dust and smelling of horse sweat. He bowed respectfully and waited as Bertie and Adele presented the third place ribbons to the St. Lucidis rider and then the young female rider of Blue Streak.

"Really, Josie? Second place. You don't think you could have pushed him harder?" muttered Bertie unkindly to the young woman who blushed furiously beneath her freckles, tears filling her brown eyes.

"I'm so sorry, Your Highness, Blue and I just couldn't keep up."

Bertie only grunted in reply.

"Prince Rainere, congratulations on your victory," interrupted Adele as the prince stepped forward to receive his ribbon. Bertie put his hand out to take the ribbon from Adele and pin it to Rainere's chest.

"Yes, my heartfelt congratulations, Your Highness," agreed Bertie dolefully. "It was a wonderful race, and your Titor really was fantastic out there. Who would have thought, eh?"

Prince Rainere nodded and stepped back again. "Titor had a hard time taking the length back from Blue Streak, Your Highness, so I believe a certain amount of luck was involved in our win today," he said graciously.

Bertie looked up hopefully. "You really think? There is a steeplechase this weekend, you know. Do you think you would be interested in running Titor in the woods? Perhaps he wouldn't do as well without a pack to follow?"

"I couldn't say, Your Highness, but it is very kind of you to invite us to race again. I'm sure we would find it a great challenge," said Rainere and Adele could tell he was amused by the twitch at the side of his mouth. She remembered what his lips felt like on her skin and bit the inside of her cheek to keep from sighing.

Rainere turned to her and the sunlight hit his eyes, illuminating their deep velvet green. Desire rocketed through Adele's already over heated body and her ears started ringing as her vision shrunk down to a pinpoint. "Your Majesty?"

Adele heard a female voice shriek, then the clatter of a falling tray and a baby's cry before the world went dark and she was falling.

Chapter Thirty-Three

"What Comfort There Lies in Dreaming"

Adele awoke to the feel of a cold compress on her forehead and the scent of lavender in the air. There were people talking softly in the room.

"I'm not at all surprised she collapsed this afternoon, Pere Raven." It was the voice of Lady Olivia. "The queen has been trying to be discreet, but she had been ill the entire time we've been here. I have not seen her keep one meal down for more than a few hours."

Adele was mortified that Lady Olivia had seen her throwing up. *Surely it couldn't have been that often, though?*

"Hmmm, I wonder if perhaps she has an ailment of the gut caught from the water here? The water at Belvoir can affect visitors oddly sometimes," said Pere Raven.

Adele decided she had been discussed enough and opened her eyes, yawning widely to alert her audience to the fact she had woken up. She tried to sit up, but her head swam again and she lay back down, groaning. The cheerful visage of Pere Raven came into her view, followed by the concerned smile of Lady Olivia.

"Your Majesty, it is good to see you awake finally," he smiled and patted her shoulder before taking the pulse on her wrist. "You gave us quite a turn for a while there."

"What happened?" croaked Adele.

"I believe you simply fainted, Your Majesty. What with the heat, lack of food and that terribly restrictive dress you are wearing, it was just all too much for you."

Adele groaned, embarrassed. Fainting had been almost a regular occurrence on Earth, but she had never had an episode here in Unisia. She hoped it wasn't something new that was starting. This certainly wouldn't help General Ohrig's opinion that she was a fragile female in need of his protection.

"Luckily, His Highness, Prince Rainere was at hand to catch you before you fell to the ground," said the Priest shaking his head. "I swear I've never seen a man move so fast!"

"The prince carried you the whole way to your bedroom, Your Majesty," said Lady Olivia giving her a wide-eyed look. "He even refused to give you over to General Ohrig who wanted to carry you himself, and he would only leave your side when Pere Raven promised him that you were just asleep. He was *very* concerned for you."

"How kind of him," murmured Adele, laying back on her pillows and avoiding Lady Olivia's curious gaze. She smoothed her hands down over the embroidery of the sheets and tried to ignore the frisson of excitement that Lady Olivia's words caused in her chest.

"Did the children see me faint? Were they frightened for me?" she asked, and at the same moment heard her children in the corridor beyond her bedroom door. She smiled at the sound of them battering someone with questions.

The children burst into the room with Prince Rainere and Bertie in tow. Bertie held Stella in his arms and Natalie had clamped hold of Rainere's forearm. Only Aaron jumped on the bed to kiss his mother, but he soon jumped off again when a maid came in carrying a tray of cakes and fruit. Aaron greeted the young woman by name and she ruffled his hair affectionately.

"That's Mary," said Aaron as the maid bobbed to Adele and left. "She makes sugar buns, too."

"So wonderful to see you looking better, Your Majesty!" Bertie beamed at her.

Adele gingerly pushed herself up to sit, feeling very self-conscious in a room full of people with her in bed and her bodice ribbons untied. "I'm so sorry to have made such a fuss, Bertie. I have no idea what came over me."

Bertie waved her apology away with large flapping gestures. "We are just relieved you are well, Your Majesty."

Adele finally dared to look at Rainere. He was freshly showered and dressed in a clean suit of black silk instead of his tight velvet coat. He looked uncomfortable surrounded by the domestic scene in the bedroom, and his eyes shifted from person to person restlessly. Adele wanted his gaze back on her.

"I understand it was you who caught me, Your Highness," she said. "Thank you so much for saving me from falling off the podium."

Natalie giggled. "You could have fallen onto a horse poop, Mummy!"

"I suppose," answered Adele with a wan smile, but she was distracted by watching Natalie lean into the prince's leg and hold his hand in both of hers, gazing up at him adoringly. Adele decided, then and there, she really had to teach her daughter some personal boundary rules.

Prince Rainere acknowledged her thanks with a modest gesture. "It is a prince's duty to aid his queen wherever he can."

Adele smiled and felt a flush creep across her cheeks. She made to reply, but Rainere wasn't finished yet.

"In fact, Your Majesty, the good doctor, Pere Raven, has noted that it is the heat that has brought you so low today, and perhaps on other occasions during this week. I have suggested that perhaps a brief respite in the cooler microclimate of the Grey Palace might help you to recover some of your strength. I would be delighted to host you and your family again until you are better recovered."

Adele felt her smile stiffen and become brittle. *What the hell was Rainere playing at? Did he want to be more obvious?*

Too shocked to respond, Adele heard the children fill the silence with their shrieks of "Can we? Can we, Mummy?" Her eyes travelled to the door and she saw that General Ohrig stood in the hall wearing a horrified expression. Obviously, he had just heard the prince.

"Of course, you can take a little holiday from the Belvoir Estate if you would like to, Your Majesty," Bertie grinned at the prince and Adele instantly saw that the two were in collusion. That was interesting. "I would love to come myself, truth be told, but I have this carnival to host and I can't very well miss my own party!"

"If you don't need me here, Bertie, I would love to go to the Grey Palace in your stead?" said Pere Raven looking pleased. "I have wanted to see inside of that wonderful place since we were young fellows daring each other to run and touch those forbidding front gates."

"Gosh, we were just boys," said Bertie, smiling wistfully at the memory.

"Of course, you are all welcome to join Her Majesty at my home," said Prince Rainere graciously, disentangling himself from Natalie's passionate hug with gentle hands. "Though my hospitality won't compare to that of Prince Bertrand's, I am sure."

The children all cheered, jumping about the room and their hysterics made everyone smile, but Adele was still troubled. *How would the court interpret the royal family leaving the Belvoir carnival to be alone with Prince Rainere for a non-state visit?* It would almost be an outright admission of a relationship between them, and that could only mean trouble when she went back to the Golden Palace and had to explain herself to High Wizard Ohren.

As if he had read her mind, Tilburn came striding into the room with his bouncy little steps. He marched straight over to Adele and presented her with a scroll mounted on a wooden board.

"I need you to sign this letter directly, Your Majesty. It's addressed to High Wizard Ohren, and just lets him know that all is well with you after your little episode this afternoon. I've been instructed to keep

226

him informed of your health while you are here at the estate."
Tilburn handed her a quill and pointed to the place she needed to
sign with his manicured finger. "You caused quite a commotion at
the race today. I can only imagine the stories and rumors that are
flying back to the Golden Palace, as we speak. The high wizard will
be most concerned about you, I'm sure."

Adele felt a surge of anger at her majordomo's words. *If High Wizard
Ohren is so concerned about me, then why isn't he here?*

She remembered Ohren's open smile and his radiant blue eyes that
twinkled with humor and had to admit that she also felt a little hurt
that he hadn't tried harder to see her at Belvoir. *Didn't he care what
happened to her anymore?* The fact that he was only communicating with
Tilburn and not her directly was infuriating.

A bolt of rebellion stirred Adele's anger at the high wizard. Ohren
had sent her to the Belvoir Estate and told her not to go back to the
Golden Palace, but he hadn't told her why. His secrecy disturbed her
and made her feel vulnerable at the same time. If events were afoot at
the Golden Palace, then they could very well follow her to Belvoir
where most of the court of the Golden Palace had decamped for the
carnival. Maybe it *would* be much safer for her and the children if they
were at the Grey Palace? Nothing could touch them there with
Rainere by her side and the protection of Marchant magic
surrounding them.

Adele scribbled her royal insignia across the page. She looked up into
the expectant gaze of her three children and Prince Bertie's excited
grin. Rainere's eyes were hooded and his face didn't betray any of his
emotions. When she glanced at him, General Ohrig gave her an
almost imperceptible shake of his head. She ignored him.

"I think going to the Grey Palace is a wonderful idea. Thank you for
your kind invitation, Prince Rainere." Adele's fragile stomach did
some nauseating flip flops with excitement. "I have been feeling quite
ill with the heat since I got here so a little break would be a relief."

"The heat never bothered Your Majesty so much in Sandar,"
commented Ohrig quietly. Adele chose to ignore him again but

noticed that Pere Raven had also heard the general and sent him a curious look.

Adele turned to Bertie. "But I am sorry we will miss the famous Steeplechase, Bertie," she said. "There is no way we will be back in time for it if we leave today. The Grey Palace is a day's travel each way, and the Steeplechase is only in three days."

"Ah-ha! Don't you worry about that, Your Majesty," said the old prince, tapping the side of his nose. "Tomorrow, I will show you that I can have you there and back in just a twinkle!"

Chapter Thirty-Four

"Passions Stirred and Emotions Tumbled"

Tonight, Adele's bedroom was as busy as a backstage dressing room. At least half a dozen people bustled about, with maids bringing in more candles, hot water, and whatever else was required to prepare for the beautification of the queen and her royal entourage. A heavy white moon shone in through the open window, but the room was lit up as bright as day with candelabras of all sizes.

"Not too tight, Lady Olivia," said Adele as she held her hands to the stays that pulled in hard on her ribs. She had already fainted once today and she didn't want to do it again.

"But your waist is so tiny, Your Majesty," smiled Lady Olivia and gave the ribbons an extra yank. "No one would ever think that you have had three children."

Adele smiled to accept the compliment and stared at herself in the mirror. On Earth a night out would have meant clean hair and a nice blouse instead of a t-shirt, but here in Unisia it took hours of primping and preening to dress for a ball.

Adele patted her hair that had been piled up high on her head and threaded through with gold silk and gems. Her wine-colored gown was cut low on the shoulders and showed off her modest bust to great effect. The fabric of the bodice was heavy with violet and emerald gems which flowed onto the stiff silk skirts in a wave pattern. Forest green lace peaked out from behind slashes in the hem of the gown and decorated the short train behind her. Adele turned her painted face this way and that, admiring her eyebrows that had been plucked into two elegant arches and the rose-tinted blush that colored her cheeks so prettily.

She was getting used to looking like a queen, and it was a little disconcerting to realize that she now preferred it to how she dressed on Earth. The beautiful clothes she wore felt like a suit of armor. The dress, the hair, the makeup: it all helped to cover her up and keep her safe inside her queen's disguise. Dressed this way, Adele felt confident enough to push back her shoulders and smile at her image until Lady Olivia stepped into the mirror behind her. The young blonde was truly beautiful with her large blue eyes, long dark lashes and high cheekbones. She was at least four inches taller than Adele and had a willowy elegance that was impossible to fake. Lady Olivia was wearing a gown of sky blue that pushed her fuller bust high, reducing her small waist to miniscule proportions. She had draped a sparkling necklace over her décolletage that drew the eye in towards the last dangling gem that fell between her breasts.

Adele wasn't a prude, and she applauded young women who were proud of their bodies, but she suddenly felt ancient beside her gorgeous young lady-in-waiting.

"Are you looking forward to dancing with Prince Rainere tonight, Your Majesty?" whispered Lady Olivia with a giggle. "I remember watching you two at the coronation ball and the prince looked like a very good dancer."

"Oh, you remember that?" said Adele and brushed on a little more lipstick to hide her smile. "Well, I suppose I'll have to, he did win the big race today."

"I wouldn't mind dancing with Prince Rainere," sighed Lady Olivia, as she replaced a pin in her hair, leaning close to Adele's ear. "I know I shouldn't be saying this, but he is so handsome and mysterious, it makes me wonder how long it's been since a woman gave him any attention." She giggled again, but Adele could only stare at her wide-eyed.

There was a knock at the door and Adele was disappointed to see General Ohrig enter, she thought perhaps she could have avoided him surrounded by the protection of her beauty team and their preparations. Ohrig looked out of place and terribly masculine in the midst of all the strewn gowns and make-up stations.

"Your Majesty, I was told that you are close to finished preparing for the ball. Perhaps you would have a minute to talk privately," said the general over the chaos of the crowd in Adele's bedroom. He stepped back to allow a maid carrying armfuls of tulle to get past him.

"I guess I'm as ready as I'll ever be," said Adele reluctantly. She dismissed her staff with a kind word and was dismayed at how quickly everyone cleared out of the room.

"Doesn't Queen Adelena just look radiant tonight, General Ohrig?" asked Lady Olivia as she floated past on her way to the door and flashed him a beautiful smile.

The general nodded curtly. "Yes, very nice."

Adele sighed and sank onto a chair. General Ohrig was already tense so this wasn't going to be fun. "Please sit, Ohrig," said Adele and gestured at a tiny tapestry chair opposite her. The general moved a tray of jewelry from the cushion and sat stiffly, his leather weapon belts creaking as he arranged himself, pushing his sword to the side.

Adele folded her hands in her lap and waited for the general to start. Ohrig was a man of action so it wouldn't take long.

"Your Majesty," he began, but paused and rubbed his hand over the rough five o'clock shadow on his chin, searching for the right words. The general was really worked up if he couldn't even begin what they both knew he wanted to say.

"Ohrig, please just speak frankly, otherwise we are going to be here forever," said Adele and her nerves made her sound more short than she meant to.

Ohrig gave her one of his grim smiles. "As you wish, Your Majesty," he said, but there was a warning in his tone. "Here it is. I want to know why you are risking your life and the lives of your children by returning to the Grey Palace with the Marchant prince tomorrow morning."

"Well…"

"Because," he interrupted. "From the moment I met you, you have done nothing but make decisions that kept you with your children at all times. And never have I thought you were being reckless with their safety when you obviously know best how to look after them. But now…now there is something going on, and you are not telling me what that is."

"Really, Ohrig, I…"

"I mean, I understand that as a foreigner to our land that you might not understand the full implications of aligning yourself with an outcast like the prince and what that could mean in Unisia. But Your Majesty, I have to tell you that rushing in blindly to this relationship will be political suicide, if not outright death at the prince's hands. The Marchant family has never sought anything but the fall of the kingdom."

"General, enough!" yelled Adele. She felt a flush heat her cheeks as she fought to control her fury. "Believe me, I'm not the only one who is acting blind here and I think you are angry with the wrong wizard! You are so dead-set against Prince Rainere that I don't think you have even stopped to consider why we are here at the Belvoir Estate in the first place. The High Wizard Ohren sent us here for a *horse carnival!* Are you kidding me?" She waved her arms about to express her outrage further. "People could be dying of the terrible Summer Influenza right now all over Unisia and we are stuck here in Belvoir with the cure because the high wizard told us we can't go back to the Golden Palace!"

"That is beside the point, Your Majesty," interrupted Ohrig, but Adele wouldn't let him finish.

"And I have heard just enough about your prejudice against Marchants," she continued, but the general was too loud to be shouted down.

"Prejudice!" he snapped. "Your Majesty, I may not be a great student of history, but even I know that the Marchant kings were all murderous tyrants. There has never, *ever*, been a good Marchant king!" He raised a hand to count on his fingers. "The last Marchant king on the Unisian throne was King Rainov the *Cruel*. Before that we had King Rainmon the *Berserk*. Before that we had King Rainfor the *Depraved* whom Rainmon murdered to steal the throne. Shall I go on?"

"But that's all ancient history, Ohrig," Adele protested. "Don't you see? Prince Rainere is as judged for his family name as I am for mine." Adele got up and started pacing behind her chair, warming to her theme. "How do you know he isn't as misplaced in his role as the black prince as I am in mine as queen of Unisia?"

"Don't ever say that, Your Majesty!" hissed Ohrig, checking the door and Adele realized she was shouting. She lowered her voice but couldn't stop now that Ohrig had her so angry.

"He has nothing! No lands, no servants, no money. He lives alone in that decrepit palace suffering the punishment for the sins of his fathers. You tell me how is that fair?"

"He doesn't need anything," said Ohrig through gritted teeth. "He is a wizard, and despite what you might think of his pitiful life he is still the second most dangerous man in the kingdom, behind Wizard Ohren."

"You think Ohren is dangerous?" asked Adele, shocked that Ohrig had even said such a thing as loyal as he was to his family of St. Lucidis.

"Of course!" snapped Ohrig, obviously frustrated by her stupidity. "High Wizard Ohren is an insanely powerful immortal, older even than Prince Rainere. If he wanted to, he could take this entire kingdom to its knees. Just as Prince Rainere could."

"Wait, what? High Wizard Ohren is *immortal*?" Adele was stunned. He had never mentioned that little detail about himself.

"Of course he is," said the general with a roll of his eyes. "How do you think he could live so long? Good health? The man is over two hundred years old!"

Adele's mind was spinning with this new information about the high wizard. Again, she was being forced to doubt everything she thought she knew in this world of Evendaar. She felt a horrible sense of vertigo as the ground beneath her seemed to tip. She grabbed the back of the chair to steady herself.

"But Ohren told me only Marchants could be immortal as they were the Chosen Ones, chosen by the Goddess herself, you know with all that green magic."

Ohrig's expression was grim. "Like I said, I'm not a great student of history and I can't recall how Ohren managed to achieve immortality, but I do know that he has no Marchant blood in him. That's why he has been slowly aging this whole time and looks like the old man we know him as today. But rest assured, the high wizard needs a peaceful kingdom as much as the kingdom needs him. If he does not want to be a despot ruling in chaos, then he must abide by the laws of men and subject himself to the wishes of the court and the Constitution of the Golden Palace."

"I never even thought about how he could have been there when I was born," whispered Adele, still grappling with her shock. Suddenly she snapped back into focus. "Ohrig, have you ever heard of the Prophecy of the End of the World?"

Ohrig shook his head. "No, Your Majesty, but despite its cheerful title, I'm guessing it's not good."

"It's why Ohren brought me back from Earth," said Adele and watched Ohrig closely for his reaction. "He said that he accidentally triggered the prophecy when he sent me away as a baby, and then had to follow the portents the prophecy gave him to bring me back and crown me queen. He did it quickly, so no one could stop him, not even his own court."

Ohrig looked genuinely puzzled but not angry as Adele thought he might after she had revealed such a huge secret to him and finally explained her presence in Unisia.

"What else does the prophecy say?"

"I don't know," Adele frowned. "I haven't even seen it myself. I was hoping Prince Rainere had a copy of it. Apparently, more copies were made…"

The general put his hands up in a gesture for her to stop right there. "Your Majesty, in no way would I advise you to ask one wizard to help you with a problem you have with another wizard. They do not work as we do. They are not truly men any more than I am really a cat."

"But where is High Wizard Ohren so I can ask him all these questions!" Adele's voice was shrill and she started pacing again. "He sent me off to Sandar before I could find out anything more about this prophecy and then he sent us here, with no more explanation than 'don't be alarmed'!"

"Look, Your Majesty, the ways of wizards are mysterious, I agree, but you cannot lose faith in Ohren just to drop it in the lap of Prince Rainere. Whatever else I might think about him; the high wizard loves Unisia and has only ever done his best to see the kingdom flourish and prosper. The only reason that he is not with us now is because he is immortal and the curse on the estate might cause him real damage."

Adele was already upset and Ohrig's stubborn tone was irritating her. *First, he calls Ohren dangerous, and then he tells me to trust him completely. It was so confusing!*

"But he abandoned us!" she protested hotly. "We haven't seen him in weeks. He hasn't bothered to collect the Fire Orchid stamens and he sent me to Sandar all on my own with no help…"

"Yes, and look how well that turned out," interrupted Ohrig, triumphantly making his point. "You retrieved the stamens and repaired trade relations with Sandar *and* made a friend of the Empress Sanda'hani. It couldn't have gone better, if you ask me."

Adele stared at General Ohrig for a long moment. The desire to tell him what had happened in the Holy Caves with the Mage of Sandar sat at the tip of her tongue. She looked into his honest face, his eyes shining with the determination to save her from making bad choices and stopped herself. It would not help him to know just what she was capable of before she understood what had really happened herself.

Adele walked back to her chair and sat down.

"You are right of course," she said quietly, but squared her shoulders and braced herself for his anger when she said what she had to say right now. "I just need to know what I'm doing here in your world, Ohrig. I know we should trust Ohren but I hate that I am just a pawn in a wizard's game. Though you don't agree, I need to know what Prince Rainere can tell me about this prophecy and I need to know now. So, I *will* be going to the Grey Palace tomorrow morning and if you don't agree then I give you permission to remain here at Belvoir."

General Ohrig dropped his head in his hands and rubbed his face muttering what sounded like curses. Adele could almost see the steam coming out of his ears and she sought to calm him. "Look, Ohrig, I think the prince is just lonely, politically he..."

"As lonely as a toothless viper in its nest," Ohrig barked rudely.

"What?" Adele was getting irritated with Ohrig all over again when she had been trying to be nice.

"A toothless viper is a serpent who cannot hunt because he has no teeth to catch prey, but he builds a nest underground in exactly the same way as a mouse does," said Ohrig, his eyes narrowed in anger. "He slithers into the hole and lays at the bottom and waits. Until one day a little mouse comes creeping along, looking for a safe place to sleep without having to build a nest of its own. The viper waits while the mouse sniffs about, then waits while it eats the seeds in its cheeks. The viper waits while the mouse climbs into the hole. It waits while the mouse crawls all over it and scratches it with its tiny claws. The viper waits until the mouse lays itself down and falls asleep. All this time, the viper has not moved, not twitched, not a breath had passed its thin lips, until it is sure that the mouse is completely vulnerable and then...*chomp!*"

The general clapped suddenly making Adele jump in her seat and glare at him. She had received his message loud and clear.

"I think we're done here," she snapped.

General Ohrig did not apologize but got up and headed for the door. Adele wanted to scream with frustration! She couldn't stand having Ohrig just walk away like that when they should be working together on finding out about the prophecy, not arguing like children. She needed his help and as crazy as he made her she trusted him.

"Then what would you have me do, Ohrig, when I've already accepted his invitation?" she asked and couldn't keep the plaintive note out of her voice.

Ohrig had his hand on the doorknob but turned to hit Adele with the full force of his icy glare.

"The only advice I can give you, Your Majesty, is to let me do my job guarding the viper's nest and stop acting like such a bloody mouse." Then he turned and left, shutting the door behind himself with a slam that made Adele flinch.

She got up and fought the urge to kick the door behind her angry general. He had absolutely no idea what he was talking about. None at all!

Adele grabbed the tiny embroidered bag containing her lipstick and silk handkerchief and roughly pulled the strap over her wrist. She was going to dance with Rainere tonight, at least a hundred times, and she hoped General Ohrig watched that! Adele left her bedroom and slammed the door herself out of sheer pique.

*   *   *

Natalie poked her head into her mother's bedroom. She was supposed to be in bed next door but couldn't get to sleep with all the noise in the hallway, and then doors slamming.

She saw no one was in the room and stepped inside heading straight for the tray of makeup on the dressing table.

Natalie loved make-up. The feel and smell of it were just so nice. She painted her lips with a bright-pink lipstick brush, and then dabbed some on her cheeks for good measure. Picking up the large fluffy powder puff, she covered herself in a vanilla-scented cloud. But the powder made her sneeze and she dropped the puff on the floor, sprinkling the carpet with white dust. Natalie knelt down in a panic and tried to wipe the dust away under the dresser. Her hand hit something, and she pulled it out from under the table leg.

Natalie could see right away that the little box was something special. The sides of the box were shiny like glass and it was all black with no pictures at all. She shook it at little but didn't hear anything rattle inside. She turned the box over looking for an opening and saw right away that there was a tiny little button, perfectly flat, in the center of one side. She used her little pinky to press it down, and the top of the box slowly creaked open on its stiff hinges.

Inside the velvet-lined box, Natalie saw something that made her gasp. She reached in and pulled out the beautiful necklace. It was very tarnished and old, but the green gem glowed as if it had a fire inside.

A noise outside the door made Natalie jump and she heard Siobahn call her name. She quickly shoved the necklace into the pocket of her dressing gown and pushed the little black box back under the dresser. She would ask Mummy later if she could keep the necklace. Mummy had so many, Natalie was almost positive that she wouldn't miss this one.

Quick as a wink, Natalie ran to the door of her mother's bedroom and stepped out into the hall before Siobahn came calling again.

CHAPTER THIRTY- FIVE

"Time Travels Backwards as Well as to the Side"

"I give you - our secret passageway!"

Bertie gave a dramatic flourish and grinned proudly at the crowd of people surrounding him in the dim light.

Adele stared at the Prince of Belvoir, utterly gobsmacked. It was the morning after the ball celebrating Rainere's win, and her awful argument with Ohrig, and she was standing in the middle of a dusty basement under the laundries of the manor. Her entire QG were pressed in around her, as well as her children, Tilburn and Lady Olivia. The three nannies and Pere Raven were peering in from the doorway. Prince Rainere stood close by Bertie's shoulder, towering over the smaller prince.

"This tunnel is very special as it leads to a portal on the very edge of the Belvoir boundary. It is said that the portal opens directly into the dungeons of the Grey Palace. The portal itself is fueled by a very powerful spell and it still functions today as it has done for hundreds of years!" said Bertie giddy as a schoolboy, as he gleefully explained the history of the tunnel to his silent audience.

"You see; this tunnel was used mostly during the time of King Rainov the Cruel. After the Grey Palace massacre, we had lots of refugees flooding through here seeking asylum in the magic-free Belvoir Estate. Of course, in those days we would have had guards posted around the clock, but our honorable Prince Rainere is a very quiet neighbor, and such precautions aren't necessary now." Bertie grinned at Prince Rainere.

"What's a massacre?" asked Natalie but Adele shushed her quickly.

General Ohrig and Captain Lucky both stepped forward to examine the entrance to the tunnel. It had been lined with rough stone blocks and had wooden supports holding up the walls. The floor was dry, natural dirt, packed tight. The tunnel was tall enough for a man to stand straight, and for three to walk side by side. It was very dark.

"We'll need lanterns," said Captain Lucky and Prince Bertie told QG Bear where to find some in a nearby storeroom.

"Do you think it will be safe for the children to travel through this magic portal?" asked Adele anxiously.

Bertie looked to Prince Rainere for the answer.

"The magic is quite safe, Your Majesty," said Rainere, nodding at Adele. "I will give everyone my personal protection as we pass through the portal. The magic, though strong, is essentially secure. As long as I am touching the portal at all times no harm shall come to anyone. I imagine my ancestors had no wish to injure the refugees as they escaped the Grey Palace."

There was a moment of awkward silence as the small crowd politely avoided making eye contact with the grandson of Rainov the Cruel. Bertie coughed breaking the tension.

"Err... quite, Your Highness," he replied non-committally.

QG Bear returned and made his way through the crowded room with the handles of several lanterns in one hand and Charlie's arm in the other.

"Your Majesty," said the big QG. "I found the royal...escort hiding down here. Did you want to take him with us?" QG Bear looked to his general for confirmation that he had properly maintained the secret of Charlie's existence and was confused by Ohrig's glare and QG Owens's muffled snigger.

"Not escort, QG Bear, Charlie is an *en*-voy," said Captain Lucky covering the gaff with some quick thinking and a fake laugh, but the damage was already done.

"Hey, it's Cheeky Charlie!" said Natalie before Adele could do anything but blush furiously. She had no idea her children had met Charlie before.

"Hello Charlie, want to come to the Grey Palace with us?" Aaron piped up. "It's not scary, you know."

Charlie muttered something incomprehensible and yanked his arm out of QG Bear's meaty grip. His gaze flicked from Adele to Prince Rainere as he addressed her.

"I beg your pardon, Your Majesty, but I was just down here looking for you when your QG found me," Charlie said, as he drifted off.

Adele was completely mortified. She gave Rainere a quick glance and her stomach dropped when she saw his frozen expression as he stared at Charlie, his dark eyes hooded. Charlie dropped his gaze to the floor and groaned quietly.

"I can hold your hand, Charlie," said Aaron kindly, misunderstanding the groan and taking Charlie's hand in his own. "It's fun there, I promise!"

Adele peered into the tunnel entrance now lit by lanterns. A shiver ran down her spine as she was vividly reminded of walking into the Holy Caves of Sandar. Her brain tried desperately to come up with an excuse to back out of the situation without humiliating Rainere any further, but it was impossible. He had invited her, and she had accepted. To refuse now would shame him horribly.

"Your Majesty?" Her majordomo gently touched her shoulder. Adele turned and saw that Tilburn was white as a sheet. "If you don't mind, I might remain here at Belvoir. I am so very sorry, but I have a rather big problem with small spaces. I just can't... er-herm." Tilburn pulled at the tight collar of his jacket, and Adele saw the sweat streak down his temple.

She grimaced sympathetically. "Of course, Tilburn. In fact, anyone who is feeling nervous about the tunnel and the portal can feel free to remain at the manor." She looked about and saw quite a few relieved faces.

"I'm definitely coming, Your Majesty," said Lady Olivia. "It is such an honor to be included in the prince's invitation. I wouldn't miss this chance for all the world." She smiled at Prince Rainere and bobbed a curtsey, but Rainere didn't spare her a glance. He was staring down into the tunnel as if he wanted it to swallow him. Adele was almost surprised that no one else had noticed the change in the prince's mood, but she didn't look at General Ohrig. If anyone could pick up on the tension it would be him.

"No time like the present!" said Pere Raven cheerfully and stepped into the mouth of the tunnel. "This will be a story to tell our grandchildren about."

The priest's words seemed to stir Rainere from his frozen state and, with a gesture, he motioned the group forward and strode off down the dark tunnel, his lantern swinging about with his long strides and throwing yellow splashes of light on the walls. General Ohrig jostled his men into formation and the rest of the party hurried to catch up with him. Adele swung a whimpering Stella up into her arms, pleased to see Lady Olivia take Natalie's hand. She glanced behind and was disturbed that of all the nannies, only Siobahn was left to help. Aaron allowed Siobahn to scoop him up, and Adele forced herself to smile at the young woman. Things had been strained between them ever since Adele had caught Siobahn in the garden with Benjamin and Adele didn't know how to make it any less awkward as Siobahn couldn't even hold her gaze.

As their small party walked down the dark tunnel, the smell of damp soil pervaded the air. Adele tried not to think of the weight of all that earth above pressing down on them, but it must have been on everyone's mind as the entire group was silent except for the squeaks of the swinging lanterns and Stella's whimpering.

Sooner than she thought it would be, they reached a glowing green wall. Adele could see the sparkles around the edges of the portal glitter and flash, though the door itself looked like a dirt wall. She felt a thrill of excitement at the sight of living magic.

Natalie edged up beside her mother. "Cool!" she whispered. Aaron joined them and took Adele's hand.

Rainere had put his lantern down and stood next to the portal. "Your Majesty, I will place my hands into the portal and that will be enough to take you through to the Grey Palace. Please step through as quickly as possible and don't look back but wait for me on the other side. No more than three shall pass at a time."

"Alright, everyone hold hands," instructed Adele and with a quick glance at Rainere she pulled her children in and through the portal.

It was dark on the other side, but the air was fresher. Adele barely had time to step out of the way before General Ohrig and QGs Bear and Owens joined them. They were quickly followed by the rest of the QGs with Pere Raven, and then Captain Lucky escorting Siobahn and Lady Olivia through. Prince Rainere stepped through a moment later with a very pale Charlie.

Adele looked about in wonder as green flames sprang to life on sconces around them. The lights illuminated the cavernous underground chamber and continued around the curved walls to show the doorways of at least a dozen other portals. The ceiling was so high it reached up into darkness, and the walls were vaulted with stone ridges, like an enormous ribcage. There were large, chunky, black pebbles underfoot and a long loop of railway track lay bouncing and jittering on the ground. Adele soon saw the reason for the movement as a carriage came tearing down the track like a train, only to lurch to a stop directly in front of Rainere. The door to the carriage opened and Grotto stepped out and bowed low to Prince Rainere. "Master, you are returned. Welcome home."

He gave Adele only the most perfunctory of bows and a sneered "Your Majesty" making her QGs bristle at the insult.

"If Your Majesty and the children would like to accompany me with the ladies to the top of the palace first, then the carriage will return to pick up your men-at-arms and the envoy later," said Rainere and his tone was acidic on the word 'envoy'.

Adele felt a jolt at his words, but it was energy that coursed through her and not anxiety. She felt amazing! The lethargy and nausea that had plagued her constantly at Belvoir Estate had completely passed and she felt like her old self again. She smiled at Rainere even though she knew he was furious with her at the idea that she had taken a teenage lover. It was just so wonderful to be well again!

Adele was so distracted by her return to health that she didn't even notice how angry General Ohrig was at being separated from her in the Grey Palace and she didn't see his thunderous expression when Grotto held up his hand to physically stop the general from squeezing into the carriage.

In all the fuss of settling the children and fitting everyone in, Adele was surprised to find that Lady Olivia had taken the place next to the prince and had squeezed Natalie out of the way. Though it was nice that Lady Olivia didn't share the fear of the prince that everyone else did, it still made Adele uncomfortable to have a much younger, and very beautiful, woman gushing at Rainere and casually touching his arm where it rested against hers.

The journey up to the palace was very fast and Adele couldn't even see the track that they travelled on. She just knew that they were lurching up and around lots of stomach-bending twists. The children were delighted and laughed as they were thrown about the carriage. Adele held onto Stella for dear life and tried not to notice Lady Olivia falling against Rainere and giggling her apologies.

When the carriage finally slowed to a stop, a grim-faced servant opened the door for them and everyone stumbled out onto the platform, admiring the grand chamber they had arrived in.

Portal Station. First Stop. read Adele on the stones engraved on the wall above an enormous archway. "Oh, I see! It's like a giant train station!"

She could see at least four other carriages like the one they had arrived in, on different tracks leading to different tunnels. More archways lined the platform, but these were dark and empty. They walked across the stone platform and through the biggest archway, lit by the green-flamed sconces, which took them out to a corridor.

Prince Rainere had only led their little party a few steps before Natalie boldly stepped in front of him and raised her arms. The prince looked down at the little girl before him and a flash of confusion crossed his face.

"Pick me up," demanded Natalie giving Rainere her best smile. "Please."

"Natalie!" Adele was shocked by her daughter's cheekiness but Prince Rainere bent down and picked Natalie up under her arms, holding her suspended in the air as she kicked her dangling legs and giggled. Aaron and Stella giggled too.

"Is that long enough, Your Highness?" asked Prince Rainere.

"Yes, it is," interrupted Adele. "Natalie, stop it right now!"

"No, you have to put me in your arms," giggled Natalie ignoring her mother. "I want you to carry me."

Adele could feel Siobahn's horror poking her like a stick in her back as the young nanny whimpered in fear for the little girl.

Prince Rainere swung Natalie around and cradled her in his arms like she was made of crystal.

"Yes, like this," nodded Natalie, satisfied. "Mummy, look! I'm Sleeping Beauty." Natalie dropped her head back and pretended to snore loudly.

"Who is Sleeping Beauty?" asked Rainere staring down at Natalie with something like wonder on his face.

As Natalie explained the story of Sleeping Beauty to the prince, Adele followed behind feeling relieved that Rainere seemed as charmed by her precocious little girl as he had last time he had seen her, and also despite the fact that he was angry with Adele.

As they continued down the corridor more sconces burst into flame and lit their way, extinguishing themselves again when the party walked past. Adele flinched as a movement from above caught her eye. She almost called out to Rainere, but she stopped herself just in time when she saw that the large bird glaring down at her was made of stone and his glittering eye was a polished jewel. Her gaze travelled down the corridor, and she saw there were a hundred more like it lining the walls. She let her breath go in relief and pointed them out to Stella and Aaron, whose eyes widened in shock as hers had.

After walking down through many drafty corridors and up cold stone staircases they finally came to a more familiar part of the palace, and Rainere led them all up to the laboratory at the request of the children. As they neared the room Adele sidled closer to Rainere, surreptitiously stepping between the prince and Lady Olivia who was walking at his side.

"…and then true love's kiss woke her up!" finished Natalie.

"So, his kiss was the antidote to the poison of the witch?" asked Rainere with genuine interest.

"No, *true love* woke her up," explained Natalie. "He was just the prince who loved her, but if her Mummy or Daddy had kissed her, she would have woken up for them, too. It's just that everyone else in the palace was asleep and couldn't get to her."

Adele smiled at Natalie's answer. She had given Natalie that little caveat to the classic fairy tale. God forbid her daughter should believe in fairy tale princes and their penchant for proposing marriage within minutes of meeting beautiful girls. Of course, that was before Adele had found out that they really did exist.

Rainere frowned. "Perhaps the kiss symbolizes a transfer of power, his to the princess. If the witch had based the spell on a simple matrix designed to endure for sixteen years, then certainly the prince could break it very easily with a touch at the most vulnerable point. Or, if it was a poison that was used, then the prince may have needed to apply the antidote to her mouth with a kiss so she could inhale it, thereby allowing the princess to wake up."

"Yes," agreed Natalie knowledgeably. "That's why Mummy kisses all my bumps and cuts when I get them. Kissing makes everything feel better."

"Indeed," answered Rainere, but there was something in his tone that made Adele want to blush.

Rainere's laboratory was much cleaner than the last time they had visited. The four long tables of scarred and stained wood had been polished underneath the clutter of odd mechanisms and potion making paraphernalia. The children were in heaven, leaping about the room and pestering Rainere with hundreds of questions. As always, the prince was patient and concise with his answers as well as helpful volunteering advice on which potions would scar irreparably and which sharp instruments could cut through bone. Adele was pleased to see the joy that her children took playing with Rainere, but she was very relieved when Siobahn had the bright idea to ask where the royal nursery was, to get them out of the laboratory.

"Nursery?" Rainere frowned for a moment, his elegant brows beetling. "I don't suppose it has been touched in over a hundred years, but I believe it is still located in the east wing of the palace, in my old boyhood suite."

"Are there toys there?' asked Natalie.

"Toys and books," nodded Rainere and his mouth quirked with amusement when the children broke into raucous cheering.

Just then Grotto led in her Queen's Guard, Charlie and Pere Raven. Grotto had obviously hustled the pace as Pere Raven looked quite winded and everyone had pink cheeks. Except Grotto of course, the manservant looked as pale and cold as ever.

"Ah, you've arrived." Rainere welcomed the newcomers with the barest of nods. "Grotto, please assist the queen's children in finding the royal nursery, they have an interest in seeing the toys there."

Grotto turned to glare balefully at Siobahn and Lady Olivia. "Bring the children this way," he barked and immediately set off, the older children scampering after him. Siobahn scooped up Stella in her arms and hurried to join them, but Lady Olivia remained where she was until Adele gave her a look.

"Me too, your Majesty?" Lady Olivia placed a hand on her chest in a gesture of surprise. She obviously wanted to remain with Adele.

Adele nodded and chose to ignore Lady Olivia's pique as the young woman gave her a hurt look. Olivia was a lady-in-waiting, not a common servant, and to be treated as such wasn't polite, but Adele had more than Lady Olivia's pride to worry about right now.

"General, could you please take the men to follow the children. His Highness and I will be in the study and meet up with you all for lunch."

General Ohrig stared at Adele and communicated much with just a twitch of his heavyset brows and Adele could see how anxious she was making him. But there was no way around it, she needed to get Rainere on his own.

"I will leave Pere Raven with you, Your Majesty," said the general obviously hoping to leave a witness to protect Adele.

"Actually, I'm very much looking forward to exploring this wondrous palace, general, so I'll be coming with you, if it pleases the queen?"

Adele nodded. Pere Raven's enthusiasm was heartening. "I will see you all later."

A still-pouting Lady Olivia took the arm of Captain Lucky without waiting for the young officer to offer it and pulled him out of the room though not before she threw Prince Rainere a lingering look.

As soon as everyone left Adele realized too late that Charlie had not had the good sense to leave with the rest of the men and stood frozen like a rabbit by the door, watching the prince, his eyes wide with fear. Prince Rainere cocked his head, listening to the receding sounds of the Queen's Guard before slamming both the doors shut with a flick of his wrist. Adele jumped at the noise, but Charlie almost fell over and only then did Adele realize that he had been held fast against his will. She turned to Rainere intending to protest, but her words died on her lips when she saw the prince's expression.

Though Rainere's posture was casual as he leaned back against one of the workbenches studiously examining the nails of his right hand, the tension rolled off him in waves. Charlie, however, looked like a cat suspended over a bucket of water. His eyes flickered repeatedly to the windows and doors as he tried to put as much space as he could between himself and the prince.

Rainere broke the silence, his gravelly voice tight with the strength of his emotions. "So have you taken a royal escort, *cara mia?*"

"Rainere, come on! It was just a stupid misunderstanding," said Adele and forced a laugh as she moved to stand next to him. "It's all quite funny really." She leaned against him to make him to look at her.

"Tell me the joke then," he said softly.

Adele shrugged in an attempt at nonchalance and gave Charlie a nod. "Charlie was in my room one night giving me the box you had given him for me, which I couldn't open by the way," —she poked his arm playfully— "when one of my QGs caught him before he could wake me up. Charlie came up with the only story that would account for his presence in my room at night and I went along with it to keep Charlie's work for you a secret. But afterwards I told the general and my QGs that Charlie is really a spy working for me, not my escort. He's only a boy for goodness sake, the very idea is just wrong."

"Were you dressed?" Rainere's voice was almost a whisper and Adele felt him shudder against her. He was so upset and she needed to calm him down before he lost his temper.

"Rainere, look at me," she begged and pressed in closer against him. "It was just a misunderstanding and it's fixed now, no one thinks Charlie is my escort."

"Did he see you naked?" persisted Rainere and Adele saw the suspicion and hurt in Rainere's gaze. This wasn't a game to him.

"For the love of the Goddess in her Garden, Your Highness, I can swear on the Blood that I never saw an inch of the queen's skin, nor did I touch her! Ever! I would never lay a finger on her, I promise," burst out Charlie, near hysterics, his face blanched white and his green eyes round with fear.

"And what do you suppose is the price of a poor urchin's promise, Charlie?" snapped Rainere, his lip curled in a sneer. "Considering he is trying to save himself from a fate worse than death."

"Rainere!" admonished Adele, matching his anger with her own. "Charlie is just a boy *and* he was working for you. You can't punish him for doing his job. It is ridiculous to be jealous of a child!"

Rainere turned back to her. "I'm being *ridiculous?*" he said, his voice holding a darkness that made her shiver and burn at the same time. Her magic rose and surged inside of her, eager to taste his energy again. Adele held Rainere's gaze for a long moment, enjoying the feel of the heat of him beneath the thin silk of his shirt. Her heart thudded erratically as she watched her prince struggle with his emotions. A crazed look flickered in the background of his dark green eyes. It only partially frightened her as she was reminded that Rainere was as unfamiliar with this love between them as she was.

"Yes," she whispered, but she was really answering the question that Rainere hadn't voiced: could he trust her?

In one fluid motion, Rainere lifted Adele up and spun her around to sit on the workbench, he pressed his forehead to hers, their lips only a breath apart.

"Boy, go and watch outside," commanded Rainere over his shoulder. "If anyone from St. Lucidis should approach, knock once, loudly."

The door nearest to Charlie creaked itself open and he didn't need to be asked twice. He scarpered and the door slammed behind him with such force it made the windows rattle.

Adele pushed at Rainere with both hands. "You are so melodramatic!" she said, rolling her eyes.

Rainere smiled his beautiful almost-smile at her teasing, but it died too soon.

"I hate that other men get to see you and touch you when I'm not there." He raised his hand to silence Adele's protest, leaving it to rest on her shoulder. "I feel like you belong to them, and the world outside, more than you belong to me," he said and his sadness made her ache.

"Rainere," whispered Adele. "No man will ever have me the way that you do, I promise."

She leaned in and kissed him softly on his perfect lips.

No more needed to be said. Rainere cleared the table top behind her with a wide sweep of his arm, all the bottles and instruments crashing to the floor, and laid her down on its scarred surface. They came together with a swiftness borne of desperation and frustrated desire. Three long days they had been parted, not knowing when they would see each other again. Adele cried out and pulled Rainere in deeper. He could only silence her with his kisses.

*　　　*　　　*

Charlie stood outside the door that had literally hit him in the arse on the way out. He heard Adele's muffled cries through the door and cursed his misfortune at ever having met the woman who kept dragging him into these life-threatening situations.

For the hundredth time, he fantasized about leaving the queen to her own dangerous life. He had almost done it, too—left her—but a message from the Boss had arrived and let him know he was being watched at Belvoir Estate. Charlie didn't dare leave after that. *Anyway, if he bailed out now, where would that leave him?* He'd have the Boss and the black prince coming after him, and even with his overblown sense of confidence he knew he had no chance. Charlie had no doubt that the prince had wanted to melt his bones just now, and it was only Queen Adelena who had stopped him.

Charlie sighed and rubbed his sore backside. *Could all be worse,* he told himself ruefully. *I don't know how, but I'm sure it could all be worse.*

CHAPTER THIRTY-SIX

"I Think That's What It Is"

Lunch was to be served in the Glassroom and it was a far more informal affair than the last time they were here.

Adele wandered to the wall of louvered windows and tweaked one to get a better look at the gardens outside. The gardens were wild and untamed. The grass and weeds grew to knee height and had only been roughly cut back from the stone paths and benches that meandered through the garden. Weeping willows crowded together over a string of little black ponds that were crammed with lily pads and thick clumps of reeds. Lots of little creatures were hopping about on the rocks edging the ponds, catching insects and plopping into the water.

Adele turned at the sound of Stella's squeal. Lady Olivia and the children were all crowded around Rainere as the prince dug up worms and other small creatures from the old pots with a rusty gardening fork. He was presently holding a shiny blue beetle in the palm of his hand as it twirled in circles on its back, making the children giggle.

"Can I hold it, please?" asked Natalie and shrieked when Rainere carefully placed it in her hand. "It tickles!"

Adele grinned at Natalie and it was only when she glanced at the rest of her entourage that her smile faded. Her general and the QGs were all spread about the room discreetly guarding the exits and Captain Lucky had yet to take his hand off the pommel of his sword. Obviously, General Ohrig had ordered them to be prepared for anything. Even QG Bear had lost his customary sneer and was as white-faced and tense as the rest of the guards. Charlie moped in a corner, looking as if he was trying very hard to be invisible. After what had happened this morning with Rainere, she wasn't surprised. The poor boy had only been doing what he was told and Rainere had scared him horribly. Siobahn sat at the table jumping in fear every time someone approached.

Adele sighed, but accepted that she would never make her St. Lucidis company feel comfortable at the Grey Palace. They were too fearful of Marchant magic and prejudiced against the Marchant prince even to give him a chance.

Stalking back into the room, Grotto announced lunch and delivered Pere Raven's apologies. The priest apparently wanted to stay in the chapel library and study texts all afternoon.

The usual whey-faced servants served up the soup and vegetables along with platters of cold cuts and hot rolls stuffed with cheese. Only the women and children sat to eat with the prince. General Ohrig made it clear the Queen's Guard would rather stand.

"Oh my goodness, Your Majesty," giggled Lady Olivia as she looked over at Adele's loaded plate. "It is good to see that your appetite has returned after your illness. That is enough food for two of you!"

Lady Olivia gave Adele a big smile, but Adele couldn't shake the feeling that Lady Olivia was trying to embarrass her in front of the prince. Was Lady Olivia really trying to compete with her for Rainere's attention?

"Yes, Your Majesty, how are you feeling?" Rainere asked over Lady Olivia's next remark. "Is the climate of the Grey Palace making you feel better at all?"

Adele felt a surge of energy zinging through her bloodstream and instinctively clenched down on her magic before it made her feel too wild. She had been so careful not to invade Rainere at all when they were together this morning, but it had been a struggle to control herself when desire had rocked her willpower. She knew he was remembering the moment, too, as his gaze traveled down her body before returning to her eyes. She smiled back at him.

"I do feel so much better, Your Highness," she answered formally. "Thank you so much for your concern."

After lunch Rainere took everyone out to the gardens just as the sun broke through the clouds. They wandered about the ponds and Adele marveled at the sunlight that made little rainbows form on the top of the murky water, and the wings of the dragonflies that sparkled as if they were made of glass. Natalie and Aaron had a wonderful time catching the tiny frogs, but the fun ended when one jumped onto Stella's chubby cheek and made her scream hysterically.

The party retired inside to let Stella go up to her room for a much-needed nap with Siobahn, while the rest of them continued on their tour into the east wing and home of the royal nursery. As they passed by, the children collected some four-wheeled scooters to help them get about. They were delighted that Prince Rainere had no problem with them scooting up and down corridors as fast as they could, endangering vases on pedestals and suits of armor everywhere.

Despite the dusty spookiness of it all, exploring the Grey Palace was incredibly interesting. Many times, Adele had such clear feelings of déjà vu that she had to shake herself. Especially when they were in the highest part of the palace where Rainere's parents had once lived. Natalie and Aaron had scooted off down the corridor well ahead of the group but had stopped in front of a giant portrait. When the adults had caught up to them Adele saw that the children were staring open-mouthed at the painting.

"How did you get a picture of my Mummy?" asked Natalie, pointing at the figure in the image.

Rainere smiled and knelt down to the children's level. "That isn't the queen, that's my step-mother, Princess Rainestra," he said. "She died when my baby sister was born."

"Where's your baby sister?" asked Aaron, placing a hand on the prince's shoulder.

"She died too," said Rainere turning to Aaron, his dark eyes hooded. "There are some things that magic just can't do, and one of them is bringing people back from the dead."

Adele regarded the portrait closely. The figure was standing by a piano, one hand resting on the edge of it, and the other on her hip. She had long dark hair falling in waves over her shoulders, and her gown was high-necked and long-sleeved, but completely sheer, with only the swooping folds concealing the intimate curves of her body. Adele looked curiously into the face of Rainere's mother and couldn't for the life of her see any similarity. The woman in the picture was self-assured, even arrogant looking, with a cruel smile playing at the corner of her mouth. Her hazel eyes wore a wicked glint and were hard at the edges, as if she had just made a mean joke and was hoping the other person felt bad. She was also radiantly beautiful.

"I don't think she looks like me," said Adele doubtfully.

"She is definitely *much* younger," said Lady Olivia behind Adele's shoulder, but when Adele turned to her the lady just smiled. "But you are much prettier, Your Majesty," she whispered, leaving Adele wondering if she was just being over-sensitive to innocent comments.

"Do you miss your Mummy?" asked Natalie of the prince.

Rainere let out a breath almost like a sigh and his eyes looked into a distant past. "I don't really remember her," he said. "It was many years ago, and Princess Rainestra was not like your own mother. She didn't have very much to do with me because I was little, but I do remember her dancing with my father at the parties they held here, and I remember her kissing me good night. Sometimes I dream about the sound of her laughter." Rainere came back to the present with a blink.

"Is there a painting of your daddy?" asked Natalie.

"It should be here, right in this spot next to her," said Rainere, frowning as he stood up. "Grotto, where is the portrait of Prince Rainold?"

The manservant bowed. "I had it taken down for cleaning, master. The frame was corroding."

"A disappointment," said Rainere to the children. "My father was a very handsome man. I would have liked you to see him."

"It's okay, Prince Rainere. I know what he looks like," smiled Aaron as he scooted off to chase his sister down the hallway.

Adele turned to Rainere and smiled at his puzzlement, she shrugged. "I have no idea what he meant by that," she said. "But I think he was just trying to make you feel better."

Rainere looked down the hall after Aaron, his expression inscrutable. "What a delightful boy," he said, and led their party onwards without another word.

CHAPTER THIRTY-SEVEN

"Sometimes Love Just Tastes Like Loyalty"

After her long nap, Stella woke up still tired and irritable, and made everyone crazy with her incessant whining at the dinner table that night. Adele had chosen to pass on Rainere's offer of a family dinner. She selfishly wanted to get the children tucked away in bed as quickly as possible, so she could spend the whole evening alone with him.

They were planning to leave tomorrow morning to make it back in time for the steeplechase at the Belvoir Estate, and then the royal family was to return to the Golden Palace the day after. Unless another ominous letter arrived from High Wizard Ohren, of course. So far as Adele was concerned, it meant that she only had this one night to ask Rainere every question she had concerning the prophecy and her magic. It wasn't exactly a secret to him that her magic was powerful, but Rainere still didn't know what she had done in Sandar. It was the time to come clean and tell him everything.

Adele dressed quickly for her dinner with the prince. Her gown was a violet silk with an embroidered neckline and a wide sweeping skirt that rustled like dry leaves when she walked.

"You look so lovely, Your Majesty," said Lady Olivia as she draped an amethyst necklace around Adele's neck. "I think you might need to be careful tonight. It is said that Marchant princes fall in love very easily with beautiful St. Lucidis women!" The young woman laughed gaily and gave Adele's shoulder a squeeze to let her know she was only joking.

"The prince and I have only boring political business to discuss, Lady Olivia, I doubt he'll find me very interesting this evening." Adele hoped that she had put the young woman off the subject but Lady Olivia merely grinned.

"Would you like me to come to dinner with you, Your Majesty?" she asked as she cocked her head to the side. "Or would you prefer to be alone with His Highness tonight? Not that I would blame you, he is so incredibly dashing!"

Adele leaped out of her chair as she saw General Ohrig cross the room to approach her and prayed he hadn't heard Lady Olivia's suggestion. The last thing she wanted was a chaperone who giggled and flirted as much as Lady Olivia.

"I'm sure I'll be fine," she said quickly and made her way to the door to try and avoid Ohrig, almost tripping over Aaron in her haste. Adele was annoyed that the children were still running around the room as Siobahn hadn't managed to get them into bed yet, but she was in too much of a rush to get back to Rainere to care overly.

General Ohrig followed her to the door of the apartment and stopped her just as they passed out of earshot of everyone else. "Your Majesty, a word?"

Adele turned to the general with a sharp retort on her lips, but she stopped when she saw the expression on his face. The general's eyes were red-rimmed, and he looked almost desperate.

"Queen Adelena," he said, surprising Adele because he almost never used her name. "I know you don't want me there tonight to protect you, but please, for the love of the Goddess, don't do anything stupid, or promise the prince that you will do something stupid."

Adele was shocked by his honesty. Obviously, the time for discretion had passed. "General, I…"

"I've seen the way you look at him, and I've seen the way he looks at you. Only a man in love would do something so crazy as to defy the curse of Belvoir and risk his own life just to see a woman, even when he knew he could never have her."

Adele froze. She felt like the general had just ripped off her dress and stared at her naked. Ohrig's eyes softened as he held her gaze and he lowered his voice even more.

"Ever since I saw you at your first coronation and the high wizard told me to guard you with my life, I have felt a loyalty to you that I do not question. You looked so tiny and alone that day, and I knew immediately that the Queen's Guard's only purpose was to protect you from all of the dangers in our world, both political and physical. I believe the Goddess herself sanctions the vow I made to keep you from danger, and I will not be forsworn. Queen Adelena, I know you don't believe it now, but you really *are* our Goddess-given queen. Unisia needs you, and Evendaar needs you. But no one will *ever* want a Marchant ruler in the Golden Palace and if you join yourself to this prince then your union will only lead to one thing: war, in the capital and between every nation. Unisia will be destroyed."

Adele looked down as General Ohrig covered her hand with his own and squeezed it tight. He never touched her and the intimacy of the gesture made her feel his emotions so much more keenly.

"Please, Queen Adelena," he whispered. "That wizard will eat you alive."

CHAPTER THIRTY-EIGHT

"Up Until the Stars"

"Would you like to see the observatory, *cara mia*?" Rainere asked. "We should have a fine view tonight, as the sky is cloudless. Perhaps that would please you?"

"I would like to see the stars," said Adele, forcing a smile as she took Rainere's hand in hers. She knew she was being too quiet with him.

Their dinner had passed quickly, supervised by Grotto, who had watched Adele like a hawk the entire time. Though her appetite was healthy again, Adele waved away dessert and asked Rainere if they could go somewhere more private. His eyes had lit up at the request, but since walking the hallways to his bedroom, Rainere had picked up on her somber mood and led her to the portrait gallery in an attempt to amuse her. Unfortunately, seeing paintings of Rainere's terrible ancestors had just made her feel worse.

One nasty ogre of a man particularly caught her attention. His long black hair hung over his face in strings and his mouth was drawn in an ugly smirk, he wore animal skins over his king's robes and the crown of Unisia perched crooked and tarnished on his large head. He sat on a throne made of bones and each foot rested on a human skull. Engraved in the little gold plaque on the frame was his name:

King Rainex the Savage. Commonly known as Rainex the Raper, reigned 112 years.

It had made Adele cringe and Rainere had hurried her away out of the gallery, and then offered to show her the observatory.

They walked back through the east wing of the palace and made their way up to a large hallway lined with white marble statues that they followed along to an enormous ballroom.

Moonlight shone down through a huge domed window in the ceiling of the ballroom and made a large silver circle on the parquetry floors. Piles of chairs had been heaped into the corners, their spindly legs broken and askew, and gilt wallpaper hung off the walls in great long lengths.

"Oh!" breathed Adele struck by the dismal grandeur of an entire ballroom left to dust and decay. "It must have been magnificent in here."

It was so sad that this palace had obviously been as wealthy and thriving as the Golden Palace was now. Adele wondered again how it didn't drive Rainere mad to be living in the ashes of his family's once-great fortune.

"The observatory is just through here, Adelena," said Rainere, gently laying a hand on the small of her back as they walked across the floor. Adele paused as they stepped into the circle of moonlight and looked up at the bright white globe. It was nearly a full moon.

"Do you remember the first time we danced, Rainere?" Adele asked. "At the coronation ball." She stepped in to lean against him and stroked a hand along his cheek, "I thought I had died and gone to heaven in your arms."

"I was so anxious," smiled Rainere. "I kept doubting my wits as you felt so fragile in my arms," – he caught her hand and kissed it – "I couldn't believe my dreams had come true."

"Would you care for a turnabout the floor with me, Your Highness?" Adele asked formally, twirling off without waiting for an answer. A moment later, she felt herself caught up in Rainere's arms, as he seamlessly joined her in the steps.

"Why are we dancing?" he asked curiously. "There is no music here."

"Of course there is," said Adele, feeling drunk on melancholy. "Can't you hear it playing? And all the ghosts are dancing around us. Listen to their whispers."

She looked up at Rainere and tried to smile, but her lips just wouldn't curve upwards. "And no one is staring at us or thinks we are wrong together. It's only the ghost ladies who are thinking, 'Who is that stunning young prince? And who is that extraordinarily happy woman he is dancing with?'"

"Perhaps they are thinking that they had never seen two people more in love than that prince and his beautiful queen?" said Rainere and laid a soft kiss on her forehead.

"This is one of the happiest moments of my life," whispered Adele, but when she closed her eyes tears wet her lashes.

Rainere waltzed them over to the bottom of a wide staircase at the other end of the ballroom and swept Adele up in his arms, cradling her against his chest. He carried her up the steps to a wide balcony, which overlooked the ballroom, and then up another smaller staircase off the balcony that brought them to the ancient observatory.

As she entered through the narrow door, Adele was struck by the beauty of the bare room. The ceiling of the observatory was made of rectangular glass panels and the walls were curved to make the chamber a circle. The plaster walls had been painted with the images of the constellations of Evendaar and though they were faded now, the blue and gold paint peeling and flaking to the floor, Adele could still read the map of this alien universe written out in a long stretch around her. A huge brass telescope dominated the center of the room, poking out through a wide hole in the glass ceiling. There was a little padded stool next to the telescope and a large chaise longue near the empty fireplace. A desk stood behind it, covered with piles of old papers and yellowing scrolls. Dust covered the floor like a pale blanket. Adele shivered in the chill air.

"You're cold," said Rainere, concerned for her comfort and he carried her to the chaise longue, laying her down as gently as a child. He moved to the fireplace and built a little fire, striking the first spark with a flint, but then there was a flash of green and the fire roared to life. Rainere fed it with the logs stacked close by. He returned to sit next to Adele on the chaise.

"What is it, *cara mia*?" he asked, stroking her arm and collecting her hand in his own. "What troubles you so much this evening?"

Adele felt the magic inside her stir and pulse at Rainere being so near. The Chime Voices sang sweetly in the background, suggesting all the wonderful things she could do to him and how good they would feel. But they were muted, like having a radio on in the background of her thoughts.

"I don't know where to start," said Adele honestly. Adele turned to gaze at the fire and picked the easiest issue that was bothering her. "Even if you come to the steeplechase at Belvoir tomorrow, we leave for the Golden Palace the day after. It makes me anxious not to know when I'm going to see you again."

Adele looked up when she felt Rainere's smile light upon her, sending a thrill of energy over her skin. She saw the happiness in his eyes.

"*Cara mia*, dearest heart, I can fix that. I have a plan that means we will be together for as long as I please you." He leaned over her and kissed her once on the mouth.

"You always please me," whispered Adele and slipped her hand around the back of his neck, pulling him in for a deeper kiss. She felt a moment of guilt that they weren't talking about all that needed to be said, but the urge to have Rainere's skin against hers was too strong. The talking could wait.

*   *   *

Adele wasn't sleepy so much as completely satiated. The Chime Voices hummed happily in her head. She had tasted the magic inside Rainere and twisted it up in her own but gently this time. At his first cry of pain she had let go and pulled her power back into herself, letting Rainere take the lead and give her an orgasm so powerful her legs still shook. Adele was proud of herself. This time she had been in full control of the lust and hunger of her magic and Rainere had not suffered like before. At least, not much more than he liked to.

The two of them lay on the floor before the fire, using Rainere's clothes as a rug. Adele had draped herself across Rainere's chest, as he lay on his back, one hand tucked behind his head for a pillow and the other playing with strands of her thoroughly messed-up hair. Too relaxed, an errant thought passed through Adele's head and headed straight to her mouth without her checking it first.

"Do you think Lady Olivia is pretty?"

Rainere raised a perfect eyebrow at her. "Do you?"

Adele grinned and gave his stomach a poke. "She is *very* beautiful, and she obviously likes you."

"Is she the insipid blonde or the bitter looking brunette?"

Adele rolled her eyes. "You know she is the blonde."

Rainere ran his hand across her back, lightly dancing his fingers up and down her spine. "I find the fragility of modern women disconcerting and slightly repulsive," he answered matter-of-factly. "I couldn't imagine being with a woman who couldn't completely consume me with her power. Such strength as you have over me, *cara mia*, is nothing less than intoxicating, and very addictive."

Adele sat up in surprise at his response, but then threw back her head and laughed. "Right answer," she said happily and then leaned over to kiss her perfect, alien prince on the lips. "Would you like me to consume you again?"

Rainere stretched languidly after her kiss but winced at a pain in his side. "Perhaps in a few minutes, *cara mia*," he said and rolled onto his stomach. "I need to regain my strength."

Adele sat up and tickled Rainere in the spot he had winced at before, making him growl – "That feels delicious, don't stop" – so she continued, running her hands all over the incredible tattoo that covered every inch of the skin on his back. If she hadn't been told it was a powerful spell etched into flesh she might have even guessed for herself. The pattern was tightly packed and intricate. But within the long swirling lines she started to see small geometric shapes tangled in the branches and vines travelling across his shoulder blades and down his lower back and along his side. She touched a small diamond that had been drawn inside a leaf.

Rainere hissed at the same time that the Chime Voices sang a clear word of command in her ears.

"Oh!" she was surprised at both reactions. "Did I hurt you?"

Rainere smiled at her over his shoulder. "You always find ways to hurt me," and his voice rasped with desire. "That's one of the reasons I love you."

Adele smiled back and bent over to kiss the little diamond, running her tongue over the tiny shape and laughed as Rainere's deep groan. The Chime Voices sang prettily in her head, a song that made her feel happy and reckless.

Adele ran her hand up and over Rainere's ribs, right at the edge of the tattoo. Long tails of ink licked across his ribcage and hipbone. Adelena hummed the same tune that the Chime Voices were singing as she trailed her fingers over the bumps and undulations of Rainere's wing muscles and ribs. Rainere's body was one of the most beautiful things she had ever seen and she loved touching him.

"Adelena, *cara mia?*" Rainere rolled onto his side and gazed at the fire, but Adele could still tell he was entirely focused on her.

She kissed his shoulder to let him know she was listening.

"Let's get married now, tonight."

Adele could feel his fear. The chill of it rippled off his skin and against her lips. He wanted her so badly to say, yes.

"Darling," she said soothingly. "I am already yours. We made promises to each other, you and I. What more could a priest give us that we need to belong together. I love you and you love me." She kissed his side and pressed against him.

"*Cara mia*, you know why we need to be joined in marriage. It will be so much safer for you and your family and the world must see us as united as we see ourselves. Please, my heart, do me this honor."

Adele found it easier this time to resist such a political proposal, but she was also finding it hard to take Rainere seriously as the Chime Voices in her head sang and laughed, and his power rolled deliciously through her veins. She decided to have some fun with her serious prince.

"Rainere, answer me this: will you be mine forever, to love, to cherish, to protect and to obey."

Rainere flipped onto his back and faced her, his eyes wide, as he recognized the sound of vows.

"I will, Adelena. Forever."

Adelena trailed her hand across his stomach and grinned as she saw he was ready for her again. She teased him slowly then let go and let her hand rest on his side. She spoke the words that the Chime Voices whispered in her ears:

"Then in front of this fire and the stars looking down on us I pronounce us joined forevermore." She signed her name on his skin with a flourish and giggled. "See, now we are married!"

Rainere constricted in pain suddenly and sat up, gasping. He held his side where her hand had been. "Gods, what is that?" he winced and gritted his teeth. "It's burning me!"

The light, loose feeling instantly left Adele. "I didn't do anything did I? I was just touching you," she protested. "Rainere, please, let me look at it."

Still wincing Rainere pulled his hand off his ribcage. A silvery grey swirl now joined two of the long tails of the tattoo together. It was a swirl in the shape of her insignia.

Adele covered her mouth with her hands. "Oh Rainere, did I do that to you? I didn't mean to! I was just thinking about…"

"That's a Mark!" said Rainere, gazing down at the silvery scar in shock. He looked up at her and all trace of his sexy huskiness had gone and he just looked angry.

"You Marked me!" he repeated. "How did you do that? How did you know *how* to do that?"

"I didn't mean to," said Adele desperately. "I'm so, so sorry Rainere, please let me fix it. Maybe I can take it off?" She reached out, but Rainere flinched from her touch.

"Don't," he said coldly. "If you don't know how you put it there, you might make it worse."

A silence fell between them as Rainere awkwardly examined his side and Adele mentally kicked herself for ruining their time together with her stupid magic yet again. How did she manage to do these things?

As if he heard her thoughts, Rainere glanced up at Adele. "This is powerful magic, Adelena. You would have had to counter an element of my immortality spell to actually change something on my body."

Adele shrugged miserably. "I was just thinking about how beautiful your body is and how much I love you and love the feeling that you are all mine." She blushed, explaining her thoughts aloud made them sound so childish and flip. "We were talking about marriage and I just said some wedding vows that we use on Earth. I never thought I was drawing anything on you." Adele hung her head. "I'm so sorry Rainere, I didn't mean to hurt you again. I just never seem to learn my own strength."

Rainere moved forward and wrapped her up into his arms, holding her tight to his chest. She felt his breath hot on her neck as he spoke, "My love what you have done to me binds us now. You have Marked me as your own and it means we will be together forever, always. Your Mark is part of my immortality now."

Rainere lifted her chin to meet his gaze. The fine rings of silver twirled around his black pupils and shimmered with his power.

"Marriage banns are nothing compared to the gravity of this bond. Do you understand, *cara mia?*"

"I understand," whispered Adele, though her head swam and a nasty feeling of dread clawed its way up from her belly.

Rainere smiled and kissed her lightly. "We should dress and I will find the priest. Tonight we will start the rest of our lives together. Adelena St. Lucidis, you have made me the happiest immortal in the world of Evendaar."

He kissed her again before turning away to pull on his trousers and shirt. Adele reached over to grab her dress from the chaise longue, but she only pulled the fabric over herself to cover her nakedness.

She couldn't really believe what she was going to say now to the only man she had ever truly loved. Her heart was shrieking at her to stop, but her head was determined and had been this whole time. She looked up at Rainere as he threw his shirt over his shoulders. He looked so happy and she knew how rare that had been in his life before her.

"Rainere, stop," said Adele. "Don't get the priest, please. We cannot get married tonight, my love."

Rainere frowned at her and opened his mouth to protest, but she held up her hand for silence. "Rainere, I will give you my heart and my body. I will give you my very soul, gladly and with both hands." Adele's voice trembled with tears. "But, Rainere, I will not give you the crown, and I will not make you a king in Unisia." Her tears fell as she struggled to finish what she had to say. "My love, I have a responsibility to the people of Unisia and to you. There would be war if I married you and too many people would die trying to take you off the throne again. I just can't be responsible for what others will do if I bring you back to the Golden Palace with me."

Adele wasn't sure how Rainere would take her heart-breaking proclamation and she watched him carefully. She wouldn't blame him if he screamed at her or smashed things and howled in frustration. She felt awful. This was all her fault. She had promised to marry

Rainere and now she was breaking that promise. She had torn his magic out of him and Marked him as her own. Whether it was by accident or not, she always seemed to be hurting him and he was always having to forgive her. Maybe that would stop now.

"Oh, *cara mia*," Rainere sighed, defeated. "My darling, *cara mia*, you just can't understand, can you? The danger is already surrounding us, my love. War is here."

He pierced her with a look that was so poignant with despair that she burst into tears. In a few steps, Rainere was there, holding her tight. Yet again, comforting her, though she was the one who had wronged him. Adele sobbed against his bare chest.

"Shah, my love, don't be afraid. I will find a way to keep you safe," Rainere murmured into her hair, as he stroked her back. "You will be safe from harm, I promise. I know you love me, but if you do not want to marry me now, I understand."

Rainere was gentle as he helped Adele back into her long gown. With deft fingers and a tweak of magic, he did up all her buttons and ribbons. Not for the first time, Adele wondered what it would be like to go back to Rainere's room with him and wake up next to him and plan her day with him like a normal couple. *Why did it have to be so impossible?*

Adele and Rainere held hands as they walked slowly back to the guest suite. When they reached the hallway of the suite they paused and gazed at each other in the near-dark. Suddenly, Rainere pushed Adele up against the wall, making her gasp.

"Your guards are patrolling tonight, I can hear them at the other end of the hall," he whispered in her ear. "But I cannot let you go with the sound of your tears in my ears."

Careless of who could hear them, Adele threw herself into kissing Rainere, wanting to say with her lips all that she couldn't with words. She reached down between his legs and stroked him firmly before fighting with the buttons to free him from his pants. Rainere groaned in her ear and scooped her up, pressing her up against the wall and managing to push her long dress aside. He ran his tongue down her neck and pressed his teeth against the fragile skin as they reached a climax within moments of each other.

The tryst was over in minutes, but they were both sweating and breathing hard. Adele felt something tickle her neck and swatted it away. In the dim light she saw her fingers came away dark.

"Rainere, I'm bleeding," she whispered.

Rainere handed her a handkerchief and his apologies. "You just bring out the beast in me, *cara mia*," he growled in a hoarse whisper and kissed her again. She could taste her blood on his tongue.

As reluctant as she was to leave Rainere, Adele knew she had to get back to her general. It must be past midnight now and Ohrig would be frantic with worry that Rainere had whipped her off to rape her and force her to marry him. She gave Rainere a lingering kiss and promised to see him tomorrow. He pulled his handkerchief out of her hand and melted away into the dark.

She was still dazed by a weird emotional mix of heartbreak and carnal satisfaction when Adele met Captain Lucky and QG Leith in the hallway outside the door.

"Good evening, Your Majesty," said Captain Lucky in a voice filled with relief.

"Something wrong, Captain?" asked Adele as she heard a commotion behind the doors to the suite.

"It's just the little Princess isn't feeling well and has been asking for you all night, Your Majesty," said Lucky.

"The general went out to look for you half an hour ago, but we haven't seen him since," added QG Leith, looking worriedly over Adele's shoulder at the dark hallway behind her.

With a sigh, Adele pushed her way into the apartment and was confronted by a sight that made her stomach drop. Siobahn was pacing the floor with a pale and screaming Stella, the nanny almost as upset as the baby.

"Oh, Your Majesty!" Siobahn sobbed with relief when she saw Adele walk in. "The poor princess isn't well. She hasn't slept since dinner time and she is so hot, I think she has a fever."

Adele took the weeping Stella into her arms and expertly felt her baby's forehead with her cheek while checking her tummy with her other hand. "Yes, she has a temperature, but it isn't too bad," she said quickly. "Send someone to fetch Pere Raven from wherever he is and bring me some cloths and cold water."

It was just a virus, Adele was sure. The kids got them all the time, it was nothing to panic about. Stella had already quieted in her mother's arms and just hiccoughed a few sobs now and again. Adele noticed the other two children were also out of bed. Aaron was almost asleep in QG Pepper's arms, but Natalie was sitting up beside him and listening to Pepper's story with wide eyes. Lady Olivia was sitting comfortably in an armchair listening, too.

"Lady Olivia, please see the other two are put to bed somewhere in the other bedroom," instructed Adele, frowning at the lapse in routine when there were so many adults who could have helped Siobahn. "They should have been asleep hours ago."

"I'm sorry, Your Majesty, I think the poppets were just so concerned about their baby sister that they wanted to be up with her," said Lady Olivia with a slightly defensive tone, but as she approached, she gave Adele a curious look. "Your Majesty, you have something on your neck. Is that blood?"

Adele was too busy to feign surprise at the trickle running down her neck. "Let me get this baby settled," she snapped. "She needs sleep to feel better. Please don't come in and disturb me with Stella unless there is an *actual* emergency."

She didn't stop to look at the reaction to her command but took Stella into the dark bedroom and shut the door.

CHAPTER THIRTY-NINE

"And Back Down to Hell Again"

Rainere wandered aimlessly through his laboratory. He had lit a few candles, but it was the near full moon that bathed the room in silver light. Rainere tried not to look up at it. He only had what was left of this one night to come up with a plan to save Adelena from the Spider Empress.

Rainere wasn't accustomed to suffering such anxiety. Melancholy, loneliness and bitter depression, these had been his constant companions over the years, but this debilitating fear was just too difficult to bear. Never before had someone else's life mattered to him more than his own.

Before Adele had come into his life and he had been confronted with her passionate and desperate love for him, Rainere had never considered his immortality as anything but a curse to be endured. He had thought little of wasting his years studying the most esoteric of magic, keeping his body weak and malnourished from his abuse of the Blue Tonic, and staying away from the world outside the Grey Palace. But now he had given his heart to a St. Lucidis queen who was a figment of the prophecy, and he wanted nothing more than to see her live through it all even if he had to sacrifice himself to do it.

Rainere bent down and picked up a few tools that the children had left on the ground and placed them back on the bench next to a pile of broken glass. It was the same bench on which he'd taken Adele so recklessly just this morning. He placed his hands where her body had lain and tried to drink in the memories the old wood might have stored. He closed his eyes to better imagine her gasps and the way her body had moved under him.

He felt a pull in the Mark at his side and his eyes snapped open, his breath coming out in a hiss. Rainere placed his hand on his side and winced as the Mark shifted and rippled, stirring, like it was trying to pull him back to her. It was such an odd feeling, uncomfortable and irresistible at the same time. *She is so close, just in the next wing of the palace, if only I could go to her.* But Adelena was distracted and she lost her focus on him. The Mark settled down and Rainere felt hollow again.

Adelena was probably with her children right now. Rainere did not enjoy the knowledge that he was not alone in Adele's heart. She had three other people in her life who would always come before him. He knew they were the real reason she would never risk a marriage to him, since it meant putting the children in danger. But now time had run out. The full moon rose tomorrow night, and the time of the prophecy was at hand.

By the Goddess, why did everything have to be so complex!

With a wave Rainere picked up the broken glass from the table and watched as it danced in mid-air, sparkling in the candlelight. He waved his hand to and fro and the glass fragments swirled into an image of Adelena's face.

"Prince Rainere?" A tiny voice behind him caused Rainere to break his concentration and the glass tinkled in a heap on the bench again.

Natalie came into view wearing a frilly white nightgown, her dark hair tumbled about her pale face, looking for all the world like a tiny Adelena. She walked over to the table and saw the mess of glass. "Did I break it?" she asked, looking up at him through her dark lashes, a tiny frown creasing her forehead.

"Not at all, child, it was my own fault," Rainere replied, brushing the glass aside. On a whim he picked up Natalie and sat her on the bench. "What are you doing out of bed, little princess?"

Natalie looked down at the glass in case it might dance again. "Stella won't stop crying and it's keeping me awake. Mummy told me to go sleep in the other room with Aaron, but I wanted to come and find you."

"And why is that?" Rainere was shocked by the little girls' courage. Surely the Grey Palace at night should frighten a little thing like her?

Natalie didn't answer but pointed to the glass. "I saw my Mummy's face in there." Natalie smiled and turned to Rainere. "Do you love her?"

Rainere's heart stopped beating for just a moment before he heard the innocence behind her question. Natalie was fascinated by love and gave out her own generously. Rainere supposed it must have been because her mother had shown her how to. "I love her as my queen," he replied gently. "As all her subjects do."

Natalie considered this. "Do you love me as my subject too?"

"I will love you all as your mother has instructed me to and as is my duty," he answered.

"Why aren't you married?" asked Natalie curiously. She picked up a pair of fine-nose pliers and began trying to separate the shards of glass.

Rainere paused and decided to skip the history lesson. "Because I have never met anyone I wanted to marry before?"

"And so you've never left a wife before either," remarked Natalie. "My Daddy left my Mummy, you know? She used to cry all the time about him, but she stopped when we moved here." Natalie frowned. "I don't think Daddy is my father anymore because we are so far away from him. Would you like to be my father?"

Rainere was dumbfounded. "Why would you want me as your father, child?"

"Because you are the handsomest man in the kingdom and you are nice to Mummy all the time. She said you are a wonderful prince and you can't always believe what other people tell you about other people; and you are so kind and your magic is more fun than Ohren's is; and I think that the Grey Palace is better than the Golden Palace because there are less people here and no one tells me to leave Mummy alone all the time. You know, lots of reasons."

Natalie looked up at Rainere and her clear green eyes were wide with earnestness. "And I love you very much. Remember I gave you that picture of us together? I haven't changed my mind, you know."

Satisfied with her speech Natalie gave up on picking at the glass shards and drew her hands up to pull her hair into a ponytail, just as her mother always did.

Rainere caught a glimmer of silver at her throat. "Natalie, where did you get this?" he asked, pulling the intricate chain from beneath a cotton frill. "I meant this to be for your mother."

Natalie had the decency to look chagrined. "Oh, it was a special present for Mummy? I found it in her room hidden in a shiny black box." She took it back out of his hand and dropped it under her collar again. "I *think* she wanted me to have it, but she was just too busy to tell me before we left Belvoir. Also, I can't get it off."

Rainere was horrified. If Adele wasn't wearing the necklace when they went to the Spider Empress she wouldn't be protected by its powerful magic. His mind flew in a hundred frantic directions, but he couldn't pull the necklace of Natalie's neck now without hurting her, badly. He had no time to prepare the complicated magic needed to break his own spell, so it would have to run its course. Already Rainere could feel dawn approach as the stars shifted in the sky and the moonlight slanted over the bench, illuminating Natalie in its light.

Rainere froze as a wicked through crept into his head and circled about, looking for a place to settle.

"You don't mind if I borrow the necklace for a little while do you, Prince Rainere?" Natalie asked, smiling up at him.

"Of course not, princess," Rainere whispered hoarsely. He reached out to lightly touch Natalie's head and ran his fingers through her silky locks. She was so much like her mother. "Just promise me you'll keep it hidden and Mummy will never know."

Natalie threw her arms around his middle and gave Rainere a sudden, strong little hug. "Oh, thank you, Prince Rainere," she said into his chest.

Rainere felt guilt like a knife twisting in his gut and he steeled himself against the pain. "I think it is time you rejoined your mother, princess," he said and lifted her down off the bench, trying to ignore the fragile feel of her ribcage beneath his hands.

Natalie skipped to the door and sent him a little wave before she turned and left.

Rainere walked to the window and gazed out over the landscape of his moonlit garden. He let the thoughts pounding through his head wash over him. A firm tug of the Mark brought a clear image of Adelena into his mind, but now it was overshadowed with her daughter's face. She could be his one day, his daughter, and he would be a good father to her.

Rainere opened his hand and looked down at the strands of dark hair laid across his palm. He pulled the blood-stained handkerchief out of his pocket and carefully wrapped the hairs in it.

But first he had a vow to keep.

CHAPTER FORTY

"Innocent Dreams of Safety"

Natalie trailed her fingers along the wall as she got closer to the brightly-lit hallway where the apartment was, but she was in no rush to get back.

She was enjoying the warm, bubbly feeling that Prince Rainere gave her. She knew that no one believed her when she said that she loved the prince, but she really did. He was everything wonderful about this new world of Evendaar. When her Daddy had left, Natalie had lived with a big hole in her chest that had ached at night, but Prince Rainere had filled that hole and she felt full again when she was with him. He really was her friend and when he looked at her, she could tell he was really waiting to hear what she had to say. When he carried her in his arms, he hadn't complained or said "Ooff, you are too heavy, Natty!" or pretended to drop her like QG Leith did. He was strong enough to hold her for ages. He gave her presents, too. Well, he gave Mummy presents, but he didn't mind when she kept them.

Natalie skipped around the corner, but froze when she saw Captain Lucky, QGs Leith and Owens and Lady Olivia standing in the hallway discussing something with serious faces. They all turned to look at her.

"Oh, Natalie, thank the Goddess!" exclaimed Lady Olivia and put her hand on her heart. "You scared the life right out of me when I couldn't find you."

Lady Olivia bustled down the hall to grab Natalie's hand and pull her along.

"You really shouldn't go wandering about the palace like that, princess," said Captain Lucky, smiling at her. Natalie liked him a lot, but he was too young to be a daddy.

"Yes, it's not safe with Mr. Grotto lurking about," added QG Leith with a pretend shudder.

Natalie didn't say anything. She was too embarrassed by the fuss everyone was making. She let Lady Olivia yank her through the door.

"Now, you need to go to bed, young lady." Lady Olivia dropped the smile she used when other people were around. Other important people like Mummy and Captain Lucky, not maids or nannies of course.

"What do you think your mother would say if she caught you out of bed? I'm sure she would think you needed a hard slap," snapped Lady Olivia. "You are so naughty to run away like that."

Natalie pulled her hand out of Lady Olivia's and frowned. She hated it when people told her what her mother would do and say. She knew her Mummy better than anyone and she knew her Mummy thought she was "beautiful and terrifyingly bright", and she knew that was really wonderful.

"What do you think Mummy would say if she knew that you lost me?" Natalie answered tartly. "I think you would get the smack then."

Lady Olivia spun to face Natalie, her blue eyes narrowed and her mouth was pursed as if she was going to spit. Natalie watched the variety of emotions flash across the young woman's face. Everyone thought Lady Olivia was beautiful, but Natalie just thought she was mean.

"It's late. You need to get to bed now, little princess," said Lady Olivia wearing a weird smile. "After all, princesses need their rest if they wish to grow up big and strong, or at all."

Natalie trailed behind Lady Olivia as she went into the other bedroom where General Ohrig and the guards had slept last time they were in the Grey Palace. She saw Aaron curled up in the middle of the big bed with Siobahn sleeping next to him.

Natalie sighed. She didn't like Siobahn very much either, but Aaron was such a cry-baby now that he had nightmares and dreams all the time and he always wanted someone to hold him or pat his back until he went to sleep. Normally Mummy did it, but Natalie did it a lot too when he woke up in the night.

She crawled in next to her brother and leaned over him to give Siobahn a poke in the arm. Siobahn was lying on her back and snoring loudly, but with the poke she rolled over and quietened. Natalie wrapped her arms around Aaron's shoulders and he instantly turned to snuggle into her.

He's such a baby, thought Natalie, but thinking that made her feel lonely and cold so she hugged him even harder. Looking up she saw that Lady Olivia was still standing in the doorway, staring at her. Natalie decided she hated the lady. *Why did she just stand there?*

"You can go now," she ordered Lady Olivia in her best bossy voice. But she was glad when the lady didn't say anything else, just left and shut the door.

Natalie snuggled into her brother and kissed his hair like Mummy did. As she closed her eyes she imagined sleeping in a big bed with Prince Rainere and Aaron. That would be so warm and cozy. No way would Lady Olivia stare at her from the doorway then.

Natalie didn't know how she knew, but she was sure that the prince didn't like Lady Olivia either. He hadn't looked at her once today even though she was wearing a dress that showed her big boobs.

Aaron kicked her gently and Natalie shifted a bit to let him move. She kissed his hair again and he settled.

All I have to do is get Mummy to marry Prince Rainere, she thought. *When I wake up, I'm going to tell her that Prince Rainere should be my new daddy.* She was glad that she had already told Prince Rainere of her plan, so he could talk to her Mummy about it, too.

Natalie felt for the necklace at her throat and, still smiling, drifted off to sleep.

CHAPTER FORTY-ONE

"One Fine Morning"

Charlie had woken up when Blondie brought Princess Natalie back to bed. From his couch tucked away in the corner, he couldn't see much of the lady, which was a shame, as she was showing off plenty of rack in a low-cut dress today.

He heard the door close and shut his eyes, feeling comfortable. The reason he had chosen this room was because the royal children were sleeping in it, and he had figured it was probably the safest room in the palace. Charlie had no trouble admitting he was terrified of being caught alone by the black prince. He also had the little problem of the prince or the queen realizing that there had been a terrible mix-up and that he didn't really work for either of them. But he was hoping that they were too busy with each other to bother about him.

It was cozy curled up on his couch, with a heavy blanket and a pillow under his head. Charlie heard the little princess sigh and found the noise comforting.

He let himself fall into a dreamless slumber.

CHAPTER FORTY-TWO

"A Devil Came Creeping"

Adele opened her eyes and squinted in the morning light. She hadn't slept, of course, but she had at least managed to close her eyes and rest a little. She checked the limp baby in her arms, but Stella was sleeping soundly, her breathing steady and her forehead cool.

Relief swamped Adele and she lay back down on her pillow with a happy sigh. Though she had known from experience that it had just been a normal virus that Stella was suffering from, she had felt the natural terror every mother has when a child is ill. The fact that she hadn't had her usual arsenal of child medications had given her a flutter of panic as well, but good old-fashioned cold water and cuddles with Mummy had fixed everything.

Adele heard a noise and saw Siobahn and Lady Olivia were quietly moving about the room, laying out the wardrobe for the day for the family. Lady Olivia noticed Adele was up and tip-toed over to her. She nodded at Stella with an inquiring frown.

"She's fine," whispered Adele, giving Lady Olivia a smile that the lady returned with a little silent cheer.

"We are just organizing your things, Your Majesty," Lady Olivia whispered. "We must leave before lunchtime to make it back in time for the Steeplechase today."

"Where are the other children?" asked Adele quietly as she extricated herself from Stella's damp little body."

"Still sleeping, Your Majesty," whispered Lady Olivia. "They were busy little angels last night and are all tuckered out."

Adele climbed out of bed and stretched out the cricks and kinks in her back after having lain with Stella in her arms for hours.

"I'm going to take a shower and get dressed," said Adele on the way to the bathroom. "Don't bother waking the children. We'll have breakfast late today."

"With Prince Rainere, Your Majesty?" asked Lady Olivia, but when Adele looked at her, the lady wore a perfectly innocent expression. It was only a natural question after all.

"I'm not sure what our host is doing today," Adele replied even as her heart thudded hard in her chest. "Perhaps you can check with Mr. Grotto for me?"

Adele made it to the bathroom just as the tears filled her eyes. She leaned against the back of the door and silently let them fall. A horrible cloud of premonition enveloped her and she covered her mouth with her hand and stifled a sob. Though they had ended last night with passionate sex in the hallway, Adele was suddenly very afraid that it might be the last time that Rainere let her close to him. She felt sick at what her decision not to marry Rainere might mean now. She couldn't be with him, but neither could she live without him.

Adele turned on the shower and, dropping her nightgown to the floor, she stepped into the hot spray and let it fall on her face, washing away the tears. The bite on her neck stung as the water touched it.

I have screwed this up so badly, she thought. First, she had declared her undying love to Rainere, then she had magically marked him with her initials—*how incredibly humiliating for him*—then she had refused to marry him, despite him asking her for the third time. *How much more is my poor prince supposed to take!*

Adele turned and lathered her hair with soap.

It was so incredibly complicated and, any way she looked at it, Adele had been right to say no. General Ohrig had just confirmed what she knew in her gut: no one would want Rainere in the Golden Palace and they would kill him before they let him sit on the throne.

Adele rinsed her hair and picked up the little razor from its shelf and soaped her legs for shaving.

Adele hated to admit it, but she supposed that Rainere was just as prejudiced against the court of the Golden Palace as much as they were against him. That must be why he kept warning her against the danger of trusting the wizards. This prophecy that underlay it all was just as dangerous, and Adele cursed herself for her distraction with Rainere that she still hadn't asked him about it.

Adele held her back under the water and let the pounding of it block her ears and thoughts. She wasn't going to be getting out in a hurry this morning. The longer they could stay at the Grey Palace the better. Who knew when they would be back again?

CHAPTER FORTY-THREE

"And Creeping Around the Corner"

The door in the paneled wardrobe creaked open and a figure studied the room in the grey light of the new morning. A long, white hand slid around the edge of the door and pushed it wider, allowing the hollow-eyed man to get out and pad quietly across the floor to the big bed.

Prince Rainere looked down on the two tiny bodies wrapped so tightly together. He could not remember what it felt like to cry, but right now, it was as if his eyes were swimming in acid.

He leaned down over the children and gently took Natalie's hand. "Princess," he whispered, though his voice was more of a croak.

Natalie's dark eyes fluttered open and, sleepily, she smiled up at the prince. "I knew you'd come," she said enigmatically.

Rainere almost gasped when his heart squeezed painfully. "Princess, I have a present for you."

Rainere knelt by the bed and pulled the bracelet from his pocket.

"It matches my necklace," grinned Natalie, already bright and awake. She sat up in bed and swung her legs over the side.

"Let me put it on you," whispered Rainere, as he took her tiny hand in his and slid the silver chain over her wrist.

Natalie began to shimmer and change before his very eyes. Her limbs grew longer, her body taller, and her face matured into a woman's. Within moments, the transformation was complete.

"There, now. You look just perfect," said the prince and ran a tender hand over the cheek of the Natalie-as-Adelena.

"Thank you! Oh, thank you, Prince Rainere," sighed Natalie happily, as she admired her new pretty thing. "I'm just sorry I don't have any presents for you."

Rainere winced and paled even more. "All I need is your happiness, Princess Natalie," he whispered, but Natalie didn't know why he looked so sad. "Your happiness, and a kiss."

Natalie grinned. Kisses were easy to give.

Prince Rainere always smelled so nice, like the wind when you played outside on a winter's day. She leant over and pursed her lips to kiss his smooth cheek, but at the last moment, the prince turned his head and she kissed his lips instead. They were cool and soft.

"Oh!" giggled Natalie. "I kissed your mouth. Only mummies and daddies can do that."

Rainere caught the little girl as she fell forward into his arms. He cradled her gently and checked the pulse at her throat. Sleeping curses were tricky things to engineer, but far less dangerous than an opiate or poison on one so young. To his relief, her pulse was strong and her breathing steady as the illusion curse continued to work, changing Natalie's features into those of her mother's.

"And only true love's kiss shall wake you, princess," Prince Rainere murmured, and Natalie's eyelids fluttered, as if she dreamed of pleasant things. "Your mother will be with you soon."

With the back of his hand, Rainere wiped off the rest of Adelena's blood that he had painted on his lips. He looked down at the sleeping face of the princess-queen in his arms. The illusion curse wasn't perfect, but it was the best he could do with the strands of hair he'd taken from Natalie and coated with Adelena's blood, before wrapping them around the links of the bracelet.

He carried Natalie-as-Adelena over to the cupboard and stepped through. The door creaked quietly shut again.

*   *   *

Only when he was sure that the prince had left did Charlie let out his breath again.

Charlie uncurled himself from his frozen position and sat up. Watching the prince perform his evil magic on the little princess had turned his bowels to water. He was trembling from head to toe and could barely organize his scrambled thoughts. His instincts screamed at him to leave immediately and to run as far from the Grey Palace as he possibly could. This was not his mess to get mixed up in.

Queens and Marchant princes, dark magic, and kidnapping! Charlie was already in enough trouble with the Boss without letting himself be dragged into the middle of a regicide.

But if he didn't tell the queen what had happened to her daughter, then who would? *It's not my problem,* his sensible side told him.

Marchant blood runs in my veins, so what if this St. Lucidis queen thinks I'm working with the prince on this, too? As she very easily could if I don't get the hell out of here.

What would stop the prince from killing him if he tried to help the queen, anyway? *He had wanted to before, hadn't he?*

But a fierce sense of chivalry the likes of which Charlie had never known before raised up its head inside of him and drowned out the other voices in his head. It suggested that he should do something very, *very* stupid.

CHAPTER FORTY-FOUR

"But Even Devils Can Be Sorry"

Rainere felt his heart pounding uncomfortably hard in his chest as he made his way down the dark tunnel into the Spiders' Nest. Though the bundle in his arms was very light, the burden he carried was heavy.

Rainere had never doubted his magic before, but as he looked down at the Natalie-as-Adelena he could see so many faults in his illusion spell. Natalie looked younger than Adelena did in real life, perhaps no more than a teenager of eighteen or nineteen, flat-chested, and too thin. It was how she would look in the future, he supposed, and his heart cracked under the pressure of the guilt that weighed on it. She didn't deserve this.

Rainere could feel the sweat dripping down his neck and under his collar. He prayed to the Goddess Serena that the sleeping curse would hold for as long as it needed to. He had been inspired by Natalie's story of Sleeping Beauty. *What could be more perfect than putting the princess to sleep while this whole terrifying ceremony took place?* Once he had taken Natalie-as-Adelena down to the empress and shown her the wedding band she wore on her wrist, then the empress would release him from his oath and he could finally be free of her power to control his will. The necklace would repel the Spider Empress from biting Natalie, with its hopefully undetectable magic, and they would both be free to leave the nest. Adelena would kiss her daughter awake and he could explain why it had to be Natalie in place of Adelena. More importantly, Adelena would not have to endure the horror of meeting the empress and she would never have to know of his humiliating oath of fealty to the monstrous empress beneath the ground.

Rainere, normally so sure-footed, tripped on a tree root sticking out of the ground. He cursed softly but savagely.

"Master, please reconsider what you are about to do," whispered Grotto, who walked close behind him on his heels. "There is still time before noon to convince the queen to come herself."

"Silence," snapped Rainere. He had heard enough of Grotto's opinions, since he had told the old man his plan to present Natalie in place of Adelena. He understood Grotto's fear. If any of the three over-lapping spells should fail, and the empress discovered the deception, they would all be eaten on the spot. Or worse.

Rainere swallowed on his dry throat, as the cloying humidity in the tunnels made him want to gasp.

There was no room for error.

As he neared the cavern at the center of the nest, Rainere could hear the noisy clicking and rasping of a large crowd gathered there. He flinched as he felt the flow of hundreds of spiders pass over the walls of the tunnel, all heading into the cavern and the court of their empress.

Unconsciously, he slowed his pace and felt Grotto bump into him.

"Master, please," begged Grotto one last time.

Rainere felt a moment of rare empathy for his loyal manservant. If Grotto had ever felt for him the love Rainere now felt for Adelena's children, then he could understand why Grotto would not give up trying to change his mind while accompanying him into certain death. But this new knowledge would not stop him tonight.

Rainere stepped into the cavern and noticed that a large stone table had been moved into the center of the space. The sides were rough-hewn rock, but the top was intricately carved and polished. A small lip had been carved at each corner and deep glass bowls sat under the runnels.

Rainere didn't react when Grotto hissed behind him, but he felt the anxiety of the old man intensify immediately. *What was the table for?*

The empress was watching the entrance and pulled herself to stand upon her eight mighty legs when she saw the prince enter.

"The new bride and groom have arrived," she screeched in the language of men. She bowed to Rainere by lowering her first two legs, but she didn't take her eyes off him or the limp woman in his arms. "Shall I call you 'king'?" she cackled gleefully, and her face contorted itself into a hideous semblance of a grin.

"In all but name, Empress Ka-kik." Rainere bowed stiffly and pulled Natalie tighter to his chest.

The movement wasn't lost on the Spider Empress. She waved a foreleg at Rainere, beckoning him closer to her. The empress had painted herself in lurid colors for the occasion and her pincers were shiny with viscous poison. "Let me see your new wife, Prince Rainere."

Rainere was loath to take another step, but he straightened his spine and approached the dais where the empress had settled down, her legs splayed to each side and her thorax molded into the pile of filthy silk cushions.

The empress looked more closely at the woman in Rainere's arms. "Why does she sleep? Didn't she want to meet me?"

Rainere tried to control his breathing, keeping it at a natural pace. Though he may doubt the strength of the illusion spell, he was almost positive the empress wouldn't be able to judge the age or true appearance of a human woman. The empress hadn't been above ground in almost a thousand years and her knowledge of humans was, therefore, safely limited.

"As I have mentioned before, Empress Ka-kik, the queen is a fragile woman, plagued by many fears. A fear of dark, enclosed spaces and spiders being chief among them." Rainere bowed as low as he could. "I felt it prudent to render her unconscious for this meeting, so as not to offend you with her screaming."

"But I like the sound of their screaming," cackled the empress, who was answered by a rippling wheeze of laughter from the crowd of Spiders in the cavern.

Rainere bowed again but remained silent. Sweat trickled down his temple. The empress was leaning over as far as she could to get closer to the queen.

"She doesn't look like she would be strong enough to kill a warrior like my son, Oki. Perhaps she is more formidable than you would have me believe, my prince of Marchant?" The empress's tone was thoughtful and she regarded Rainere with her canny gaze, an animal intelligence lighting the many eyes that studied him. "Perhaps you wish to join your power to this Child of Prophecy and claim her strength for yourself?"

The pit of dread in Rainere's stomach started to curdle and turn. *What was the empress talking about, joining powers?* With a belated clarity, Rainere finally saw beyond his own fear and noticed that every one of the empress's guards had surrounded the cavern, standing in front of each exit, with their knives drawn. The crowd of spiders had pushed back out of the way and sat hunched on the walls and ceiling. This was highly unusual. *Were they expecting him to cause trouble?*

"Empress Ka-kik," said Rainere, forcing his voice to remain firm. "This Queen Adelena is but a human female, as you can see. At your order, I forced her to marry me and give me the throne of Unisia, which she did last night. When the full moon rises tonight, I will make her sign, in blood, the decree releasing you from your status as monsters and your people will once again be free to walk the Above Lands. The light of the Goddess Lune will shine down upon you and the Golden Palace shall be yours. As king, I will allow you to reign as you will over the land of Unisia."

Rainere felt his lungs constrict as he finished his speech. Panic was making his mind scramble. The Spider Empress should have been pleased with this night, but instead, she looked irritated.

"You will *allow* me, my king-in-all-but-name?" hissed the empress, snapping her jaws. "You will *allow* me nothing, boy! I saved *your* life. I gave *you* your freedom in return for a miserable little oath! All I ask in return for my kindnesses is that you marry one of your own and take the throne of Unisia."

"And I have done so, empress," interrupted Rainere, once again scanning the exits. This was not going well.

"Really?" snapped the empress. "Then show me proof of your loyalty. Give me the queen."

Rainere felt the blood drain from his overheated cheeks.

"But, Empress Ka-kik," he croaked, as he saw the shamans by the empress's side shudder and shake into their human forms with a wet, ripping noise. They approached him, arms extended.

Rainere instinctively hugged Natalie tighter.

"Give me the queen, *Prince* Rainere," ordered the empress in a voice full of triumphant spite. She watched Rainere closely. She could smell the fear in him so strongly, that she could almost taste it. Empress Ka-kik was ready to shriek for joy. She had the Marchant prince right where she wanted him. He would do anything to keep his bride.

Reluctantly, Rainere laid Natalie-as-Adelena in the ropey arms of the nearest shaman. His brain whirled, but he couldn't think of a way to escape the cavern with the empress here and her guards armed and ready. He watched helplessly as Natalie was placed on the stone table and was arranged with her arms pulled out from her sides and her legs parted. He made on involuntary move toward her and felt Grotto pinch at his sleeve, uttering a warning hiss.

Empress Ka-kik lumbered off her dais and to the floor, making her way to the stone table. She felt the prince's fear for the queen vibrating the hairs on her legs pleasantly. "Wake her up!" she commanded Rainere, as he stepped in beside her.

"I cannot, Empress," replied Rainere. "The spell is organic and will wear off on its own, naturally."

"Pity," sniffed the empress, sounding petulant. "I would have this evil one look upon the face of the mother whose son she killed. My favored, dearest Oki is dead because of this evil human woman!"

The empress emitted a high keen that was echoed by the crowd about her. The sound brought a hot burn to the back of Rainere's eyes, but it wasn't the communal grief that had affected him. The empress had her pincers, shiny with poison, perilously close to Natalie's fragile skin. One more inch and she would be burned, but the empress lumbered around to face the prince and the danger was averted. Rainere almost sighed in relief.

The shaman nearest the empress leaned forward and whispered something too low for Rainere to hear, but it caused her to grind her jaws with a horrible clicking noise. "You like to lie to me don't you, little prince," said the empress suddenly.

Rainere's relief evaporated and his blood ran cold. He snapped a shallow bow to hide his expression. "Never," he croaked.

"Oh, I think that you do," corrected Empress Ka-kik. "I know that you would like me to think you care nothing for this skinny excuse for a queen, and I know that you believe the Hidden Child will make you her king for love alone, giving you the throne and raising the Marchant family from the ashes of history. You will rule over that kingdom, then, won't you, little prince? You will rule with her by your side and the wizards at your back. I know all of these things, little prince."

Her eyes glittered malevolently at Rainere. "Do you know *how* I know these things, my little betrayer?"

In mute horror, Rainere shook his head.

With a flick of her front leg, the empress gestured one of her shamans forward. The shaman shook out something small and black from his hand. In his other, he held out a crumpled piece of paper, covered in a pencil sketch.

"Shift!" ordered the empress.

The tiny black spider shifted into his human form. Schiss, broken and battered, shimmered into view. One of his arms hung limply and his feet were a bloody mess of exposed bone and gouged flesh. He could barely stand and leaned against the arm of the shaman.

"I believe you know my son, Schiss," hissed the empress, narrowing her thousand eyes. "I believe you ordered him to lie to me. Lie to his own mother!"

The Spider Empress spat and a gob of poison landed on the ground next to Schiss, splattering him and making him whimper in pain.

"He is dead to me now," she hissed. "As dead as your plan to take my Lost Child and join with her St. Lucidis family. You will never rule this kingdom with her. It will be mine! For a thousand years, I have waited while you Marchant kings and princes grew too weak to keep your ancient promises. I have been patient, Prince Rainere, but I will be patient no more. The queen is mine and her crown is mine!"

"Empress, no!" shouted Rainere, desperately. "I was never going to tie myself to the queen's family. She will abdicate the throne as soon as I can be crowned at the Golden Palace. When the moon rises tonight..."

"*When the moon rises tonight!*" mocked the empress. "My young prince, when the moon rises tonight, I will *eat* your nasty queen whole. She will satiate my hunger and grief, and I will take her St. Lucidis power into my blood." She grinned hideously, her eyes gleaming with triumph, as she delivered her final blow. "Then with the power of the old St. Lucidis blood flowing in my veins, I will be able to walk in the sun once more. You see, Prince Rainere, now I realize that *this* is how the Hidden Child will bring us out of the shadows and into the light!"

She wheezed with laughter and it was echoed around the cavern. The Spider Empress took another step closer to Rainere, until he could feel her foul breath on his face.

"Your oath to me is unfulfilled," she whispered in a soft rasp. "You will continue to be beholden to me until you learn to do as you are told."

Rainere felt a wave of despair wash over him and nearly staggered on his feet. He had been unutterably stupid to believe that the Spider Empress would ever keep her word. He was chained to her forever and because of his stupidity, Natalie's life was forfeit.

"Grottonski, take your prince home," ordered the empress, as she lumbered back to her dais. "He is looking a little feeble tonight."

Rainere felt Grotto pull him by the arm and mutter something, but he couldn't make his feet move. Rainere's spinning brain had slowed to a stop. Was he really going to leave the nest without Natalie? But that was impossible! He needed to give her back to Adelena. None of this made sense anymore.

Grotto pulled him more forcefully toward the entrance of the cavern and Rainere fell into step.

"Prince of Marchant," called the empress. "Remember to take your servant with you. If you leave him here, I will eat him after I eat your queen."

Unthinking, Rainere stumbled over and picked up the cowering Schiss in his arms. Though he cradled the small man gently, Schiss still cried out in pain at the touch.

"Now go!" ordered the empress with a wave of her lurid yellow foreleg. "I have much to prepare before I feast on the Hidden Child tonight. When the moon rises, I will no longer just be the Empress of the Under Lands, but I will become Queen of the Above Lands. The Hidden Child and I will be as one and *my* favored will roam the lands, eating everyone in our way!"

Rainere walked out of the cavern, pushed and pulled by the anxious Grotto, with the sound of the empress's words ringing in his ears. As the darkness enveloped them, he automatically led the way out of the mile of tunnels to the surface.

Rainere was surprised when they stepped out into the warm, dappled sunshine of mid-morning. Surely the world should have gone still and the birds fallen silent. Natalie was lost and it was completely his fault.

Rainere passed Schiss to Grotto and then, with shaking hands, conjured a pulsing green portal. He paused before stepping through to look back down the tunnel to the nest.

"Leave her, master," said Grotto gently. "You did everything you could. The child is lost to us now."

"The Lost Child," whispered Rainere, as Grotto took his arm and pulled them through the portal and back to the Grey Palace.

CHAPTER FORTY-FIVE

"And Wish to be an Angel Instead"

"But you must have some idea where the prince went, or when he'll be back?" insisted Adele. She was starting to lose her patience with the whey-faced servant before her.

The man wiped his nose on the back of his filthy sleeve and shrugged. "'E doesn't tell us nuffink," was the terse reply.

"Can you at least tell me how many servants are working in the palace and help me organize a search party? My daughter could be hiding anywhere!" Adele knew she was getting shrill, but it had been a couple of hours since Lady Olivia had gone to wake the children and discovered Natalie had disappeared.

"I wouldn't know 'ow ta," said the servant as he started to lean to the left before righting himself. The man was clearly drunk. "Tha's Mr. Grottonski's job, innit?"

"And, where is he?"

But the servant just shrugged again.

Adele huffed with frustration. Of all the days that Natalie could start playing her games, she had picked the worst of them. Adele knew her daughter loved it here in the Grey Palace and that she didn't want to leave again, but after last night Adele was loath to have to ask Rainere's help for something as silly as Natalie playing hide-and-seek in the palace. A thorough search of the apartments hadn't turned up any trace of her, and though Adele wasn't ready to panic she was close to it.

"Your Majesty. No luck, I'm afraid," said General Ohrig, as he and the rest of her Queen's Guard returned from another search, filling the room with their noise and clatter but no Natalie.

Adele frowned at her general and Ohrig frowned back. "We explored where we could, Your Majesty, but there are lots of places we could not enter that were protected by magic."

Adele heard the undercurrent of concern in his voice, but she fought to avoid feeling it herself. Natalie was just hiding and would be found soon. Adele chewed her lip. But where was Rainere, or even Grotto for that matter?

"Your Majesty, we've also had no luck finding the priest, Pere Raven, or Charlie either."

"Where is that priest?" muttered Adele to Ohrig as he approached her. "Surely he wouldn't want to miss the steeplechase?"

"Your Majesty, when was the last time we saw Pere Raven?" asked General Ohrig, keeping his voice low and casting his eyes about to make sure they weren't overheard. The servant Adele had been questioning had wandered off to scratch himself and ogle Lady Olivia as she played on the couch with Stella.

"The last time I saw him was when he went for a tour with all of you," replied Adele.

"The priest accompanied us as far the royal nursery, then left us there and went with Mr. Grotto to the Marchant's family chapel," continued Ohrig. "He seemed excited about it, and almost ran out of the room when Mr. Grotto offered to show it to him. After that, all we've had is Mr. Grotto's word that Pere Raven has remained in the chapel or the library attached to it. I thought nothing of it until this morning, but the man still hasn't shown up and its almost time to leave. And now Natalie has gone."

The unwanted fear uncurled in Adele's gut. "And no Prince Rainere or Grotto either," Adele added reluctantly. "This is very odd."

A dark frown was Ohrig's only reply. He didn't need to say anything else. Adele knew what he was thinking.

Lady Olivia walked over to Adele with Stella on her hip, giving the leering Grey Palace servant a wide berth.

"Your Majesty, all is in readiness for our departure. The steeplechase is scheduled to start at midday. We should probably be on our way if we are to make it on time."

"We can't leave without Natalie."

"No, of course not, Your Majesty, but perhaps Siobahn and I could take the little ones back and await you at Belvoir?" the young woman suggested. "I'm sure the prince would understand if we split the party in two. It's probably best I go with the nanny and children as Siobahn is terrified of His Highness."

Adele locked eyes with Ohrig as she realized if Rainere didn't appear to help them pass through the portal they were all trapped here in the Grey Palace.

"He'll be here," she promised her general, but didn't quite know what made her so confident. *Where had Rainere gone with Grotto and Pere Raven? Was this something to do with the wedding I refused to have? Had Natalie seen something?*

Adele shook the dark thoughts from her head and turned to the Grey Palace servant. "You there! Do you know the way to the palace chapel?"

The man shrugged and nodded at the same time, which Adele took for assent.

"General, let's leave three men here with the children and three of you come with me to the chapel." Quickly, Ohrig organized his men and they set off after the swaying servant.

As they left the palace interior, Adelena and her men made their way across the unkempt gardens to an enormous building separated from the rest of the grounds by a rusty wrought-iron fence. More church than chapel, the building loomed over them, casting a somber form in the sunny sky. They stopped at the large stone doors and the servant leading them muttered a short prayer, which was echoed by Ohrig, Owens and Bear. It was a prayer intoned out of respect to the Goddess Serena before they entered the sanctity of her house. One of the doors had already been pushed open, so they could pass through silently.

As she stepped into the chapel Adele felt a sudden flash of the familiar. Like many of the Gothic edifices back on Earth, the stone walls were decorated with stained glass windows portraying scenes both hideous and sublime, and which filtered the sunlight into different colors. Long wooden benches sat in tidy rows, ten on each side of the carpeted aisle. Adele heard the sound of roosting birds in the eaves and noticed the pews were decorated with dry, white splotches. She shivered as a cold draft blew in behind her and remembered that Natalie would still be in her little nightdress.

Adele walked down the aisle and saw that candles had been lit at the altar: row upon row of tall black candles that filled the air with a dusky perfume.

With a start, Adele realized there was a figure kneeling on the steps before the altar and her heart leapt. This was why her men hadn't been able to find him. He was here, in this unfamiliar part of the palace. As soon as she told him that Natalie was missing he would help to find her immediately.

Rainere rested on his knees, his long black hair hanging down his back, his head bowed as if in prayer. It only struck her as odd that he didn't turn when she called out his name. Adele mounted the steps and came close enough to touch him.

"Prince Rainere," she used his title as her men were within hearing distance. "I'm sorry to disturb you at prayer, but we have a problem. Natalie has gone missing." Adele stopped when Rainere gave her no reaction, but kept his eyes closed and his hands clasped in front of his chest.

"My love," whispered Adele more urgently. "Please I need you to help me find Natalie."

Adele was shocked to see a glittering green tear slowly trace its way down Rainere's cheek.

"Rainere, what's the matter?" she asked and touched his shoulder. She heard her men fall silent as they witnessed her gentle gesture.

Rainere finally opened his eyes and Adele saw his lashes were wet and his eyes glowed strangely, swimming with bright green tears.

"*Cara mia*, I know where she is," he whispered and turned to her, grief and despair marring his beautiful face. "But, my darling heart, she is lost."

Adele's hand flew to her mouth and the Chime Voices shrieked so loudly and so forcefully that she blacked out.

CHAPTER FORTY-SIX

"But Devils Don't Have Wings"

"The prince should be back soon," General Ohrig muttered. His heavy tread paced close by to her.

Adele woke up but didn't open her eyes. There was something on the other side of her eyelids that she didn't want to face, a terrible thing. If she stayed here in the dark she could ignore it.

"What happened to Queen Adelena?" A panicked young voice roused Adele and almost tricked her into opening her eyes. Carefully, she kept them shut tight.

"Where have you been, boy?" asked Ohrig gruffly. "We thought you had been taken, too."

"I haven't been, yet," answered Charlie. "But I know the princess has been. That's why I'm here."

The princess, thought Adele dreamily. That word had something to do with the 'terrible thing'.

"What do you know about Princess Natalie's disappearance?" demanded Ohrig.

Adele's eyes flew open at her daughter's name and she woozily climbed to her feet. She had been lying on a velvet couch and the dust from it clung to her. A large blanket had been draped across her but was now pooled at her feet and threatened to make her tumble.

"Where is Natalie?" she croaked and looked wildly around the unfamiliar sitting room. "Where are Aaron and Stella?"

General Ohrig was by Adele's side in an instant and he pushed her gently back down to sit. "Easy, Your Majesty, you've had a shock. Charlie, pour the queen some wine."

"I don't want wine," coughed Adele and noticed that General Ohrig had his sword in his hand. "I want my children."

"Prince Rainere, is guiding the children with the nanny and Lady Olivia back through the portal to Belvoir. The men have gone down to see it done. We still don't know where Natalie is, but the prince has promised to tell you everything when you are revived."

Ohrig handed her a glass of red wine. "Drink this, Your Majesty, it will help you feel better."

Adele doubted that. She felt horribly hollow and sour inside. Her mind was still so dull and kept flitting about, noticing insignificant things, like the broken braid trim on the side of the couch, and that Ohrig smelled of peppermint and tobacco, but she had never seen him take either. With an effort, Adele forced herself to sip at the wine and swallow it.

"Where have you been, Charlie?" she asked and saw the boy had huge sweat patches under his arms, making the fabric of his shirt stick to his ribs.

"That doesn't matter just yet, Your Majesty." The boy was in a great hurry to tell her something. Adele watched incuriously as he dropped to his knees before her on the carpet.

"Your Majesty, I don't know where the princess is, but I know who took her from her bed. It was the prince himself." Charlie's voice was low and urgent, and when he reached out to take her hand, she could feel how cold and clammy his fingers were.

Why would he lie to me like this?

"Careful lad, she's still in shock," warned General Ohrig. "If what you're saying is true then…" The general was interrupted by the arrival of Captain Lucky and the rest of the Queen's Guard. Prince Rainere and Grotto followed close behind.

Rainere. Adele breathed a sigh of relief at his arrival. He would fix all this confusion, and he would help her find Natalie.

"The children and women are all off the grounds and were safely put through the portal, general," said Captain Lucky. His voice was loud in the quiet of Adele's head.

Adele found Rainere's eyes with her own. She smiled and was happy when he came to sit next to her on the couch. Without thinking about the room full of men around them, she leaned into him as his arms encircled her. She breathed in his spicy cold scent and felt a warmth spread inside of her. She knew he felt it too.

"*Cara mia*, I am so sorry," he whispered into her hair. "She is gone, my darling. I did everything I could, but the Spider Empress has her now."

Wait. What?

Adele's shock shattered like a glass wall around her, and the real world came rushing in too fast and too bright. She pushed herself out of Rainere's arms and stood up. She raised his chin with a finger so she could look into his eyes.

"What did you just say?" she asked and her voice was brittle.

"Your Majesty, I really don't..." interrupted the general, his tone betraying his disapproval.

"Shut up, Ohrig," snapped Adele and waved Ohrig to silence while keeping her finger under Rainere's chin. She saw green tears leak from his eyes.

"*Cara mia...*"

"No," corrected Adele sharply. "After all of that, you said Natalie was *where?*"

"With the Spider Empress," whispered Rainere. "Darling, I did what I could to save her."

Adele dug her fingers in Rainere's chin, pinching hard. The Chime Voices began chanting low and intensely in the background behind her gradually stoking rage. "Are you telling me that Natalie is with spiders? What does that even mean?"

"*Cara mia*, let me explain," said Rainere and pulled his chin from her grasp, clasping her hand in both of his.

Adele could already see the guilt in his dark green eyes, and she stepped back to let General Ohrig and his men move forward. As she got further from him, the prince climbed to his feet. He didn't seem to notice the swords surrounding him or the glass manacles that General Ohrig proffered at him.

"Your Highness, Prince Rainere, I am arresting you under the authority…"

"Adelena, I need to tell you what happened," said Rainere, and with a twist of his hand, all of her Queen's Guard were hurled back against the walls of the room, their swords clattering to the floor as they were suspended a foot above the ground.

"What did you do to my Natalie, Rainere?" asked Adele. Her voice sounded as cold as the fear that was spreading through her chest, freezing her heart and making it splutter frantically, then pause for too long.

"He took her, Your Majesty." Charlie surprised her by jumping between her and the prince. "He came to the children's bedroom this morning while they slept. He put something on Natalie's wrist and kissed her on the mouth. She passed out and he carried her out of the room, through the great wardrobe. Your Majesty, you must believe me. I saw the whole thing."

Charlie was pale and desperate, but his eyes burned with an intensity that sent the silver rings glittering and spinning about his pupils.

"I have no reason to lie," he added more quietly and turned to face the prince. "Stay behind me, Your Majesty. I can defend you from him where your guards can't."

Adele looked from Charlie's trembling hands then to her Queen's Guard pinned helplessly against the walls by Rainere's magic. She almost laughed, but it would have been joyless and it would have wasted even more time. Adele didn't fear Rainere's power. She could take him down with one hand. An image of the Sandarian Mage in his death throes came to her mind.

"I'm waiting, Rainere," she said.

Rainere moved toward her, but her little bodyguard, Charlie, put up a hand to stop him, the other slipping inside his vest.

"Adelena, please do not blame yourself for what has happened," said Rainere, his tone pleading with her to understand. "The prophecy and the actions of those forces of darkness here in Evendaar were all fighting long before High Wizard Ohren brought you here."

He looked into her eyes and sighed at the confusion he saw there. Rainere sat back down on the couch and ran his hands through his hair, pulling it back and away from his face.

"I have never lied to you, *cara mia*, but there are things about myself that I have hidden from you." The prince took a deep, shuddering breath. "At the very beginning, I was coerced by the Spider Empress, Ka-kik, into helping her bring the Hidden Child of the End of the World Prophecy into our world. She used my blood to fuel her Spell of Retrieval. What she didn't know was that the wizards of St. Lucidis also wanted you and attempted their own Spell of Retrieval at the exact same moment. The empress's spell failed with the interference and I was lost among the stars for a time, but when I returned to the world, I saw that you, the woman who had haunted me for so long, was here in Evendaar. High Wizard Ohren crowned you queen in accordance with the prophecy, but he didn't know that the empress also feels a claim to you and believes that you will be the one to bring her species back to power. The Spider Empress is evil, and she holds a great deal of power over me, Adelena. The only way I could protect you from her was to marry you and take your throne from you, ruling as king of Unisia. Empress Ka-kik and her Spider People would then have the freedom to rise up from their nest and once again walk in the light. My oath to her satisfied, you and I would have been free to live as we wished. With the Spider People once more in power, the St. Lucidis wizards would have been so busy defending their precious Golden Palace, that they would not have troubled us again."

Rainere shook his head sadly.

"But you would not marry me, *cara mia*, though I begged you to so often. I wanted to save you so much from knowing the terrifying truth about our world. I thought our love was strong enough that you would marry me for me alone."

"Get to the part about Natalie," said Adele over the cries of General Ohrig, who had renewed his efforts to get down off the wall with louder shouting.

"The empress gave me until the full moon to convince you to marry me. She wanted to rise on a night when their dark Goddess Lune is at her strongest. That is tonight, *cara mia*."

Rainere stood up and came toward her but stopped a few feet away. She could see his desperation in his tightly held jaw and the vein that throbbed at his temple.

"Adelena, I vowed that I would never give you reason to fear me and I would never force you to bend to my will, so I had to come up with a plan to save you from yourself. In the little black box, I gave you, there was a very special necklace which would have been enough to protect you from the Spider Empress's poison but Natalie took it for herself. It was imbued with powerful magic and I couldn't take it from Natalie to give it back to you so I thought perhaps I could just," - Rainere took another deep breath - "I disguised Natalie with an illusion spell to look just like you and put the Marchant wedding band, a bracelet, on her. I then put her under a sleeping curse so that she would not suffer when I took her underground to the Spider Empress. That was what the boy saw me do." He gestured at Charlie, who tensed at the motion. "I took her down into the cavern this morning and showed her to the empress, wearing the band, as proof of our marriage, but the empress betrayed me. I can see now that all along she planned to keep you for her own."

"She is keeping my Natalie?" repeated Adele.

"Please, my dear heart, do not blame yourself for what has happened to your daughter," begged Rainere again, his face etched in pain.

Adele felt the cold comfort of shock creeping back over her mind. She clenched her fists and forced herself to breathe. She wanted to listen to Rainere's words, but the Chime Voices were ebbing and flowing, making her feel lost.

"So, you just wanted to marry me to make this Spider Empress happy with you?" she asked, bewildered. "And when I wouldn't you gave them Natalie instead of me."

Rainere raised his chin, his eyes flashing with frustration. "Adelena, I love you with every fiber of my being and with every drop of the Blood in my veins. You knew this was true, even before you knew me as a flesh-and-blood man. You must believe that I had no knowledge of this prophecy before the empress took my blood for her Spell of Retrieval. But when you appeared as the Hidden Child, I knew it was the hand of the Goddess that had brought us together. Neither the wizards nor the Spider Empress know what we mean to each other, but I couldn't risk the empress hurting you in an effort to get to me. I would not risk your life or safety, no matter what it costs me, Adelena."

He gathered her hands in his own and kissed them gently, his eyes closed to her shocked expression.

"You were scared the empress would hurt me, so you gave her my *daughter* instead of me?" she asked. Adelena was asking the same question, but Rainere kept answering it in different ways.

"I made a vow to you Adelena. I vowed on my life to protect you in this world and I would never break that vow. I have little left to me but my honor and I will never be forsworn, my love."

Adele considered this man who had loved her so passionately and intimately. Rainere's face was beautiful even with its mask of fear. She had given herself to him body, heart and soul and he had loved her fiercely in return. He had not broken a single one of the promises he had made to her.

But he was completely and utterly insane.

"Release my men," she said quietly, and pulled her hands out of his.

She heard the sound of gasping as all six of her Queen's Guard dropped to the floor with a thud. General Ohrig was at her side in an instant.

"Tell me where the princess is now!" he ordered the prince.

Rainere ignored him. "Tell me you understand, *cara mia*? I had to give Natalie up to save you. Even if I had revealed her true identity the empress would have eaten Natalie and I immediately, and you would still be at the mercy of the Spider People. I saved myself so I could come back to protect you from what is to come in the Days of Darkness."

Adelena turned to the general and saw his cheeks were pale beneath his weathered color. His blue eyes were clouded with worry, and he looked at her as if he had never seen her before.

Suddenly, and sharply, Adele felt very much alone.

She looked at the men surrounding her and every single one wore an expression of fear and, what she imagined was disappointment. She was supposed to have been their good Queen Adelena, sweet, helpless and in need of their protection. Her affair with the evil Marchant prince had destroyed their image of her and had made her a different kind of woman in their eyes. Only Grotto met her eye, and he snarled at her with a glare charged with venom.

Well. Fuck them all. Adele was no one's saint, but neither was she anyone's whore. At the force of her anger, the Chime Voices went quiet in her mind and Adele felt a fissure crack open deep within her body. Magic came pouring out from where she had shoved it down deep, flowing through her veins and around every organ in her body, filling her with strength and fanning the flames of her rage.

In a heartbeat, Adele knew that everything she had ever thought about herself was wrong. The insecure, trembling woman, always crippled by anxiety, had only ever been a disguise for her true nature that she had hidden from for so long. The real Adelena was ferocious and wild and could crush a man with one hand. But the real Adelena was also a mother and now she would show them what a mother was capable of.

"I will only ask you one more time, Rainere, where is Natalie?" asked Adele, as she stepped toward the prince, shaking off General Ohrig's warning touch.

Rainere shook his head. "I will not take you there, my love. It is far too dangerous."

Adele stepped up to the prince and placed a hand at the back of his neck. Rainere leaned down, almost as if he expected a kiss. They exchanged a breath and Adele whispered a word of command so powerful that it made her tongue burn.

This time there was no gentle throbbing of power, or sweet delicious dive into green magic. Adele gritted her teeth as her power stabbed into Rainere like a blunt metal bar.

"Luckily, that isn't your choice to make, Rainere," she said through clenched teeth. "You will tell me where she is now or I will be climbing over your corpse to ask that evil skeleton over there."

Rainere dropped to his knees, unable to fight her off or even catch a breath. Within moments he fell to his side on the floor. Adele followed him down.

"Let him go!" shouted Grotto striding over to Adele and ignoring the sword that Captain Lucky pointed at him. "You are killing him, you filthy monster!"

Grotto was beside himself with rage and kneeled down next to his prince but was too frightened to touch either him or Adele.

"Watch your tongue with our queen," snapped Lucky defensively.

Grotto spat on the ground next to Adele. "She is not my queen, she is not even your queen," he screamed. "She is an abomination!" He pointed a long bony finger at her. "How can no one see what you truly are? You are more a monster than the Spider Empress herself."

Adele smiled coldly as Rainere silently writhed beneath her hand. "Your master is dying, yet you are taking the time to insult me?" she remarked. "If you know where my child is, old man, then you had better tell me quickly. He won't last much longer like this."

But Adele was lying. She could feel the depth of Rainere's power like it was an ocean into which she had dipped a straw. The pure strength of him was flowing into her own body and she suddenly understood something important about the magic she was using. She needed this! Rainere's magic was giving her own power the fuel to grow beyond itself.

Grotto paused to glare fiercely at her for a moment before betraying his master. "The cavern of the Spider People is in the Dark Forest, far beneath the ground. I can take you to the entrance. Now, let him go, witch!"

Adele released Rainere and climbed to her feet. She was vibrating with the churning, swirling power and the feeling was incredible.

"Take me there now," she commanded.

"No, no don't," Rainere protested, struggling to sit up and clutching his shoulder where she had touched him. "Grotto, I forbid…"

"I will take you there," insisted Grotto. "Master, forgive me when you live through this."

Rainere wiped the hair out of his eyes and the cold sweat off his brow. He looked like hell, and he was trembling all over in convulsive waves, but still he did not give up.

"Adelena, please, *cara mia*. You will need to kill me before I would let you go into that kind of danger. Your daughter is lost and I will not lose you too. The empress betrayed me and cannot be trusted. To ask her for anything is to invite more lies." He climbed clumsily to his feet.

Adele stared at Rainere in disbelief. "I'm not going to *ask* her for anything, Rainere. I am going to *take* back my daughter and anyone who gets in my way will be destroyed."

Rainere swayed on his feet. "You will never find your way through the tunnels," he protested stubbornly. "And I will not help you on this suicidal mission."

The silence that fell after Rainere's admission was stifling. Only the crackle of the fire and their breathing could be heard. Adele's heart constricted as fear squeezed it tightly. Her only hope had been bullying Rainere into doing as she asked.

"I will help you, Your Majesty," said a quiet voice, and a small skinny man stepped out of the shadows of the room looking directly at Adelena. He limped painfully as he made his way over to bow before her. His sharp shoulders poked out of the fabric of his tattered shirt and his huge eyes were dark with bruises.

Adele narrowed her eyes at the newcomer. "Do I know you?"

"You know me, my queen, but not in this form," croaked the little man. He stood no taller than Adele and his head was slightly too large to be unremarkable. A streak of perfectly white hair swept down the center of his head.

"Schiss, no. Don't! I order you..." gasped Rainere, staggering forward to grab at him, but instead fell on Grotto, who held him back.

"Your Majesty, you saved my life once." Schiss bowed again, though it obviously pained him to do so. "I owe you a life in return." He righted himself and sent Rainere a defiant glance before continuing. "I can show you the way through the nest to the cavern where the empress is keeping your daughter. But we only have a few hours to rescue her because as soon as the moon rises, Empress Ka-kik will perform the ceremony and eat Princess Natalie whole."

Adele let out an involuntary cry and covered her mouth with her hand. "My baby," she whispered.

"Think of your other babies," begged Rainere. "Stella and Aaron are all you have left now, *cara mia*. You must get back to the Belvoir Estate to be with them. The empress cannot touch you there."

Adele froze at his words. She heard the despair in his voice. He had given up on Natalie, and now he only hoped to save her, his beloved. Adele's stomach roiled instinctively at the idea of returning to Belvoir, but if Stella and Aaron were safe there, then she could go after Natalie by herself. She felt the flex of Rainere's power combined with her own. These men could quail here like frightened birds if they wanted, but she had to rescue her daughter.

"Right, let's go Mr...." she said.

"Schiss, Your Majesty," said Schiss, with a little smile that lit up his odd features. She saw his many pointy teeth, and instantly knew who he was.

"You're a spider-person," she accused him, though her shock wasn't as great as it would have been earlier this morning.

Schiss nodded and his sharp tongue poked out to lick his cracked lips. "Yes, but the empress tried to kill me and then gave me to the prince. I am free of any loyalty to her wickedness."

"I will crush you if you are lying to me," said Adele. "And I imagine you will take a lot less to kill than the prince here."

Schiss nodded and, strangely, smiled again. "Should you wish it, my queen, I would put my own head under your foot."

Adele nodded. "Good."

"We should bring the boy too, my queen," suggested Schiss politely. "He is filled with the Blood of the Marchants, I can smell it on him. If we are caught, we can offer him up to the empress as tribute. She never misses a chance to taste the Blood."

"Oi! I'm no Marchant..." Charlie protested, but it died when Adele's eyes fell on him. What he saw there made him bite his lip and murmur an apology. "I'll come with you if you need me, Your Majesty."

Grotto made a noise of disgust, as he carried Rainere back to the couch to sit. "Look how she hypnotizes them to do her bidding, master. Do you not now see what she *is*?" But his protest fell on deaf ears as Rainere had turned his focus to General Ohrig.

"General, surely you cannot allow your queen to put herself in such danger. If she goes near the nest she will die along with her daughter. You *can't* let her do this. The future of Unisia depends on her," Rainere's voice pitched hysterically at the end as he begged for someone to see the sense of his words.

General Ohrig looked from the desperate prince and back to his determined queen. "If this nest is as dangerous as the prince says, it would be worse than foolish to go charging in there by yourself with only a traitor and a Marchant boy to help," Ohrig said slowly. He looked at Adele and his light blue eyes were clear.

"Your Majesty, we are going to need a plan."

CHAPTER FORTY-SEVEN

"Deep and Dark is the Rage of Betrayal"

The war room of the Grey Palace was an appropriate setting in which to hold their meeting. The room was not large, and the walls and ceiling had been covered in blood-red silk to match the scarlet carpet. That, coupled with the fact that there were no windows, gave the visitors the disturbing feeling of sitting inside a womb. There was a long table set in the middle of the room surrounded by heavy oak chairs. A map of the kingdom of Unisia had been carved into the wood of the table itself and was still marked by the various miniature flags and figurines that had been required to plan the last Marchant war in Unisia.

Adele sat at the head of the table and looked at every one of the men in front of her, examining them with a critical eye for their strengths and weaknesses. For once in her life, she couldn't care less what they thought of her in turn.

Inside her, the Chime Voices wanted magic and they wanted blood and they sang their desire to Adele in a low chant that made her mind reel. A terrible thirst for revenge had dried up all the compassion and softness inside of her. A red tinge of rage colored the outside of her vision and throbbed in time with the blood pounding through her head.

General Ohrig sat to her right and Charlie to her left with Schiss next to him. Captain Lucky and QGs Bear, Owens, Pepper and Leith were in a row next to their general. Prince Rainere sat at the end of the table, his back straight and his face expressionless. Grotto sat at his master's right hand, glaring savagely back at Adele.

"Rainere, you are the strongest here amongst us, why can't you help us fight this Spider Empress?" Adele demanded.

"Because of the vow I made to her when she caught me, over a hundred years ago," he said and his voice was heavy with regret. "I have wanted to take it back a thousand times since, but I was young and I thought I was dying at the time I made it. I had no idea what a lifetime of servitude would feel like."

"What would happen to you specifically if you broke your vow?" asked Adele

"My magic does not work against her," said Rainere. "Anything I tried to attack her with would just backfire and hit me instead."

"Have you tested that theory?" asked Adele and didn't even flinch as the hurt in Rainere's gaze stabbed her through the heart. Her heart wouldn't be worth much anyway if Natalie died tonight.

"Of course I have, many times" said Rainere quietly and unconsciously ran his fingers over the delicate web of scars on the backs of his hands.

"But could you still protect us from the empress and the other spiders?" Adele persisted. "Anything helpful that wouldn't be the same as a direct attack on the empress."

Rainere frowned doubtfully. "Perhaps. But even if we can get to Natalie at the center of the nest, the empress will be alerted by our very presence. There are thousands of spiders living in every tunnel of the nest, and any one of them could let the empress know where we are."

"Not while she sleeps they wouldn't," said Schiss nervously, speaking for the first time.

"Go on." Adele gestured for him to speak up.

"Well, Empress Ka-kik will rest before the big occasion tonight when the full moon rises. She will need to prepare herself to accept her new power when she eats your daughter."

A fresh wave of panic swamped Adele. Her daughter was going to be eaten by a monster who thought she was Adele and they were all just sitting around talking about it.

Adele felt General Ohrig's hand on her arm and realized she had risen out of her seat. "Calm yourself, Your Majesty," he said. "We will move when the time comes."

He was right of course. They had a way to get into the nest with Schiss, but no way to fight the empress or to get Natalie safely out again.

"How big is the empress?" asked Adele. "Because as a spider, Schiss is no bigger than my hand."

"The empress is enormous, my queen," answered Schiss. "She would fill half this room with her body alone."

"She is as tall as me but ten times wider," said Rainere, more accurately.

"That's disgusting," whispered QG Pepper and for the first time Adele could see just how pale and shaken her young QGs were. Pepper and Leith were barely out of their teens and had yet to see anything of their own world, and now she would ask them to face this monstrous foe. Maybe she should leave them in the Grey Palace rather than risk their cowardice when she needed them most, when Natalie needed them most?

"Can metal or glass weapons kill her?" asked Captain Lucky of the little man-spider, but had trouble looking Schiss in the eye.

Rainere answered for Schiss. "Yes, if you can get past her hundred strong royal guards and ability to spit venom and if you could trap her somehow, then yes, your human weapons would kill her."

"And my magic?" asked Adele.

"Your magic works in close quarters, Adelena," said Rainere, softening his tone for her. "You would have to be touching to do what you do, and by that time you'd be dead."

There was a minute of silence as everyone stared at their hands and thought furiously.

"Your Majesty, there is one thing that would kill the empress and indeed every spider in the nest," said Charlie quietly. He pulled a scrap of cloth from his vest pocket and lay it on the table, then, with a nervous look at the prince, he took out a small glass ball from inside his shirt and placed in on the cloth so it couldn't roll. Captain Lucky and General Ohrig leaped back from the table at the sight of it, making everyone else jump or yelp in surprise. Everyone, except Rainere, who only gazed morosely at the small blue flame flickering inside the clear glass.

"Cunt of a cat, boy!" swore General Ohrig, clearly shaken beyond decorum by the appearance of the glass bauble. "Where in the name of the Goddess did you get that?"

"It's mine," sighed Rainere and Adele watched as a dark fatality suffused his beautiful face, rendering him old and sad.

"Is that really...?" whispered Lucky, pointing a shaking finger at the ball and staring at it in horrified fascination.

"Charlie," said Adele sharply. "Tell me what it is."

"It's Dragon Fire, Your Majesty," said Charlie, looking her straight in the eye. "One small flame of living Dragon Fire. It is the most dangerous weapon ever invented by the ancient wizards." Charlie cast his eyes down the table to Rainere. "It is one of only two ways that an immortal can be killed," he added.

"Whoever breaks the Sticking Glass and has enough power to direct the flame can be its master," explained Rainere to her inquiring look. "It will then burn eternally, obliterating the fuel it has been commanded to consume. It is powerful enough to destroy any magic it touches, including God-given curses." Rainere gave her one of his sweet half-smiles. "It was given to me by someone who knew from experience just how painful immortality could be."

"So, we have our way into the nest, and we have a weapon to destroy the spiders. Now we only need a way out," said Adele, not allowing herself to be drawn in by Rainere's smile. But her heart cracked a little under the pressure.

"I imagine that's when we pick up our arses and run as fast as we can to escape the tunnels once the fire is released," said Ohrig, gingerly sitting back down as far from the delicate glass ball of Dragon Fire as he could and still be at the table.

Schiss looked to Adele. "I will hold them off until you escape, I promise," said the little man-spider, bravely.

"But the Dragon Fire will destroy you, too, won't it?" asked Captain Lucky. "You won't have much of a chance to help if you get incinerated." Lucky gave Schiss a sympathetic look, finally meeting his eye.

Captain Lucky turned to Adele and she knew what he would say before he said it, she could see the goodness of his soul as it shone out at her from the depths of his sky-blue eyes.

"Your Majesty, have we considered that there will be females and infants down in that nest? What if not all the creatures are evil? Surely there will more Spider People like Schiss, who would be willing to help us. They are an ancient race of beings, Your Majesty, to kill them out of hand for the actions of their empress, well, it wouldn't be…"

"It wouldn't be right," agreed the general and he turned to Adele too, beseeching her to reconsider using the devastating Dragon Fire. "Maybe the empress acts alone, Your Majesty? The Rules of Combat state that the enemy must be given mercy and the right to surrender before being engaged in battle. Dragon Fire will show no mercy, Your Majesty."

Adele took a deep breath and placed both hands on the table in front of her. She stared down at the whorls in the wood grain and could see the scratches that had been etched and covered with polish for who knew how many times in this palace, in this nation, in this alien world, in this part of the universe. She stood up and looked at each man in turn as she spoke.

"I think that there is something you all need to remember. My children and I, we were brought here to your world against our will. Since we arrived six weeks ago, I have been terrified out of my wits, crowned queen by wizards, and forced to deal with magic and power that I have no comprehension of." Adele paused to take a breath and stop her voice from shaking. "I have killed a man and destroyed the life of another to protect myself and my children from the scheming of the wizards of the Golden Palace. And now…now I find out that the only man I thought I could trust, the man who claimed to *love* me has betrayed me and given my daughter up to be eaten by a monster!" Adele's voice broke on the last word, but it was anger and not fear that choked her. She glared about the table and saw the shock on all the faces of the men before her at her revelation of murder. Ohrig, a frown on his pale face, opened his mouth to question her but she raised her hand for silence. She was not cowed by his authority anymore.

"Please listen, as I'm going to make this very clear: I *don't care* about your prophecy, or your rules of combat! There will be no mercy for the nightmarish creatures who have my daughter." She pointed down the table at Rainere. "And there will be no mercy for the man who took her from me."

Adele could feel her eyes flashing as the rage pulsed around her in a cloud, and her magic surged within her, moving with the chanting of the Chime Voices.

"But I will tell you what there *will* be. There *will* be blood and there *will* be dead spiders everywhere! I will not rest until every last one of them dies for what they have done to Natalie. If you don't have the stomach for genocide then I command you to stand down before we go any further, but if anyone so much as suggests the word *mercy* to me again then your corpse can join the thousands of monsters that will soon stain the earth with their blood."

There was complete silence, until:

"Hell, yes!"

The exhortation was so unexpected that Adele didn't even recognize the voice that shouted it.

"Hell yes, Your Majesty," QG Bear corrected himself. "Let's kill all those demon pricks and save the princess from being eaten." He gave Adele a nod of respect and a wide smile.

"I'm with you too, Your Majesty," agreed QG Owens and sat up taller in his chair, exchanging a grin with QG Bear. "Killing mythical creatures is something I joined the Queen's Guard to do."

QG Owens turned to General Ohrig. "It is in our oath, Sir."

"... to protect our queen from the Dark Entities and the Deeper Mysteries found between the Known and the Unknown of this world," murmured Ohrig, acknowledging that their archaic oath was now curiously relevant on this dark day. He gave Adele a firm nod. "Your Majesty, we will join you and we will lay down our lives for you. We will follow you into hell if you should ask it of us, just please, don't waste our sacrifice."

The red haze slowly dissipated from the edges of Adele's vision. General Ohrig was intelligent, brave and strong. He was also incredibly loyal to the men under him and she would be wise right now to listen to him.

"I will not ask any of you to go where I will not," said Adele. "And when we find Natalie, we will either leave with her or die trying. If anything should happen down in the Spiders' Nest, you are not to come back for me. Natalie is the only person who matters. That is an order." She looked heavily around the table at the men, avoiding Rainere's eye at the last moment. "We have only a little time left, so let's get started on a real plan."

CHAPTER FORTY-EIGHT

"Down We Go Into the Darkness Below"

The journey through the portal had shaken everybody up. Rainere had taken the party through in pairs, as they each had to hold his arm to make it through the long green void without getting lost.

Rainere had brought them deep into the Dark Forest, far from the main entrance to the nest, but close to a little-used waste channel that Schiss had claimed would be a discreet entry point. Their party now had time to rest and survey their surroundings, while Rainere closed the portal from the Grey Palace and opened another one, which would lead them to the border of the Belvoir Estate. It was to be their escape route if they made it out of this nightmare alive.

Adele stood apart from the others and watched Rainere work. She couldn't help it. As if from nowhere, a swirling matrix of particles and clusters of green dust appeared before him as he swept his arms in small circles and formed the portal. She could feel him pulling magic out of the air and mixing it with the power within himself, as green sparkles of energy flowed from his elegant hands and coalesced in an oval shape big enough to fit a human form. It was beautiful. *He* was beautiful. As if she had spoken aloud, Rainere turned to look over his shoulder at her, catching her gaze and holding it for a moment. Her eyes ran over the planes of his face, those fine cheekbones she had held between her hands, and the perfectly-formed mouth that fit so well against her own, and tried to deny the urge to throw herself into his arms. Her anger toward him had been eclipsed by her nearly-petrifying fear of walking into a cave of giant spiders and finding her daughter dead.

A cold breeze blew into the forest glade, swaying branches and rustling the dead leaves at their feet. Adele shivered and pulled up the collar of her riding jacket, dragging her gaze away from Rainere. Schiss shuffled over and gave her a welcome distraction.

"I never got to thank you, m'queen." Schiss smiled shyly. "You saved me from that horrible Mage in Sandar. I would have died in that little box if you hadn't set me free."

Adele nodded. That was a week ago, when she'd had mercy for spiders. "Who did this to you?" she asked, gesturing at his injuries.

"The empress, my mother," whispered Schiss and a bleak look passed over his face. "She never liked me, I think, or any of her children who walk in the Above Lands. Though I once would have kissed her foot for a kind word, I know I am dead to her now. Should she see me again she will eat me or feed me to her new hatchlings." He looked closely at Adele, his big eyes bulging even wider. "I do not think, my queen, that you would ever eat your children?"

Adele shook her head, no, but couldn't say another word. *What madness have I been caught up in? Mothers eating children, monsters eating her daughter. Wizards who could love you and turn on you in a heartbeat.* Adele wanted to scream in fear and frustration. This wasn't what her life was meant to be like!

"Your Majesty, we are all as ready as we'll ever be," whispered Ohrig close to her shoulder. Adele took a deep breath and struggled to bring her hysteria under control. Natalie needed to be rescued and that was what she had to focus on.

Adele surveyed the group standing under the trees. General Ohrig looked as grim as she had ever seen him and was staring about the glade in sharp, jerky movements like he was trying to catch something that kept darting out of his view.

Captain Lucky stood tall but was pale in the dim light of the late afternoon. QGs Leith and Pepper looked scared out of their wits and stood close to each other, jumping each time there was a rustle in the thick undergrowth. QG Bear and Owens, on the other hand, looked almost relaxed as they discussed the odds of their survival and laid bets on it. A woman named Bess featured a lot in their bargaining.

According to Schiss, most of the larger spiders would be near the empress when she prepared for the moon rising. This meant they only had to worry about the thousands of tiny spiders who lived in the labyrinth of tunnels, but even those spiders would most likely be close to the center of the nest, awaiting the call of the empress when the time came.

Charlie moved to stand on the other side of Adele. She noticed he kept his hand in the pocket which held the glass ball of Dragon Fire. She had always known that Charlie was capable of magic, but that he was a Marchant as well was not a great shock. How else could he have handled the magic sand in her room the first time she had seen him if he wasn't a Marchant?

"I cannot believe I was scared of this lot when I first met them," said Charlie and cast a disparaging look at the Queen's Guard. "That Leith looks like he might have filled his britches already, and we haven't even started yet."

Adele realized the joke was an attempt at battlefield humor, meant to jostle the others out of their fear, and it worked when QG Leith's head snapped up, his eyes sparking with derision. "Shove a cat in it, Charlie," the young QG sneered. "Did the queen lend you that pretty vest today or you wearing your own for once?"

"Oi, Charlie, why don't you take a message down to the Spider Empress, seeing as how you're so brave," added QG Bear. "Or maybe you could shag her for us..."

"Steady," growled Ohrig in a warning tone, but Adele was too far from herself for jokes that could make her blush now.

Rainere walked across the clearing and made his way through the soldiers as if they were so many trees. He only had eyes for Adele and she felt herself leaning into him even before he reached her.

"Adelena, *cara mia*." His rasp sent a chill over her skin. "I am begging you, please do not do this. Send the men in your place if you must, but please, don't go down there yourself."

'Down there' was a cave in a mound of rotting tree trunks, no more than a yard across and a yard high. A tiny creek flowed out of the cave and carried out the waste from the nest. The smell of the sewerage was acrid and caught at the back of the throat like ammonia. Schiss had assured them that even though the entrance was small, it opened into a much-larger tunnel, one that was high enough for a man to walk upright.

"You brought my little girl down there," Adele replied softly, and Rainere flinched at her accusation. "I'm going to get her back."

"But, Adelena, think of the prophecy," Rainere beseeched her, and came a step closer. "I have read it and it only travels in one direction. *The Hidden Child shall defend the throne from the Favored and cast the Shadows into the Light, to restore the glory of my Chosen Ones on the throne of my kingdom'*. Adelena, the Favored are the St. Lucidis Wizards, the Shadows are the spiders and the Chosen Ones are the Marchant family. Our marriage was foretold, but our future doesn't have to be. Listen to me when I say…"

"Does it say anything in the prophecy about the Shadows eating little girls given to them by a Chosen One?" asked Adele.

Rainere shrugged helplessly and opened his mouth to speak again.

"Then we are done talking about this," she snapped. "You and the wizards and the demons can all follow your cursed prophecy, but I'm taking my part in this out."

Adele squared her shoulders and stepped up onto a nearby tree stump to raise herself above Rainere. She didn't want to speak loudly and they all crowded close to hear her. It felt passing strange to be comfortable with the mantle of leadership, but Adele knew she had become someone else the minute she found out Rainere had stolen her daughter.

"Men, I want to thank all of you for coming with me tonight to save my little girl, Natalie. You are all heroes tonight going into battle with mythical creatures, fighting a war we never expected to be faced with. But we will be united and I will do everything in my power to get you out and back to Belvoir before the sun rises. Remember the rules are simple: Stay close to each other and if you see a spider, kill it. We will get the princess out alive."

There was nothing else to say. Adele stared hard at each man in turn, then hopped off the tree stump and led the group to the hole at the side of the clearing. She wiped her hands down her leather riding pants and made sure her shirt was tucked in tightly and the sleeves pulled down to her wrists. The less flesh that was exposed, the better.

Despite her inner transformation, there was a part of Adele that wanted to scream and cower back at the Grey Palace and let the men around her rescue Natalie from this deep hole in the ground. She patted her tightly-braided hair and could already feel imaginary spider legs getting tangled in it. She suppressed a shudder as a lifetime of arachnophobia washed over her in a suffocating wave. Adele pulled on her gloves.

There was no choice. Natalie needed her. She gave her magic a squeeze and felt it pulse back in response. She was stronger than she had ever been in her life.

"Kill them all!" she muttered hotly and was the first to push through the dead tree branches into the hole.

"Fall in," whispered General Ohrig and the men moved into position behind Adele as they all filed into the cave. Their feet splashed quietly in the shallow creek and Adele didn't even hear Rainere until he was by her side, a small globe of light was suspended in front of him to light their way.

"The tunnel opens out just pass these tree roots, m'queen," whispered Schiss. Just a few yards in, Adele could see the giant tree roots from the forest above them hanging across the tunnel in an immovable curtain.

"Cut these down, Lucky," ordered Adele. "As quietly as you can."

But Rainere had stepped to the front and with a flick of his wrist the tree roots disintegrated into a cloud of tiny shards. Rainere caught

Adele's eye and held it for a moment in the blue light of the globe. "You can still turn back, Adelena."

"Err, m'queen?" Schiss coughed nervously. "It seems we are expected."

Adele looked past Rainere to the tunnel beyond. Thousands of eyes glittered in the blue light, and a soft rustling and clicking noise could be heard as a blanket of spiders moved toward the intruders.

CHAPTER FORTY-NINE

"Where is the Fire to Light Up the Darkness?"

"Stop!" shouted Schiss, as the horde of spiders rustled their way up the walls of the tunnel toward him. At his command, the spiders all stopped moving and sat in eerie silence, waiting. With a quick glance back at the queen for confirmation, Schiss started speaking in his native tongue, clicking and wheezing oddly as he flailed his arms about his head. When he stopped, the carpet of spiders undulated as they all rose up on their back legs and waved their forelegs in the air.

Rainere's gaze flew to Adelena when he heard a whimper escape her. She was deathly pale and sweat trickled down her temple, her fists clamping and unclamping at her side. She was clearly terrified out of her wits despite her brave speeches. He saw her close her eyes and heard her mutter a prayer to the God of another world. His heart clenched hard and he wanted so much to catch her into his arms and carry her away from this dreadful place, but he knew she would just find a way back down here by herself. He had never before witnessed such maternal love and he was struck dumb with admiration at its power. For love of her children, Adele would face a terrible foe and drag her little army into battle with her, knowing she was doomed to fail, yet still hoping to save her daughter. It was tragic, yes, but tragically beautiful.

Schiss turned to smile at Adelena. His sharp little teeth gleamed in the blue light. "I have told them that we are on our way to the empress already, m'queen," said Schiss. "So they will not stop us. Of course, these are just little Brown Stripes. Most of them can't morph into human form yet, and some of them don't even have venom in their fangs."

"Comforting," sniffed Charlie. "At least *some* of them can't bite you."

"Oh no, boy, they can all bite," Schiss assured him. "It just wouldn't kill you."

Rainere watched as Adelena turned to exchange a look with General Ohrig. She still doubted Schiss, as well she might. He was betraying his own people and committing them to death at her hands. *What was to stop him from betraying her to the empress?* Rainere gritted his teeth. He would pull Schiss limb from limb if he tried it. Rainere hoped that Adelena would look back at him, but she didn't.

As they splashed their way down the center of the stream the Spiders slowly dropped to their eight legs and edged back from the water to avoid getting wet.

"Steady, steady men," said General Ohrig. "They are just backing up. We will pass them by, peacefully now."

Continuing down the tunnel the stream became much wider and deeper. Though the current wasn't strong, they were soon walking in water up to their thighs. But Rainere noticed Adelena was now up to her waist in the filthy stream. He wanted to offer to carry her but he feared she might attack him again. His shoulder was still sore from when she had stabbed him earlier with her power. It had been awful to feel his magic leaking out of him as it was conducted into her hand. It was odd that she could do that. Normally her touch had felt exquisitely painful, but always it had been tempered by desire and the heat of lust. Rainere touched the Mark on his side. He could tell that Adelena wasn't thinking of him at all right now. No doubt, all her thoughts were taken up with fear of spiders touching her skin, and touching Natalie.

Their party made their way along the stream and travelled further and further underground. Rainere could feel the familiar sensation of tons of stone and rock pushing down on the curved roof of the tunnel. To their credit the soldiers did not complain or show much discomfort at being so far under the Earth.

Rainere felt Adelena tense up beside him. "What's that music?" she whispered.

She looked around, but everyone shrugged.

"There is no music in the nest, m'queen," whispered Schiss.

But Adele was unsettled and Rainere could see that she still turned her head from side to side, as if trying to find the source of it. He heard her whisper something that sounded like, "Chime Voices." And strained his own senses to listen for music but heard none. Adelena sent him a worried glance, but she looked away too quickly for him to reassure her.

Schiss held up his hand for silence and pointed to a fork in the tunnel. They took the right fork and had enough room now to clamber out of the water, and rest on the dirt path by the side of the stream.

Schiss had told them that they would have to pass the hatching chambers. It was Schiss's belief that the chambers would be empty, as he hadn't heard the empress birthing in the last days he had spent in the nest. But if he was wrong they were all in serious trouble. The baby spiders had a keen sense of smell and ravenous hunger. If they smelled fresh meat they could well swarm and overpower the humans.

As they walked the corridor to the chamber doorway, Rainere could feel his heart pounding. Unlike the humans with him, being eaten alive wouldn't kill him. He would remain alive and conscious as the flesh was stripped from his body and his soul remained attached to his bones, feeling every last moment pain until there were no nerves left to feel.

Reaching the doorway, the whole group froze and Rainere's arm instinctively curled around Adelena's shoulders to hold her back against his side. He decided, then and there, that should a wave of carnivorous baby spiders flood out the doorway, he would kill them all before they could touch her. His oath to the Empress Ka-kik would be broken and he would forever be her puppet, but Adelena would live a moment longer and that would be a comfort.

Rainere felt Adelena's trembling stop as she held her breath. Schiss had crept forward on all fours to peek inside the first hatching chamber. Rainere only felt her breathe out again when Schiss lifted his hand to give the all-clear. Schiss then crept onto the second chamber doorway. Adelena leaned into Rainere's side, and because of the Mark he became suddenly and acutely aware of how relieved she was to have him by her side. Rainere almost gasped with pleasure at her psychic touch but too soon it was gone and she pulled out of his arms.

Schiss raised his hand a second time and everyone breathed a sigh of relief. Then Schiss pointed down another pitch-black tunnel indicating it was time for their party to split up.

Rainere looked at the boy, Charlie—that little piece of catshit who had dared to call himself Adelena's escort. Though any fool could see the Blood ran strong in the boys' veins, Rainere felt no loyalty toward him. He was a Marchant bastard; no doubt he was born in filth and he would die in filth. It irked Rainere to no end that the boy had earned himself a place in Adelena's maternal affections. Rainere watched as the boy gave Adelena a frightened glance and she squeezed his dirty hand in return. Charlie checked the precious ball of Dragon Fire in his pocket and turned to follow after Schiss into the darkness. The little cretin was brave, at least, as he headed off to find the empress in her sleeping chamber with only a spider by his side.

Schiss and Charlie would wait outside the chamber until the rest of them could retrieve Natalie from the central cavern and carry her back down the tunnels and out to the portal that Grotto was holding open for their escape. It was Charlie's job to ignite the Dragon Fire and unleash it on the empress, killing her and most of her royal guard immediately. His chances of survival were pretty slim but he seemed determined enough, and Rainere was sure the boy had enough magic to do what he had to.

Rainere tried to calm his pounding heart as it thudded out of control. So much could go wrong with their flimsy plan, but now it was time for Rainere to do his part and take the lead. He was the only other person who could take Adelena into the cavern where her daughter was. He dismissed the idea of leading her out of the nest along different tunnels, instead of to the center. At least if he went along with her plan he could remain by her side until the end.

Rainere reached out to take Adelena's hand. Despite the situation he took a moment to enjoy the sweet thrill that her squeezing his hand back gave him. He fantasized about kissing her, they were so close here in the dark, but quickly pushed the thought away. General Ohrig was antsy enough to skewer him for trying such a move. He satisfied himself with pulling her closer until her felt her breast pressing against his arm and her leg push against his.

Then he led her to their mutual doom.

Rainere's little blue light had faded to almost nothing when they reached the torch lit passageway that took them to the cavern. As they approached the doorway Rainere held up his hand to silently signal to Adelena's Guard to be alert. The empress would probably have guards watching over Natalie. General Ohrig and his men had orders to dispatch them before Natalie could be freed.

Just outside the cavern doorway he hesitated. Something was wrong. Little spiders scuttled passed them, no doubt too frightened to stop. He held Adelena so tightly he felt her squirm against his grip.

"What is that music?" she whispered and looked wildly about for its source. She looked up at him, but he shook his head sternly. Rainere needed her to keep it together right now.

Peeking around the corner of the doorway, Rainere risked a glance into the main chamber. A large crucible sitting over a smokeless fire had been placed next to the stone table with little Natalie, still asleep, laying on top. At least she was still alive, so far. Now they had only to move in and grab her and make it back to the juncture of the tunnels to send Charlie the signal to detonate the Dragon Fire and get out as fast as they could, back along the sewerage stream.

Rainere gestured to the general and his men before quietly stepping into the chamber and pulling Adelena in after himself. It was only when she pulled her hand from his and dashed headlong to the stone table that he realized that they had missed a step.

Where were the guards watching the princess? Ohrig and the QGs stood around with their swords glinting in the torchlight wearing expressions of confusion.

"Princess?" Rainere straightened up as the awful reality dawned on him. Natalie was herself again, and she was the bait in a trap.

"Adelena, no!" Rainere's shout came an instant too late as the empress's guards launched themselves out of the shadows and grabbed Adelena, pushing her to her knees.

"Well, well," cackled the disembodied voice of Empress Ka-kik, sending a sickening thrill down Rainere's spine. He cursed in terror as the enormous body lowered itself from the ceiling of the cavern. The four back legs pulling a chain of wet rope from her obscene spinneret.

"Finally, you bring me the real queen I asked for, and some delicious manly gifts to go with it." She wheezed with laughter. "I knew you wouldn't disappoint me! You shall be richly rewarded for this my young Marchant prince. When we are married I will be pleased to keep you by my side."

"Adelena, no! It's not true," shouted Rainere, as he felt a vicious stab in the Mark. She could not really think he had betrayed her yet again, but the look on her face brought him to his knees.

CHAPTER FIFTY

"The Fire is Deep Within"

Adele fought as hard as she could to get off the ground. Natalie was lying on a stone table just in front of her. Out of the corner of her eye, she could see the enormous mass coming down from the ceiling, but she wouldn't let herself look at it. Instead, she glared at Rainere, as he fell to his knees in the dirt, two guards pinning his arms to his back. She would have to wait all night for him to shake them off, though. He was beholden to this monster spider and wouldn't do a goddamn thing to protect himself. If she was going to get Natalie out of this hell, she would have to do it herself.

Adele surprised her guards by lurching to her feet as they were watching their empress and managed to get two steps closer to Natalie before they stopped her again. Adele cast a desperate eye over her daughter and watched for some sign of life. When she saw Natalie's eyelids flutter she almost cried out with relief. Rainere hadn't lied about the sleeping curse, at least.

Adele tried to turn and see her men, but they were all on their knees, swords on the ground, with their arms held painfully behind their backs. QG Bear had managed to wrestle his way out of the guards' grip, but now he had four of them holding him low to the ground. Captain Lucky had chopped the arm off another before they had taken his sword and he was covered in the black blood of the spider-guard who lay on the ground. The guards holding Adele suddenly jerked her hard, pulling her to her feet and face to face with a walking nightmare.

The Spider Empress was truly a monster. Her great black body loomed massively in the dimly lit chamber and the legs that stretched out from her body were muscular and covered in long black hairs. But it was her face, with its gaping maw and heavy white fangs, that directed all of Adele's attention. There were two soft, tubular feelers that uncurled from behind the fangs and scented the air, moving as if of their own accord. Adele was speechless with horror. She could feel her bowels churn and her bladder beg for release, but a whimper near the door snapped her head around.

QG Pepper was pale and close to passing out as his eyes rolled back in his head and he vomited on the dirt in front of him. For some strange reason his show of naked fear helped to galvanize Adele's trembling bravery.

This was just like the Holy Caves in Sandar. Except this time the monster was seven-foot-tall and had her daughter held hostage.

Adele thought furiously. There was a hideous dark monster before her, a monster who had lived for a thousand years and who had only ever dealt with one human being: Rainere. That told Adele something, it told her that the empress was frightened of something, something that she needed a prophecy to solve. If Adele took away the prophecy, then the empress would have nothing.

The Spider Empress gasped and croaked in a confusing babble that Adele had no hope of understanding, but she needed to communicate with the monster somehow. Adele noticed lurid pink stripes had been messily painted on the first few legs of the empress, and that yellow paint dotted the white of her fangs. *Was this hideous creature actually vain?*

What was it that Rainere had said? The empress had wanted the Hidden Child for herself to walk in the light of day. Was I supposed to protect the spiders from the wizards of the Golden Palace? If that's so, then the empress always expected to have a relationship with me, of some sort.

Adele's thoughts spun wildly and morphed into a clear plan only when the music began again. The music was beautiful, and it reminded Adele of the ballets of Earth, if Tchaikovsky was played at double time by ten different orchestras. She felt her blood sing in time to the vigorous beat and had no more time to wonder at it. She reached into herself and grabbed at her magic that was still vibrating with the strength attacking Rainere had given her. It jumped at her touch and held firm.

Adele drew herself up to her full height and shouted over the wheezing noises of the monster empress. "Just who do you think you are? I am here to meet the Empress of the Spider People. Go now and fetch your mistress for me!"

The empress broke off and trained her thousand eyes directly on Adele. "I am the great Empress Ka-kik, mother to the Spider People and leader of Those Who Live in the Shadows." The empress spoke slowly this time, and her accent clicked and jumped over the syllables of the human language as if her mouth wasn't made to make such sounds.

Adele assumed what she hoped was a sufficiently arrogant expression. "I have come for my daughter," she said, enunciating each word clearly.

The Spider Empress was silent finally and her many eyes swiveled from Adele to Rainere and back again. "You are the Hidden Child of the Prophecy of the End of the World."

"What? What are you saying? I can't understand any of this," Adele interrupted the empress and cast a despairing look about the room, as if anybody else could get it. "Rainere, get off the dirt and come and translate for me."

Rainere shook off his surprised guards and climbed to his feet, his expression was neutral, but his eyes showed confusion. "Empress Ka-kik would like to know if you are the Hidden Child of the prophecy," Rainere translated politely, giving Adele a subservient bow.

"Oh, that!" Adele waved her hand as if to brush away such nonsense and gave a hollow laugh. "Oh, of course she would think that given the circumstances. Rainere tell her: I – am – not – the – Hidden – Child." Adele shook her head to emphasize her point.

Rainere dutifully repeated Adele's words. He had never seen the empress so unsure of herself as she watched Adele.

"But the wizards at the Golden Palace brought you to Unisia, did they not?" asked the empress.

"Is she talking about the wizards?" snapped Adele at Rainere. Rainere nodded and gave Adele a warning look that she ignored.

"The wizards made a mistake. I am not their Hidden Child. I'm not even a St. Lucidis," Adele flicked her dark braid over her shoulder. "I am Marchant."

Adele tried to ignore the gasps of her men as they all watched her performance before the empress. "But!" she raised her finger imperiously. "I *am* the queen of all Unisia and you have stolen my daughter, Empress of the Shadows, and I have come to take her back."

"You killed my favored son, Oki," spluttered the Spider Empress. "And for that I require vengeance."

The empress was plainly angry, but she still waited a moment for Rainere to translate her words to Adele despite everyone understanding them as the Empress spoke more and more clearly.

"What? The thing who invaded my bedroom in the night was your son!" Adele raised her voice and shook her finger at the Empress. "Perhaps you should have taught him better manners. He had no right to be in my private chambers!"

"My son," wheezed Empress Ka-kik, gnashing her great fangs. "He will be avenged!"

Adele felt herself losing ground as the monster shuddered and rose up on its back legs to hover over her.

"If it is revenge you require, you cannot have my child, but I will give you my royal escort in recompense," said Adele quickly, as she pushed Rainere toward the empress. She ignored his shocked glance. "I could never marry him. The union would never be allowed by the wizards of the Golden Palace. Take him. He is yours."

The empress stretched even higher, resting only on her four back legs. Her shock at Adele was wearing off and she was now becoming irritated.

"He is mine anyway, little queen. The boy prince made a vow that binds his soul to my will. If he should forswear his promise to serve me then he shall become my slave in body, and soul."

Adele frowned darkly. "But I have Marked him for my own. Look!" She snatched at Rainere's shirt and pulled it up for all to see the silvery Mark tattooed to his side. Her royal insignia was clear even in the dim light of the cavern.

"He is my property now," she said as if that ended the subject. "But I will give him to you as a gesture of goodwill."

"No!" The empress's shout was shrill and pierced Adelena's eardrums painfully. "Enough of these games! The prince said he would marry you and put himself on the throne as king. He didn't! Instead, he brought me this little girl who wears the wedding band of his people, but she is not the queen. Now you stand before me as the queen, but claim you are not the Hidden Child. Who is to blame for all of this?"

"The wizards are," shouted Adele right back again. "I tricked the wizards into making me the queen, and once again Marchant blood sits upon the throne of Unisia. I think the Marchant prince here was too enamored with me to understand the truth though," – she forced a laugh – "why would I marry a poor Marchant prince when I have all of the powerful men in the kingdom to choose from? But he is quite helpful with keeping my magic strong, so I Marked him and wanted to keep him as an escort."

A bustle of noise at the door interrupted them and Charlie was dragged kicking and flailing against his captors to fall at the feet of the empress. Schiss was thrown down a moment later.

Adele could feel the blood drain out of her cheeks. She had hoped that Charlie had managed to hide. "Ah, good, the tribute is here," said Adele smoothly, borrowing Schiss's word for Charlie. "See,

Empress Ka-kik, I am not so rude as you might think. I have brought a gift for you."

The Spider Empress's feelers waved madly over Charlie's head. "I smell magic," she snarled.

"Of course! The boy is just reeking with magic," replied Adele. "He has the purest blood I could find, after Prince Rainere, that is."

"And now that we are speaking of blood again," said the empress and lurched toward Adele, unsteady on her back legs. Adele bit her lip to keep from yelping in fear. The undulating feelers were just inches from Adele's face. Up close, Adele could see that the white fangs glistened with slime. The empress breathed out and a smell like warm sewerage enveloped Adele. "I will need to taste your blood to verify you are not lying to me, and we will burn it on the Sacred Fire to ignite the power."

Adele was looking directly into the mouth of the empress and saw the black tongue pulsating within. It was terrifying to think about being eaten by that mouth. She heard Rainere cough and shook off her fear. Two short men were approaching her, their heads were too big for their squat bodies and their arms were very long, giving them a simian look, but the thing that drew Adele's attention were the great machetes they each carried.

The music was building in Adele's head. The swirling waltz had descended into the low notes of anticipation. Her blood ran cold, but she knew the time was coming when action would be needed. The end of this scene was drawing near.

"Go and get Natalie," Adele muttered to Rainere and was relieved that he gave no sign of having heard, but simply melted away behind her.

Adele took a couple of steps back from the empress and grabbed the arm of the still-struggling Charlie and pulled him to her side, out of the grasp of his guards.

"Quiet down, boy," she instructed him firmly. "Empress Ka-kik would like to taste your blood. It is a great honor to be a tribute to such an empress. You should be grateful your miserable Marchant life will be worth something. The time is almost upon you to give the empress *your tribute*."

Charlie stopped struggling, as the two shamen shuffled to each side of Adele and him. Adele kept her arm firmly around Charlie's shoulders. The boy was trembling so badly, that Adele feared he would collapse soon. He stood still as he held his arm out to the man-spider shaman with the big knife but gave a little sob of fear that vibrated through Adele's ribcage. Adele held out her opposite wrist.

The slice on her wrist was slow, but not deep. She gritted her teeth and didn't cry out as she watched with dreadful déjà vu as her blood dripped into a bowl. She heard Charlie whimper and squeezed his shoulder hard.

The first shaman approached the Spider Empress with the little bowl containing Charlie's blood. Carefully, he dripped the blood onto the empress's great black tongue as it appeared, quivering, to take the offering.

"He is Marchant, it is true, but the strain is impure, though the magic is strong. He is a very humble tribute," said Empress Ka-kik, narrowing her hundreds of eyes at Adele and clicking her fangs together irritably.

"Get ready," Adele muttered and felt Charlie flinch. "When her mouth opens again, do it."

Slowly, the tongue extended a second time to receive Adele's blood. Adele gripped Charlie tightly. She had no idea what the empress would taste in her blood and they had to be prepared to act fast. But Charlie stared at the empress with his mouth open and fear held him frozen.

The empress smacked her jaws together with a resounding crack.

"I taste St. Lucidis," mused Empress Ka-kik. "But something else, something darker than Marchant blood, something far more ancient."

Suddenly her many eyes grew wide and the empress shivered all over her great body. Droplets of venom sprayed out over Charlie and Adele. Charlie cried out, but Adele held him firm as he struggled to escape the acid shower.

The Chime Voices sang in time with the beat in her head. It was almost time.

"But no, you can't be," creaked the empress and seemed to stagger in shock. "Abomination! You are an abomination!"

Empress Ka-kik fell to her eight legs and backed away from Adele. "Guards! Shaman! To me!"

All the spider guards ran to the side of their empress, leaving General Ohrig and the QGs to pick up their weapons. Adele saw her only chance as the Spider Empress opened her mouth to shriek again.

"Charlie, now!" she shouted, as she pushed the boy toward his worst nightmare.

Quick as a snake, Charlie pulled out the little glass globe from his pocket and smeared it with the blood from his wrist.

"*Arachanea!*" he screamed and he lobbed the ball into the empress's open maw.

Everything slowed for a moment, as the air glowed green and the world paused to watch the glass ball shatter against the white fang of the Spider Empress and a tiny blue flame leap into the void of her mouth. A moment later, the blue light exploded and a blast of heat radiated out from the empress. Adele stared in shock at the pile of black dust where the empress had been just seconds before. She looked up in a daze, as her eyes followed the almost-invisible flames of blue fire as they danced and reached out for more victims in the crowd of panicking spiders.

Adele's gaze was caught by a vision of Rainere by the exit. He was carrying Natalie in his arms and silently mouthing something at her. She felt pulling and looked down to see Charlie ever so slowly yanking at her arm.

Time caught up to itself in a screeching crash of noise and movement.

"Run! Adelena, run!" screamed Rainere as he stepped outside the door.

They had to go! The fire would consume every spider in the nest, but that wouldn't stop the spiders from killing the humans before they died.

Adele streaked through the chamber, right into the pile of black empress dust and through the blue flames. She smelled her clothes singeing but the fire didn't burn her skin.

"Men, to me." Adele heard General Ohrig yell. "We follow the queen."

The tunnels of the nest were in chaos. Adele felt the touch of spiders scurrying across her face as the blue flames of Dragon Fire licked out of the cavern and into the tunnel, eating up every spider in its path.

Adele ran as fast as she could after Rainere's retreating back. He was carrying Natalie and she was determined not to lose them, but Rainere's legs were longer than hers and her QGs kept getting in the way of her sight.

When they hit the sewerage stream Adele felt something fall in front of her, knocking her sideways. Instinctively she kicked it away, but a flash of blue fire lit the hallway as a clump of spiders were incinerated and in the light Adele saw Schiss's white face drop under the filthy water. She reached down and dragged him up into her arms.

"Get up, Schiss," she hissed at him. She felt a shadow fall over her and turned to see QG Owens behind her.

"Girl, you're with me," he said and caught her as she staggered under Schiss's weight.

"No, take Schiss," she protested. "He'll die here and I can run."

QG Owens did as he was told and grabbed the little man from her as if he weighed nothing at all and threw him over his shoulder. Looking behind, Adele saw General Ohrig bringing up the rear, and almost froze in fear when an enormous wall of blue flame filled the tunnel just yards behind him. There were spiders everywhere, on the walls, the ceiling, on their bodies, in their hair. They would be burned alive along with the spiders.

Adele turned and fled down the churning stream. She prayed hard that Rainere had made it close to the exit with Natalie by now. She was running as fast as she could, but the waist-deep water was pushing against her and she started to panic. Even with the roar of the fire in her ears, she could still hear the screams of the Spiders about her as they were burned alive. Adele joined the screaming when she felt an iron bar wrap itself around her shoulders and her feet were lifted clear of the water. She was thrown over General Ohrig's shoulder with a *whump* that knocked the wind out of her. It was hard to catch a breath as she was jostled and bumped against his armored shoulder, but as Adele watched the wall of Dragon Fire edge even closer, her desire for air was swallowed by her fear.

Adele could tell by his speed that General Ohrig had reached the shallow part of the underground stream. He was almost running by the time they reached the entrance. Adele twisted and then fell through Ohrig's arms, but she mis-stepped and dropped to her hands and knees. She scrabbled as hard as she could, up and toward the hole they had entered through. She saw a flash of green in the clearing and knew that the portal held.

Ohrig pushed out of the tunnel behind her and they both lurched across the clearing to stand in front of the shimmering portal. Adele looked around wildly but didn't see Grotto or the prince anywhere.

"Pepper!" shouted Ohrig and Adele looked down to see that her QG was lying behind the portal, only his legs were sticking out to the side, and his body was covered with a sickly green light. General Ohrig pulled Pepper up into his arms and shook him. "Pepper, are you with me, man? Speak!"

But Pepper's eyes were wide and his face was white with shock. He looked at the general but didn't say a word.

"We cannot wait for Rainere to help us," shouted Adele over the dreadful roaring of the fire in the tunnel. "We must go now!"

Tentatively, Adele stuck her hand into the swirling green light. She reached for Ohrig and held his arm as she had seen Rainere do when they had first come through. Her courage quailed at taking that first step, but a wave of hot air blasted them from behind and they were pushed into the portal.

The three of them were surrounded by flickering and flowing green light. It was like being inside an ocean wave. *Keep walking*, Rainere had instructed them. *Never stop walking inside a portal. The structure is as fragile as water, and you will sink through and drown just as easily.*

Adele pulled on Ohrig's arm and he hefted Pepper tighter to him. Adele led them through in what she hoped was a straight line. She concentrated hard on the image of her daughter's face and prayed that Rainere had got her to safety. The magic about them hissed and zapped at their steps, and Adele saw a door appear, surrounded by shadows. It was the only exit in front of them and she headed toward it. Walking was taking all her energy, and she was working hard to concentrate on keeping her steps steady and constant.

Suddenly, Rainere appeared in front of her. He looked weary and was covered in the black soot of disintegrated spiders.

"This way, *cara mia*," he said gently and took her hand. "That way lies darkness."

Obediently, Adele followed Rainere along the invisible path in the portal, Ohrig dragging Pepper with him. She heard the Chime Voices complain about not heading toward the door, but they only whispered and chimed quietly in the back of her head so she ignored them.

Though she felt like they were curving back on themselves, Adele soon saw a gap in the green wall. Through it, she could see the forest at the edge of the Belvoir Estate. Rainere stepped out first and pulled her through after him. Adele stumbled like she had gotten off a boat when she left the portal.

It was night now, and the full moon lit the forest floor so she could see Natalie, still asleep, lying in the arms of Captain Lucky as he leaned against a tree. With a cry, Adele ran the short distance to her daughter and grabbed her out of Lucky's arms, sobbing great, hot sobs of relief. She sank down to her knees still holding Natalie and thanked every God in Unisia and on Earth that she had got her daughter back in one piece. Natalie was alive.

She felt Rainere's touch on her shoulder as he crouched down beside her. "True love's kiss will wake her, Adelena," he said, his gravelly voice even hoarser after the fire. "A kiss from the person who loves her most in the world will wake her and she will be fine. But perhaps wait a moment, the dark and the forest may frighten her. Get her back to the Belvoir Estate where she will be happier."

Adele could understand his concern, and it made sense even though she wanted nothing more than to see Natalie's green eyes open. She felt Rainere watching her, but she didn't look at him or say anything and after a minute he moved away.

General Ohrig dropped next to Adele, sitting on the ground and stretching his legs out with a groan.

"How is the princess?" he asked and lay a gentle hand on Natalie's cheek.

"Rainere says she'll be fine, but to wake her up when we get back to Belvoir." Adele nodded to the forest around them. "All this would frighten her to pieces."

"Well, if she is anything like her mother, she might take a bit more than that to scare," said General Ohrig, as a smile yanked up the corner of his mouth. "Never has a woman showed me the true meaning of courage like you have tonight, my queen."

Adele returned his grin. Natalie was back in her arms and she could smile again. "But if anyone ever asks you, General, I ran the whole way out of that tunnel by myself."

Ohrig managed a dry chuckle. "And if anyone ever asks you, Your Majesty, the smell of piss on my trousers is all spider waste."

Adele pulled Natalie tighter to her chest and took a deep breath. The horrible fear that had held her lungs tight was gone. She had won. She had killed yet another monster in Evendaar and had kept her family safe again.

Adele sucked in a breath and felt a sob rattle through her.

Long live the queen!

CHAPTER FIFTY-ONE

"Fire Lights the Way as it Burns"

Adele looked up to see Schiss staring at her from just a few feet away. He had crawled over to her on his knees and when her tired eyes took him in, she could see his shabby black jacket was crawling with spiders the size of her hand.

Despite everything they had been through tonight in the spiders' nest, the sight of those creatures—hairy and long-legged—moving over Schiss's body still made her shiver.

"Queen Adelena," Schiss ducked his head respectfully, but his large eyes were full of fear. "I'm sorry to interrupt you and the general."

"What is it, Schiss?" asked Adele, something about Schiss's manner made her nervous. She handed Natalie to Ohrig and struggled to her feet to stand before him. Adele cast a glance in Rainere's direction. He was starting a fire, but he looked up suddenly as if she'd called his name. She turned away from his dark stare.

The little man-spider was as tall as she was, but he tried hard to make himself as small as possible, hunched over his wringing hands.

"My queen, congratulations on your victory tonight. The Spider Empress is dead and all the Favored Children with her. All that remains of our once great people is myself and these few babies who crawled into my jacket before the fire could eat them too."

Adele didn't like the word 'babies' being used to describe the tiny Spiders they had all trampled on their desperate run out of the nest. It made her feel uncomfortable. Schiss looked terrified as he trembled in front of her, and the moonlight did his large features no favors.

"Queen Adelena, it was an honor to fight by your side and serve you in this war."

"I'm sorry Schiss, it's been a long night," said Adele, her eyes narrowing. "Please just get to the point."

Schiss coughed and plucked a spider off his face as it crawled out of his hair, tucking it protectively in a pocket. He smiled at her. His thin lips stretched hard over his pointy teeth in a valiant effort to be brave. "My family and I would like to know what you mean to do with us, m'queen," he squeaked. "If you mean to take our lives then I will place my own head under your foot. For I could think of no nobler way to join the Great Darkness beyond this world than by…"

"Stop," interrupted Adele. "I'm not going to kill you, Schiss. I saved your life in that tunnel and I'm not going to take it now, or any of those ba…babies."

All the quiet conversations around them stopped to listen to her speaking to Schiss.

Looking down at the fragile Schiss and the spiders crawling about him, trying to hide themselves in his clothes she couldn't help but feel a cold stab of guilt. *How many more Spider People just like Schiss had been hidden in those tunnels and caverns?* Now they were all burned to ashes by the Dragon Fire. The fire that would continue to burn underground until every single spider and object touched by spider magic was dust. Schiss and what was left of his family could never return there. She had killed their empress and destroyed their home. They were now refugees in their own world.

Adele took a deep breath and tried to order her jumbled thoughts. "I only killed the empress because she took my daughter from me and would have killed us both. She wanted to rule Unisia and eat my people. I couldn't let her have her way." Adele shook her head. "But if you mean me no harm, Schiss, then you are free to go your own way. Your loyalty and faith in me have earned you your freedom. Without your help tonight we would never have been able to save Natalie and for that I will always be grateful to you. Thanks to you, Schiss, I will never have to fear another spider again."

Adele forced herself to grasp Schiss shoulder. She felt his tiny bones beneath her hand and tried not to flinch as the little spiders on that part of his arm scattered.

"Schiss, you are now Emperor of the Spider People," said Adele. "You should gather up the last of your family who live under the sun like you do and let them know of the danger for them in the nest. Let them know that you are their new leader and that the queen of Unisia considers you her personal friend and hero."

"Hero," whispered Schiss and his lip trembled. Adele's speech was too much for him. He dropped to her feet and kissed her filthy shoes. "Queen Adelena, your mercy is only equaled by your power and beauty. I give you my deepest…"

"Get up, Schiss," insisted Adele, and took Schiss by his shoulders pulling him to his feet. "You are an emperor now. Stand tall and be proud. I know you will do well by your people. And if you ever need anything you only have to ask it of me. I will never forget what you did here tonight for my family."

Schiss bowed deeply. Adele bowed in return and smiled. She felt good that she had restored some balance to what she had done tonight, and she felt the rightness of it down to her bones.

"I will leave immediately to search the forest for the rest of my people, m'queen," Schiss grinned. "I will let them know we can walk in the light of Queen Adelena's Unisia. The Above Lands are once again safe for the Children of the Shadows."

Schiss bowed once more and scuttled away from her and into the deep gloom of the Dark Forest.

Adele's stomach had dropped away at Schiss's words and she could see Rainere had heard as well. Though she couldn't hear him she saw his lips move in the words of the prophecy.

So, it looked like she had cast "*the Shadows into the Light*" after all, but it was still difficult to see Schiss as a shadow creature when he had been so selfless in helping her to save Natalie. *Perhaps the prophecy was wrong about that, too?*

"Your Majesty, we should probably get to Belvoir now," said General Ohrig. "It's getting close to dawn break and we need to prepare to return to the Golden Palace."

Adelena nodded. Despite his warning not to return there, Adele had to tell High Wizard Ohren about the death of the Spider Empress and everything that had happened. Though she still didn't have all the details of the wretched prophecy, the fact that it was unfolding before her very eyes was disturbing. Ohren would have to help her whether he liked it or not.

By leaving her in the dark about everything, Ohren had sent her to the Mage of Sandar woefully unprepared. Then he had sent her to the Belvoir Estate, with not a word about why. Had Adele known anything about the details of the prophecy, she never would have left the grounds of Belvoir Estate and she never would have run into Rainere's arms and all of his psychotic plans for their 'happily ever after' in a world run by giant monster spiders and no Natalie.

Adele felt cold. High Wizard Ohren was a mystery himself, but he was also the only source of answers for all the questions she had about her magic. On this journey she had experienced so much and learned even more about herself. She was no longer the frightened, trusting girl she had been when she had left the Golden Palace three weeks ago. But what exactly she was now she couldn't say. But she was stronger, certainly.

Stronger, and angrier.

CHAPTER FIFTY-TWO

"But When the Fire Goes Out"

Rainere watched as the men around him pulled themselves to their feet and made to follow their queen back to Belvoir Estate. He had designed the portal to land at a point at the border closest to the Belvoir manor. They would only have a short walk back, no more than a mile.

Through the Mark on his side, Rainere could feel Adelena's thoughts flash to him and away again. He couldn't make out her every thought or read her mind, but the Mark let him feel a connection to her so deep that when she thought of him, it was as if she spoke to his face. The connection was fascinating, but, at this point, also very painful.

He could feel that Adelena was confused and bewildered. She longed to take comfort from him but couldn't find her way back to trusting him as she had once. He would have to be gentle with her. Though with the danger of the Spider Empress now passed they no longer had to marry with such haste, he could not imagine having her so far from him again. Leaving her alone at the Golden Palace with her children would be impossible. Until Rainere could be sure of what the High Wizard Ohren wanted from Adelena, he would be keeping her safely by his side at the Grey Palace.

Rainere was surprised Adelena didn't even turn to look at him as she walked to the edge of the magical boundary between the Dark Forest and the Belvoir Estate. *Surely she doesn't mean to leave me here alone?*

"Adelena," Rainere called out, not caring who heard the desperate note in his voice.

Adelena froze, and though her back was to him he could feel her feelings toward him churn and swell in her mind.

"Adelena, don't leave me like this," he begged, pouring every ounce of passion into his plea. "You have to know everything I did, I did to protect you. If I had had any idea the Spider Empress would betray me like that, I would never have taken Natalie to her. I love you, *cara mia*, and I love your children."

Adelena finally turned to face Rainere. He drank in every feature on her finely-drawn face. She was exquisite. She was the image of love painted on his heart.

"Love," she said quietly. "That's a funny word to use to describe your deception and ambition, Prince Rainere."

Rainere gasped and grabbed at his side where the Mark burned him with the force of her emotions. "*Cara mia*, please, don't!" His voice was rough with pain.

"I am not your *cara mia*!" Adele suddenly shouted. "I never was! You *lied* to me and you *used* me, and all you ever wanted was the crown off my head."

Rainere took a step toward her, crossing the fire. If he could just hold her again, he could make her understand. She had to understand he had done it all for her.

"No!" And his shout was as fierce as hers. "I *do* love you and it was for that love that I have turned my whole world upside down, Adelena. I betrayed my family name, my vows, and the Blood itself for you, woman. You have no idea what it cost me to protect you from this world!"

"What is it exactly that have you protected me from?" asked Adelena, and swung her arms wide encompassing the whole group of tired men and her sleeping daughter. "We almost *died* tonight!"

Even now, in the shuddering firelight, covered in disintegrated spiders and wet with the filthy water from the tunnels, she still looked beautiful. But the hatred that she felt for him was flooding through the Mark and filling him with despair. Her love was the most precious thing that Rainere had ever been given, and he would not let it go without a fight. After all he had been through to get her into his arms, she couldn't just walk away from him tonight.

"I might have lied, but you lied, too, Adelena," he said, and the green tears dripped down his cheeks unnoticed. "After all those years we had together in our dreams, and then finding you here, you told me you had waited for me, then you refused to be my bride. You told me you had no magic and then you hurt me worse than I had ever been hurt before. You told me you didn't think you were a queen, but you wouldn't give your crown to me. I trusted you to tell me who you really were and it turned out that you are one of the Blood and not St. Lucidis at all, and you knew that. You promised to marry me. You vowed that you would love me always."

"You forced that promise out of me," Adelena hissed back. "I *never* wanted to marry you, or anyone else, ever again."

Rainere gasped. Finally, he had the truth. She had never wanted to keep him forever. A painful stab of self-loathing slipped between Rainere's ribs and this time the emotions had nothing to do with Adelena's.

Of course she had lied. How could she love me when no one else ever has?

Adelena continued screaming at Rainere, but he no longer heard her words. It was enough to know the way she truly felt about him. His eyes dropped to the ground and his knees soon followed.

But how could she hate him so quickly now when he had only ever loved her and risked his immortal soul to protect her in this world? Rainere closed his eyes against her tirade of pain and hurt. Her language had turned ugly and guttural. She was no longer his sweet Adelena. This night had woken a monster inside of her and he didn't know this part of Adelena at all. This part she had kept hidden, even from herself. Rainere could feel the undercurrent of mad joy that Adelena took in screaming at him now. The monster was daring him to speak, daring him to retaliate.

"Adelena," he whispered, opening his eyes to look up at the twisted demon she had become. Before him, she was wreathed in shadows, her eyes burning with an eerie mix of green and gold lights. Her face was transfigured with rage and she spat down at him words of hate. He searched her face desperately for the woman he loved. "Come back to me, *cara mia*. Please."

She finally stopped speaking and dropped her face down close to his. Her mouth was close enough to kiss.

"You need to go and find the deepest pit in hell. You will crawl to the bottom of that pit and there you will spend every last day of your endless life knowing with absolute clarity just how much I hate you. Right up until the day I stop thinking of you at all." Adelena placed her hand over Rainere's hand where it was pressed to his side. He ached for the touch and leaned into her only to recoil from the vicious blow she sent him through the Mark.

Rainere fell to the ground. His ears were ringing and his head buzzed and spun sickeningly. He couldn't pull a breath into his lungs and didn't feel Grotto when he dropped to the prince's side and started banging on his chest.

Rainere fought to gain control of his neck muscles, just enough so that he could turn and follow Adelena with his eyes. His heart stuttered and burst in his chest and he was aware, dully, of just how frantic Grotto was now.

Am I dying? But the thought was almost a relief. This way he wouldn't have to live without her again. He saw the doorway into the Great Darkness beyond and felt his soul reluctantly step toward it. Freedom blew in the doorway and tasted like the North Wind. If he could just pass through, he would be free.

He could make out Adelena's ruined shoes as she walked away from him, but hot tears kept blurring his vision and burning his eyes.

"Your Majesty, is he? I mean…" Charlie asked, giving Rainere a look that was heavy with pity.

"I said, we are done here," snapped Adelena, not even sparing Rainere a glance, as she took her daughter back from Captain Lucky.

As she passed through the magic barrier between the two lands, Rainere gasped as he felt Adelena's emotions instantly withdraw from his body. He cried out in agony as the immortality curse forced his heart to beat again and pulled air back into his lungs. Within moments, he was recovered. The doorway to the Beyond receded and left his vision.

Rainere howled in rage, as the tears slipped from his eyes and cursed his eternal life. If he couldn't have Adelena, then he didn't want to be alive anymore. He wouldn't go back to the hollow, empty hell that had been his life before her.

He just couldn't.

CHAPTER FIFTY-THREE

"And They All Lived…"

Adele felt the curse of Belvoir this time. The Chime Voices called out and went silent as the magic left her or was covered by something. She couldn't be sure which. Just as instantly, her savage anger left her and she felt weak enough to need to grab General Ohrig's arm for support.

Natalie murmured in her arms and shifted her head. Adele gazed down at her little girl and smiled. "Natalie, I love you, my precious girl." She bent down and lay a light kiss on her daughter's lips. She held her breath, frozen in that position, until she felt Natalie's mouth move against her own.

Adele pulled back and watched closely as Natalie's eyelids fluttered and ever so slowly opened.

"Oh, Natty!" Adele clutched her daughter tight to her chest. "Oh, baby. You are okay. You are okay, my sweet girl."

Adele let the tears stream down her face, as she relished the feel of Natalie's living, breathing body in her arms. Her daughter was healthy and alive.

Natalie pulled her face from her mother's heaving chest and looked around in confusion. She searched the faces of the Queen's Guard before looking over Adele's shoulder. She sent Charlie a small smile and an inquiring look.

"Hey, Charlie! Where is Prince Rainere?"

CHAPTER FIFTY-FOUR

"Outrun the Storm, Little Queen"

Adele and her group returned to find Belvoir Estate in an uproar and though she could understand why, she still had no patience for it.

Tilburn was nursing a horrible case of guilt and could not believe he had left Adele to the mercy of the Prince Rainere's household because of his claustrophobia. He chose to make it up to Adele by following her every command to the letter, without question. So when she asked for the royal party to be ready to leave by noon, Tilburn ran and screeched about the manor until it was done.

Adele had marched right up to her suite and after ordering her Queen's Guard to do the same, she had headed straight for her bath and vigorously scrubbed herself clean of dead spider-dust and the filth that felt ingrained in her pores.

The children were happy to be welcomed into the bathroom and Adele took solace from their conversations and teasing. Stella was clingy after being away from her mother for the day and wouldn't let Adele out of her sight again.

After washing, Adele dressed in her regular travelling clothes and ignored the long gown that Lady Olivia had laid out. She saw the children were dressed the same way and then hustled everyone down to the carriages at Tilburn's word.

In the entrance hall, Adele saw her Queen's Guard all wearing clean uniforms and somber expressions on their pale faces. She felt a stab of pity for them. Draining Rainere of so much energy had left her feeling strong, despite the curse of Belvoir, but she could imagine how exhausted they all were. She approached General Ohrig and gave him a reassuring smile.

"We must get back to the Golden Palace as soon as we can, Ohrig," she said. "But I will keep one of the carriages free for the men to take breaks when we are clear of the estate."

"It's kind of you to have that concern for your Queen's Guard, Your Majesty," said Ohrig, loud enough for his voice to carry to the men gathered in the doorway. "But if, Your Majesty, can carry on after what you've been through this day, then your Queen's Guard will carry on right beside you."

Adele smiled as the men cheered their general, and all bowed to her respectfully. General Ohrig gave Adele one of his dry smiles and quietly added, "Or until we collapse. The money is on Pepper as the first one to fall."

Adele gave Ohrig a pat on the arm as they descended the steps to the waiting carriages to let him know she appreciated the humor, but she wouldn't ever bet against any of these wonderful men. She couldn't believe that her Queen's Guard had been to hell and back for her in the last twenty-four hours. QGs Leith and Pepper looked older than they had before, and QGs Owens and Bear looked more humble. Only Captain Lucky appeared unchanged, but perhaps his blue eyes were a little less open, and a little wiser now.

"Your Majesty!" A panicked voice called out from the doorway of the manor. Adele motioned the nannies to stuff the children and their dogs into the carriages. All except Stella, who clung to her mother's arms.

Prince Bertrand II flew down the steps of the manor, his riding coat waving behind him like a cape. He was red-cheeked and sweating, as if he had ridden hard to be here now.

"Your Majesty, we were all so worried about you. What happened at the Grey Palace?" asked Bertie. "When you missed the steeplechase yesterday, I was terribly concerned, but then you arrived this morning, out of the forest and across the fields, only to leave again in such haste. Has something happened to Pere Raven? I haven't seen him yet."

"Pere Raven hasn't returned?" said Adele sharply. "We left him at the chapel, I thought…"

Adele went silent at a warning cough from General Ohrig. He was right to be cautious. With all that had happened and the mysterious disappearance of the priest, they couldn't yet know who to trust.

"You lost him!" squawked Bertie before recovering himself enough to lower his tone. "Do you think he is still at the Grey Palace, Your Majesty? If he is there, then I will need your help to recover him. By the Goddess, I had no idea that Prince Rainere was capable of kidnapping a priest. He seemed like such a nice man."

"Consider it done, Bertie," replied Adele quickly. She had no idea what Rainere would or wouldn't do to a priest of the Church, now that he had no bride to marry anymore. "Now, if you will excuse me, I must get back to the Golden Palace immediately."

But Bertie would not be thwarted so easily. He looked up at Adele as she awkwardly mounted the carriage steps with Stella still in her arms. "Your Majesty, is there is anything I should know? If there is trouble coming, then…well, then, I hope you know that the Belvoir family will always stand at your back, sure and true. You are a gift to our land, Queen Adelena, and we are your subjects, despite, and I hope you understand me when I tell you this, despite the whims of wizards."

Adelena looked into Bertie's concerned frown and noticed his blue eyes were flecked with green shards. Adele smiled at the old prince and touched his hand where it gripped the carriage door. "I understand, Bertie, and thank you," she said quietly. "Keep the curse of Belvoir safe. We may need your hospitality again soon."

Bertie nodded, frowning even more deeply, and stepped back from the carriage. He lifted his hand in a half-hearted farewell before returning to the doorway of his manor to watch the carriages leave.

Adelena sat back against the plush cushions of her seat and felt the familiar roll of nausea in her stomach, but now she knew that as soon as they left the grounds of the Belvoir Estate, she would be well again. She stroked Stella's back and noticed her daughter had a slight temperature. The baby was almost asleep in her arms, which was unusual at this time of day, but not if she was feeling unwell.

General Ohrig rode alongside Adele's carriage window. He looked in, giving her a nod. "Ride hard, Your Majesty?"

"As hard as we can, General Ohrig," said Adele grimly. "I've got a feeling that this time we are bringing the storm with us."

To be continued...

Continue reading for a sample chapter of The Demon Revealed, Book Three in the World of Evendaar series.

BOOK THREE – AN EXCERPT

"The Defeated Prince"

Prince Rainere stood naked before the mirror in his bedchamber. His dark eyes travelled down the length of his body, then back up again to meet his own hooded gaze. Goosebumps prickled his pale flesh, making the skin tighten over the hard lines of his well-defined muscles. His hands hung by his sides looking as limp and impotent as the member between his legs.

The North Wind blew in through the open window, splattering the floor with raindrops, blowing papers about the room and whispering nonsense in his ears. As if moved by the breeze, Rainere swayed this way and that. His eyes were searching for that invisible aspect of his body that had fired such passion in his beloved and made her pant with lust for him. Adelena had always praised his beauty and had taken such delight in his nakedness. Rainere raised a hand and lightly traced the muscles of his stomach, outlining each of the eight pillows where Adelena had kissed him so often.

How could it be that her worship of this body had filled me with such strength, when now I feel so very weak without her? Rainere rested his hand on his chest and felt the dull vibration of his heart, still beating though it should have been ripped out by Adelena's delicate hands; ripped out and crushed into a pulp, until only the pain remained. The pain, and her Mark.

Twisting in front of the mirror, Rainere angled himself to examine his right side. He pulled his long hair out of the way, its silky, black lengths still matted with sticks and mud from the Dark Forest. Caught between two tails of the black tattoo that covered his entire back and licked out and over his lower ribs, the royal insignia of Queen Adelena St Lucidis could be seen, grey and soft, like an old scar stamped on his body, forever marking him as hers.

Rainere winced as the Mark undulated and pulled tight. An answering jolt of adrenaline raced through him, making his hands shake with the desperation to return its call and go to her. She must be thinking of him now. The magical bond that linked them was a spell that he had never encountered before. Its power was intense and consuming. Even after she rejected him, and even after her violence in the Dark Forest, he still couldn't resent this connection between them. It was all he had left of his love: only the Mark and the memories of their too-short nights of passion together. Those things at least, remained with him.

Rainere looked deeply into his own eyes. The circle of silver surrounding his pupils spun slowly, still tarnished and fragile after Adelena's attack. Even then, he had failed her. Instead of giving her the comfort of his death, the cursed immortality spell had forced the air back into his lungs and strength into his limbs, giving him back the life that had been Adelena's to take. Rainere watched numbly as a sparkling green tear traced its way down his cheek. After over a century of nothing, suddenly his eyes wouldn't stop crying.

The chamber door opened and Rainere didn't have to look to see that the quiet tread belonged to his manservant, Grottonski, nor did he bother to cover his nakedness. Grotto had held the prince on the day he was born and had been by his side every day since.

Grotto appeared in the mirror behind Rainere, his almost-iridescent green eyes meeting Rainere's deep, forest green gaze. Grotto looked old tonight. The thin black hair on his head was plastered down with a slick of grease and his tattered black suit hung on thin shoulders. Though almost as tall as his master, Grotto stood hunched under the burdens of his responsibilities.

"What do we do now, Grotto?" asked Rainere, his voice only a dry rasp. "What do we do now that your precious Prophecy of the End of the World was broken apart by Adelena? Alone she brought the Shadows into the Light, and alone she rules from the throne of Unisia with the blood of Marchants, and something stronger, flowing in her veins. She has no need of me, and she never did. So I ask you, what do we do now?"

In the closest he ever came to embracing the prince, Grotto rested his hand lightly on Rainere's shoulder. "Master, the prophecy continues, despite our disappointments. There is a future for you with the queen, but we must look now to the past for the answers. Your father…"

"My father is dead," interrupted Rainere. "He cannot help any of us."

"Your father," persisted Grotto, "was a terrible prince. But he was a very great wizard. Although it is his fault the Marchant family lies in ruin, it is also he who can help us heal."

"You speak in riddles, Grotto," sighed Rainere and turned from the mirror's reflections to face the open window. The North Wind blew his hair into his eyes, as if teasing him.

Grotto shook his head, a sly smile dancing across his lips. "The queen is aware that the St Lucidis wizards have lied to her about her heritage, yes? She knows now that more than gold magic flows through her veins, she fears that she has the blood of another and thinks it is Marchant?" He paused to enjoy his moment. "Let me remind you, master, of the prophecy; it says the Lost Child was stolen *from* the Light but it doesn't say that the Child is *of* the Light. You see, High Wizard Ohren had been tricked into hiding another child away from Evendaar, the daughter of your step-mother, Princess Rainestra after her affair with the St Lucidis king, Octavius."

"But that's ridiculous," replied Rainere, turning to Grotto and rising to the bait. "If she is my step-mother's daughter then that would make Adelena my younger sister-by-marriage."

"And by right of the Laws of Marchant, everything your sister has belongs to you." Grotto's smile was triumphant. "As your younger sister in the descendency, and with both of you being orphans, then you are the senior heir and the crown of Unisia is yours, master!"

Rainere was shocked. Wanting to get out of Grotto's reach, he walked to the window, staring sightlessly as the dark rain lashed at him. It was summertime in the rest of the Unisia, but the Grey Palace lived in an eternal winter of Rainere's own making. Weather magic could be powerful, but he had only ever used it to reflect his moods, wreathing the palace turrets in gloomy, grey clouds and constant rain. Only when Adelena had stepped foot in the palace had the sun shone. *Adelena, his lover, was his stepsister? Impossible!* Though they were not bound by blood, this was still a legal tie almost as binding. Rainere spun to face Grotto again.

"In the Nest of the Spider People, Empress Ka-kik called Adelena an abomination after she tasted her blood." Rainere's glare was accusing. "Is that what she meant? That Adelena has damaged herself by being with me, the way she did, using magic and going so deep inside me? Did I hurt her by letting her do that when we are," - Rainere almost couldn't bring himself to say the word – "related."

Grotto hid his impatience badly. "The false queen's damage is not your concern, master, you did nothing wrong. It is her own wickedness that has brought about…"

"No!" Rainere's hoarse shout silenced Grotto. "This is *your* fault, Grotto. Adelena endangered herself to be with me, and now you would have us tell the world that I am brother to the queen I lay with? They will destroy her in the court of the Golden Palace, and she will be dead within a day. I will have to kill anyone who even suspects…"

"*Could* you kill High Wizard Ohren?" Grotto's gaze was crafty. "It was he, after all, who took the child away as a favor to your father when Prince Rainold couldn't bear to see his wife's bastard killed by the Eldars like she ought to have been. The high wizard knew she was your half-sister when he brought her back from Earth and presented her to the court as the child of the King Octavius and his own sister, Queen Olivia. He knew she was a false queen, a bastard with Marchant blood in her veins, and yet he still crowned her and had the gall to invite you to the coronation!"

Spittle flew from Grotto's mouth as he became more and more livid. "He thought you would be too weak and addled by the Blue Tonic to protest. He thought that you would never know that the crown he gave that wretched demon was yours as soon as it touched her head and by Marchant law, you now have every right to swoop in and take it. He thought I would never tell you the truth about Princess Rainestra as it negates your…"

"It negates my what?" Rainere's eyes narrowed at his manservant as Grotto's mouth snapped shut. "If Adelena is technically no closer relation to me than a step sibling, once removed, I have no claim to her kingdom, just as she has no claim to mine."

Grotto dropped to his knees and clasped his hands in front of his chest, beseeching Rainere, "Master, please, you must stay focused on the crown. The high wizard doesn't suspect you know about the queen's heritage, and he knows nothing of your relationship with her. The queen has no interest in marrying you after the…*incident*…with Princess Natalie, so you must go to the Golden Palace and steal that crown off her head."

Grotto climbed to his feet, mistaking Rainere's silence for assent. "I will pack immediately. We should move into the Marchant townhouse in Concordis to prepare for our assault on the palace. We will need the most dangerous magical weapons we can find. I will ask my contacts in the city for supplies and men."

Turning away from Grotto's insanity, Rainere looked out again at the black night. Rainere hadn't thought it possible to feel any worse about what he had done to Adelena, but Grotto was trying to destroy the last beautiful thing about their shattered relationship by saying that their love had been cursed from the very beginning. Yet, Rainere's heart fought to deny it. Grotto only spoke like this because his sanity had finally cracked. To speak of the long-dead Prince Rainold as some sort of phantom savior in Rainere's hour of need was worse than ridiculous. Grotto was insane and nothing that he said could be believed any longer. Rainere didn't say a word when Grotto gently laid a blanket over his shoulders, and Rainere saw the determination in his old servant's face.

"Shall I pack the carriages and follow you, master?" Rainere remained silent. "Yes of course, you travel faster through the portals anyway, and then I will come later with the baggage, as is right. I'll pack everything we need, don't you worry, Master. You can be in Concordis by tomorrow, me the day after that, and we can plan our attack when the demon queen least expects it of us. I have friends who can help us. Strong friends." Grotto became incoherent as he continued muttering of all that needed to be done and left the room.

A sigh welled in up in Rainere's chest, but when he exhaled all he felt was a deeper hollow in his being. There was nothing left for him in this world. Everyone he loved had left him, either by walking away or retreating into madness. There was no way that Rainere would be going to Concordis to steal Adelena's crown. He didn't want to rule Unisia, he had just wanted to be part of her life, and that was impossible now.

Stepping away from the window, Rainere made his way to the bed to see that Grotto had already laid out his clothes and grooming kit on the coverlet. Rainere spied the long narrow blade of the razor and picked it up, twirling it in his hands and watching the candlelight flash on its keen edge.

Rainere caught sight of himself in the mirror again, his wretched eyes had filled with tears and they glittered greenly against the whites. Rainere held the razor to his throat and pressed lightly. The cold blade felt good against his skin, but he could cut a thousand times, and bleed from a thousand wounds, and it would not end his life. His immortality would keep him here in this world, a prisoner of his own misery.

Did the Eldars not think of this when they dragged their own unwilling descendants into this living hell? Rainere wondered. Rainere's only hope of an early death had been the Dragon Fire, but he had given it to Adelena when she needed it to kill the Spider Empress.

A gust of wind rattled hard at the window and the shutter flapped, crashing against the wall and sprinkling glass on the stone floor of his chamber. The North Wind came shrieking into the chamber once more, scattering fat drops of rain over everything. Rainere's long hair tangled and got into his eyes, he grabbed a handful and pulled it away.

"What do you want?" he whispered to the gusts blowing about him.

"*Go to the Eldars,*" chortled the North Wind and its many voices chilled Rainere to his core. "*They are waiting for you. Go to them. The Eldars know what you want. They want you. Go, go, go!*" The North Wind howled in glee, pulling at Rainere's blanket and picking up all the tiny things in the room only to dash them on the floor again. It often spoke in riddles, but tonight its message was oddly clear.

Of course, the Eldars can take what I do not want to have any longer, thought Rainere with a flash of dark joy. *Only they can flay this immortality curse off my back and take away the Mark Adelena gave me.* Rainere had come to the end of his patience with this world and the loveless, lonely life he had pursued for over a hundred years. *I will go to the Eldars. I will make them take back this cursed tattoo, and I will be Marchant no longer.*

His hair blew about like the branches of a tree as the North Wind plucked and pulled at it. Rainere felt a sudden urge to strip away every aspect of his Marchant heritage. Dropping his blanket on the floor, Rainere grabbed a thick hank of his hair and gripped the razor tightly. The strands pattered to the ground and Rainere didn't stop until he had cut it all off.

The blade scraped across stubble and revealed the undulations of his skull. Staring at his handiwork, Rainere was almost relieved that he couldn't recognize himself in the haunted visage that stared back at him. Without long hair to frame his face, his features seemed larger and uglier. His nose was now too beak-like and his brow was too hooded and low over his red-rimmed eyes; his scalp gleamed, as pale and naked as the rest of his skin. Rainere twisted to see the enormous black tattoo that covered his back and the edge of the Marchant family crest stamped on the back of his neck. His eyes lingered on Adele's Mark as he watched it twitch and pulse. Rainere gave a hoarse yelp at a savage pull that yanked at his heart. Adelena was thinking of him, and hating him.

Soon he would be free of this agony.

Not wanting to waste another moment, Rainere took the clothes from the bed and pulled on his leather trousers, snapping the studs at the front as he shrugged on a simple shirt and his heavy tailored jacket. The rain wouldn't bother him but it would be cold where he was going, so Rainere pulled on his winter cloak. Grabbing an old leather duffel bag, he looked about the room for the things he would need. It wouldn't be much. He shoved in an extra shirt and the blanket from the floor, shaking off the mess of cut hair, then made his way to the mantelpiece above the fireplace.

Rainere's expression softened when he picked up a piece of parchment covered in a penciled image of two smiling stick figures holding hands and wearing crowns. He carefully folded the paper and put it in his pocket. He slipped a tiny wooden box into the same pocket as it had been a gift from the artist who had drawn the endearing portrait. Rainere spied the portrait of his father, Prince Rainold, in its tiny pewter frame, but he only let his eyes rest on it for a moment before he gently placed it face down. Rainere gave the room one last glance. He already felt disconnected from the chamber where he had slept every night for the past one hundred and forty years. In his heart, he had already left.

The prince walked to the door and checked the hallway for Grotto. There was no point in saying good-bye to his old servant. The words would never be enough. Better just to leave. The door clicked shut behind Rainere and a pale green glow pulsed briefly as the protective wards re-aligned themselves.

Acknowledgements

This page is for my outpouring of gratitude to the people who helped me write, or supported me, while I wrote this book.

I would like to thank my unpaid, yet tirelessly enthusiastic editors, Monica Hall and Lisa Clausen, for their supportive and careful criticism, not to mention their uplifting compliments, when working with me on this last draft. To Alison Clausen for her devotion to keep the story 'right', thank you. Thank you to all my Beta readers for reading and giving me feedback of any kind. I deeply appreciate it. I would like to thank my friends (you know who you are) for their support in listening to me either waxing lyrical or bemoaning the writing of this book, and taking it all with a pinch of salt. I would like to also thank Anastasia Ward for her beautiful rendering of my little Queen Adelena, creating an image that helped keep me grounded and focused on making my mess of notes a proper book once again.

Finally, I would like to thank my family. You are a constant source of inspiration to me and I thank you from the bottom of my heart for being as mad as hatters, every one of you.

To find out more about the author A.R. Winterstaar or the World of Evendaar please visit:

www.evendaar.com

A. R. Winterstaar on Facebook

www.ingramcontent.com/pod-product-compliance
Lightning Source LLC
Chambersburg PA
CBHW051321250626

47155CB00007B/2400